UPROOTED

THORNS AND FANGS

GILLIAN ST. KEVERN

Recovering vampire Ben is discovering that life after death is hard work. It will take more than a reflection to impress his boyfriend Nate's religious mother. And Nate's twin brother, Ethan, openly resents Ben's presence at the family farm. Nate is confident they can build a normal life together, but Ben's not even sure he knows what normal is. He can't face his reflection, let alone his past, while Nate refuses to divulge his family's supernatural secret. Can they build a future on such shaky foundations?

When a supernatural hunter is found dead on the family farm, Ethan becomes the main suspect in a murder investigation that puts Ben and Nate at odds. Nate wants to protect his family and stay silent about what he is, but Ben knows no one is safe until the demonic agent responsible for a string of murders is caught. Defying Nate to investigate alone, Ben can't let the demon claim another victim. But as his investigation continues, he discovers links to a past he thought he'd buried—and a past Nate refuses to acknowledge. With a desperate killer on a deadline, Ben must face the literal demons in his past if he wants to have any chance of saving himself and Nate from a fate worse than death.

Published by
NineStar Press
PO Box 91792
Albuquerque, New Mexico, 87199
www.ninestarpress.com

Print ISBN # 978-1-945952-42-5
Cover by Natasha Snow

DEDICATION

Thank you, Kaje, for spotting a story that needed to be told, Sera and Melissa for supporting me through the writing of this, Julia for perfectly timed feedback and Raevyn for her endless patience.

CHAPTER ONE

Heat burned a line across his exposed skin.

Ben startled awake instantly. He knew he was in trouble, even before he saw the dim light filtering through the drawn curtains. No ordinary light. Sunlight. Death.

Ben grabbed the blankets lying around him, tugging them over his body as his heart raced.

How did this happen? I never take chances! Other vampires might play chicken against dawn's slow approach, but Ben was always back in the crypt well before daylight. Along with the fangs, the blood lust, and the lingering sensation of something missing, being a vampire brought with it an ever-present awareness of the coming sun. Ben's body should have screamed at him, every sense straining with the awareness that dawn—and a horrible second death—approached. Instead, he felt nothing beyond the adrenaline of his near escape.

Ben dug deeper beneath the blankets. *Something is seriously wrong—*

He collided with something warm. It shifted, murmuring a sleepy protest.

Ben froze. That was a body. A warm, living body—

A rough hand reached out to wrap around him, pressing him against the almost indecently hot body lying beneath the blankets. Naked, Ben realized. And most definitely male.

Most definitely *aroused* male.

"Not a morning person?"

The words were slurred, but Ben was confident he understood them. His heart switched gears, accelerating in a different way. "Says the guy who sounds more asleep than awake."

Nate chuckled, shifting to press a sleepy kiss to Ben's neck. His movement dislodged the blankets covering Ben, leaving him exposed to the light, but Ben didn't try to hide.

I'm alive. The sun couldn't hurt him now. *Alive.*

Ben turned his head to catch the next kiss fully on his lips. Nate's mouth was just as hot as he remembered, searing like the sun but infinitely kinder.

Nate seemed happy to share a tender moment, too sleepy or too content to pursue needs beyond the reassurance of Ben's presence. When Nate broke the kiss to burrow back into the pillow at Ben's neck, Ben left his eyes open. He followed the curve of the sheets over Nate's body to the sliver of sunlight coming through the curtain that made his dark hair shine. Everything about Nate was warm, from his healthy tan to the heat of the arm around Ben's waist.

Their first night together, he'd watched Nate sleep, but he'd retired to the crypt before Nate woke, leaving Nate to be unceremoniously bundled into a taxi. That should have been it. A simple tryst Nate didn't remember and Ben didn't regret. And here they were. Him, a vampire, lying in sunlight next to a man who looked human but remained a mystery.

Ben shifted so he could study Nate's sleeping expression. Nate made a vague sound of protest but relaxed as he realized Ben wasn't going anywhere.

This shouldn't be possible. Ben frowned, reaching out to stroke his fingers through Nate's hair. *I shouldn't be awake at all. And Nate...*

Ben looked quickly away, but the memory came too fast to avoid. Nate, paler than he should ever be, lying still in the dirt, his blood mingled with the dead leaves and his throat—

Ben's fingers stilled to a halt. *Nate shouldn't be alive.*

ARX had a clear procedure for encountering an unknown supernatural being. Ben sat up, mentally running through the checklist. First, assess the immediacy of the threat.

Ben bit his lip. *Unless the threat is never getting out of bed again, I'm safe.* Nate clung to the pillow with the dedication of a poor swimmer to a flotation device. He didn't bat an eyelid, even as Ben shifted and the crack of light fell directly on him.

That's dedication. Ben studied the rise and fall of Nate's chest and the slight flutter of his eyelashes until, with a guilty start, he remembered step two—gathering all available information.

What do I actually know about Nate? Apart from the fact that he is incredibly distracting, even when half-asleep? Ben considered his companion.

When they'd first met, Nate displayed the sleek, self-satisfied confidence of a well-fed tomcat, too smug to know he should be ashamed of himself. Given his job as an escort, it made sense. Nate was polished, confident, and annoyingly, gloriously sexual. Ben had disliked him purely on principle. He could never have imagined that Nate concealed a thoroughly selfless heart, or that he would risk his neck—literally—for Ben's right to feel.

Now that Ben looked closely, he could see traces of the intense strain of the last week. There were exhausted shadows beneath Nate's eyes, bruises on his arm from their narrow escape in the cemetery. Holding his breath, Ben leaned forward to get a closer look at Nate's neck.

Where there should have been an ugly gash, there wasn't even a scar.

Not even a werewolf heals like this. Nate made a plaintive grumble, and Ben settled back, thinking hard. *A skilled magic user might have been able to pull it off, but there was no way they could do it without leaving their magical traces all over Nate.* The only thing Ben detected was a warm, gooey feeling that he suspected had its origin less in Nate's magical state and more in Ben's proximity to him. *Which leaves what Nate told me. He healed himself.*

Ben had four years of the best supernatural education under his belt—just enough to know how inadequate his knowledge was. First, the middle ages had hunted the supernatural into hiding, while the church, the greatest authority on unlawful magic, guarded what knowledge they had to prevent it falling into the wrong hands. With the Renaissance had come rationality, the lessening of the church's grip on knowledge and a lack of belief in magical beings the supernatural were quick to exploit, fading almost entirely from sight. The lore that remained was piecemeal at best, focused more on killing the supernatural than studying it.

Not undead. Not a witch. Well—probably not a witch. Nate had potential but lacked the knowledge. He'd also walked through wards aimed against anything of magical or demonic origin... *No matter how you look at it, Nate shouldn't be possible.* Ben tapped a finger thoughtfully against his chin. *Maybe I'm looking at this from the wrong perspective—*

"Like what you see?" Nate tilted his head back, watching Ben through half-lidded eyes. His smirk was lazy.

Ben started. "Um—"

Nate chuckled. "That's not a difficult question. You're here, after all."

Here. Ben's mouth quirked. Accompanying an unknown supernatural being and his equally unknown brother to an unspecified location without telling anyone of his plans was not ARX procedure—unless they were talking procedure that resulted in Ben's instant dismissal. *Perhaps it's a good thing I quit when I did. ARX wouldn't know whether to fire me—or investigate me as a supernatural threat.* "Where is here?"

"You don't remember the drive?" Nate relaxed, leaning back against the headboard.

"I remember *a* drive." Ben stayed sitting. "That's about it." He looked around the room. He remembered peeling off his clothes as he fell onto the bed, but nothing else.

His location was a mystery, but his surroundings were definitely prosaic. The morning light gave the wooden walls and floor a pleasant warmth. An old-fashioned wardrobe with a mirror built into the door stood against the wall. On its far side was a table with a sewing machine and a basket of fabric scraps at its base. The bookshelf above it sagged beneath the weight of its paperback burden, and an armchair was positioned in front of the drawn curtains. The sunlight fell across the floor in a direct line. "Are we in your mother's bedroom?"

"Spare room." Nate's fingers rested on Ben's waist, playing with the sheet fabric. "Doubles as Ma's sewing room."

That explained the sewing machine and the quilt covering the bed, which was old, probably a family heirloom, with a solid carved headboard and footer. The mattress was just as old. It sagged in the middle, inviting Ben to roll against Nate. Tempting, but a sound from outside caught Ben's attention. "Are we near the ocean?"

"What?"

"I can hear waves."

Nate snorted. "Look out the window."

How late in the day is it? Without the vampire's internal alarm, Ben felt lost. He slid out from under the quilt, discovering that the only thing he wore was his briefs. "Am I going to alarm your neighbors?"

"Nearest house is a five-minute walk." Nate shifted so he lay on his side, supported by the pillow as he watched Ben. "You're fine."

The emphasis he put on that made Ben feel warm in a way that had nothing to do with the sunlight, warming the wooden floor beneath his feet. To counter his confusion, he lifted a hand, drawing back the curtain fully.

All he saw was green. The fresh green of the grass stretching all the way to the fence and the glossy dark green of the bushes there. Beyond that, willows, their long branches dragging on the ground. A breeze lifted them, and Ben heard the sound he'd mistaken for the sea. Beyond the willows, extending all the way up into hills, was a varied collection of deep greens. "Forest?"

"National reserve," Nate explained. "Borders the farm. You're allowed to gather fallen wood and hunt if you've got a license, but nothing else. Not without permission. We can go hiking later if you're interested."

Ben looked out the window again. If he looked away from the hills, following the line of the willows, he could see more trees, these spaced regularly, with the bright green of new leaves.

"It's quiet, compared to New Camden. Nothing ever happens out here." The bed shifted as Nate sat up. "I wasn't kidding about the place being small."

There was a large building, the faded red paint worn away in patches to reveal weathered board, and fences, but no other buildings in sight. Only trees.

"Ben?"

"You could murder someone out here, and no one would ever know."

"What the hell?"

Ben flushed, turning back to the bed. "Sorry. Was that weird?"

"Just a little." Nate patted the bed next to him. "But considering that you used to be a vampire, I'll give you a pass. *This* time."

Ben took the invitation, curling up against Nate's side. It wasn't cold exactly, but separation gave the rush of warmth to their reunion. "I'm not used to so much...country."

"You know we don't actually marry our cousins out here, right?" Nate settled his arm around Ben's shoulder automatically. "Or fuck goats or dismember people with an ax or whatever else you city people think we do to pass the time."

"It's the quiet," Ben said. "Growing up in the city, you could always hear your neighbors, even if you couldn't see them." He settled his head on Nate's shoulder. "This... I don't know how to take this."

Nate laughed. "You can take down any number of revenants without batting an eye, but peace and quiet have you beat? That's... I don't know what to say, Ben."

After a moment, Ben smiled. "When you put it like that..." He settled his arms around Nate's torso, enjoying the solidness of his body. This was real. "I have to get used to the idea that I'm not a vampire—not even an ARX employee anymore. From now on... I'm ordinary."

Nate nodded. "You're going to need new business cards. 'Ben Hawick, Totally Normal Human'."

"Jerk." Ben elbowed him. "What are you going to put on yours? Nathan..." He didn't even know Nate's last name. *What is wrong with me? That should have been one of my first questions...*

"You sound like our principal. No one calls me Nathan. Not since high school."

He'd attended high school, then. There would be records—
Ben caught himself.

Nate's not a case! He's... Ben sought through the various options. Boyfriend? Even given the tumultuous circumstances of their first meeting, it was too soon for that. But someone who defied death and necromancers for you went beyond friend... *Complicated*, Ben decided at last. *Nate was complicated.*

"It's too early in the morning to look so serious." Nate settled back, looking up at Ben through half-closed eyes. His lashes were long, almost ridiculously delicate. "What's up?"

Seeing Nate like this felt intensely personal. His hair wasn't styled, and he needed a shave. So different from the highly polished appearance he displayed at the club.

Ben ran his fingers through Nate's hair, brushing it straight before deciding that he liked it better spiking in odd directions. Nate had slept with many people, after all, but how many had he woken up with? This—

This was special.

"I forgot." He explored the rough stubble of Nate's chin with his fingertips. "The sunlight. When I woke up and felt it, I thought I was dead."

"Shit!" Nate sat up. "You— I didn't even think about it. Are you okay?"

The transformation from sleepy to alert was sudden. Ben couldn't regret it, not with the blankets pooled around Nate's waist, the sunlight playing over his bare skin.

"I'm fine. I'm alive." The words still gave him a thrill. *Alive. Human.* "We met the dawn together, remember?"

Nate let out a deep breath. "Yeah, we did. Scared the crap out of me then, too. I thought—" Instead of finishing his sentence, he reached out, pulling Ben into a sitting hug.

Ben smiled apologetically against Nate's neck. "It's going to take getting used to. You don't lose a year of fear overnight."

Nate's arms tightened around him. "You're fine now, Ben. You're safe here."

Safe. Ben's mouth twitched. The word felt like a foreign concept when it was applied to him. The definition of a vampire was unsafe, after all.

"Ben?"

Had he been silent too long? "Is it bad that being alive is scarier to me than being dead?"

Wrong thing to say. Nate kicked himself free of the sheets and climbed out of bed. He threw the curtains open, flooding the bed with sunlight.

Ben threw a hand up reflexively, even though he knew the sun couldn't hurt him. "It's so bright."

"But it doesn't hurt, right?" Nate held out his hand. "Come here."

Ben's mind screamed that he was burning. Or was that just the blush as Ben realized they stood in front of the window, entirely exposed? "Your family—"

Nate guided Ben to where he wanted him, back from the window, entirely in the light. "Still asleep."

Ben got an unrestricted view of the body he'd been pressed against. There was something powerful in the way Nate's body worked, muscle and confidence combining in a way that made Ben's heart beat faster just by proximity.

Nate knelt between Ben's legs, any submissiveness in the gesture immediately counteracted by the assurance with which Nate placed his hands on Ben's thighs, urging them further apart. "How's it feel, Ben?"

It took him far too long to realize Nate was talking about the sunlight. "Good. Warm. Like being touched by you." Ben's hands gravitated towards Nate's hair. "Only, you're better—" He gasped.

The warmth of Nate's hands on the tender exposed skin of his inner thigh was nothing to the warmth of his lips, pressed against Ben's stomach. "Shut your eyes. Imagine yourself entirely surrounded by sunlight." His hazel eyes sought Ben's, glowing with an earnestness that was ridiculously endearing.

Ben felt it as a surge of warmth within his chest, not dissimilar to the blood pumping through his cock. He swallowed back unexpected emotion. "Sunlight?"

"Maybe the problem is that you don't have any positive associations with sunlight." Nate planted another chaste kiss to Ben's hip. "I think we need to fix that."

"I don't think it works that way." But Ben didn't tell Nate to stop. He shut his eyes and steadied himself. Nate's mouth had traveled to the soft hair at Ben's navel, brushing over highly sensitive skin. *No arguing with that mouth. Or his tongue...* Ben heard himself gasp in appreciation. Color rushed into his cheeks. He'd never believed he was capable of making a sound like that, but Nate showed him things about himself he had never suspected.

"Feels good, doesn't it? Entirely surrounded by warmth and light." Nate punctuated each statement with a burning kiss. "This is where you belong now, Ben. In the light."

"That was terrible, Nate. God. I don't know why I put up with you." The sunlight felt good on his bare shoulder blades, just as the smooth wooden boards did beneath his feet. "Okay. I'll admit. I could get used to this." Ben stroked his fingers through Nate's hair, down to the base of his skull, tipping Nate's face up to meet his as he bent down. "But it's not the sunlight I'm imagining surrounding me." Keeping his eyes closed made the maneuver difficult. Ben hoped Nate would get the hint and kiss him.

Nate did. He stood as he kissed back, tongue slipping against Ben's even as they readjusted their balance. It wasn't graceful, but being unable to see gave it something else. Not uncertainty, not exactly—Ben trusted Nate not to let him stumble. But the unknown was a definite enticing factor, especially as Nate stepped back.

"Don't open your eyes."

"What are you doing?"

"Relax, okay?"

Ben heard a zip being undone. The bag Nate had brought with him.

"I got this." There was another sound, a soft plastic pop.

"Is that what I think it is?"

"That would be telling, wouldn't it?" Nate's reply was frustratingly unhurried. "Concentrate on thinking sunlight."

Ben heard Nate kneel in front of him and braced himself for the return of his searing touch. Instead, he was left to wait, hands grasping only air. "Nate."

No reply.

"Maybe I'm not going to be afraid of sunlight after this." Ben listened for any sound that might give away Nate's location, or any shift in the air surrounding him that might reveal Nate's movements. "But replacing fear with frustration isn't going to help me any." He gasped as warm breath ghosted over his cock.

"I don't know. I can think of definite advantages to you getting aroused in the sunlight."

Ben reached out, finding Nate's shoulders with his hands. "Are you just going to tease— Oh, fuck."

Nate had taken the head of Ben's cock into his mouth and sucked at it, surrounding it with warmth.

Ben was unable to stop himself pressing forward, seeking more of that heat. "You're so hot, I— God, Nate."

Impossibly, Nate's mouth had got tighter around him. Had he swallowed? Fuck but that was hot. Ben bit his lip to hold back his disappointment as Nate pulled away. "You like that?"

Ben could picture the lazy smirk as Nate said that. He felt his cheeks heat. "You know I do." He could feel his pulse beat in his erect cock, demanding more of Nate's attention.

Nate's hand wrapped around his base, pumping him lightly as his other hand toyed with Ben's balls. "Talk to me, Ben. Tell me what I do to you."

"I hope you're don't expect anything coherent because— Oh fuck. That. I like that." Ben's fingers sought out Nate's hair, tangling in it with the surety of a boat returning to harbor. "Do that."

Nate's reply was a low chuckle, muffled as he took Ben's other ball in his mouth. He was slow on purpose, taking his time.

Not going to act until he gets what he wants. "Your mouth. I just want it. You—you feel so hot." It felt like there were two voices within him, one that was holding up a mirror to catch his words and throw them back at him, letting him know just how inexperienced and needy and embarrassing he sounded. "Seriously, forget the sun. You're all the light I need. Especially when you do that thing with your tongue— Oh god, yeah, Nate. Just like that." And the other part of him, the part that felt stronger with every word, confident enough in himself to push forward as Nate's tongue traveled deliberately up the underside of his cock.

"This thing?"

Ben hummed agreement, shifting one hand to tighten in the hair at the base of Nate's skull. "Mm," he said, keeping his voice deceptively mild. "I also like the thing where I fuck your mouth."

The words were still strange to say, and as he waited for Nate's reaction, Ben wondered if he'd gone too far. They were new, and he was still learning how to use them. With his eyes shut, he couldn't gauge Nate's reaction, and Ben held his breath, listening for any indication that he'd assumed too much.

He shouldn't have worried. Nate made a desperate sound that made Ben as awed as it made him needy, and then Nate's mouth was around him, taking him in almost to Ben's groin.

"Yeah...like that." Ben's control wavered, and he pushed forward.

Nate squeezed his thigh. It didn't feel like *stop*. It felt like *come on*. Ben carefully rocked forward.

Nate met him. He worked over Ben's length for what seemed like an eternity of glorious heat, before pulling off to alternate with sucking at Ben's head as he pumped him.

"I don't know if it's the morning or not being able to see you, but everything you do... It just feels more. I— Oh fuck. I just want more—"

Nate casually thumbed the sensitive ridge at Ben's cock head. "You want to come in my throat?" he asked with an innocence that was entirely put on but didn't prevent Ben from jolting eagerly into his touch. "I'm going to take that as a yes."

"You're a jerk. And also, yes." Ben gripped Nate's shoulders tighter than absolutely necessary, steadying himself as he felt Nate reposition, one hand at Ben's base, the other urging his legs apart. He had a moment to catch his breath as Nate lined himself up, and then all hope of self-control was gone as Nate swallowed him whole.

"Yeah, you're going to make me come. I'm going to—" Ben thrust into Nate's mouth with abandon. Not pausing as he felt a slick finger press against his crack. *That explains the plastic sound from earlier*, the part of his mind that still worked supplied helpfully. "Oh god—" Nate's finger pressed inside, seeking that one spot. He should say something. Warn him. "I'm close—" But Nate had found the spot, and it was all Ben could do to stay on his feet. Sunlight seemed to grow within him, the light building behind his eyelids until all his senses were consumed with the rush of sensation.

When he remembered that he could open his eyes, it was to see Nate gently laving the head of Ben's penis before letting it slide from his mouth. He met Ben's gaze and grinned up at him, mouth way too pleased with itself, as he shifted to sit on the rug. "You like that?"

Ben let himself be pulled down to straddle Nate's waist. "I lo—" Ben swallowed back a spike of fear. "*Like* your mouth," he said hastily, leaning into the kiss Nate pressed against his neck. His heart beat hard. *What is wrong with me? It's just a word! There's no need to be afraid of it!*

"Nate—" Ben reached for Nate's erection, hoping to lose his unwanted visceral reaction in a more pleasurable one but found Nate's hand already there. Even the feel of Nate's rough fingers beneath his own felt good, and Ben wondered if Nate felt the same thrill of contact as he moaned, free hand coming to a halt on Ben's back as his hips jerked.

If Nate's mouth felt good wrapped around him, wringing from him phrases Ben never thought he'd hear himself say, then it felt equally good to hear those same words from Nate. "Fuck, yeah, Ben. I want—" Even his come felt good, putting the sun to shame with its heat as it hit Ben's chest.

Finally they were still, Nate leaning back against the foot of the bed, eyes half closed, fingers idly caressing Ben's hips as Ben leaned against him. "Feeling better?"

It took Ben a moment to think back and catch Nate's meaning. "Actually, yeah. I am." He wrapped his arms around Nate. "You know you can't give me a blowjob every time I have a bad morning, right? It's impractical."

Nate gathered him close. "I can try. Though, um..."

"Um?" Ben raised an eyebrow. Nate had just initiated sex in front of an open window, and now he was embarrassed?

Nate squirmed. "When we talked at your apartment, we hadn't decided what we are to each other. I don't want to pressure you or anything, but last night, when Ma asked, I told her you're a friend."

Ben nodded. "That makes sense." Nate was complicated on many levels.

Nate ran a hand through his hair. "Can we keep things casual in front of my family? Ma is... I only just told her I'm bisexual."

"Are you blushing?" Ben poked his cheek. "You are." Unashamedly sexual Nate could blush. The discovery was weirdly endearing.

"Stop that." Nate swatted his fingers away. "You don't mind, right? I mean—I figure give her time to get to know you, and then break the news. If there's news to break."

Ben nodded slowly. "Right." This wasn't that weird, surely. He couldn't expect Nate to act the way he did at the club in front of his family, after all.

The grin Nate gave him silenced Ben's lingering doubt. "Thanks, Ben." He squeezed his hand, helping him to his feet. "C'mon. Let's introduce you to the folks."

☆☆☆

"I hope you like toast, Ben, because that's all I have in the house." Ma put the plate down in front of him. Golden brown toast, a dollop of butter melting on it. Before Ben could muster an 'It's fine,' she'd turned back to the coffee maker on the bench. She was a small woman, almost ridiculously tiny next to Nate and Ethan, but there was something of her sons in the set of her jaw. "And we're out of cream, too."

"I usually take my coffee black," Ben assured her.

Nate squeezed his hand under the table. "Ma's just annoyed she can't go full country hospitality on you. She took one look at you last night and decided you needed fattening up." His smile was amused.

Ma set Nate's plate of toast down on the kitchen table with a bang. "And whose fault is that? A sixteen-hour drive and it doesn't occur to you I might like to know I have a guest! Look at the state of this kitchen!"

"The kitchen looks great," Nate said promptly. "Like it always does. You really know how to make the place feel welcoming."

It wasn't an empty platitude. The kitchen was small, crowded with the everyday clutter of the family living in it, but that only added to its welcome. The wooden walls were warm, even if the pictures that hung on them were faded, and the furniture solid despite showing the passage of time. The kitchen table was large and bulky, reminiscent of a time when families were bigger, and the chairs had an irregularity to them that suggested they'd been hand-made. The blue-and-white floral design of the curtains had faded, and the bench and cupboards had lost their shine, but it was scrupulously clean.

A bowl of deep-purple flowers (African violets, Ben learned later), sat on the table. A row of herbs lined the windowsill over the sink, while ivy waved in the breeze beyond the kitchen window. A trio of spider ferns, possibly relatives of the one Nate had brought home with him, occupied the top of the fridge.

Ma flitted around the kitchen like a bee in a garden, never settling for long in any one place. She paused with one hand on the coffee pot, the other on her hip, to give Nate a severe look. "If it's so welcoming, why do we never see you? No visits—not even a phone call to let your mother know you weren't being murdered!"

Ben flinched, snatching his hand back from his slice of toast. Nate *had* been murdered.

Ma noticed. "Eat up," she told Ben. "Don't mind me. Nate should know better—"

"Here we go." Nate settled back in his chair.

Ma immediately bristled. "Here we go indeed! A city in a state of emergency—a new murder every time you turn on the news!—And you not even answering your phone so that we know you're all right!"

"I told you! My phone's broken—"

"Didn't stop you calling when you had something you wanted to ask." Ma banged a cupboard open with energy. "Or from using a payphone! But no—a necromancer on the loose and nothing to let me know you weren't in trouble!"

Ben stared at Nate. *He has to have told his family he was one of the necromancer's victims. That wasn't something you could hide!*

"I didn't want you to worry." Nate adopted a soothing tone. "The place I worked at closed and I was out a place to stay. I ended up crashing with a friend and—well, I knew you'd be anxious."

"Anxious is right!" Ma placed a cup of coffee in front of Ben. "Here I am not knowing whether you're alive or dead—"

He hasn't told her. Ben swallowed. Nate radiated honesty like a teenager radiated AXE body spray. Ben could not have believed him capable of hiding something of the magnitude of his own death, but the evidence was unfolding before his eyes. *And if he can hide that...what else is he hiding?*

"I'm fine," Nate assured Ma. "And I'm home now. Nothing to worry about."

Ben frowned at Nate. *If Ma had any idea of what we'd escaped from—*

Across the table, Ethan rolled his eyes.

Seeing his thoughts mirrored on Ethan's face disconcerted Ben. Nate's twin had not spoken once, applying himself methodically to the toast and coffee set in front of him. Although physically the brothers were identical, Ethan's indifference was a marked contrast to Nate's easy display of emotion. Ben had no idea what Ethan thought or felt about his presence at the family table. That grimace was the most emotion Ben had seen on him to date.

Is this an ongoing argument? Ben only half listened to Nate assuring Ma that he could be trusted to take care of himself, struggling to reconcile the Nate he thought he knew with a Nate who routinely deceived the people closest to him.

"Easy for you to say." Ma's scolding was undercut by the fact that she stroked Nate's hair as she gave him his coffee. "You're not the one who was worried sick. And I don't know what you're smirking about, Ethan. The only reason I knew you'd gone to New Camden was because Dan saw you topping up the truck at the gas station and asked where you were off to. Nothing wrong with your phone."

Ethan hastily reached for his coffee.

Ben bit back a smile. Ethan was an enigma, but knowing he reacted like a guilty child to his mother's scolding made him less intimidating. "So, Ethan," he said quickly, before Ma could regain her steam. "Nate tells me you take care of the farm all by yourself. That must be a lot of work."

Ethan grunted, putting down his coffee and picking up his toast.

Ben paused. *At least he responded.* Which was more than Ethan had done their previous encounters. Ben cast a look at Nate and received a thumbs up in response. *This is...good?* Ben took a deep breath. "I'm really interested how you knew about flying rowans. Usually, that sort of knowledge is limited to witches or—"

"There's no talk of magic in this household," Ma said in tones that didn't brook any discussion. "Or witchcraft."

Ethan smirked.

Ben looked down at the untouched toast in front of him. He felt stung, more upset than he should by the abrupt interaction. *It was only a question!*

Nate's hand found his under the table and squeezed it. "You never told me what you decided to do with the pruning, Ethan. Did you get help?" The gesture should have been reassuring, but instead Ben was uncomfortably aware just how out of place he was in the farmhouse.

Ethan snorted at Nate's question. "Don't need it."

"You realize being independent doesn't mean you have to do everything yourself, right?" Nate nudged his brother with his elbow.

Ethan looked at him. "You're here now."

"What a good idea," Ma said briskly, wiping down the bench with a cloth. "Nate, you can help your brother in the orchard once you finish breakfast. He can show you all the progress he's made."

Nate put down his coffee. "Ben—"

"Ben will want a shower and a fresh change of clothes." Ma wiped her hands on her apron. "I'll take care of him."

And that settled that.

☆☆☆

The bathroom was down the same hall as the spare bedroom. Ma smoothed out the rugs covering the floor as they went. "Mind your feet. It's an old house, the boards have shifted over time."

"It's beautiful," Ben said. "It's been in your family for a long time, hasn't it?"

Ma gave him a pleased smile. "Mitch was the third of his line to live here. Ethan and Nate are the fourth." She paused a moment. "We don't get many visitors out here, so our manners are a little rusty."

Apology for Ethan? Or warning? Before Ben could decipher Ma's statement, they reached the bathroom.

"You don't have anything to change into?" Ma took a towel from the hot water cupboard.

"We left New Camden in a hurry." Ben winced. Ma would not like that! "There wasn't a chance to shop."

"Shop?" Ma looked back, her hand on the bathroom door.

"I—found myself out a place to stay unexpectedly." True, if leaving a lot unsaid. "I left everything behind."

"The necromancer?"

Ben bit his lip. "I'd rather not talk about it." That was definitely true. "It's still very recent."

Ma's hand rested on his shoulder gently. "I'll find you something of the boys for the time being," she said. "But first, let's get you that shower."

Ben nodded thanks, feeling more than his usual awkwardness in comparison to Ma's brisk efficiency.

She led the way into the bathroom. "Leave your clothes outside the door, and I'll get them into the wash straight away. We can't offer you a bath because..." She shrugged. "Look at it."

Ben smirked. *Definitely Nate's family.* There were three ferns in pots at the end of the bath and what looked like egg cartons filled with dirt took up the majority of the tub. "What are those?"

"Seedlings." Ma picked up a carton so Ben could see the tiny green shoot with two round leaves. "A frost right now would kill them. Here they're protected until Ethan can plant them outside."

"Are they flowers?" They didn't look like any plant Ben knew, but plants Ben knew was not a large category.

"Radishes. A heritage variety. Ethan gets them out of a catalog."

Ben understood 'radishes' and nothing else. As he tried to parse the sentence, Ma turned on the water inside the shower. "There you go. Help yourself to anything you need."

"Thanks." Ben stepped forward. As he did, he caught a movement in the clear glass above the bathroom sink, a pale face with sunken eyes and limp, dank hair. *Revenant!*

Ben jumped back. His foot caught on the edge of the hallway rug, and he landed flat on his ass in the hall.

"Are you all right?" Ma bustled forward before he could warn her. "What happened?"

He stared at her. There was no sign of the monster, nothing—but the bathroom mirror above the sink.

Ben swallowed.

"Ben?"

"I'm fine." Carefully, Ben lifted himself up off the ground, ignoring the protest of his aching muscles. "I wasn't expecting the mirror there. The sudden movement gave me a fright."

Ma didn't laugh. She didn't even smile, her lips pressed thinly together. "You take it easy," she said and left him to the shower.

Ben heard the bathroom door close behind her with a sense of relief. He leaned over the bathroom sink, listening to the water hitting the shower sides until his heart rate had calmed. *Wonderful. Nate's brother doesn't like me and his mother thinks I'm weird.* Bracing himself, Ben raised his face to the mirror.

No wonder I jumped. This doesn't look like me at all. Ben had seen his reflection since regaining his humanity, but it was uncomfortable to look at, not matching his mental image of himself at all. His cheeks were thin, and he was so pale he opened his mouth to make sure there weren't any fangs. But it was the hair that bothered him most. Ben looked like a refugee from a history book. "All I need is a stupid hat, and I'm a dead-ringer for Richard the third." *I told Hunter and Godfrey to let me know when I needed a haircut.*

Ben bit his lip. Neither member of his vampire family was up to date with modern fashion. Hunter might still consider Richard III a fashion icon. "That's behind me now." Ben turned away from the mirror. "No more vampires. No more vampire haircuts."

He was alive.

CHAPTER TWO

Ben's vampiric hangover went down the drain with the last of the hot water. He returned to the spare room entirely transformed, a towel around his hips and his skin tingling with the shock of the cold water. *Who says water doesn't have any magical properties?* Ben felt alert, alive, and aware enough to be amused at his earlier reactions. *Had I really thought Nate kidnapped me?* Just because someone was unknown didn't make them suspect—despite numerous ARX employee memos on the subject. *None of which apply to me anymore.*

But no amount of magic—or showers—could transform Ben into someone capable of pulling off the clothes left out on the bed. Ben held the jeans up to his hips. The ends trailed on the ground, and the waist had inches on Ben's. Fortunately Ma had provided a belt. And underpants.

Ben felt his face heat. Not two weeks into meeting Nate, and he was borrowing underwear from him. At least, Ben fervently hoped he was pulling on Nate's briefs. Nate and Ben had some form of relationship, even if it wasn't one Nate wanted to share with his family. Borrowing Ethan's on the other hand? *No. Just no.*

Ben stepped into the jeans. Even with the belt on its tightest loop, one good tug would cause the jeans to slide off. Still, the voluminous T-shirt Ma had left would prevent him from flashing anyone. The faded T-shirt would adhere snugly to Nate's torso. On Ben it was a tunic, the collar stretching almost to Ben's bony shoulder. Tugging at the neck to see if there was enough give to tie it, Ben caught the smell of dried grass and sunlight. *Nate's smell.* He smiled, smoothing the fabric down, remembering Nate's hands on him only a few hours earlier. Nate had brought Ben home, introduced him to his family. Actions counted more than words. *And Nate's actions... Nate's actions said a lot.*

Ben took one step and immediately tripped over the ends of the jeans.

When he stepped out of the room, it was with the cuffs rolled up to mid shin. *I look like a kid playing dress up.* Nate was going to have a field day with him. "Nate?"

Ma stood at the kitchen sink, up to her elbows in dishwater. "If he's not still with his brother, he'll be down by the river. Do you have everything you need, Ben?"

"Yes, thank you." Ben rubbed his elbow. "Can I help?"

Ma shook her head, adding another clean plate to the rack beside her. "You're a guest. You just relax."

Ben nodded. "Thank you." He wasn't sure what to say to Ma, uneasily aware that he stood in her kitchen under false pretenses. *Then again, she gave me Nate's underwear. She must suspect something—*

"How long have you known Nate?"

Ben took a deep breath. "Not long. About two weeks." *It's a totally normal question!* It was only the coincidence of it coming so soon after his thought that made it feel interrogative.

"How did you meet?" Ma continued doing the dishes.

"A party at a friend's house. Nate was one of his guests." Technically true, but the party had been the anniversary of Ben's death, and Nate was there professionally. *Am I blushing?* Ben fought to keep his expression calm.

"Do you usually accept invitations to stay from people you've known for two weeks?"

Put like that Ben's spur of the moment mistake sounded even worse. *She must think I'm an idiot.* "No." Ben tugged at the hem of the T-shirt. "Nate..." How to explain Nate without giving away that Nate was not merely a friend? "Nate was really welcoming."

Ma pursed her mouth. She finished the plate she was washing and reached for the next. "Nate's got a good heart, but he doesn't think things through."

Ben rested his hand on the kitchen table. *Didn't think me through. That's what she means.*

Ma continued calmly. "Your family will be wondering where you are."

Ben snorted. *A hint?* "They're dead."

Ma stared at him. "Dead?"

I should have put that better. "I'm an only child. My father died a year ago and my mother when I was nine."

Ma lowered the plate she was holding. "Not the necromancer?"

Ben grimaced. Technically his father had been the first of Peter's victims, but the connection was not public knowledge. "Not much is known about it." Which was true. ARX covered it up the best they could.

A home invasion in the house of one of their senior executives would have been damaging to any firm that specialized in security, even without revealing that Hunter was a vampire and Austin's duties as butler sometimes included occult research.

"I'm sorry." Ma watched him a moment and then turned back to the sink. "To get to the river, take the back gate. There's a path."

That was clear dismissal. Ben took it with relief.

☆☆☆

I'm over-thinking this. Ben followed the path worn in the carpet to the front door. He carefully navigated around the jacket dropped on the floor to open the door and step onto the porch. *Any concerned mother would ask those questions! Nate's family just met me. No way—*

His foot skidded out from under him. Ben flung his arms out as his body pitched backward. He caught the doorframe, the impact jarring his body.

Ben let out a shuddering breath and lowered himself to the welcome mat. *No way they're out to get me?* His arms ached, and a muscle throbbed in his leg.

At least the quiet had one thing going for it. If Ben had skidded like that anywhere in New Camden, his near-miss would have been greeted with a chorus of jeers and sarcastic applause. Here, the only sound that greeted Ben's disaster was the shuffling leaves of the wisteria that overhung the porch.

With a grunt, Ben levered himself to his feet. He took a moment to stuff the too-big socks into his pockets—a vampire only had to be bitten once—and stepped onto the porch.

No wonder Ben slipped. The wooden porch must have been as old as the house, big, broad slabs worn smooth by generations of feet. The warm timbre of the timber didn't match the coolness Ben felt underfoot, but his bare feet had grip. Certain he wasn't going to fall again, Ben looked for his shoes.

A pair of sneakers sprawled next to a prim pair of crisp blue gardening boots. Those could only be Ma's, too small and dainty to be either sons'. Ben thought the sneakers were Nate's, but there was no sign of his own shoes.

I know I had them yesterday. Ben vaguely remembered leaning on Nate's arm as he kicked off his sneakers the night before, but that was all. *Could I have taken them inside with me?* He didn't remember carrying his shoes, but Ben didn't remember much at all besides Nate's arm, guiding him down the hall. *Careless.* He bit his tongue. Given the interview he'd just had with Ma, he didn't exactly want to go back through the house. *I'll look later.*

Ben cast a look down the porch just in case and smirked. *So much for country stereotypes.* No rocking chairs here. Instead, a faded sofa, presumably retired from the living room, occupied the far end of the porch, looking out at the farm. A sawn-off stump acted as a side table, holding a stack of farming magazines. *How much time has Nate spent here?* Ben wandered over to take in the view.

The house perched at the highest point of the property, commanding a view of the entire valley. Presumably, the original homesteader had enjoyed surveying the fruits of his labor after a long day's work. To Ben, the surrounding countryside looked like nothing so much as a carelessly thrown quilt. Beyond the lush lawn and the border of flowering shrubs, the paddocks formed a patchwork pattern, either brown speckled with green where the field was planted with lines of crops, or the uniform rich green of pasture. The road continued to the left of the farm, the land on the other side varying hues of dusty yellow. Even the barn, the biggest of the scattering of small sheds Ben could see, matched the color scheme. Its red paint might once have stood out against the dark, forested peaks of the mountain range framing the valley, but faded with time and cracked to display the wooden boards beneath, it now appeared a natural part of the landscape.

Not that the farm lacked color—or even brightness. Ben's initial impression of overwhelming green faded as he stepped off the porch. The thick grass of the lawn was speckled through with yellow dandelions and the glossy, dark green leaves of the bushes forming the border between garden and farm, featured richly colored blossoms of pink and crimson. Flowerbeds surrounded the house and made small islands of color within the ample lawn. There was so much color, in fact, there were only a few places where the wooden fence was visible at all. The picturesque effect was lessened by the chicken wire nailed to it to stop the gaps.

Not pretty—but definitely practical. Ben studied the fence, wondering what it protected the garden from. *Cattle? Pigs?* He hadn't seen any stock in the fields. *Wild animals?* He turned to consider the forest, rising above the farm on all sides.

It went on as far as Ben could see. The only things showing above the hilltops were more hilltops, all carpeted in the same impenetrable green. It hid the road and blocked out the world they'd come from entirely. Ben rubbed the back of his neck. *I grew up surrounded by skyscrapers! No way I feel claustrophobic!*

Resolutely, he faced the hills, looking for the variations in color. By focusing, he could pick out individual trees among the mass. But breaking it down only made it worse. Where before there had been a single entity, now there was a faceless mass, waiting—

Ben snorted. *Two minutes alone in Nate's backyard, and I'm freaking out. If anyone should be teased about conforming to stereotypes, it's me—total city boy. Not a Starbucks in sight and my heart starts racing.*

Was it the lack of Starbucks or the lack of people? Ben had come outside to find Nate, but there was no sign of him—or anyone else.

Ben balanced on one leg to remove a blade of grass from the underside of his foot. The sun was warm on the back of his neck and shoulders but didn't reach beneath the surface of the grass. His feet were clammy and cold, reminding him of the more basic kind of revenant.

I feel—vulnerable. That's all it was. His bare feet made him more keenly aware that he lacked vampire strength and senses. That pressure he imagined on his shoulders, the weight of the mountains pressing down on him, was his body's way of trying to fill in for an awareness that any human lacked. After all, the idea of anything magical lurking in the mountains was ridiculous. How many times had Nate apologized for how plain ordinary Little River was?

Of course, Nate also insisted he was human, and look how that turned out.

Ben pinched the bridge of his nose. *I really need to find an off switch for my paranoia.* The sooner, the better. There was still a lot he had to learn about Nate, but Ben knew no one with Nate's confidence would be turned on by paranoia—

Something moved in the grass behind him. A chicken raised its head, stepping out of a bush, its strange, unblinking eyes fixed on Ben. He watched it. Chickens were a favored ingredient in many magical rites, but this was the first time he'd seen one in the wild, so to speak. Encouraged, other hens appeared, heads bobbing above their brown, feathered bodies, as they stepped through the grass with exaggerated daintiness.

Now I get why cockatrices are a thing. There was something really unnatural about the ladylike movement of the hens coupled with their ungainly claws that Ben could see easily appealing to a medieval imagination. Or maybe it was their beady stare? *I'm being unfair. Vampires dislike roosters because they signal the coming dawn, not because they're inherently nasty.*

The hens were coming toward him. "That's enough. Stop now." Ben raised his hands in a shooing motion. "I don't have any food if that's what you're looking for."

The first hen tilted her head, ruminated on Ben's words. With a shrug of her speckled feathers, she continued to advance.

"I mean it. Go away!" Ben wiped his hands on his jeans as he stepped back. None of his ARX training had prepared him for being confronted en masse by your almost-boyfriend's family's chickens. He caught sight of a side gate left ajar. *Not like anyone's here to see me run.*

One quick dash later and Ben slid the chain of the gate home. The chickens cast him baleful looks, but Ben was firmly on the other side of the fence with no one to witness his undignified retreat. *Score one for quiet!* Ben turned and plunged his foot directly onto an upturned twig.

His yelp was swallowed immediately by the surrounding woods. Eyes watering, Ben balanced precariously as he looked at his throbbing foot. It felt like he'd been stabbed, but the skin wasn't broken. Ben cautiously lowered his foot to the ground. *First step, find my shoes!* Maybe Nate remembered what happened to them?

Come to think of it, how am I going to find Nate?

A dirt path meandered through the grass in front of him. The path Ma spoke of? *Maybe I am finally getting somewhere.*

A loud crack called Ben's attention to the trees that surrounded him. They were planted in rows, with gnarled gray bark and light green leaves. Moss grew between their roots. *The orchard?* Ben peered down the first row. He couldn't see anyone, but another sharp crack indicated someone was present. Hesitantly, feeling out the grass before resting his full weight on it, Ben made his way through the trees.

One of the twins stood with his back to Ben. He stuck the secateurs he used under his arm, stretching out his hand to the trunk of the tree in front of them. Two clipped branches lay at his feet, the source of the noise Ben had heard.

Ben hesitated. *Nate? Or Ethan?* Neither twin had worn that jacket at breakfast, and the breeze whispering through the row of trees, lifting Ben's hair into his eyes, could easily have undone Nate's meticulous styling. The man's silence brought to mind Ethan's quiet demeanor, but the casual ease with which the twin peeled off his gloves and stretched indicated a comfort with himself and his surroundings that was all Nate, perfectly at home with himself in any situation. Ben fought the urge to shift, feeling very uneasy. He'd never seen Nate when he was alone—obviously, that was the definition of alone—but the lack of any facial expression alarmed him. Nate's face so readily expressed what he was feeling, that to have that missing felt like a trick.

The breeze lifted the branches of the tree the twin stood in front of, brushing its leaves across his cheek. He smiled slowly, an inward, unpracticed smile, catching the leaf between his fingers.

Ben knew. "Hello, Ethan."

Nate's brother turned his head to give Ben a half-second glance. The smile, slight as it was, disappeared entirely.

Ben carefully picked his way through the grass to join Ethan. "Still working?"

Ethan grunted.

We're talking! "So, this must be the orchard? It's bigger than I thought." Ben glanced around, searching for something to say. "Not that I've seen many orchards, of course."

Ethan snorted. He reached for the back pocket of his jeans, the matching pair of the ones balanced on Ben's hips, and pulled out a knife.

Ben raised an eyebrow. The knife was impressively big, but as Ethan removed its sheath, Ben saw the shape was completely wrong for a dagger. The blade was sharp but in serious need of a good wipe down. "You know, you really should clean that."

Ethan paused, hand around one truncated branch-stump, to give Ben a look. Had Ben thought Ethan lacked emotion? There was enough annoyance there for both twins. "Does its job."

"I didn't mean to criticize. It's just, I'm just good with knives." Ben rubbed his elbow. Way to go! Ma thought he was weird, and now Ethan was going to think he was some kind of violent nutjob. "I've helped clean a lot of them. I could help you, if you'd like."

Ethan placed the knife across the center of the stump and began to work it down in a gentle sawing motion. He did this until there was a crack through the stump, about a thumbnail deep.

Ben took a step closer to better see the stump. He watched Ethan kneel to take a twig from the bucket at the base of the tree. "Are you...grafting?"

Ethan might have nodded.

Ben leaned in, watching as Ethan took the knife to the base of the twig, whittling it to a fine point. "My botany professor described the process, but I've never actually seen it done."

Ethan didn't respond verbally, but he took a step sideways, making it easier for Ben to observe. He carefully inserted the twig into the cut he'd made in the stump and then, once satisfied with its position, placed his hand around stump and twig and let it rest there a long moment. Finally, he knelt to pick up the ball of twine at his feet.

"And you just bind it?" Ben shook his head, watching Ethan wrap the twine carefully around stump and branch. "And that branch is going to become a part of the tree, just like that?"

Ethan gave Ben a flat look. "That's what grafting is."

"I know." Ben set his hands in the pockets of the voluminous jeans as he explained. "It's just—it still seems incredible. Humans have spent thousands of years studying medicine, made all sorts of advances, and even the most skilled surgeon can't guarantee that an organ transplant will work. And yet anyone can take a branch from one apple tree and attach it to another and it grows." Ben caught himself abruptly. *Did I just imply that Nate's brother is stupid?*

Ethan picked up the knife. "Don't underestimate trees." He turned toward Ben, waving an arm toward their surroundings with the most animation Ben had seen him display ever. "Look around. These trees. How old are they?"

Ben fought the urge to step back. Showing alarm would only escalate the situation. "What do you mean?"

"How old do you think the trees are?" Ethan shoved the knife into sheath.

Ben took his eyes off Ethan to glance at the trees. They weren't big, not like the oak in Mason's Park, but their trunks were twisted and wrinkled, putting Ben in mind of a stooping senior citizen. "Um... Thirty years old?"

"Seventy. Planted by our grandfather." Ethan rested his hand on the trunk of the tree beside him. "How many seventy-year-olds you know who are still growing?"

"That is—" More words than Ben had ever heard Ethan say. "—impressive." Ben gave the surrounding apple trees a considering glance. "And they still produce fruit?"

Ethan smirked. "More productive in one season than some people in their entire lifetime." He smiled at the tree, giving it an affectionate pat before bending to pick up his bucket.

When Nate said his brother liked plants, he meant *really* liked plants. Ben couldn't help but be amused. *Ethan's a geek for plants!* Finally, something he could relate to. "If they still produce apples, why are you grafting?"

Ethan scowled. "Heard of Winesap?"

"Is that an emulator?"

"Type of apple. Popular seventy years ago." Ethan waved his hand in the direction of the road. "Used to be this valley was full of orchards."

Ben winced. Ethan's scowl gave him an inkling where this conversation was going. "Now not so much?"

"Apple trees live to one hundred. But they just cut them down. Perfectly good trees, gone." Ethan clenched the secateurs tightly. "Grafting is easy. Saves the tree, grows different apples to sell. Win-win. But they don't care. Just chop down the entire orchard. Know what they replace them with?"

So much for thinking Ethan lacked emotion. The heat in his voice coupled with the angry rise of his chest was bringing home his relationship to Nate in a very immediate way. Ben swallowed. "I...don't know?"

"Christmas trees." Ethan punctuated the sentence with an angry snort. "Grown just to be cut down." His scowl deepened. "It's a criminal waste. Lots of people don't earn their keep. But no one chops *them* down."

"Ha."

Ethan shot Ben a raised eyebrow and turned back to the tree in front of them.

Ben's smile faded. Ethan's face was completely flat, wiped clean of the emotion of a moment ago... *Is he serious?*

Ethan sized up the tree, weighing his options before coming to a decision. Tapping the tree in mute apology, he used the secateurs to clip a branch.

Ben watched the branch fall to the ground. He felt very out of his depth. "So... I can see you're busy."

Crack! Another branch fell to the grass.

Ben resisted the urge to shift. "Looks like you have a lot of work to do." He tugged at the edge of the T-shirt. "It can't be easy, running a farm this big by yourself."

"Nate helps." The words were sharp and punctuated by the crack of another severed branch. "It's his home too."

"And it's beautiful." Ben cast around for something to say.

"Nate belongs here." Ethan turned to face Ben, the secateurs casually resting in his hand. "Not New Camden."

Ben blinked. There was a definite note of challenge in Ethan's voice. He ignored the grass tickling his bare ankles, holding himself still to meet Ethan's gaze. "That's Nate's decision, don't you think?"

Ethan matched him gaze for gaze.

They really are identical. It was too easy to imagine that cold look coming from Nate, the thought of it sending a shiver over Ben's spine.

As if also feeling the weight of the conversation, the breeze dropped entirely. The strange pressure Ben had imagined earlier seemed to bear down on him again, a palpable weight. The gentle rustling of the tree leaves died away, and even the grass that tickled Ben's bare feet ceased.

There's a word for this. Hyper-awareness, or something. Being a vampire was a traumatic experience. This was probably a hangover of some sort. Ben forced himself to look away. *Not every encounter I have is life or death. I need to stop thinking like a vampire, start thinking human.* "Speaking of Nate, is he out here?"

Ethan turned away but not fast enough to hide his smirk.

Ben gritted his teeth. *This is Nate's brother. Don't start anything.* "Your mother mentioned a river?"

Ethan ignored him, running his thumb over the stump of the branch he'd just cut.

The silence had an unexpected bonus. As he weighed his options, Ben became aware of a gentle trickling sound, previously obscured by the plants' rustling. "That must be it. I'll go check it out." He gave Ethan his blandest smile. "Nice talking to you."

Ethan shot him an unimpressed look. "River's rocky. You'll want shoes."

Ben paused.

The grass he stood in was long, long enough that his bare feet were entirely covered. Ethan had spent most of their conversation trying to ignore him. It was hard to imagine a moment where he might have noticed Ben's lack of shoes. *Does that mean...Ethan took them?* Ben narrowed his eyes. *That's ridiculous—utterly childish! Ethan's a grown man!*

Ethan unsheathed his knife with unhurried ease. His posture was entirely casual.

Ben wasn't fooled. "That's fine. I'm tougher than I look." He walked as fast as he dared through the long grass, determined that Ethan would not see him flinch.

☆☆☆

Why did I think this was a good idea? The dirt path that wound toward the river allowed Ben to see what he stepped on, but that was no guard against rocks. Ben hobbled toward the trickling sound. *If this is just another bunch of trees...*

The path led him around a corner, and abruptly apple trees and grass gave way to willow trees and ferns. Ben walked beside the path, using the carpet of fallen leaves to cushion his aching feet. *Have I somehow wandered into the forest?* In a matter of minutes, the farm was entirely lost from view. Ben could no longer hear Ethan working in the orchard. Only the gurgling river, getting closer with every bend in the path.

Ben limped grimly forward. No way was he turning around, but without a cell phone, he had no idea where he was. *I didn't think I'd need a map just to find Nate! Seriously, who has a forest in their backyard?*

The path took a dip, and there it was—the river. It shone as clear as a mirror, the smooth brown and gray rocks breaking its surface barely distinguishable from those that made up its bed. Its soothing whisper was echoed by the ferns on its bank, raising their fronds in gentle welcome.

Ben stood still a long moment. He didn't want to like the river, but all the same, there was something peaceful about its regular movement. He continued down the path at a much more relaxed pace.

Another bend in the path, and Ben saw a flash of red amongst the trees on the bank. "Nate!" Ben grinned, leaving the path to scramble up the bank. "I am so glad to see you—"

"Stop!" Nate half slid as he scrambled to his feet, throwing out a hand urgently. "Don't move!"

Ben froze. "What is it?" He hadn't heard anything, but with his newly dulled senses, that was no guarantee of safety. *No weapon.* Ben strained his ears for any indication of the threat. Daylight was no defense against all supernatural entities. Isolated locations had a way of amassing volatile spirits. *And being incorporeal just makes them harder to fight. I should never have left the house without salt—*

Nate edged carefully towards the river. "Just stay where you are." He peered at the surface of the water, his body tensed for sudden movement.

The clean surface of the water was only obscured where it reflected the sunlight overhead. It was plain to see there was nothing there—and even plainer that nothing could be there. The water was shallow, barely ankle-deep. No room for a lurking nyx, and running water deterred most forms of ghost. "Nate? There's nothing there."

Nate exhaled, running a hand over his face as he straightened up. "Nothing. Yeah." He smiled ruefully as Ben approached him. "Sorry about that. I am not a lunatic, I promise."

Nate's words were so close to Ben's own thought processes that only Nate's bashful expression stopped him laughing out loud with relief. "I know the feeling. What's up?"

Nate reached for Ben's hand, tangling their fingers together. "You'll laugh... But I had this dream, back in New Camden. About you."

"Me?" Ben let Nate lead him to the tree he'd been sitting by. "Is this TMI? I mean, we're not technically dating..."

"Not that kind of a dream! Well, not exactly." Nate sat down, leaning back against the tree. Tugging at Ben's hand, he invited Ben to join him. "At first it was really nice. You were here at the farm, wearing what you're wearing now." Nate's fingers traveled up underneath Ben's T-shirt, lingering on the bare skin of his hips. "I was just thinking how hot you looked, when Peter exploded out of the water all skeletal and vengeful and—" Nate shrugged, dropping his hands. "—I woke up."

Ben looked down at himself. *There is already one skeleton here. Me.* The turned-up jeans only made his pale legs look even skinnier, his ankle bones jutting out excessively. "You pictured me dressed this way?"

Nate nodded. "Exactly those clothes." He chewed his lip, frowning up at Ben. "That's weird, right?"

"Extremely weird." Ben tugged the T-shirt down, settling next to Nate. "There is absolutely nothing sexy about this."

Nate's mouth curved, as if he knew something Ben didn't. He settled his arm around Ben's shoulders. "I don't know," he drawled. "Seeing you in my T-shirt, looking like you could slip out of it at any moment..." He leaned in, tickling Ben's neck with his words. "Kind of does something for me."

That throaty note in his voice did major things for Ben's everything. He resisted the urge to shiver, cocking an eyebrow at Nate. "What sort of things?" he asked in his most unimpressed tone.

There was a twinkle in Nate's eye that indicated he wasn't buying it, but that wasn't going to stop him from enjoying himself. "Things."

"I'm not following you." Ben shrugged, the T-shirt sliding further down his shoulder and taking Nate's attention with it. "Maybe you could give me, I don't know...some kind of demonstration?"

Nate grinned. "I could be up for that."

"Then what are you—" *Waiting for?* Ben gasped as warm fingers brushed over his unsuspecting skin. The wrinkles of the T-shirt had screened Nate's hand from his view.

Nate stroked his fingers lazily across Ben's chest. "That." He used the arm around Ben's shoulders to draw Ben closer, even as his free hand ghosted beneath the T-shirt. "Fuck, Ben. When you let yourself go—"

Ben ended Nate's sentence for him, with his mouth on Nate's. The kiss was unhurried, much like Nate's explorations. *I could get used to this.* In New Camden, they'd been fighting against time, against Ben's family, against each other. Now, Ben felt time stretch out before them, slow and meandering like the river. He hummed happily against Nate's lips.

A loud splash came from the river. "Fuck!" Nate started to his knees, throwing out his arms protectively. "Stay...back?"

There was nothing there, only a trail of bubbles on the water's surface.

Ben fought to keep from laughing. "Frog?"

Nate groaned, burying his face in his hands as he collapsed back into a sitting position. "I wanted to bring you here so you could relax. Instead, I'm jumping at every loud noise. You're going to think I'm nuts."

"I know what you went through." Ben ran his fingers through Nate's hair. "I'm not going to judge." Nate's skin was cold, his heart racing. "You want to talk about it?"

Nate hesitated a long moment. "Peter. He's dead, right?"

"Twice dead." Ben squeezed Nate's hand. "He's not coming back."

"How do you know that? He set one trap; he might have others!"

"And if he does, ARX will find and eradicate them." Ben watched Nate closely. "Are you worried that he's coming back—or that he's not?"

Nate flinched.

"That's a good thing." Ben settled his hand on Nate's arm. "He tried to kill us, murdered dozens of people. His death was entirely his own fault."

"I know, but—" Nate looked down, avoiding Ben's eyes. "—I feel responsible in a way. Because it was my magic... I don't like it."

"Hey." Ben nudged Nate with his elbow. "You told me being a vampire didn't make me a monster."

"Well, yeah." Nate's shoulders hunched. "But we don't even know *what* I am. What if..." He bit his lip.

"We know *who* you are," Ben told him. "That's the important part. Being human didn't make Peter a good person, any more than being—whatever you are—makes you a monster. It's what you do that counts." He stroked his fingers through Nate's hair. "Would a monster be worrying about the death of a guy who actively tried to kill him?"

That produced a slight smile. "Guess not."

"So, what's up?"

Nate leaned back against the tree. "Seeing you appear exactly as in my dream really freaked me out. I feel like something's going to happen at any minute." He sought Ben's hand. "You don't think it's a premonition? Some kind of warning?"

"Against Peter?" Ben shook his head. "Sunlight is the most effective weapon against vampires."

Nate's frown deepened. "I had this feeling, the night Hunter came to the club. Like my world was about to change—and it did."

Ben snorted, removing his hand. "Hunter has that effect on people."

"I'm serious, Ben. I've never had a feeling like that."

"So am I. Premonitions are incredibly rare, Nate." Ben stood, stretching. "Does your family have a history of foresight?"

"Of what?"

"Seeing the future. Someone who always gets the weather right or had a knack for being in the right place at the right time."

Nate shook his head. "Nothing like that. We're solid, church-going farmer types, as far back as anyone can remember."

Ben poked Nate with his foot. "Then that answers your question, Nate. It wasn't a premonition."

Nate refused to budge. "It was really vivid. When Hunter showed up at the club—I've never felt anything like it."

"That's your flight or fight response kicking in."

Nate looked up. "You really think so?"

"Take it from a vampire—former vampire." Ben couldn't resist nudging Nate. "This explains so much about your inability to stay out of danger."

Nate laughed, standing up. "You had something to do with that, you know." He stretched out his hand to rest on Ben's arm. "Thanks. I needed to hear that."

Ben smirked. "I will happily remind you of your reckless behavior anytime."

"Jerk." Nate cheerfully folded his arms around Ben, drawing him into a hug. "Seriously, though. Thanks."

A shot of warmth went right through Ben—*That's all my doing!*—followed immediately by a stabbing guilt. *What kind of sick person delights in his boyfriend's—almost boyfriend—insecurities?* Ben's fingers gripped Nate's T-shirt. "Nate—"

"You want to go for a hike or something?" Nate squeezed Ben's arm before he stepped back, stretching.

"A hike?"

Nate grinned, his eyes lingering over Ben. "The views from the mountain are something else."

Ben raised an eyebrow. *What views is he talking about?* "Pass. Don't know if you've noticed this, but I don't have any shoes."

"What?" Nate's gaze snapped to Ben's feet. "Why would you come out here without shoes?"

"I couldn't find them." Ben hesitated, running a hand through his hair. "Don't take this the wrong way, but I think your brother might have put them somewhere."

Nate snorted. "He didn't waste time."

Braced for Nate's anger, it took Ben a moment to parse his sentence. "Does...Ethan do this a lot?"

"Only for people I date. And never right off the bat like this." Nate was regarding Ben with a warmth entirely at odds with the situation. "Guess you made an impression."

"Lucky me."

"Don't worry. I know how to deal with him." Nate quickly dusted off his T-shirt and knelt before Ben. "Hop on."

Ben didn't move. "Are you offering me a piggy-back ride? I walked out here, I can walk back." His feet throbbed painfully, but Ben resolutely ignored them. *Vulnerable, sure. But I'm not weak!*

"Trust me." Nate stayed put, turning his head to talk to Ben. "If Ethan sees you hanging over me, us acting all cozy because you have no shoes, then I'm willing to bet your shoes are going to appear real fast."

Ben blinked. "That's unexpectedly devious."

Nate smirked up at Ben. "Younger brother. It's my job. So, Ben. Are we doing this?"

Ben placed his hand on Nate's shoulder, deliberately running over his biceps. Nate took pride in his body, and it showed. The interplay of muscle was endlessly fascinating. *This could be a very interesting ride.*

From Nate's silence and the way his body went taut, Ben was certain the same thought had occurred to him. "Sure. Let's do this."

CHAPTER THREE

The return trip was vastly preferable. Clinging to Nate's shoulders, his legs locked around Nate's waist, Ben felt every step Nate took. The shifting of his powerful muscles, supporting Ben with barely a protest, produced a strong response in Ben. He shifted, hoping to alleviate some of the friction.

Nate careened off the path. "Geez, Ben! Warn a guy!" The urgency in Nate's breathing was entirely at odds with the ease with which he carried Ben.

Interesting. Ben leaned in, keeping his mouth close to Nate's neck. If he remembered right, this was a sensitive area. "Having trouble?"

He felt the thrill that went through Nate. "That depends. You want to make it back to the house or not?"

"Or not sounds nice—" Ben gloried in the groan Nate was not fast enough to muffle. "—but unless your definition of casual involves fucking in your mother's garden, we'd better concentrate on reaching the house." He squeezed Nate's bicep.

"You're an evil, evil man, you know that?" Nate released Ben's legs a moment to adjust his jeans, setting off back down the path with renewed determination.

"This was your idea," Ben reminded him. "Though I'm no longer convinced we're doing this for Ethan's benefit."

Nate increased his pace, but by the time they reached the garden gate, they were both flushed and out of breath.

Ethan sat on the sofa porch. He shot them one unimpressed look and got up, slamming the screen door behind him.

Nate let Ben slide off his back onto the lawn. "What did I tell you?" He leaned into Ben, his hand lingering on Ben's back.

"What have I told you boys about minding the door—" Ma appeared in the doorway, a kitchen towel across one arm. She blinked. "Ben. Has Nate been showing you the farm?"

Nate snatched his hand away as if he'd been burned. "Ma! Ben lost his shoes. We came back to look for them."

Ben shot him a sideways look. *I didn't lose them.* "I left them by the door, but they're not there now." He tugged at the edge of the T-shirt, aware of Ma's eyes on them both.

Ma stepped forward, pursing her lips. She looked at Ben's bare feet, giving the scattering of shoes on the porch a scant glance. "No," she agreed. "They're not. Nate, try the back door. And, Ben. Can I have a word?"

It was all over. "Sure." *She'd already figured them out.* Ben climbed the steps with a feeling of doom.

Ma led the way down the hall to the spare bedroom in silence. *Angry?* Of course she was. Nate said she was religious. She probably saw him as some kind of pervert leading her impressionable son to hell—never mind that Nate had done all the leading!

Ma waited for Ben to enter the spare room and then shut the door behind him. "I finished washing your clothes."

They were spread out on the bed, neatly folded and ironed, and looking better than they had in days. "Thank you!" Ben took a step toward the bed, before collecting himself and turning back to Ma. "I really appreciate this."

Ma didn't smile. "I don't mean to pry, but are you in some sort of trouble?"

Ben froze. The rush of wind in the trees outside suddenly seemed very loud. "What?"

"Your T-shirt." Ma nodded towards it. "When I was ironing, I noticed there seemed to be a lot of blood on it. Do you need to see a doctor?"

"No!" If he didn't seem suspicious before, that hasty denial would have done the trick. "No," Ben repeated, forcing himself to smile. "I'm fine. It looks worse than it actually was." He felt underneath his voluminous sleeve for the thin ridge that was all that was left of the injury. "It's already healed. Department Seven had one of their people look at it when they interviewed me."

Ma didn't relax. If anything, her mouth got tighter. "Department Seven. They're the ones in charge of Supernatural crime?"

"That's them."

"I won't have my boys involved in anything like that." Ma pulled her apron straight, smoothing it down as she drew herself up. "We're law-abiding people here. I don't want either of my sons involved in anything that's against church or law. Do you understand me, Ben?" She fixed a sharp stare at him.

She was tiny! Tiny and human, with nothing more behind her words than the force of her personality and love, but Ben found his tongue sticking to the dry roof of his mouth as he nodded. "Yes, ma'am."

"Good." As Ma turned toward the door, it felt like a pressure lifted off Ben. "It's about time for lunch. Change into your clean things and wash your hands. And Ben?"

Ben looked up from his jeans. They were still warm from the iron.

Ma's hand tightened around the door handle. "I don't hold with sex before marriage," she said firmly. "Not while you're under my roof. I trust you'll respect that while you're here." And clearly feeling she'd made her point, Ma shut the door.

Ben looked down at the jeans in his hands. He absently smoothed out a wrinkle, his mind replaying Ma's words. *She knows. There's no way she doesn't know.* So much for keeping things casual! Ben bit his lip in an effort to suppress his laugh. *How? How had things got so massively out of control?*

The sound of chairs being drawn back in the kitchen called Ben back to the present. He unhooked the belt, freeing himself from the borrowed jeans. The familiar rub of his own clothes against his skin brought him slight relief. If nothing else, his jeans were right. With a frown, Ben held out the T-shirt.

Now he was looking for it, the stain was very visible. All down the under seam of his arm, and in patches where it had seeped into the body of his shirt. Not immediately noticeable, but too great a risk to take. *I need to go shopping. Fast. Until then...Nate's shirt is my safest option.* Ben felt his mouth curve, despite his discovery. Nate's likely interpretation of Ben's choice was an added bonus. Nate's family's interpretation of Ben's choice, however...

Ben groaned. He couldn't win. *It's like being a vampire all over again.*

☆☆☆

"Lunch isn't anything special." Ma set a bowl of macaroni and cheese in front of Ben. "If I'd known we'd have a guest..." There was an abruptness to her words that undid their attention.

Still, after a year without food, Ben found the homely macaroni and cheese nothing short of amazing. Ma added frozen vegetables, bacon pieces, and hard-boiled egg to the cheese sauce, making it a hearty meal. There was bread on the side, but Ben never managed to finish his bowl.

Nate and Ethan had both cleared two bowls and a couple of slices of bread when Ben put down his fork.

"Finished? You've hardly eaten anything." Ma frowned at Ben.

He felt very conscious of how thin his arms were, especially compared to Nate, sitting beside him. "It's delicious. But I can't eat another bite. I'm full."

"If you're sure." Ma continued to frown at him. "If you want something else, you only have to ask. A cookie perhaps, or some fruit—"

"He's fine, Ma," Nate assured her. "Ben eats like a bird. This is the most I've seen him eat, ever."

Ben looked down at his bowl, trying to hide his embarrassment. He thought back over everything he'd eaten since becoming human. *Nate's right.* But the bigger realization was that Nate cared enough to notice what Ben ate. *Still looking out for me?*

"It's a waste," Ethan said loudly. "Not eating." He sat at the opposite end of the kitchen table, glaring at Ben between spoonfuls of macaroni.

"Ethan!" Ma scolded him. "Ben's our guest, and he hasn't been very well—"

Oh great. The last thing Ben wanted was to be an invalid. "I'm not—"

"It's cool, Ethan. Ben doesn't want it, more for us." Nate reached over to take Ben's bowl, and before Ben could react, had spooned the remaining macaroni onto the slice of bread on his plate. He folded the bread around it. "See? Macaroni sandwich. You should try it."

Ethan gave Nate a sour look. That could have been because Nate followed his statement by putting the sandwich into his mouth in one go, but Ben suspected he was the real cause.

"Nathan! I don't know what this house is coming to. Between both of your behavior, Ben's going to think we have no manners at all." Ma stood, wiping her hands on her skirt as if relieving herself of responsibility for the situation. "Ben, would you like some coffee?"

He was too full to want the coffee, but the macaroni was starting to have a soporific effect. "Yes, please."

"You go and make yourself comfortable in the lounge." Ma stepped towards the coffee maker on the bench. "And Nate—"

"Way ahead of you." Nate spoke around his sandwich. He stood up, bundling the empty bowls into a stack on top of the collected plates. "I haven't forgotten all my manners."

"Just most of them." Ethan stuck his elbow in Nate's ribs and then rolled up his sleeves.

"I don't know what I'll do with the pair of you." Ma's statement was fond rather than exasperated.

Nate grinned back, swallowing the last of his mouthful. "Don't know what you'd do without us, you mean." He set the dishes down on the counter, where Ethan was already busy filling the sink.

Ben stood, resting his hands on the back of the chair. "Can I help?"

Nate shook his head, picking up a dishcloth. "Nah. We got this. You're the guest. Make yourself at home."

How am I supposed to do that when you treat me like a guest? Ben bit his lip. He caught Ethan's smirk reflected in the coffee maker, but there was nothing he could say.

I'm being ridiculous. Ben caught himself pacing the living room. He halted in front of a portrait of a dour matriarch and patriarch and what were presumably their assorted offspring. *Breathe out.* Nate's family had their own patterns and habits. He couldn't expect to be a part of them from day one. *It's a natural reaction. Nate would be just as strange visiting my family.* Ben bit his lip. *If I still had one.*

"Do you take milk or sugar?" Ma set down a tray down on the coffee table.

"Yes, please. To both." Ben watched Ma stir in his milk with the same spoon she then used in her own cup. The hallmark of magic was precision. If Ma was a witch, she was an unusually careless one. *Or wants you to think that.* Ben ignored his inner voice to take the cup. "Thank you."

"Don't mention it." Ma sank back into what was evidently her armchair, judging from the roll of knitting beside it. "Take a seat."

Ben sized up the options. The remaining armchair looked the most comfortable, but set back from the rest of the furniture, felt somewhat isolating. Instead, he chose the middle of the sofa opposite Ma. He had a moment's alarm as it sagged, almost spilling his coffee as the cushion gave way beneath him. Not too long, and the sofa might replace the one on the porch.

Ma pursed her lips, but if he'd made some huge social faux-pas, she chose not to mention it. Instead, she poured herself a cup of coffee. "Did Nate mention he found your shoes? Seems they were brought inside by accident."

By an accident named Ethan? "That's good news."

Ma settled back in her chair with her coffee. "You mentioned you're an only child? Brothers like to play jokes on each other. You shouldn't pay much attention to it."

This is the second time she's apologizing for Ethan—and it's barely noon. "It's fine. Nate said the same thing." Ben carefully settled back against the sofa. The cushions welcomed him, but did not give way. "They seem really close, even for brothers."

"Like two peas." Ma's gaze traveled to the wall, a fond smile lightening the hard set of her face. "We had a difficult time telling them apart as kids."

Ben turned to see what she was looking at. Over the fireplace, among the collection of family photos, was a framed photo of the twins aged no more than seven and dressed in identical shirts and trousers, standing side by side before a letterbox. The house was in the background, the focus clearly on the boys, looking freshly scrubbed and vaguely uncomfortable. "First day of school?" he guessed.

"That's right." Ma gave Ben a considering look. "I have some photo albums, if you're interested."

Ben set his coffee down immediately. "I'm interested."

"Beneath the TV." Ma waved to a shelf of big, leather bound albums. "That red one. It's the most recent."

Ben knelt before the TV. The album was heavy and wide, with an embossed leather cover. Clearly a family treasure. "This one?"

Ma held out her hands for the book. She flipped through the pages, finding the picture she wanted with ease. "There. Graduation. You'd hardly know them for the same boys, would you?"

Ben took the album eagerly. High school Nate was too good to pass up. "No way you could confuse them," he agreed. Nate and Ethan stood side by side in identical shirts and uncomfortable ties, but while Nate grinned broadly, his arm resting around his mother and hair gelled into the style of the moment, Ethan's wooden expression and stiff posture made his shirt look ill-fitting. They were still obviously brothers, but Ben wasn't sure he could have identified them as twins with certainty. Ethan's awkward posture made him look like a younger brother roped into a family photo, while Nate's confidence put him well above his years. He looked to the fourth figure in the photo. "Is this Pa?"

"That's Mitch." Ma held out her hands for the album again. "Nate's told you about him?"

Ben nodded. "Losing our fathers is something we have in common. Nate helped me a lot." He hesitated. "I hope this isn't painful to talk about."

Ma shook her head. "It's been years. Still hurts, of course, but it feels good to remember him." She flicked through the album before finding the picture she wanted. "Mitch wasn't the easiest man to live with, but no other man would have suited me so well. People tell me its stubbornness on my part, but I don't believe I'll find another like him, so why look? Ethan keeps me company, and Nate does too—when he remembers to call."

"You offering to buy me a new phone? I won't say no." Nate wandered into the living room, wiping his hands on his jeans. "Talking about Pa?" He spotted the album on Ma's lap and froze. "Ma! You're not boring Ben with photos, are you?"

"Don't be so rude." Ma passed the album back across the table. "Ben's enjoying your photos."

"I certainly am." And even if he hadn't, the look of horror on Nate's face was too good not to make the most of. Ben looked down at the album quickly to hide his smirk.

This time, the album showed the family seated on the porch, just like the old portrait Ben had been looking at earlier. Ma sat primly at the side of a man just as wiry as she was, with round glasses and a surprisingly bald head. He had his hands planted on his knees and his legs apart, suggestive of an expansive personality. Ethan and Nate stood behind them, looking uncomfortable in shirts buttoned all the way to their necks. "Special occasion?"

"Mitch's last birthday." Ma blew steam off her coffee and took an unhurried sip. "Remember, Nate? It was a year more than the doctors told him he could have. Gave himself full credit for that."

"Yeah, I remember." Nate apparently resigned himself to his fate, plonking himself down on the sofa beside Ben. "Look at us all. You'd never guess we were enjoying ourselves."

"You look very nice," Ma said immediately. "It's lovely to have a picture of the two of you looking like gentlemen for once."

"I think you look charming," Ben added helpfully.

Nate gave him an unimpressed look. "You can't even tell which of us is me."

"Want to bet?" The twins were uniform in their discomfort, but Ben tapped the twin standing closest to Pa without any hesitation. "This is you."

Nate was non-plussed. "How'd you know?"

"Only one of you bothered to comb your hair."

"It was such a hassle getting Ethan into the shirt that we gave up on his hair," Ma said. "I'd almost forgotten that. Fancy you noticing." The look she gave Ben was speculative.

Nate took the album, flicking backward. "Try it again. Can you tell who is who here?"

It was clearly a school trip. Ethan and Nate wore backpacks and hats and were surrounded by students similarly attired. It was break time, and the twins were seated next to each other, wearing identical expressions of boredom but looking in different directions.

Ben didn't miss a beat. "You're on the left." Looking at their classmates. "Ethan's on the right." Staring fixedly ahead, as if counting the minutes until he could leave.

"Got it again. When'd you learn us so well?"

"I just spent sixteen hours in a car with the two of you." Ben flicked through the photo album with interest. High school Nate was just as he'd imagined him. He'd escaped the awkwardness that had plagued Ben's teenage years, confidently facing the camera. He was less polished, lacking the sophistication and sense of style he'd developed at Century, but the earnest charm that so attracted Ben was there in abundance. Photos of school or community events showed him as part of a group of students, equally tanned and cheerful. Ethan, when present, ignored the camera as he did everyone else.

"Let's find you a real challenge." The sofa dipped wildly as Nate stood up. He knelt in front of the TV cabinet, digging through the books. "How about this one?" He sat next to Ben, spreading the album across both their knees.

Nate and Ethan must have been around twelve or thirteen, with shaggy haircuts that fell over their eyes. Dressed identically in long flannel shirts that obscured the T-shirts they wore, one looked at the camera with a startled expression, while his brother clutched his arm, wearing an expression of deep unease.

Ben frowned at the photograph. In their own ways, both twins were very individual. Seeing them so young wasn't as shocking as seeing them so similar. For the first time, he hesitated.

"Your first day of high school?" Ma nursed her cup. "You know, I'm not sure I could tell you apart."

Ben laid a finger on the boy looking at the camera. "Ethan." He tapped the other one. "You."

"How on earth did you get that?"

Ben lifted his own cup. "That's my secret." Nate cared a lot about people. Ethan not so much. If either twin worried about what people thought of him, it would be Nate.

"You just guessed." Nate flipped through the rest of the album.

Ben had a flash of forewarning. He looked up to find Ethan looming over him. Ben drew back, but with the photo album on his lap and his coffee in his hands, he couldn't move. He just managed to stop his coffee from spilling as Ethan shouldered his way between Ben and Nate, taking up his position in the middle of the sofa.

"Geez, Ethan! Some warning?" Nate grabbed the album just before it slid off his lap.

Ethan grabbed the remote from the coffee table. Any further comment was drowned out by the blaring TV.

Ben cautiously lowered his coffee cup. He craned his neck back to catch Nate's expression.

Nate shot his brother a look of mingled annoyance and fondness. He caught Ben's glance and lifted his elbows as if to say 'what can you do?'

Ben narrowed his eyes. *This is getting beyond a joke.*

The sudden silence was just as loud as the TV had been. Ma removed her hand from the TV's power switch. "Ethan Granger. I taught you better manners than that." She fixed him with a meaningful glare and then turned to Nate. "Why don't you take Ben into Little River?"

"Aren't we in Little River?" Ben asked.

Nate patted his arm as he stood. "She means the shops. Not a bad idea. You'll probably want to pick up a toothbrush, stuff like that."

Ben resisted the urge to run his tongue over his teeth. "That sounds great."

Nate led the way down the hall. "Don't get too excited. Little River is—"

"Little. You may have mentioned it." Ben patted his back pocket to make sure his wallet was there. A town. With shops. And toothbrushes.

"Whatever expectations you have now? Lower them." Nate held the door open.

"I'm legitimately excited about a toothbrush." Ben looked down at his shoes. They looked no worse for whatever adventure they'd been on. "I don't see how anything could get lower than that."

☆☆☆

Little River more than lived up to its name. The road crossed the river at what Nate explained was the border between their property and the next and then continued to follow it down through the valley, taking in numerous twists and a railway crossing before descending a hill and revealing a scattering of buildings either side of the road.

Ben had just decided this must be the outskirts when Nate pulled the truck off the road and onto the large stretch of concrete before the nearest building. "This is Little River?" He frowned out the window. "Where's the rest of it?"

"Told you." Nate grinned as he slid out of the truck, but there was a worried frown that didn't quite leave his eyes. "We like to think of it as convenient." He waited for Ben to join him, waving his hand across the road. "That's Town Hall—fire, police, and library, all in one."

"And library?" The building was straight out of the 1930s, art deco stucco, with a grand façade and nothing much behind it, but its paint had been redone sometime in the last decade. "If you return a book late, do you get fined or arrested?"

"I've never been curious enough to find out. But at least we have a library." Nate waved his hand in the direction of the mountains. "Hearn doesn't have one at all."

Even here, in the middle of what Nate optimistically called 'town,' the mountains could be seen. Ben looked at them a moment, one solid dark green mass, before turning to see where Nate pointed now.

"The school. It only goes up to sixth grade. Then there's the Lutheran Church. And on this side of the road, we got the business district—gas station, general store and farm supplies. Baptist church is down the road, along with the cemetery."

Ben looked. He estimated there were four times the number of houses as businesses, and that still wasn't saying much. Beyond the houses, the patchwork of fields continued. An occasional silo provided color. "Where did you go for high school?"

"Rockford. There's a bus."

The houses were similar, variations on a theme that included a porch, a prim fence, and a truck with mud-splashed wheels in the yard. "When you said 'shops,' did you actually mean 'shop'?"

"The gas station sells ice creams and fish bait. And if you wanted, you could buy a tractor from the supplier." Nate tugged at his T-shirt collar. "But, if you're talking shops that sell toothbrushes, then yeah, there's only the one." He grimaced. "Look at it this way. Maybe we're not spoiled for choice, but we don't take hours getting the shopping done either."

Ben, who could spend days happily weighing different models of laptop against each other before making a purchase, raised an eyebrow. "I'm not convinced that's an advantage." He nudged Nate with his elbow so he'd know he was teasing. "So. Toothbrushes?"

There was a bell, an actual brass bell, hanging over the door to the general store. As soon as Nate opened the door, an older man with a scraggly salt-and-pepper beard, wearing denim overalls liberally splattered with oil, stopped his conversation with the young woman behind the store counter.

"Wanting to fill up?" he asked, looking at Ben. Then, his eyes traveled to Nate, and something in his expression cooled.

"Hey, Dan." Nate nodded in his direction, before turning to the woman. "Rose. Been a while."

"Nate! Now this is a surprise." Dan slapped Nate on the arm. "Didn't realize you were home." Had Ben imagined that coolness? He was all smiles now.

"Just visiting." Nate motioned to Ben. "This is Ben, a friend of mine from the city. Brought him here for some peace and quiet."

Friend? Ben started. He had to tell Nate about the conversation with his mother.

"Peace and quiet? You'll get all you want of that and more," Dan observed.

Nate continued the introductions. "Dan runs the gas station. But if he's not at the pumps, chances are good he's in here, having a yarn. Rose and her husband run the store."

"Nice to meet you, Ben." Rose was a welcoming lady, a few years older than Nate with feathery blonde hair. "You staying long?"

Ben smiled politely. "I'm not really sure yet."

"You'll find it quiet," Dan warned. "City people always do."

"That's why he's here," Nate said. "You can have too much city."

"I wondered what your brother was doing, going to New Camden like that. Fetching you, was he?" Dan resettled himself on the counter.

Nate leaned an arm against the counter, making himself at home. "That's right. New Camden's crazy right now. It feels good to be back home where nothing happens, but at least you know it's safe."

Ben, scraping the bottom of his social reservoirs in a vain attempt to find something to say, saw Rose's expression shift, and she glanced at a flyer, pinned up amongst the store calendar and other notices. *Do you know who killed Olivia Winkler?*

A murder case? I didn't hear anything about this. With a start, Ben realized that he hadn't watched the news or read a paper in days.

"Man, Rose. I'm so sorry—I wasn't even thinking!" Nate straightened belatedly.

She shook her head. "It's old news now." She saw Ben's confusion. "Olivia and I were in the same class at high school. We weren't friends, but you can imagine the impact a death has in a small community like ours."

"She was from Rockford." Dan turned to look at the flyer. "Yeah, I remember that. Sad case. You would have still been at elementary then, Nate?"

"Just started high school," Nate said. "So we knew her, but only by sight. She was the quiet type, always kept to herself."

Rose nodded. "That was Olivia all right. If you weren't in a book, she wasn't interested in you. The last person in the world you'd expect to get murdered, but there you go. It's a cruel world we live in."

Ben took a closer look at the poster. The grainy black and white photo showed a teenage girl sulking at the camera in the fashions of a decade ago. Below that, a plea for anyone with information to contact the police was followed by a reward. "An unsolved case?"

"They really think there's anything to find?" Nate asked.

"It's been ten years," Dan said. "The family's desperate for closure. You can't blame them for trying anything they can." He sighed, shaking his head. "For all the good it will do." His eyes brightened. "You hear about Scott's new irrigation system?"

Nate shook his head. "Last I heard he'd decided against it. What changed his mind?"

Dan leaned back. "Managed to swing a state subsidy. Part of a new scheme. Heard about it? Aimed at encouraging farmers to diversify."

"Yeah?" Nate straightened. "How'd you find out about this?"

The discussion quickly became technical. Deciding that they would probably be at it a while, Ben walked down the aisles.

The first four shelves were everything you'd expect from a supermarket—flour, pasta, cereal and baking powder, followed by laundry powder, shampoo, and household cleaner. Ben found a toothbrush and toothpaste. After that, the general store lived up to its name. There were clothes, gardening tools, seeds, DVDs, fans, cutlery, and more, crammed tightly into any remaining room.

The clothing selection was scant. Ben looked up at the T-shirts hanging from the ceiling. The options were washed out blue or faded black. *Small choice doesn't help when neither of your options are good.* Ben finally decided on the black T-shirt. He added a 5-pack of briefs to his basket and hesitated in front of the stationary. A notebook wasn't exactly going to break the bank, was it? He put it in the basket, added a pen, and returned to the register where Nate was still talking.

Rose rang up Ben's items without pausing her conversation. "You're very popular suddenly, Nate. We had a man in here asking after you just the day before yesterday."

"Yeah?" Nate leaned his arm against a rack of all-weather coats. "Someone from school?"

Rose shook her head. "He wasn't a local."

"Sure I've seen him somewhere before," Dan said. "Asked after your family, but it was your address he was looking for. Seems like he was planning on heading to New Camden anyway, thought he might as well look you up."

"New Camden's a long way to go just to look someone up," Nate said.

"That's what I said." Dan settled back against the counter. "He said it was nothing to him. Thought he might have been a stock truck driver. It's been years since you sold your cattle, right?"

"I guess he could have been someone from the Scouts. Ethan and I went to a couple of jamborees."

Rose shook her head decidedly, deftly ringing up Ben's total without missing a beat of the conversation. "He wasn't from the Scouts. Not with hair like his."

Nate was already packing Ben's shopping into a bag. The toothpaste slipped out of his fingers. "Was he blond? With green eyes?"

Rose nodded. "Very striking, his eyes. And politely spoken, for all he dressed like one of those alternative lifestylers." She accepted the bill Ben handed her and gave him his change.

Dan stroked his beard. His eyes lingered on the toothpaste Nate dropped on the counter and on Ben. "Know him?"

"We had a farmhand for a season. After Pa's surgery." Nate's tone was casual, as he resumed packing Ben's shopping. "Expect he was hoping for work."

Dan snorted. "Well, he didn't get any out of your brother."

Nate paused. "Ethan talked to him?"

"I wouldn't call it a conversation." Dan's eyes glittered. "Whatever your brother said to him, he didn't like. Hurried into his car, and if he was going less than sixty when he pulled out of here, I'll eat my hat." He chuckled. "Got to hand it to Ethan. Your brother's really got a way with people."

Chapter Four

"Were you going to tell me Sandy was here?"

Ma's smile of welcome froze on her lips. She stared up at Nate, hands resting on the arm of her chair. "Sandy?" At least Ben wasn't the only one confused by Nate's explosion. Standing in the hallway behind Nate, he saw Ma shake her head. "I haven't seen him."

"Ethan did. Talked to him and everything." Nate marched over to the sofa and glared down at his brother. "Well? Were you going to tell me?"

Being in the truck with Nate's anger was uncomfortable enough. Ben couldn't imagine how Ethan bore it focused directly at him, but he didn't even glance at Nate. His attention was on the documentary playing on the TV, Attenborough's dry, measured tones as he described the tropical rainforest at odds with everything else in the room. "No."

"Why not?"

Ethan did not visibly react to the question.

Nate grabbed the remote. He turned the power off, standing between Ethan and the TV. "C'mon, Ethan! You know how important he was to me!"

Ethan raised his gaze to Nate. "Sandy's not good."

Nate's fists clenched. "He was my friend, Ethan!"

In contrast to Nate's anger, Ethan's shrug was unhurried. "He hurt you. Made you miserable."

"So you decide, just like that, not to tell me about him? Ethan, you can't make my decisions for me! He's my friend! I decide if I want to see him or not!"

"Nate, dear." Ma put her hand on her arm. "Your brother's not always good at showing it, but he really cares about you. He's only thinking of what's best for you." Her tone lowered. "Why don't you take a walk? You're upsetting our guest."

"Of course you'd take his side! You never liked Sandy either—" Nate turned to face his mother, and as he did, his eyes met Ben's, still standing in the hall. He dropped his gaze. "Fine. But don't think I'm forgetting about this, Ethan."

Ben drew back to let Nate reach the door. He was tempted to let him go—Nate was obviously upset, and if he'd wanted to talk they'd had chances in the truck—but even as his brain decided that letting Nate cool off was the best choice, his stomach decided abruptly that he was not letting Nate go. "Nate, wait!"

Nate didn't. He stepped straight into his boots and stomped down the porch, leaving Ben hastily tying laces. He jogged to catch up.

Nate's anger took him past the tree by the river where they'd talked that morning. The path forked, the right side veering off towards the forest. Nate's long legs easily straddled the wooden stile that crossed the fence, but Ben lost precious seconds scrambling over it.

This must be the hiking trail. I really hope Nate's not intending to climb a mountain! Ben walked quickly after him. Nate stomped along at a pace Ben couldn't match. Forcing himself to continue up the slope, Ben thought fleetingly of the vampire's ability to run without tiring. *Never thought I would miss being a vampire!*

As he looked ahead, Ben caught himself. *What am I thinking? No vampire could run through these woods!*

The sun dappled the path ahead of him, the canopy of leaves above dimming its light to a pleasant sepia and giving the surrounding forest the faded air of a photograph. The farther into the woods they went, the more pronounced the surrounding stillness became. Ben became aware of an urge to dawdle and heard Nate's furious stride cool, wane and finally stop altogether. Ben pressed on.

Around the next corner, he caught up with Nate, standing still in the middle of the path.

Nate let out a deep breath, running a hand across his face. "Damn it."

Ben waited until he'd reached Nate to speak. "So when you described Little River as boring, what did you mean exactly?"

Nate jumped. "Jesus, Ben! I had no idea you were behind me."

Ben smiled ruefully. "I'm not surprised. You could have come face-to-face with a werewolf and not noticed." He bit his tongue. "Want to talk?"

Nate sighed. "God. I'm sorry you saw that. I just—I don't want to dump this all on you." He grimaced, running a hand through his hair. "I know you've got your own crap to deal with."

"Which you're helping me with. This goes two ways, you know." Ben nudged Nate with his elbow. "Remember, you met my family." And while Nate's family might not be the most welcoming, they hadn't tried to kill either of them, which put them miles ahead of Ben's vampire brethren.

Nate's smile was weak. "Okay."

☆☆☆

"There. Now we're completely private." Nate settled his hands on his knees.

Ben looked around. They sat side by side on a fallen log almost totally covered by emerald green moss. All he could see was trees. Thin trees, big, thick trees with broad branches and solid trunks, scraggly little trees growing at lopsided angles, and the decaying trunks of dead trees, lying as they'd fallen or caught on a neighbor. Any leftover space was filled with plant matter, whether the carpet of fallen leaves, the ferns that blanketed the bank they'd climbed down, or scrubby bushes. "Do we want to be completely private? If we get lost in here, no one's ever going to find us."

"We're not going to get lost." Nate smiled at him. "I know exactly where we are."

"Completely surrounded by trees?"

Nate shook his head. "This is nothing. These mountains used to be full of chestnut trees. The house, our barn, most of the town was built from chestnut wood. Now, you won't find a single tree on this mountain."

"Forestry?"

"Blight. Started in the 1900s, spread from tree to tree, all the way down the country." Nate looked up at the canopy above them. "They estimate four billion trees died in forty years. Incredible to think about, isn't it? Imagine something like that coming, and having no way to escape it... There's still people working on a hybrid tree, hoping to repopulate the mountains, but the forest will never be what it was."

Ben tried to imagine a forest filled with even more trees. It was difficult. "You and Ethan aren't fighting about chestnut trees."

Nate sighed, rubbing his elbow. "No, we're not."

"Who is Sandy?"

Nate leaned back, resting his hands on the back of the trunk for balance. "Sandy—man, how to explain Sandy? He just showed up one day out of nowhere. Pa hired him as a farmhand, and I hung out with him a lot. He was my first friend after Ethan—hell, Sandy's the first person outside of my family who ever took any interest in me." He made a face. "That sounds overly dramatic, but it's true. You're not going to believe this, but as a kid, I was pretty shy. Stuck close to Ethan, followed whatever he did."

"I believe it." Ben felt for Nate's hand and squeezed. "That's how I could tell the two of you apart in that photo. Ethan's not really interested in people. You are."

Nate ducked his head. "It's not his fault. He's just different. Always has been. And I'm not—at least, I wasn't." He raised his head to look at Ben. "You said my powers were latent, right? So I always had them, even before I knew they were there?"

Ben nodded. "That's my guess. The stress of your encounter with Peter woke them but didn't cause them." He brushed his hair out of his face, frowning as he studied Nate. "Are we still talking about Sandy?"

Nate's mouth flickered. How had Ben ever thought Nate dishonest? His conflicted emotions were all over his face. "Sandy's only part of it. Actually, this is not the first time today I've lost my temper with Ethan."

Ben blinked. "Does this have something to do with why I found you alone at the river?"

"Yeah." Nate's shoulders slumped. "I'd been waiting to get him alone to tell him exactly what happened in New Camden. I figured if anyone knew what was going on, he would. Far back as I could remember, he's had his thing for plants. Whatever I've got, he's got more of it." He glanced at Ben, his expression uncertain. "It's not bad to want to know, right?"

Ben smiled in what he hoped was an encouraging way. "Wanting to know is natural. When anything supernatural is involved, knowing as much as possible is essential. Did he tell you what you are?"

Nate's laugh was hollow. "No."

"But—"

"I asked." Nate's voice was taut. "Asked him if he knew. He said, 'yes.' That's it. Yes. So I said, 'well?' and he said it wasn't important. There wasn't a word for it, and he couldn't explain. It was just something you understood. And then he started telling me about this new type of pear he wants to grow."

"That's all?" Ben knew better than to expect Ethan to confide in him. But Nate was his brother!

"Maybe I shouldn't have yelled at him. But I told him that he couldn't make my choices for me, that I had a right to know. And all he said was that I hadn't wanted to know until now and that hadn't hurt me any." Nate dropped his face into his hands. "That's the worst of arguing with Ethan. He never gets angry. No matter what you say, he just gives you that look as if you're somehow a long way away and he has to strain to hear you, and then he tells you what he'd decided and that's it. You can't change his mind. Nothing changes his mind." Nate exhaled. "I should have seen this coming, but I thought—I really thought—things were going to be different now."

Ben placed his hand on Nate's leg. "I'm sorry." He hesitated. "Have you tried talking to your mother?"

Nate blanched. "I can't talk to Ma about this!"

Despite the seriousness of the conversation, Ben had a hard time keeping his face straight. "Why not? Because she's religious?"

"That's part of it."

"I don't think it's the problem you think it is." Ben squeezed his hand. "She figured us out."

"Oh god." Nate stared at Ben with open horror.

"When she took me aside this morning? It was to say she didn't hold with sex before marriage and she'd have none of it in her house, thank you very much."

"No— That's all she said?"

Ben nodded encouragingly. "Maybe you're underestimating her."

But Nate groaned, shaking his head. "This— Shit. I really worried her."

Ben bit his tongue. It wasn't his call to say anything, but... "You should tell her about what happened. Everything that happened."

"I can't do that! Ben, it'll kill her!"

Ben caught Nate's eye and held it. "She knows about Ethan, and she handles him just fine."

"She doesn't know about Ethan though. None of us do. Not—properly." Nate took a deep breath. "This is going to be hard to explain, but bear with me. Things are different in Little River. It's not just a small town, it's a small everything. You don't just grow up with people. You grow up with their ancestors too. And they don't just know everything about you, but everything your family ever did. You're always being watched. Judged."

Ben remembered the glint in Dan's eyes as he'd watched Nate picking up Ben's things. Were rumors circulating about them even now? He shivered, doubly glad he hadn't worn the blood-stained T-shirt. "I can imagine."

"It's okay for me," Nate said. "I can get away. Ethan... He doesn't care. But Ma minds. Ma minds a lot."

Ben's stomach lurched. The way Dan's expression had changed before he recognized Nate flashed through his mind. "People treat Ethan differently."

"That's putting it lightly." Nate picked at the log. "Ma's always worrying about him. She's a warden in our church, has been on the council for years. Public opinion's the kind of thing she cares about a lot. She relies on me to keep up the family reputation. Be normal." He shot Ben a pleading look. "You see?"

Ben chewed his lip. "Waking to your magic hasn't changed you that much. You can still support her. And she knows something's up. Isn't it better for her to know rather than to guess, worrying herself about it?"

"Here's the thing. If she knows, she has to do something."

Ben's hair was back in his eyes. He pushed it aside impatiently. "That makes no sense."

"I told you this was going to be hard." Nate looked to the canopy above as if for inspiration. "You know the church's stance on the supernatural is pretty grim, right? Especially out here. There's no compromise. Ma lives her faith. But she loves Ethan. If she has to acknowledge that he's supernatural, then she has to cast him out. No matter that we all know Ethan couldn't ever leave the farm. It's his life."

Ben remembered the way Ma looked at him. It felt to him now that there was a wariness in her look, a tension that never entirely dissipated. "So she just ignores it?"

"We all do. Did." Nate drummed his legs against the trunk. "It's this unspoken thing, never talked about but always there. Ma, Pa and me, we knew we had to cover for Ethan. That sounds like nonsense, right?"

Ben stared at him. He felt the press of an answering weight and swallowed. He'd never told anyone about his secret, not Hunter, not Godfrey—no one. *Do I tell him?* If anyone understood, it would be Nate. *He's all I have. If he doesn't understand...* "It...makes sense." Ben swallowed, aware his voice was rough. "Nate—"

"You're going to tell me how unhealthy it is, living with secrets. And you're right. People always guess Ma's our grandmother. All the worrying, it just wore away at her. But how do you think she's going to feel if I go to her and say 'hey, it turns out I'm not as human as we thought'?"

"You really haven't told her?"

Nate brushed his hair across his eyes. "Gunn made me call her. When I woke up after...after the park." He didn't look at Ben. "I couldn't tell her. I asked her if I was a monster, and she said they'd raised me better than that." He tried to shrug, but the movement looked stilted. "That's it. I have to do my best to keep up the family normality, otherwise it's the same story—goodbye Nate, and she's going to be taking care of Ethan all alone. And you have to admit, Ethan needs taking care of."

He's had too much taking care of. Ben frowned. The thought was unfair. What he'd seen was only the tip of the iceberg. "I get it. I don't know that I agree exactly, but I can understand why you don't want to say anything."

"Thanks, Ben." Nate sighed. His smile didn't reach his eyes. "So that's that. Back to square one, nothing changed."

"Not necessarily. There are still avenues to explore—" Ben broke off to elbow Nate. "I *am* a paranormal investigator, remember?"

Nate tilted his head back. "What is there to investigate?"

"Your family history for one. You've been here for generations. If this is hereditary—and since you and Ethan both have it, there's a good chance it is—there has to be some kind of precedent. Can you think of anyone in the family known for their green thumb?"

"Not that I can think of. But most of our family moved away after the chestnut blight. Those that are left... We're not exactly on speaking terms with." Nate grimaced. "So. First off, Pa committed the absolutely unforgivable sin of being the first and only member of the family to get a college degree. Then when Ma married him, she persuaded him to go to her church. His family isn't over it yet, and her family is mad she married him at all."

Ben shook his head. "Wow. That's— Do they know it's not the nineteenth century anymore?"

Nate snorted. "Little River. Religion is serious business."

"I can talk to Ma. Casually. And is there a history of the town, anything like that?"

"What do you want with a town history?"

"Magic can be acquired in a number of ways." Ben ticked them off on his fingers. "Inherited, granted, learned or gained via exposure to a magical source or event. You definitely don't strike me as the studious type—"

"Hey, fuck you!" Nate nudged him. "I graduated high school!"

Ben grinned unrepentantly. "But it's possible that you and Ethan were exposed to some kind of magical source here."

"How many times do I have to tell you, Ben? Little River—"

"Is the most ordinary place in the world," Ben finished. "But a magical source isn't going to advertise the fact. You've got local ghost stories, right? Superstitions about certain places, stories of phenomenon that no one can quite explain...?"

"Well yeah. What small town doesn't?" Nate's frown increased. "You're not going to tell me they're real, are you?"

"In most cases, the stories are just that—stories. But by working our way through them, sorting out fact from fiction, we might be able to find something real."

Nate studied Ben. "You're really into this."

"It's what I do. What I'm good at."

Nate reached for Ben's hand. "It's cool that you want to help. Really cool. But I didn't bring you here so you could investigate us. I brought you here to get you away from all of that. So you could just be normal."

Ben squeezed Nate's hand. "This is normal for me."

Nate didn't smile. "It doesn't have to be. You're free from ARX, right? From Saltaire. You can make a completely fresh start now."

"And leave you guessing?" Ben shook his head. "Not going to happen."

"I'm fine. I needed to vent, and talking with you... Well, I can see now that Ethan's right. I spent most of my life not knowing, and it hasn't made a difference."

"You spent most of your life with your magic dormant," Ben reminded him. "That's no longer the case."

"So I just don't use my magic. Problem solved."

"It doesn't work like that, Nate. At the very least, Department Seven needs to know where you are—"

"What, so they can roll up and start investigating us? You know that's a bad idea." Nate sighed. "The werewolf—Kenzie—she told me that I should really be higher than Class Three, but because I'd helped them out, they were going to overlook my potential danger. You think they're gonna overlook Ethan?"

Ben winced. That was a really good point. "Department Seven needs to know something."

"And they will. *When* we're back in New Camden." He nudged Ben with his elbow. "You haven't exactly been in a hurry to tell them where you are either—or even let your family know you're alive."

"That's different," Ben said quickly. "And you know why it's different."

"Hunter, Godfrey—they really care about you. Thinking you're dead, it's got to be hard for them."

Ben avoided Nate's eye. "It's better this way."

"Don't you miss them?"

"That part of my life is over," Ben said firmly. "In the past. And it's going to stay over."

Nate sighed. "I can't really argue with you, given what I've just told you about Ma. But I think you make things harder than they need to be."

Ben poked him in the ribs. "Look who's talking. Seriously, Nate." He bit his tongue. "If we investigate, we don't have to take anything we find to Department Seven."

Nate's smile was faint. "I know. But...hearing you talk about this like it's one of your cases... It kind of brought home that I'd be doing what I hate Ethan doing for me—making his choices."

"I don't follow."

Nate stood, stretching a bit. "Whatever I've got, Ethan's got it in spades. And it's been part of him as far back as I remember. He's been this way his entire life, and he's never tried to define it or look it up. What right do I have to go and change that?"

Ben slid off the trunk to face him. "So, you're just going to leave it? Nate—"

Nate set his hand on Ben's shoulder. "We've had enough craziness. I'll talk to Gunn once we're back in New Camden. Till then, I'm just a perfectly normal guy who has brought his maybe-boyfriend home to meet the family and hang out—and you're the totally normal guy I'm hanging out with."

Ben felt himself deflate. "I'm not doing a good job of perfectly normal. Your mother already thinks I'm weird, and I keep freaking out over perfectly normal things." He hesitated. "I jumped at my reflection again."

Nate brushed his cheek. "You just need time—and some decent meals to put some color into you. Let's head home. Ma usually has cookies or something in the pantry."

Ben let Nate lead him back towards the path. The weight in Nate's hold felt like an anchor, keeping him tied to normal. "I'm not hungry."

"Wait till you try Ma's cookies," Nate promised. "No one's ever been able to stop at one."

Ben snorted. For all Nate worried about his family, his fondness for them came through loud and clear in his voice. "They're that good?"

Nate's smirk was pure confidence. Ben remembered abruptly that the man holding his hand was very attractive. "Wait and see."

☆☆☆

The sun had lost its harshness, taking on the muted light of late afternoon. As they crossed the stile back into the farm, Ben noted the increase in shadows made it feel later than it really was. Framed by the steep mountain peaks, the valley would soon be covered in long shadows.

A prolonged twilight. Perfect for creatures like ghosts who occupied the spaces between worlds, or those like witches who could augment their power from the mingling of day and night—

Ben dug his fingers into his palm. *Ordinary thoughts!* He kept his expression casual, hoping Nate hadn't noticed. *Concentrate on the cookies.* He was actually starting to feel hungry, anticipating the snack. How many times had he come home from school, particularly in his senior year to find his father taking a tray out of the oven in a coincidence too perfect to be accidental— *Stop it! You're being normal.*

Instead of following the path uphill towards the house, however, Nate turned downhill, following the stream.

"What happened to cookies?" Ben followed.

"What was it Ma said?" Nate asked casually. "She didn't hold with sex before marriage...?"

Ben nodded. "'Not while under her roof.' Why?"

"It occurred to me that 'not under her roof' still leaves us with a lot of options." Nate's voice had acquired a definitely smug tone. His fingers were still tangled in Ben's, but his thumb stroked Ben's wrist. "There's the barn for one. The orchard for another. And then there's the bridge." He sounded far too pleased with himself, as if he knew Ben would follow.

And I am following. Ben didn't know whether he was annoyed, amused, or something else entirely. "Is this what counts for flirting in Little River?"

"Hey, out in the country, we make our own fun."

Fun. Ben caught his breath, stumbling to a halt. *When was the last time I did something because it was fun?*

"Are you okay?" Nate caught Ben's arm to steady him. "I didn't mean it like that— Well, not totally. Mostly, I was thinking how nice it was having you to myself and not worrying about Ma or Ethan interrupting, and I realized I didn't want to go back to the house."

Ben was very conscious of his heart thumping in his chest. Nate's hand was warm where it brushed his skin, and as Ben looked up, meeting Nate's gaze, he felt an answering surge of warmth in his chest. He hadn't felt his heart beat in a year. Now—

"Ben?"

"Would Ma approve of me kissing you here in the middle of the path?"

Nate took a sharp breath. "No. I'm pretty sure she wouldn't."

"That's too bad." It didn't take much. A slight pressure on his arm and Nate leaned down, and then Ben was kissing him. *I'm alive. And Nate—* Nate's mouth was warm. Ben sucked at his lip, trying to capture as much of that warmth as possible. Nate's breath brushed him like a caress, his mouth just as hungry. Was he kissing Nate, or was Nate kissing him? Ben no longer knew or cared which. *Nate makes me feel it. Reminds me of it, each and every touch—*

Nate pulled him against his body, and Ben reveled in the static shock-like feeling of contact that followed. There was nothing like this—nothing even close. *This is living.* He needed to be locked in Nate's arms, grinding against him as the feeling drowned out everything else. God, yes. The uncertainty and insecurity that had dogged him all day would be silenced by the rush of blood, of breath, of impulses that had nothing to do with vampiric hunger and everything to do with life—

Fuck! Ben pulled back quickly. His heart beat fast but with sudden fear. *Am I—using him?*

"Jesus, Ben. You don't mess around." Nate's tone was breathy, and his arm settled around Ben's waist. "Are we even going to make it to the bridge?"

"Nate. Do you—" Ben took a deep breath. "Do you want to do this? You're not—taking care of me?"

"You're serious?" Nate brushed Ben's hair out of his eyes. What he saw in them got his attention. "Why would you think that?"

"You're always there when I want you, before I know I want you. And you're so perfectly what I need..." Ben swallowed. Nate looked injured, but he had to get the words out. "It doesn't seem real. That I could ever be this lucky."

Nate let out a long breath. "Ben." He was wrapped in a tight hug. "I'm the lucky one. And you've got no idea..." He stepped back, taking Ben's hand. "Come on. I want to show you how lucky."

The shadows were already advancing across the paddocks as Ben and Nate stepped out from them into the paddock.

"What happened to the bridge?"

"Too far. We're going to the barn."

Ben should not have been amused, not when Nate meant it so seriously. But there was something heavy in his chest that flickered, and something in his eye. Ben blinked abruptly. It was too overwhelming to look at Nate, so he looked away.

There was a movement in the paddock. "What's that?"

"Doesn't matter." Nate continued towards the barn.

Ben dug his heels in. "I think it's an animal."

It had heard them, its head whipping up. It froze, standing next to the oddly shaped object that had its attention.

"Coyote!" Nate swore. "Get out of here! Go!" He let go of Ben's hand, jogging towards it, waving his arms.

Ben followed. "That's a coyote?"

"It's a pest! Don't want them hanging around the chickens—what are you waiting for? Go!"

The coyote finally took off. It ran with a light loping run, and Ben paused to watch it wriggle its way through the fence to disappear into the shadows. *Nothing like a werewolf.* He shook his head. *What was I thinking—*

Nate continued to run.

The coyote had left something behind in the field. It was an odd shape, too big to be another coyote, but the wrong color to be part of the field. It looked very much like a jacket and a pair of jeans...

Cold touched Ben, a sudden suspicion. He ran after Nate.

Nate reached it first. He stood a long moment, looking down, wiping his hands on his jeans before stretching out a hand.

"Don't touch it!"

Nate jerked his hand back. "We've got to check. Take a pulse or something."

"No need." Ben quietly put a hand on Nate's arm, drawing him away from the man. "Take it from a former corpse. He's dead."

CHAPTER FIVE

"What do we do?" Nate's hands hovered, fingers clenching as he fought the urge to wipe his hands on his jeans a second time. He was pale.

Ben watched him swallow. *He's shaken. Really shaken.* "You need to go back to the house." Ben quietly sized up their surroundings. *Why didn't I grab a weapon when I had the chance?* "Call emergency services. Tell them you need to report a suspicious death."

"A suspicious death," Nate repeated. He took a deep breath. "And you're really sure he's—sorry, stupid question. But you don't expect to find a guy dead on your farm."

Ben pressed his lips together. "No," he agreed. "You don't." He looked down at the man at their feet.

He'd been a tall man just on the cusp of his prime, thick brown beard speckled with gray, long hair pulled back into a full ponytail. There were no obvious marks of violence on him, but he was dead all the same. Something about the way he sprawled on the ground that just said 'wrong.' *What about sudden death isn't wrong?* Ben made a mental tally of the man's high leather boots, worn jeans, and thick combat jacket. "Who is he?"

Nate shook his head. "No one local. I don't think I've seen him before in my life." His voice took on a puzzled note. "Why would a stranger die on our farm?"

Ben bit back the urge to ask Nate who he was expecting to die on his farm. "Mention that in your report. Male, late forties, dressed for the outdoors. Probably been dead for over forty-eight hours."

"*Forty-eight?* And no one noticed him just lying here?"

Ben pointed. "See how his chest appears bloated? It's filling with gas as he decomposes. And if you look at his skin color—"

Nate shuddered. "Forget I asked." He wiped his hands on his jeans again.

Ben watched him closely. Nate was still paler than he should be. "Are you all right?"

Nate swallowed before he replied. "Just fine."

"Ask Ma to give you something when you get back to the house. A hot drink. Coffee, maybe."

Nate appeared to notice Ben's use of 'you' for the first time. "And what will you be doing?"

"Someone has to stay here." Ben motioned to their surroundings. "To make sure the coyote doesn't come back."

Nate sucked in a breath. "I can't leave you out here."

"Someone needs to call for help."

"You can call. You know exactly what to say."

Ben shook his head. "That's not a good idea, Nate."

"What if the guy's not dead-dead? You're human now, Ben! If there's any risks to be taken, I should be the one taking them."

"I'm not helpless, Nate." That came out sharper than he intended. Ben pushed his hair out of his face. "If he's a revenant, I can handle him."

"But you're not armed—"

"Combat trained. I can handle him."

"It's still a risk—"

Ben shook his head. "It has to be you who makes the call, Nate. This is your farm, right? When the police arrive, they're going to wonder what he's doing here."

"But we don't know what he's doing here."

"The police don't know that. We're all going to come under suspicion, but you—and your family—are going to come in for more of it, which is why I should be the one to stay with the body. As a stranger, I've got no reason to want to interfere with the body, but you—"

Nate's head whipped up. It wasn't nausea he swallowed this time, but anger. "Are you saying one of us did this?"

"I'm telling you how investigations work." Ben's reply was curt. "That's all. Go, make the call. A delay will look even more suspicious."

Nate looked like he wanted to argue, but a glance at the dead man decided him. Without another word, he strode back toward the house.

Ben watched him until he was almost out of sight. He looked down at his hands and was surprised to see they trembled. The discovery of the dead man hadn't penetrated beneath his composure, but Nate's anger left him shaking. *What does it mean?*

Not the time. Ben turned his attention to the corpse at his feet. The shadows were increasing. If Ben had an undead on his hands, he wanted to know what he was in for.

Careful not to disturb the corpse in any way, Ben knelt beside it. Using the fabric of the T-shirt to cover his hand, he drew back the man's lip. His teeth were yellow, stained with nicotine, but clean and there were no traces of blood.

Not a revenant. The lowest form of vampire, revenants were mindless corpses possessed by pure, animal hunger. They lacked a vampire's awareness, but imperviousness to pain and sunlight made them dangerous all the same. Ben was about to stand when something caught his nose.

Thank God Nate's not here to see this. Ben leaned over the corpse, breathing in a putrid odor better left undescribed. For a moment, his mouth contorted, fangs that were no longer present longing to bare in a hunter's grimace. The human in Ben wanted to gag. The investigator wouldn't let him. Ben pushed past the stench of human decay. *Alcohol. A lot of it.* Either the man had been drinking, or someone wanted to hide another, more incriminating scent... *There it is!* A burnt smell. Sour, mingled with something rotten and acrid, something that stuck directly to the back of Ben's throat. *Sulfur. Brimstone.*

Ben stood slowly. *Demonic interference.* He mentally reviewed what he had seen of the small town. Quiet, close-knit, god-fearing community could easily mask a cult. It was isolated enough...

You're speculating. Ben shook his head. *Facts first, then theories.* He put his hands in his pockets, taking a step back to consider the man from a distance.

From this angle, the wrongness about how he lay was even more apparent. *He didn't fall like that.* Rigor mortis had set in before he had been placed on the farm. *That's it—he was put here.*

The man sprawled in the trench between two rows. *An attempt to hide him?* Ben looked around the field. It was planted in long lines of raised beds, green leaves just protruding from the top. There was no sign of trampled plants or any other evidence of a fight—but there were signs of something being dragged along the trench.

The forest is right there. With all that available cover to hide a body, who on earth would choose an open field? Ben bit his lip. Someone who didn't think along common sense lines. Someone with no interest in or comprehension of other people. Someone like Ethan.

Nate's words flashed into Ben's head. *Ma, Pa, and me, we knew we had to cover for Ethan.*

Cover...cover for what? Ben looked after Nate, but he'd vanished out of sight behind the barn. Presumably he'd reached the house and was already telephoning the police. Or would he tell Ma first?

I should have gone with him. Leaving the three of them alone gives them time to concoct a cover story— No! Ben dug his nails into his arm. *Nate's not like that. Anyway, the man didn't die here. He was brought here.*

Why bring a dead body to a field? Especially a field by the road? Ben studied the road. *So it would be discovered?* Was the body visible from the road? He didn't remember seeing it when Nate drove him to Little River, but he'd been looking out the window on the other side on the way there, and on the return journey, he'd been focused more on Nate's obvious anger than the view.

At least the coyote seemed to be gone for good. Ben followed the drag marks towards the road, keeping an eye out for traces of footprints. There were occasional indents in the damper soil at the base of the trenches. *One person taking care to cover their tracks.* Which made their choice of location even stranger.

The grass beside the road was dry and dusty. There were no tire tracks, but Ben found a patch of grass that seemed to have been pressed down. *A vehicle was parked here. Probably a truck.* Looking up, Ben saw that the barn screened the house from view. *Meaning unless someone drove past, you could pull up here unobserved and carry the body into the field.* It was a risk but a calculated one. Someone who knew how little the road was used might feel confident in pulling it off.

Someone with local knowledge. Ben walked across the field, back to the body. *Someone aware that Ethan is different.* Ben put his hands into his pockets. In many parts of the country, just being supernatural was considered proof of guilt. *This is not going to go well for Ethan.*

He looked down at the man. Ethan had no interest in people. According to Nate, his brother rarely left the farm. His trip to New Camden to fetch his brother had been entirely out of character for someone who so enjoyed the peace and quiet of the farm he rarely ever left it. So why a stranger? Did Ethan know him?

It was tempting—really tempting—to pat down his pockets for ID. If Ben had still worked for ARX, he wouldn't have hesitated. *How long will it take the police to get here? Sure Little River wasn't far away, but a death necessitated a homicide team. They'll have to call in backup—*

Ben paused. He crouched beside the man.

The breeze had blown his ponytail aside, revealing the tattoo on the back of his neck. It was a simple design, a stylized human eye. Among the supernatural community, it was known as 'the third eye' and, done by a gifted practitioner, could grant extra awareness to its recipient.

A hunter. A supernatural hunter dead on the farm. Ben turned, but the barn blocked his view of the house. He swallowed. *First suspect in the supernatural killing is always the supernatural.* They were in serious trouble.

☆☆☆

The police arrived in a patrol car that had not only been around the block but managed to hit every puddle on the way. Ben waited for them on the road, waving them to park on the opposite side of the road.

Instead, an older woman with sandy-blonde hair stuck her head out of the window. "Who are you, and what do you think you're doing, giving us directions?"

"Ben Hawick." Ben kept his tone even. He motioned behind him to where the flattened patch of grass was. "It looks like someone parked there. I thought you'd want to look at it."

The woman whipped her head around to look at the back seat. "You didn't say anything about this, Nate."

Nate shrugged. He sat straight in the back of the car, as if called to answer a question at school. "I didn't know about them. Soon as I saw the guy was dead, I went back to the farm to call you."

The woman—clearly the senior officer—exchanged a look with the younger man driving the car. "Might as well pull over here," she conceded. "But I want to see what you think you've found."

They all watched silently as Ben pointed out the flattened grass and explained how he'd found it.

"You see any truck, Nate?" The woman asked.

Nate shook his head. "Not me, sheriff. But it's like Ben said. We wouldn't, not from the house."

The deputy walked further up the road and whistled. "Strange place to kill a guy. Anyone who drove by would see it."

"Maybe the victim thought that would protect him." The sheriff swung herself easily over the fence. "All right. Let's have a look at him."

Ben was aware of Nate at his elbow as they followed, but to his relief, Nate didn't try to talk. Ben shot him a tight smile. *Later,* he promised. Looking up, he was startled to find the woman's eyes on them.

"Nate tells me you're from New Camden?"

"That's right. You're the sheriff?"

She gave him a hard stare. "That's right. Sheriff McCall, Castanea County. And this is Deputy Ray Legapsi."

The deputy raised a hand in salute. He was lean, with hazel eyes and a smile that came easily. "Not the best introduction you could have to Little River."

Ben fought the urge to smile back. "New Camden," he said briefly. "This sort of thing happens a lot."

Nate stood beside Ben as the officers examined the body. He didn't take Ben's hand, but carefully, making sure the gesture was screened from the officers, he rested his hand on Ben's back.

The gesture was entirely unnecessary, but Ben found that it made him feel better. He brushed against Nate, lingering a moment before stepping away. He looked up to see the sheriff beckoning him. "Yes, ma'am?"

"Did you touch the body, or move it in any way?"

Ben shook his head. "I walked around it but didn't touch it."

She turned to Nate. "Would you agree that this is how you left the body? Take a moment to think about it."

Nate approached with reluctance. "Looks the same to me."

The sheriff and deputy looked at each other and then nodded. "Nate, Ray's going to ask you a few questions. In the meantime, Mr. Hawick, I'd like you to tell me how you came across this body—"

"I already told you," Nate interrupted. "Ben and I were coming back from the woods when—"

"We've heard your story, Nate." The sheriff was abrupt.

Ben watched Nate tense with alarm. *Getting defensive will only make things worse!* "The sheriff wants to hear my version of events," he said as casually as he could. "To compare our statements. It's normal police procedure." He offered Nate an encouraging smile.

The sheriff narrowed her eyes. "Do you have a background in law enforcement, Mr. Hawick?"

"No, ma'am."

"Then perhaps you can refrain from telling me how to do my job." She pointed. "The car. Now."

Sitting in the patrol car did not make for a comfortable interview, but that might have been the sheriff's intention. Ben kept his hands resting on his knees as he answered her questions. He described the discovery of the body, and at her request, what he'd done while waiting for their arrival. She jotted it all down in her notebook and then paused, frowning at what she'd written.

"And you say this man, Harriet, was a stranger to you?"

Ben raised an eyebrow. Neither the sheriff nor her deputy had checked the corpse for I.D. "A complete stranger. How did you know his name?"

"He blew through town a week ago. Making some inquiries." The sheriff fixed him with her stare. "Why?"

"I just discovered a dead man. I'm bound to be curious."

"You're bound to answer questions, not ask them." The sheriff turned the page of her notebook. "Give me your movements for the last twenty-four hours."

"Nate and I were at my home in New Camden yesterday morning when his brother arrived to take Nate home." Ben decided not to mention that Ethan's appearance had been a complete surprise. "On the spur of the moment, Nate invited me to join them. I did."

"That's a long drive. What time did you leave?"

"Maybe about nine, ten in the morning? Neither of us was paying attention to the time." Ben brushed his hair out of his eyes. "I'm not sure when we arrived. It was dark, and I was tired."

The sheriff pursed her lips. "Can you verify that?"

Verify...? Ben blinked. *The man was killed while Nate and I were in New Camden and Ethan driving there. If we can prove we were on the road, we've got an alibi.* "We stopped for gas and food a couple of times. I'm not sure where exactly—diners, mostly. Nate will be able to tell you, or Ethan." Ben shrugged. "Twins tend to stand out. I'm sure you could find staff who remember seeing us."

The sheriff shot him a glare. If she'd hoped to rattle him, she was out of luck. "Leave that to us." She put her pen down but didn't close her notebook. "What do you do in New Camden?"

Ben was prepared for this. "I was a student."

"Of?"

"Paranormal Studies. Mostly Cryptozoology."

"Isn't that interesting?" The sheriff tapped the pen against the window glass. "Our dead man was also interested in the supernatural."

"I know he was a hunter. I saw his tattoo."

"But you're not a hunter?" Ben shook his head. "What's your relationship to the Granger family?"

"Nate's my friend."

"Did you meet him during your course of studies?"

Ben gave her a flat look. "No." What had he told Ma? "A mutual friend was having a party. Nate and I discovered we had a lot in common. We started hanging out. When Nate invited me to visit and escape the craziness in New Camden, I jumped at the chance."

The sheriff considered him thoughtfully. "And Ethan?"

Ben fought the urge to rub his arm. "I'm still getting to know Ethan."

The sheriff's mouth flickered, but she didn't comment. Instead, she waved Ben towards the door. "I have some calls to make. You and Nate can go, but we'd be obliged if you stay close to home this evening. We'll want to talk to you again. Rest of the family, too."

Nate was chatting to Ray with what sounded like a good imitation of his usual upbeat manner. They paused for Ben to deliver his message.

Ray grinned, thumping Nate on the arm. "What did I tell you? Back home for dinner."

"Not that I really want dinner now," Nate complained.

"Put it aside for me."

Ben raised an eyebrow. "Won't the sheriff mind?"

Ray grinned. "Not if you save her some. Now go. Don't let our—sorry, your—dinner get cold."

"Ray seems cool," Nate said, as they walked back across the fields. "Not what you expect from a police officer."

"The sheriff on the other hand..."

Nate laughed. "She's all right. She's been deputy here for over thirty years. People are traditional. Didn't feel comfortable with a woman sheriff, but she kept at it, and eventually people came around to her way of thinking." He paused. "I'm sorry I snapped at you earlier. I get what you mean now."

"It's all right." Ben looked back over his shoulder. The deputy was a small shape in the distance. No way he'd be able to see Ben reaching for Nate's hand. "Supernatural death isn't your area of expertise. It's natural to be shaken."

"Supernatural?"

"The man was a hunter."

"Shit." Nate looked blankly back across the field. "Is that what killed him?"

Ben remembered the faint smoky smell, undercut with bitter metal. "Yeah. It is."

"Fuck me."

Ben squeezed Nate's hand. "Not under your mother's roof." And then, before Nate could respond, he continued, "If I'm right and he died forty-eight hours ago, then we all have an alibi. You and I were still being interviewed by Department Seven and Ethan was on the road."

"And no one could possibly think Ma murdered anyone. She's on the church council." Nate frowned. "Ray was telling me that they're gonna call in a special task force. That they'll have to do a scene exam of the farm."

Ben frowned. While the sheriff had interviewed him, Nate had apparently gathered a lot of info of his own. "That's normal procedure in any homicide case."

"What about supernatural homicides?"

Ben bit his lip. "They're probably going to have to call in a specialist division. One with training in handling these sorts of cases."

"Shit. This isn't good, Ben."

Ben squeezed Nate's hand. "The sheriff's smart. I'm pretty sure she's already noticed that things don't add up."

"Things?"

Ben detailed what he'd noticed. "Harriet was murdered elsewhere and moved here after the fact," he said. "I'm positive."

"But who would do something like that? And why?" Nate came to a halt. "Ethan. They want Ethan to get the rap for this."

"It's possible," Ben allowed. "Who knows about your brother?"

"That's the thing, Ben. No one."

☆☆☆

Ben had thought lunch was uncomfortable. Dinner took things to a whole new level. Ma and Nate tried to keep conversation going but paused whenever a vehicle sounded along the road. Ethan chewed methodically, unaware or uninterested in the repercussions of the afternoon's discovery. Ben tried to talk, but his attention was on the sheriff and the deputy and their silent companion.

"They got here awfully fast," Ma said. "Almost as if they were expecting something."

"Matter of fact, they were already heading over to Little River." Nate stood at the kitchen sink, holding the curtain up as he peered down the road. "Can't tell if the backups have arrived. The barn blocks everything."

Just as I thought. The place was chosen on purpose. Ben frowned. Looking up, he met Ethan's eyes watching him.

"Sit down, Nate. Things are bad enough without you jumping up every time you hear a car." Ma mechanically started to wipe the table down. "You said the sheriff will be stopping by to see us?"

"She'll want statements from everyone in the house," Ben said. "And since this is a supernatural investigation, she'll probably want to scan us too."

Ma and Nate shared a look.

"Like the kind they use on CSI Paranormal?" Nate asked.

Ma shook her head. "What will the neighbors think! Nate, why don't you take Ben into the living room and give him some coffee. I'll do the dishes— No, I'd like to do it. Nothing like a full sink to clear your mind."

Nate shut the living room door behind them. "I'm glad you're here," he said. "Not glad you're caught up in this, but glad you're here."

A good person wouldn't be pleased by that. Ben fought but couldn't suppress the warm glow that followed Nate's words. "Glad I could help." He elbowed Nate. "Please tell me you don't actually watch CSI Paranormal?"

"What's wrong with it?" Nate sat on the sofa, patting the seat beside him.

Ben took the invitation. "Everything! When the entire premise of an episode hinges on inaccuracies—"

The conversation that followed was fun—Ben rarely got to air his passion for supernatural investigations or his keen interest in mysteries—and by the time he realized Nate was teasing him, the damage was done. He'd well and truly outed himself as a geek, and Nate was laughing at him.

"This isn't funny, Nate."

"I'm not laughing." Nate's smile didn't diminish in any way as he continued to stroke Ben's hair.

"You're grinning at me." Ben folded his arms.

"I like it when you get passionate about something. Your eyes light up, and your entire attention focuses in on this one thing."

Ben felt his heart twist in fear. *Nate couldn't know—could he?* "Are you saying I've got a one-track mind?"

Nate shook his head. "It doesn't happen very often, but when it does, it's amazing." His fingers lingered on Ben's forehead, brushing his hair out of his eyes. "I know why it doesn't happen," Nate lowered his voice. "It's cool. I get it— You're reluctant to let that side of you show till you know you're safe, and you're still getting used to everything. And why not? It's a lot to get used to."

Ben swallowed, suddenly aware that his mouth was very dry. *Nate's dangerous.* No one, not even Hunter, had ever read him so accurately. The part of him that stayed cold and calculating, even in broad daylight. *I can't let Nate see that. But I can't hide—*

"Also," Nate continued in that same, unhurried tone. "I've never seen an episode of CSI Paranormal in my life."

Ben pinched his leg. "Jerk."

Nate stretched out on the sofa, smirking at Ben. He had never seemed more pleased with himself and it was infuriating, even as it was somehow pleasant. "What are you going to do about it?"

Another good question. Ben couldn't let this challenge go unanswered. He placed his hand on the sofa above Nate's shoulder, leaning in so that he was not touching Nate, only by the barest of margins.

From the kitchen came the clatter of cutlery as Ma did the dishes, but Nate made no move to draw back.

I'm dangerous, too. "I'm *not* going to kiss you."

Nate's breath caught. "You—"

A car pulled up outside. The kitchen fell silent.

Ben quickly stood up. "The sheriff?"

"Must be." Nate followed Ben to his feet. "I guess we should go see what she has to say."

The sheriff stood on the porch, taking down Ma's statement in her notebook. "And except for the women's bible study and the evening prayer group, you were home all day?"

"That's right." Ma dried her hands on the dishtowel she'd carried outside with her. "You're sure you won't come in?"

"Love to, Emma, but I'm on the clock." The sheriff leaned comfortably against the porch railing. "Notice anything out of the ordinary today or yesterday?"

"Nothing at all. I put the car away when I got back from the prayer service, and I haven't been out since. Except for feeding the hens and doing some gardening, I haven't left the house."

"Anyone to verify that?"

"The boys have been in and out of the house all day. As for yesterday, I got a phone call from Margaret Ross about noon, but nothing until the boys got home."

The sheriff made a note. "Where's Ethan?"

"Lying down," Ma said. "He drove all the way to New Camden, and most of the way back. He's tired himself out. I told him to rest after dinner."

Ben kept his face carefully blank as he leaned against the wall of the house. Funny that Ethan had energy to tend his orchard and hide Ben's shoes, but was too tired to talk to the police.

"I'll have to talk to him too." There was a faintly apologetic note in the sheriff's voice. "One last question. The victim passed through Little River last week. Did Harriet call on you?"

"Harriet?" Ma frowned, turning her head to where Nate sat on the porch railing. "Nate, you told me the victim was a man."

"His surname was Harriet." The sheriff nudged the brim of her hat back with the end of her pen. "I take it you didn't know him?"

Ma shook her head. "I'd remember a man named Harriet."

The sheriff nodded, putting the notebook into her jacket pocket. It seemed to Ben that she hesitated. "In cases of supernatural death, it's usual procedure to ask people in the vicinity for a scan."

Ma stiffened. "The man died of magic?"

"I didn't say that, Emma. But the man was a supernatural hunter. We have to do our due diligence."

"You know perfectly well I hold no truck with that sort of thing—"

"It's fine," Ben assured Ma. "It really is normal procedure. Just like testing the clothes of a suspected shooter for traces of gunpowder residue." Ben was the recipient of three blank looks. *Does no one read mysteries?* "I'll go first if you're worried about it."

Nate shifted restlessly from his seat on the porch. "You sure, Ben?"

"It's fine," Ben stood, putting his arms out, like a passenger going through security screening at an airport. "Anything the scan picks up, the sheriff will learn when she does her background check on me anyway."

The sheriff gave him a speculative look as she raised the scanner. "Hold still."

The scanner worked on the same basic principle as dousing rods or scrying, but numerous police studies had found that the general public had more confidence in an officer holding a shiny piece of plastic that beeped and whistled than an officer wielding a forked twig or metal diving fork. The scanner was a joke amongst supernatural hunters—in the hands of non-practitioners, it was about as useful as a Magic 8 Ball, and its evidence could not be relied on in court—but it did what it was meant to do: light up in the presence of magical residue.

The sheriff whistled. "You been exposed to magic recently?"

Ben nodded. "I'm from New Camden. Nate and I were at one of the sights where the necromancer was active. It's no surprise that there'd be residue from that."

"Nathan Granger!"

"I was going to tell you, Ma. But when you'd had time to get over being worried." Nate reluctantly took Ben's place in front of the scanner.

It lit up immediately. The sheriff snorted. "No wonder you need a vacation." She beckoned Ma over. "You, too, Emma."

"I don't hold with this," Ma said. "I'm a Christian, Alison. You know that."

The sheriff did not look at all like an Alison as she held up the scanner. "If necessary, you can tell Pastor Whitlock to take it up with me." This time, the scanner didn't light up at all. A single beep indicated that it was working, and no more. "All clear. That wasn't so bad, was it? Now, if I could just speak to Ethan for a moment."

Ma's mouth tightened, but all she said was "Nate, will you go wake your brother?"

"Sure thing." Nate disappeared into the house.

Ma turned the dishcloth over in her hands. "What happens now?"

"We're waiting for the specialized homicide unit." The sheriff tugged at the brim of her hat. "They'll want to set up shop on site. Is there anywhere we can put a trailer—"

"A trailer!" Ma was openly dismayed.

"It's going to be noticeable one way or another," the sheriff said quietly. "But put it right out in the open, and folks will know you have nothing to hide."

Ma looked at her. There was color in her cheeks, but she said nothing.

Undercurrents under undercurrents. Ben wondered if the sheriff knew or if she guessed. *Decades in law enforcement gave you an instinct for when people hid, if not what they were hiding...*

"And here's Ethan now." The sheriff straightened, holding up the scanner. "This won't take a minute."

Ethan slouched over to the sheriff. He was wearing the same clothes he'd worn earlier, and his messy hair all but covered his eyes. He approached the sheriff with a palpable air of reluctance.

The sheriff was evidently used to Ethan's particular brand of friendly. "Now don't be like that. This won't take a minute, and then you can get back to your nap." She beckoned Ethan to stand with his arms outstretched. "Your mother and brother have done it already. Nothing to worry about."

Ethan obediently stepped forward. His eyes flickered toward Ben, just for a moment, but for that brief second, Ben saw a flash of fear. Then it was gone, replaced by Ethan's usual wooden expression.

Ben felt a sense of incredulity. *It can't be. They wouldn't– Too risky!*

But Nate was willing to do anything for his brother.

"Exposure to magic." The sheriff raised her eyebrows. "Your brother been leading you astray in New Camden?" she laughed, slapping 'Ethan' on the arm to indicate it was a joke. "Now, I'm going to need a statement. You had no idea that anything had happened on your farm?"

Ma shook her head. "You've known Ethan since he was an infant! The very idea—"

"I have to ask, Emma." The sheriff shrugged. Her attitude indicated that the questions were mere routine, but Ben noticed that her eyes flicked back to 'Ethan' at regular intervals. "About that field. When was the last time you went down there?"

"Me? I can't even remember. But Ethan planted it maybe a fortnight ago." Ma wiped her hands on her apron, motioning the sheriff and to follow her indoors. "I don't know why we're standing around out here for the mosquitos to get us. Let's go inside."

Evidently Ma usually answered for Ethan. Which was lucky. Nate might be able to copy his twin's facial expressions, but Ben doubted he could replicate Ethan's flat tone. Already Nate was fidgeting far too much, and the speed with which he took the opportunity to disappear down the hall looked too much like haste.

"I'm on the job, Emma," the sheriff protested.

"You've never let that stop you having a cup of coffee before." Ma shooed her towards the kitchen table. "It'll be an hour at least before anyone from Chinquapin arrives."

For all her protesting, the sheriff pulled up a chair to the kitchen table readily. She placed her hat on the table. "True enough. And I don't think anyone could grudge me one cup of coffee."

"Your deputy might." Nate wandered back into the kitchen wearing the same T-shirt he'd greeted the sheriff in. He leaned over the sink to look out the window. Concerned for Ray—or avoiding Ben's eye? "You just left him out there?"

"Someone has to preserve the scene." Ben slid into a chair.

"You should have said something!" Ma bustled around the kitchen. "I'll make up a thermos."

"Emma—"

"It's no trouble, Alison. I won't have people saying we're not hospitable." She reached for the coffee pot. "Shall I give you a thermos, too?"

The sheriff conceded defeat. "Might as well. Just need to take samples, and then I'll be heading out."

"Samples?" Ma paused, coffee pot in hand.

The sheriff nodded. "Routine. I'll have to take one from everyone who produced a positive reading from the scanner. That includes you, Mr. Hawick."

Ben had seen this coming. How many times had he said the same thing to people, made the same assurances? "Of course. Hair?"

"It's preferred."

The sheriff looked to Ma. "You happen to have any plastic bags or the like? I don't really have much call for them on the job as a general rule, and I can save the forensic team paying you a visit."

However Ma felt about the samples, she opened up the kitchen cupboards readily enough. Helpful? Or keen to avoid the forensics team?

Ben caught himself. *What is wrong with me? Why can't I react like a normal person?* He tugged a hair from this head and held it out to the sheriff. "There. That's my contribution."

The sheriff nodded in thanks. "Mind calling your brother back, Nate? I'll need one from each of you too."

"One moment." Nate turned back down the hall. "Ethan?"

It was as good as watching *The Parent Trap*. Ethan, wearing a much-maligned expression and the clothes he'd worn earlier in the day appeared beside Nate in the doorway. His expression plainly said, 'What now?'

"The sheriff needs a hair. No, stop that—" Ethan turned away. "Don't be such a baby." Nate put his hand on his brother's chest to stop him. He picked a hair off Ethan's sleeve. "I'll just give her this."

Ben had trouble hiding his surprise. *No way that's Ethan's hair.* Nate was very resourceful.

"Thank you, thank you. Makes my life much easier." The sheriff carefully bagged and labeled the hairs. "No doubt I'll be back later to let you know how we're getting on." She stood, nodded to Ma, and replaced her hat. "Until then, you have our number."

Country courtesy apparently demanded to see the sheriff off from the porch. Even Ethan stood to watch the patrol car turn back down the road.

"Well," Ma said. "What Mitch would say to this all, I don't know." She put her hand on Ethan's arm. "In all the excitement, no one's fed the hens."

Ben caught Nate by the sleeve before he could follow them inside. "Have you lost your mind? Nate, you can't do this."

Nate blinked. "Do what?"

Ben narrowed his eyes. "Did you think I wouldn't notice? You move too much, Nate. Ethan doesn't get nervous."

Nate froze. For a horrible second, Ben thought he was going to deny it. "You can't tell."

"Do I sound like I'm going to tell?" Ben drew Nate back down the porch away from the kitchen. "But this is insane! It'll never work."

"It has to." Nate removed Ben's hand from his arm. "Ethan... They figure out he's not normal, you know what will happen. Department Seven said they were going to hook me up with a caseworker, that I'd have to stay in the city and be monitored—and that was being soft on me. They're not going to do that for Ethan."

Ben was silent. Ethan with his surly manner and unknown abilities was not going to be greeted with the leniency accorded his personable brother.

"You don't know what being taken away from this place would do to him," Nate continued in a whisper. "He could never handle living in the

city. He can't even handle New Camden for more than an hour. Jail...
Jail would destroy him. And you know that's where they'd want to send
him."

"Nate. I know. But I also know that you can't cover for Ethan." The
fact that Nate had put distance between them hurt. Ben's hands felt
empty. He put them in his pocket so he wouldn't have to think about
them. "Yeah, he's your brother. But this is an investigation—"

"Investigation? Or witch hunt?" Nate's voice was low and insistent.
"This isn't like New Camden. There's no Department Seven here. The
police will see 'hunter' and look for the nearest, biggest source of
supernatural power."

"And that's Ethan." Ben tried to keep his breathing calm. "I
understand, Nate. But this is a murder investigation. Everyone is going
to get investigated. There are processes to make sure that the guilty
party is found. You doing this won't protect Ethan. It might even make
things worse."

"We don't have any choice. This is the only way to protect him."

"What about protecting you?" Despite himself, Ben reached out to
put his hand on Nate's shoulder. "What if they arrest you instead of him.
What then, Nate?"

"They'll have to let me go," Nate said confidently.

"You don't know that, Nate."

"Trust me." Nate set his hand on Ben's arm. "No one could imagine
Ethan had anything to do with this. The guy was left between two
trenches, right? No way Ethan would have put a body there.
Permaculture principles, you put your sources of fertilizer at the top
where the rain will carry it down to the rest of the farm. You'll see."
Giving Ben's arm a brief squeeze, Nate walked into the house.

Ben looked after him with a sense of horror. *He's serious.* That was
the scariest part of this entire thing. *God, Nate.* Ben swallowed. *You
can't fight a murder charge with permaculture.*

CHAPTER SIX

Dawn approached. He felt it in every fiber of his body, felt it build at the back of his mind. Its cold fingers drew back the red mist of rage dominating his mind, and for one startled moment of clarity, he knew he was afraid.

With that realization came others. It wasn't the fear that made him feel cold, but the marble slab beneath him. Its smooth surface and confining walls gave him no purchase, even if he could have removed his arms from the jacket that bound him. He had fought until he was exhausted—he was exhausted still. But as the tingling awareness of dawn grew closer and closer, he began to fight again.

"You wait too long." The voice was stern, hard as the marble surrounding him.

It was answered by a sigh. "I know."

In one of his moments of lucidity, Ben had recognized the voices, knew who they were and why they stood watch. Now it was all fear, and he snarled, a savage promise to revenge himself on those responsible for his imprisonment.

"He's not aware." Impatience colored the first voice. "There is nothing of Bennet in this creature. It will be nights before he comes back to us—providing anything of Bennet survives."

"Perhaps that is what makes it so hard to close the coffin." There was movement. The speaker drew closer. Ben strained against his bonds. The presence of another vampire overwhelmed, for a moment, the pressing of the sun's imminent arrival. He would fight, kill, feed. He must.

"If only we could be sure."

"I have told you what must be done." The first voice spoke with an authority that penetrated Ben's blind fury. "You gain nothing by delaying."

"You are right. Sleep. I will follow."

The sound of stone scraping against stone followed. As the pressure of the first vampire's presence lifted, the dawn rose up to take its place. Ben fought violently. No coherent thoughts filled his mind, but he knew he must escape.

Fingers as cold as the marble that encircled him brushed his forehead. Ben opened his eyes to see Hunter leaning over him. An instinctive snarl contorted his own face, fangs bared in raw hatred.

"Ben." The word was more like a sigh. Hunter's eyes were red-rimmed, and his face strangely hollow. If Ben had been in possession of his senses, he would have known at once how wrong this was. As it was, he thrashed violently, hissing his fury.

"The first night is the hardest." Hunter's lips pressed together, as if in apology for the inadequacy of his words. "I can't say it gets easier but..." His face tightened with suppressed emotion. "But the night will never be this long, the monster never again this wild. You will sleep, and you will wake and with every sleeping you will die a little more, and with every waking, it will be harder to remember that there was ever anything before this." He looked down at Ben from what felt like a long distance. "Sleep, Ben. We sleep beside you, and we will be here when you wake." He turned aside.

Ben heard the scrape of stone again and watched as the marble lid was placed over him, plunging him in complete darkness. A few moments later, the scrape of Hunter's coffin lid followed. Ben knew himself to be alone.

Safe! Even in his confusion and anger, Ben knew the dawn could not reach him now. He would sleep, he would wake and then... Ben bared fangs, feeling their sharp prick against his skin.

Coldness stole over him, a deeper cold than before. Ben tried to move but found his legs were dead weight. His arms moved sluggishly, getting heavier with every second.

The cold spread through his body, not fast but implacable. It came into Ben's mind that he was dying, that once the cold reached his heart, he would never move again. He struggled to raise himself, but his arms didn't respond. He tried to scream, but his mouth didn't work.

The coldness wrapped around his heart. Ben fought desperately, seeking anything—

☆

—And found himself sitting bolt upright, the spare bedroom blankets pulled around his waist, as his chest heaved and his hands shook.

"Jesus, Ben!" Nate sat on the bed next to him, his outstretched arm frozen in place. "I am so sorry. I didn't mean to wake you up!"

Ben took a deep breath. "Nate." The sensation of being in the crypt was so strong, he didn't immediately recognize the spare room. "What are you doing here?"

"Couldn't sleep. I just kept thinking about the dead guy and—" Nate glanced anxiously at Ben, running a hand through his hair. "I started worrying about you."

Ben looked from the drawn curtains and Ma's armchair to Nate. "Me? But I'm used to this sort of thing."

"That's why I worried." Nate patted the blankets resting above Ben's leg. "I thought this might be too much of a reminder. That it might have brought up memories you didn't want to be reminded of." He removed his hand to rub the back of his neck. "You looked like you were sleeping, but your breathing seemed kind of rapid. I thought it might be a nightmare, so I put my hand on your shoulder—"

"And I woke up." Ben digested Nate's words slowly. "If you woke me it was just in time." He shuddered, feeling again that awful creeping numbness.

Nate placed his hand lightly on Ben's arm. "Come over here."

The prospect of being folded in Nate's warmth was hard to resist. Ben stayed put. "Your mother—"

"Ma won't object to me taking care of a friend," Nate said easily. "Come on."

Nate wore pajama bottoms and a T-shirt. It was the first time Ben had seen him wear anything in bed. That decided him as much as Nate's words, and he climbed into Nate's arms without further reservation. *This isn't about sex. It's about me.*

Ben settled his head against Nate's shoulder, leaning against him. Nate wrapped his arms around him, and Ben shut his eyes. This close, he felt the rise and fall of Nate's chest as if it was his own. Nate's presence felt more real than Ben's did. "It wasn't a nightmare. It was a memory. One I didn't know I had."

"How do you know it wasn't a dream then?" Nate's curiosity seemed real.

Ben frowned. "I just know." He searched for Nate's hand and found it, threading his fingers through Nate's and clasping them tight. "It was my first night as a vampire. I was out of my mind. The monster was in complete control. I expect that's why I didn't remember... I would have attacked anyone who came near. Luckily, I wasn't allowed to." With Nate's arms around him, Ben found that he could look back dispassionately at the crypt and its chill. "Saltaire and Hunter locked me in the crypt. They subdued me, fed me, and watched me until I could be taught to control the monster. I didn't leave the crypt until I was in possession of my mind."

Nate rubbed Ben's back. "You're not going back there. No matter what, they can't make you."

Something stirred within Ben. Tension he hadn't even known he had. He squeezed Nate's hand. *Once again, Nate knows me better than I do.* "Thanks." He lifted his eyes to Nate's. "I feel better now."

Nate grinned. The impulse to kiss seemed to occur to both of them simultaneously. Just as the impulse to linger did. It was warm, it was gentle, and it stayed with Ben even after Nate had climbed off the bed to open the curtains.

"Well, you can say this much for the police. They don't wait around."

Ben joined Nate looking out the window. A trailer was set up in the field neighboring the one where Harriet was found, a stream of uniformed officers going back and forth between it and the scene of discovery, obscured by the barn.

You could murder someone out here, and no one would ever know.

Ben shivered, his words of the day before coming back to him. The same thought had occurred to someone else, and a man was dead because of it.

Nate patted his shoulder. "Pretty sure I heard Ma stirring. Let's go see what's for breakfast."

☆☆☆

Ma was obviously off her game. Ben's coffee went without being refilled for five minutes before she noticed it, and she asked him if he didn't want scrambled eggs twice. The third time she repeated her question, Nate intervened.

"Priding yourself on your hospitality is one thing, but you're going to give Ben a food complex if you keep this up." Nate joined her at the counter, setting his hand on her shoulder. "That's the third time."

Ma looked down blankly. "I'm sorry, Ben. I don't know what I was thinking—" She seemed paler than usual, the lines in her face deeper. There were shadows under her eyes that suggested a restless night.

"You're still half-asleep," Nate told her. "Go on. Take a hot shower. I'll get breakfast."

Ma hesitated wiping her hands on her ever present apron. "I always shower last. You boys—"

"Ethan and I are fine. Aren't we, Ethan?"

Ethan chewed mechanically at his mouthful of toast and nodded. "You're just fussing, Ma."

Was it Ben's imagination or was the strain of yesterday's events having an effect on Ethan? Ben studied him closely. There had been something in his voice that had sounded fond.

Ma still hesitated. "With how uncertain our hot water is and a guest in the house—"

Ben smiled. "I'm fine. Besides, I'm curious to see if Nate actually knows how to use that skillet."

"How rude." Nate used the hand on Ma's shoulder to steer her into the hallway. "Sorry, Ma. My honor's now at stake."

Nate knew his way around a frying pan. He had two going, the eggs in one and hashed browns in the other. He was more successful at getting food on Ben's plate than his mother, primarily because he ignored Ben telling him he wasn't hungry.

"You've got to eat more than toast," Nate said, putting a plate together for Ma at the counter. "And no, before you say anything, coffee doesn't count."

His back was turned. Ben took the opportunity to tip his eggs and potatoes onto Nate's plate and returned to the slow consumption of his toast.

Across the table, Ethan paused his own breakfast to stare at him.

Ben stared back. Ethan could tell Nate if he liked—but then he'd have to verbally acknowledge Ben's presence. *Well, Ethan? Which is it going to be?*

Ethan snorted, returning to his meal.

Point for me? Ben decided he'd take his victories where he could with Ethan.

Ma emerged from her shower looking considerably fresher. She accepted the coffee Nate poured for her with a smile. "Not that I need it now. That shower did me a world of good. Oh, thanks, Ethan." She looked up with a smile as Ethan took her breakfast out of the microwave and placed it in front of her. "I hope you've been looking after Ben as well as you're looking after your mother."

"Speaking of looking after, what's happening with the police team?" Nate looked towards the trailer although it was impossible to see anything from the kitchen windows. "Nearest diner's all the way in Rockford. Their food'll be cold before it gets here."

"They've been there all night, some of them," Ma noted, nursing her coffee thoughtfully. "I wonder... Nate, look and see how much butter I have in the fridge."

When they left the kitchen, a much happier Ma was making cookies for the forensics team.

Ethan disappeared into the bedroom he shared with Nate. Ben got a brief glimpse of two twin beds, a selection of sports posters and a desk with an ancient desktop computer before Nate filled the doorway.

"Hey," he said, dropping his voice. "Ethan mentioned something about a new pear tree yesterday. I was going to go through the catalogs with him. You don't mind?"

Yesterday's argument was forgotten? Ben shook his head. "Of course I don't mind."

"We might take a while."

"And you're worried I'll get bored?" Ben raised an eyebrow. "You don't need to babysit me, Nate." He let his hand rest on Nate's arm. "I know exactly what you're doing," he said, his voice the same intimate pitch as Nate's. "And this time, I do approve."

"What do you mean?"

"You're looking after us. Your mother—you got her onto cooking deliberately."

Nate deflated, shutting the door on Ethan. "She always says baking relaxes her."

"You did the same thing for me, sitting with me in case I had a nightmare. And now you're talking plants with Ethan." Nate looked startled, and Ben smiled quickly to show he wasn't angry. "It's a good thing, Nate. Honestly. If there's anyone who needs some cheering up right now, it's your brother."

"You should see him in a bad mood." Nate managed a weak smile. "You know where to find me if you need me."

Ben shook his head. "I can occupy myself for a couple of hours. Wait and see."

He shut the spare bedroom door behind himself with an intense feeling of relief. Nate was easily the best thing to have happened to Ben since he died. He was also—and in the privacy of the bedroom, Ben could admit this to himself—overwhelming.

Ben flopped backward onto the bed. *I should be grateful to Nate for—for everything. Not glad to be alone!* But there was no denying that, left entirely to his own thoughts, Ben felt some of his underlying tension fade away. *This is the first time I've been alone—properly alone—since Saltaire tried to kill us.* Granted, Ben hadn't wanted to be alone after that. *But I'm an introvert at heart. Some space to think, arrange my thoughts... This is what I need.* Was Nate looking after him even now?

Ben spent some time marveling over Nate's caretaking instinct before a troubling thought occurred. *How do I take care of him?* Nate enjoyed talking to people. Spending time with his mother and brother was probably just what he needed. *Can't help him there. The only thing I am good at—is investigating.*

Ben rolled off the bed, coming to stand at the window. The sheriff had made it clear that she didn't want any amateur detectives underfoot, and without ARX backing up Ben's findings, he had no authority. Ben climbed into the armchair. *The most helpful thing I can do now is relax so that I'm ready to support Nate when he needs it.* And Nate would need it. The way the sheriff had looked at Ethan made that only too clear.

There was only one flaw in Ben's plan.

What do I do in my free time? Ben tapped his fingers against the arm of the chair. His time as a vampire had been mostly spent trying to assuage the guilt of his existence by tracking down and dealing with supernatural threats. What little down time he had was usually spent recovering, researching new techniques or training himself against future attacks. *I wasn't always a vampire. What did I do before then?* Ben wrinkled his nose. *I've got nothing to study—and no one to play D&D with.* He'd actually enjoyed student life, spending hours in the library on readings only tangentially related to his courses. *Read?*

Ben slid out of the armchair. He eyed the shelf of books above the sewing machine without much enthusiasm. Romance novels weren't exactly his thing. *His Bugling Bride? Really?* The spines of the books were cracked and faded. They'd obviously been read more than once. *I suppose it won't kill me...* About to pick up *The Duke's Secret Mistresses' Secret*, Ben paused. Leaned against the wall, obscured by the Harlequins were two books whose size and hard covers marked them as different.

Ben lifted both of the books out feeling vaguely guilty. They'd obviously been set aside for a reason. A glance at the covers explained why. *How to Tell if Your Child is Autistic. Special Love for Special Needs Children.* Kept carefully out of sight, these books still had glossy covers, but their pages were dog-eared, and the spines creased. Ben flipped through the pages. *Ethan. These books have to be for Ethan.* But Ethan's anti-social nature was clearly the result of his abilities. *Or was it?* Ben closed the book. There was very little research on the effect of magic on the brain. Supernatural beings had only recently made themselves known to the world at large. In many countries, they were still considered a threat to public safety and legally allowed to be killed. Even in New Camden, famous for its supernatural population, most non-humans preferred to live their lives as anonymously as possible. Test subjects for studies were hard to come by.

Or maybe they didn't know? Ben replaced the books carefully. If what Nate told him was true and the family did not have a history of magic, it would explain why Ethan's difference hadn't been correctly identified at first. *But that's impossible. There has to be some indications somewhere–*

Ben caught himself. He had found something to do.

The obvious starting point was the photo albums. Ben sat in front of the TV cabinet. The albums were arranged in reverse chronological order, and he had fun tracing Nate's development. Most of his senior high school photographs had him in company with a pretty blonde. A girlfriend? Nate was bi, after all.

The possible girlfriend was a late development. Junior high showed Nate with an assortment of friends, but the groups became smaller and smaller the further back Ben went in time. *The proverbial late bloomer?*

Ethan hadn't bloomed at all. The only time he actually looked happy in photographs was in the ones taken at what was evidently a local fair, proudly displaying a series of vegetables, all with a first-prize ribbon attached.

Once Ben reached a certain point in the albums, the friends disappeared entirely. There were individual photos of Nate and Ethan taken in the house or around the farm, but photos taken at school or church events, showed the brothers stubbornly together.

What happened to cause such a great shift? It literally occurred between pages of the album. Ben's frown grew deeper as he worked back through photos of the boys at elementary school. In many photos, the boys wore name tags. *No wonder. I can't tell them apart at all.* Ben closed the album and reached for the next.

But this album told an entirely different story. A progression of tractors, home improvements, Ma with a considerable collection of ribbon winning flowers, church groups, and community committees. *Before the twins were born.* Ben flicked through, but none of them seemed like a cover for an illegal coven, and Ma usually collected second place for her gardening. Finally, he found a candid photo of Ma blushing, one hand resting on her baby bump. *This is it.* Ben flipped to the next page.

It was empty. So was the next. The album had been abandoned partway through.

Maybe they started a new album for the baby photos. Ben examined the remaining albums, but apart from the discovery that even Little River was unable to escape the hilarious fashion trends of the 70s and 80s, he found nothing to help him.

There must be baby photos somewhere. With the care Ma had taken to put the albums together and her obvious enjoyment of them, Ben just couldn't imagine there wouldn't be. But where?

☆☆☆

Warm cookie smell permeated the entire kitchen. And no wonder—two racks of cookies cooled on the counter, and from the looks of the oven, there were two more trays on the go.

"They're too hot yet," Ma warned Ben. She sat at the kitchen table, sipping a milky cup of coffee. "But if you can't wait, there's some in the tin on the counter."

Ben was momentarily tempted but shook his head. "I'm still full from breakfast. Actually, I was wondering about the photo albums."

"The photo albums?"

Ben nodded, sliding into the seat opposite Ma. "I noticed there aren't any baby photos of Nate and Ethan. I wondered if there was an album missing?"

"Oh. Those photos." Ma put her cup down. "That's right. There should be one more album."

"Did something happen to it?"

"Oh, no." Ma shook her head. "Nothing like that. I just sent them away to be retouched. They were exposed to the light, faded. There's a lady in Greendale who does it."

"That's too bad. I'd have liked to see them." Ben reconsidered his strategy. Nate had said not to ask Ma supernatural questions—nothing about ordinary questions. "That's a nice plant on top of the fridge. The sort-of purple one."

"The violet?" Ma considered it. "It was a birthday present from the boys."

"You all like plants, then? I don't know many families who share an interest like that."

Ma sipped her coffee. "I hope it's not too boring for you out here, Ben. If it wasn't for the police, I'd have suggested Nate take you over to Rockford. There's a mall there and a cafe or two."

Ben was momentarily tempted—Rockford promised much, much more than Little River's shops did—but decided Rockford wasn't going anywhere. "Not boring at all. I think it's really interesting. We never really had a garden, so it wasn't until I saw yours that I started to understand where Nate's interest in plants comes from. Has he always been interested in plants?"

Ma studied Ben thoughtfully. "Folks around here tend to take pride in their gardens."

There was pride—and then there was carrying a spider fern around New Camden with you. Ben wondered how to phrase his next question.

He didn't get the chance. Ma stood up to check the cookies in the oven. "Almost done," she announced. "Mind giving me a hand, Ben?"

Ben got to his feet with alacrity. "Sure!"

"I need those racks for the fresh batch of cookies." Ma set a tin lined with baking paper down on the table. "Just put them into the tin."

It was hardly back-breaking labor, but doing something felt good. *Because I'm repaying their kindness letting me stay here? Or because Ma's not treating me like a guest?* Ben helped Ma transfer the fresh out of the oven cookies to the racks without being asked.

"Thanks very much, Ben." Ma considered him thoughtfully. "Did you help in the kitchen at home?"

Ben shook his head. "Not exactly. My mother didn't like being interrupted in the kitchen, and my father wanted me to study."

"Do you know how to peel a potato? No?" Ma rolled up her sleeves. "Then you're going to learn."

Ma demonstrated the use of the vegetable peeler and stayed to make sure Ben had the hang of it. "Put the peels in this bucket here. We keep them for the compost."

The potatoes were much bigger than any Ben had seen in supermarkets. "Are these home-grown? I'm not surprised Ethan wins prizes."

Ma smiled. "He puts a lot of work into the farm. Now, if you don't mind, I'd better check the boys aren't getting into mischief."

That put an end to Ben's research, but the look of annoyance on Ethan's face when he stepped into the kitchen and found Ben hard at work at the counter was worth it.

"What are you doing?"

Ben smiled sweetly at him. "Helping."

"Look at you," Nate said. "Right at home already." His hand lingered on Ben's shoulder. "Want a hand?"

"Nah," Ben deliberately mimicked Nate's easy drawl. "You go ahead and make yourself comfortable."

"Playing me at my own game?" Nate leaned against the counter. "You know you don't have to do anything, right? We're happy to have you here."

Ethan gave Nate a dark look but didn't comment and wandered into the living room.

Ben heard the television turn on a moment later. For all intents and purposes, he and Nate were alone. "It's good to be busy. These two days alone, I've had more free time than I've had in the last year. No. Longer."

"That's kind of the point of us coming to Little River. So you can relax."

"Not having anything to do isn't relaxing," Ben said. "At least not for me. I feel...guilty." He added a freshly peeled potato to the pile and reached for the next. "I'm used to doing something."

Nate fell silent.

Ben looked up to find that he was studying him, seriously. "What's that look for?"

Nate shook his head. "Have I told you how much I like how you make me look at things differently? We're different, but it's not a bad thing."

"Not today."

"Careful," Nate said, putting his arm around Ben. "Or the next time you offer to help, I'm gonna say yes and send you off to dig fields with Ethan."

"Fate worse than—" Ben was interrupted by Nate's mouth on his. He grinned into the kiss, hastily wiping his damp hands on his borrowed jeans so that he could wrap his arms around Nate's broad shoulders. "You're incorrigible."

Nate settled his arms around Ben's waist. "We have dictionaries here, you know. I'm going to look that up, and then you'll be in trouble."

"I'm quaking." Ben kissed Nate lightly but found himself lingering over Nate's mouth. Their next kiss was deeper but equally unhurried.

Is this what it feels like to have a future with someone? Nothing about the moment was inherently sexy, but the kiss produced a feeling of contentment that was equally attractive. Ben had no desire to escalate the kiss, only to stretch it out as long as it would last. He let his weight rest on Nate, secure in the knowledge that Nate could support him.

Floorboards creaked. When Ma stepped into the kitchen, Ben was peeling potatoes and Nate was reaching for one of the cookies.

"Leave those alone," she scolded. "You know perfectly well those are for the sheriff and her team."

"But Ma, you've got to let us have at least one cookie. It's torture otherwise—sitting here, the entire house smelling of them—"

Ma shook her head. "I thought you might take Ben into Rockford," she said. "He'll want a change of clothes, to say nothing of a change in scenery."

Nate glanced at Ben. "You want to go to Rockford?"

"Yes." The prospect of more than one shop was exciting.

Nate leaned back against the counter. "You think the sheriff will let us go? She told us to stay close by."

"She meant don't go back to New Camden, that's all." Ma opened the tin and began placing the cooled cookies with the rest of the batch. "But if you want to make sure, why not ask her? You can take her the cookies at the same time."

There was something in Ma's suggestion that implied it wasn't really a suggestion. Nate nodded. "Fine."

"You go with him, Ben." Ma rolled up her sleeves. "You've done a good job with the potatoes, but I'll take over from here."

Ben wasn't sorry to be displaced. All that morning, no matter what else he'd been doing, the presence of the forensics team in the field had been on his mind.

"A blight," Nate said suddenly.

Ben looked at him. They were walking across the field, without any trees in their immediate vicinity. "What?"

"Did I say that out loud?" Nate winced. "I was just thinking that having the police here reminded me of something, and I remembered the chestnut trees. It must have been awful, knowing that something bad was coming closer and closer and you were powerless to escape it. You could only wait."

What even? "Trees don't know if there's a blight. They can't."

"Want a bet? When oak trees get attacked by caterpillars, they signal to surrounding trees who know to ramp up tannin production, making their leaves taste so sour, the bugs just give up."

"You're making that up."

"Honest truth."

"Huh." They were in hearing range of the trailer and its busy stream of people now, and by mutual decision, they fell silent.

The sheriff came out to accept the present. "We shouldn't—really shouldn't. It's not exactly protocol."

Nate didn't consider the refusal serious. "Ma would be hurt if she thought the Chinquapin team were going to go away, thinking Little River doesn't know how to take care of guests."

The sheriff laughed. "She would too. And she wouldn't hesitate to tell me about it. All right, Nate. Find Ray and tell him I said you could take in the cookies yourself."

"What—go into the trailer?"

The sheriff nodded. "That's what you boys are here for," she said indulgently. "Mind you don't touch anything or ask any questions."

Nate went off in search of Ray. Ben was about to follow when the sheriff stopped him. "A word, Mr. Hawick."

She walked with him to the edge of the field. "I've been following up on everyone's statements. Phoned New Camden. Department Seven had a lot to say about you."

Ben's mouth twisted. *Busted.* "I imagine they would."

"A supernatural death occurs and there's an ARX investigative agent already on the scene." The sheriff crossed her arms. "Were you going to tell us about your very interesting history?"

Ben shook his head. "No. And if you've talked to Department Seven, you'll know why."

"Because you quit?" The sheriff tilted her head back to study Ben. She had curiously light blue eyes with lashes the same sandy blonde as her hair. *Is that why she wears her hat so low?* Hair could be cut pragmatically short, but it was hard to make delicate eyes look tough. "Or because of Nathan?"

Ben felt a cold stab of fear. "I considered ARX a second family," he said simply. "After my father died, they became my only family. This isn't a case of unjustified dismissal, or employee dissatisfaction. It goes deeper than that. It was a betrayal of my trust." He put his hands in his pockets, running a quick double-check that his tone of voice was calm. "I want to forget all about them, start over."

"And did Harriet's arrival here prevent you from starting over?"

Ben shook his head. "You asked me about him already. I never met the man."

"Old habits," the sheriff shrugged. "Matter of fact, with Department Seven confirming your presence in New Camden and security camera footage of Ethan at an out of state gas station, we can put you, Nate, and Ethan out of Little River at the estimated time of death."

"But Harriet didn't die here, did he?"

The sheriff raised an eyebrow. "No, he didn't." She stood with her hands in her jacket pockets. "You're not planning on heading back to New Camden, are you?"

Ben shook his head. "Nate and I were planning on going to Rockford."

"That's fine. But I don't want you, Nate, or Ethan crossing state lines until we say so." The sheriff hesitated and then came to a decision. "Harriet had traces of a demon on him." She narrowed her eyes. "You're not surprised."

"I noticed that he smelled really strongly of alcohol. I wondered if an attempt had been made to hide something. Another smell, perhaps. That's when I noticed the sulfur."

"And you didn't tell us?" The sheriff crossed her arms in front of her chest.

Ben shrugged. "I knew you'd notice. As soon as you got a supernatural team in here, they couldn't fail to see it. And I was trying to keep a low profile. I left ARX under strained circumstances, and I'm not keen to get their attention again anytime soon."

The sheriff studied him impassively. "Then you'd also have known we couldn't help but notice the demonic traces in your hair sample."

Ben's mouth went dry. "The what?"

"You don't need me to tell you how testing works."

"No. Of course not." Ben tried to shake off his stunned feeling. "But—you're sure?"

"The results are clear as day. You, Nathan, and Ethan show traces of demonic contact."

CHAPTER SEVEN

"And?" Nate held the top wire of the fence down and climbed over it. "It's not like we're the first people in the world to test positive for demonic contact."

Ben shot him a dark look. Nate was not taking this seriously enough! Not only that, but there was no way Ben was getting over the fence that easily—and they were still within eyeshot of the police trailer. "Demonic contact alone is bad enough to get you on a watchlist. Demonic contact while being present at a site of a demonic-caused death? You have to see how bad it is."

Nate put his hands in his pockets as he waited for Ben. "Nothing a phone call to Department Seven can't fix."

"Department Seven?" Ben took his eyes off the fence to stare at Nate.

"Gunn. He's some kind of demon, right?" Nate didn't give Ben time to process all the things wrong with his statement before continuing. "I spent a couple of days rooming with the guy, you got interrogated by him for hours. That's got to be where the traces come in. And since Gunn's the one they'll be calling in New Camden, there's no way they can miss it."

Ben bit back the first thing on his tongue. It was not Nate's fault that Little River lacked even cursory supernatural education. "Okay. First thing. Gunn is not a demon. *Lemurs* are demonic, not demons."

"There's a difference?"

"Demons exist elsewhere. You can call it another dimension, another reality, another plane—"

"Hell?"

"Or hell," Ben conceded. He took hold of the fence with both hands. "It's a hotly debated topic, even without bringing religion into it. Especially since so little is actually known about how demons work. They interact with this world through dreams and visions or—in extreme circumstances—can possess an animal or person. This suggests there is some force actively preventing them from existing in our reality."

Nate put out a hand to steady the fence as Ben climbed over it. "But if they can possess someone—"

"Evidence suggests that it is extremely difficult for them to hold down a possession without constant sustenance. If an exorcism isn't performed in time, the demon ends up cannibalizing its host in its attempt to prolong its presence here."

The fence wobbled alarmingly as Nate shuddered. "Oh gross. That's—"

"The demons don't enjoy it either." Ben hastily jumped down. "Which is why they prefer to work through agents." He cast a look back to see if any of the forensics team were looking their way.

"Agents?"

If Ben's ignominious descent had been witnessed, the police were keeping it quiet. Ben turned back to Nate. "Someone who has made a pact with a demon is an agent. There is a contract, usually signed. The common terms are that the agent will supply the demon with something he wants—"

"Souls?"

"Possibly souls," Ben agreed reluctantly. He started walking towards the house. "Life energy and suffering are also strong contenders."

Nate matched his slow pace. "So why do demons have such a bad rep?"

Ben pressed his mouth flat. "Outside the boundaries of this reality, they have access to power and energy that allows them to promise their agent almost anything they want. So whenever you deal with a demon, you've got the double problem of dealing with the agent, too."

"How does the demon even come to an agreement with an agent if it can't exist here unless it's killing itself?"

"You know the medieval woodcuts of sorcerers. Doctor Faustus, that sort of thing?" Ben abruptly remembered who he was talking to. "Any movie with a demon in it. There was a circle drawn on the ground with weird symbols, right?"

"Yeah."

"Drawn correctly, the circle both acts as a portal for the demon and screens it from the forces acting against it long enough for it to accomplish its business."

"And drawn incorrectly?"

That was the thing about Nate. He hadn't been drilled in magic precautions, so he didn't know that there was no way a practitioner would allow himself to be caught out by a demon—

But most agents weren't practitioners... Ben frowned. "Um. I guess it depends where they messed up. They might get pulled into the other side, or the circle might just fail to work at all."

"Could it ever trap the demon here?"

Ben shook his head. "Demons have had centuries of existence. The ones that made it this long know every trick in the book. Capturing a demon in this reality is thought to be the only way to destroy one."

"Only thought to be?"

Ben nodded. "Far as I know, no one's ever pulled it off. Demons are too cautious."

Nate frowned. "If they're so cautious, how come we had contact with one? I definitely don't remember summoning any demons."

"It's more likely we've had contact with an agent," Ben said. "And significant contact." He bit his lip. "Have you signed any contracts?"

"What, like to give away my soul? Do you take me for an idiot?"

"Any contract signed with an active demonic agent would leave an influence. Whether it was related to their demonic contract or not. Demons work through contracts and promises."

"There was my employee contract at Century. You're not suggesting that, right? 'Cause Denise is scary, but she's no—" Nate caught himself. "Fuck me."

Ben placed his hand on Nate's arm. "It's all right, Nate. It takes a while for a death to sink in."

"And I found her. You'd think—" Nate took a deep breath. "Sorry. I just... Denise is one of those people you think will always be there. And now she's not... I just keep forgetting."

Ben winced.

They were silent as they walked. Ben thought back over the contracts he'd signed. His employment with ARX, numerous non-disclosures, every time he'd borrowed specialist equipment—even the code of conduct at his university! *Where to even start investigating those?*

"What was the second thing?"

"What?"

Nate unhooked the gate that led into the barn paddock. "You said 'first thing.' Gunn is demonic, not a demon—I still don't get what that means."

"He exists in this reality," Ben reminded Nate. "Much as we wish he didn't. *Lemurs* feed directly on human suffering, but unlike real demons, they don't need a conduit to do it, they just absorb it. Gunn started out being possessed by an existing *lemur*—"

"He told me." Nate shuddered. "And there's nothing we can do to help?"

"Lemurs are notoriously hard to get rid of," Ben said. "And with Gunn's position at Department Seven—in many ways, Gunn *is* Department Seven—any attempt to destroy him would probably set supernatural law enforcement back decades."

"I wasn't talking kill him!"

"That's the only way to separate Gunn and the *lemur,* Nate. And even then, you'd have to do it right." Ben frowned. What had they been discussing? "Anyway. Gunn's not responsible for us testing positive for demonic contact—and even if he was, Ethan never met him." He glanced at Nate. "You're going to have a hard time explaining why your twin tests positive for demonic contact that you made."

"I'll think of something." Nate looked straight ahead at the house in front of them. "In the meantime, you can—"

Ben kicked him in the leg. "Tell me to relax and you'll regret it."

Nate came to a complete stop.

"Nate?"

"I don't recognize the SUV in the drive."

Ben looked at it. It was clearly well used, a dusty red model with dried mud on its tires. "It could be a plainclothes car…"

He and Nate shared a glance and simultaneously started towards the house. Ben was sure the same thought must be going through both their minds. *Ethan!*

Nate was first through the door and into the kitchen, Ben only a second behind.

But if the woman lounging at the table with Ethan was an officer, she'd missed the memo about blending in. Ben would not have thought twice about her heavy combat boots, low riding jeans and midriff top in New Camden, but in Little River, the outfit seemed scandalous. Or was that the look of obvious appreciation she gave Nate, her gaze lingering over his powerful arms? "And this must be your other son. You sure know how to raise them right, ma'am."

Ma put a plate of cookies on the table. "Nate and his friend, Ben. Boys, George here is hiking the trails and stopped to get directions."

"Hiking?" Ben looked skeptically at the woman's outfit. *She's dressed for a night out clubbing—not mountain trails!*

"I told you about the national park, right? We're actually listed in the official brochure the Parks and Recreation Association gives hikers." Nate pulled a chair up to the table, taking a cookie. "We get people stopping by for directions, topping up their water bottle or just leaving their cars here all the time. We've got a guest book and everything."

Ben shot Nate a look. *He can't be buying this—can he?* "Do you do a lot of hiking, George?" He gave the combat boots a pointed glance.

She grinned at him. "Not since I was a kid. My dad used to drag us out to the mountains every summer. Back then, I hated it—a week without MTV? A fate worse than death! But lately, I've been feeling nostalgic. I thought a couple of days collecting blisters and mosquitoes should fix that."

"You only need to worry about mosquitoes here by the river, and if you're going to the lake, here." Nate tapped the map. "Doing a day-hike?"

George nodded. A tightly knotted bandana covered her hair, the sole concession to hiking. "Yeah. At least, that was the plan. Now I'm not so sure. Your mother was just telling me there's been a murder."

"You don't have to worry about that," Nate said immediately. "Guy responsible will be long gone." He nodded at Ben. "Tell her what you told the police, Ben."

Ma looked up sharply. Even Ethan stopped chewing his cookie to consider Ben.

Thanks, Nate. Ben turned to George. "The victim's body was placed in the field in a way that it was obvious he hadn't died there." Ben recounted the other evidence he'd noted, conscious that Ma hadn't moved. "So it seems likely that the body was dumped here and the murderer as far away from here as he could get."

George whistled, leaning back in her chair. "You don't think he could be hiding out in the forest? I mean, it's right there."

"It's possible," Ben conceded. "But if that was his plan, he'd hide the body somewhere it wouldn't be found. Once he gets into the forest, he's on foot. The police have dogs and helicopters." Ben shook his head. "The police are already searching the woods for anything suspicious. Leaving the body in an open space so close to the woods makes no sense at all—unless he is using it to take attention away from his actual location."

George eyed Ben. "Wow. You know your murderers."

Ben shrugged. "I'm from New Camden."

"You're a long way from home."

"So are you." Nate nodded towards the porch. "I noticed Florida plates on your car." He pulled the chair next to him out and nudged it towards Ben.

"Miami," George said. "God. It's the worst in summer. You want to talk mosquitoes? Let me tell you about all forty-five species we got. And then there's the humidity..."

Ben sat, looking at the papers spread out over the table. There was a pile of glossy brochures with the National Parks and Recreation Association logo on them offering a rundown of all the state had to offer adventurous hikers. Other brochures introduced the specific highlights of the Little River and Rockford trails and nearby tourist attractions. A map was spread out all over the table, and beneath it was a rather battered looking exercise book. Ben opened it and discovered a list of names, dates and comments. *The guest book?*

"Dad used to take us to Big Cypress," George continued. "But as we got older, he got more adventurous. We climbed Springer Mountain and Blood Mountain as teens, but this is the first time I've hiked this far North. Any local sights I should know about?"

"In Little River?" Nate laughed.

"Turtle Ridge Falls," Ma said. "Especially in autumn. The fall leaves..."

"This time of year, the view from Mt. Baldtop is the best. On a clear day, you can see for miles. And at night, the city lights in the distance look amazing."

"Nathan!" Ma slapped his arm. "What are you doing climbing Mt. Baldtop at night?"

"You don't have to worry about your son, surely." George let her gaze rest appreciatively on Nate's arms. "I'm sure even a bear would think twice about messing with him."

"Not bears," Ethan said unexpectedly, taking another cookie. "Girls."

George raised her cup to her mouth, but it didn't quite hide her smile. "The local make-out spot? I want to hear more about this. Seriously—I'm all about local history. Ghost stories, random traditions, stuff like that. A place stops being just another name on a map when you know its stories."

"Does Little River even have any stories?" If Nate was embarrassed, he was doing a really good job of not showing it.

"Only stories I can think of are about people, not places," Ma agreed. "And they're all long gone."

"I heard something about a tree—"

"Ethan, if you can't keep away from those cookies, I'm sending you outside." Ma dusted her hands off on her apron. "You can check on the hens. Poor things must be so confused, wondering why they're still shut in the coop. You can take them some fresh greens."

Ethan pushed back his seat with reluctance.

"And Nate, you were going to run into town for me."

Nate blinked, hand outstretched to take a cookie. "But Ma—"

"No buts. Your guest needs to eat. And it will be nice for Ben to get off the farm."

"Chores?" George grimaced. "That's too bad. I was hoping I could get some company for my hike..." She trailed off hopefully.

Ben snorted. "You'll have no lack of police company."

George took a rueful sip of coffee. "True. Though, I can't imagine they'll be the best company." She hesitated. "You're sure it wasn't...someone local? It's just that stocking up on snacks at the local store, I saw a flyer about another murder."

"That's an old case," Ma said. "A very sad one, but years ago now..." She shook her head. "That was a stranger, too."

"You're sure?" George tilted her head. "The guy at the shop said it was unsolved."

Ma snorted. "And a good many other things too, I imagine. If Dan worked as hard as his mouth does, he'd be a rich man. No, that poor girl's death shocked everyone. But in a small place like Rockford or Little River, things don't stay secret. If there had been anything to know, anything to find out, it would have come out by now. That proves it had to be someone from out of town. Just like this new murder. After all, the dead man was a stranger."

"That doesn't exactly make *me* feel better." George's tone was dry.

"What I mean to say is that ten to one it was a stranger that killed him, and they're already miles away. People 'round here aren't the kind to get caught up in something like this." Ma took the seat Ethan had vacated. "Nate, you might go and see if your brother's got anything to add to the list."

"Do this, get that..." Nate shook his head but went in search of Ethan obediently.

"Ben, why don't you wait for Nate outside?" Ma suggested. "Now, George. If it's a short hike you're after..."

I'm being paranoid, Ben told himself. *There's no way Ma is trying to get me out of the house, any more than there's any reason this woman isn't an ordinary hiker.* He stood.

George leaned forward to look where Ma pointed at the map. The loose ends of her bandana fell forward, revealing two darkly colored bumps on her neck. The edges were jagged, but the scars were an angry color, as if they were fresh.

Ben recognized the marks at once. For a moment he saw a flash of fangs, smelt the copper tang of freshly spilled blood mingled with the foul decay of the creature that spilled it. *A revenant bite.* He looked at George, comparing the map in her brochure with the map Ma showed her. *Who is this woman?*

☆☆☆

Whoever George was, she had an interesting collection of trash in her car. Ben peered through the passenger window. The SUV was littered with Tropical Pollo takeout boxes and empty soda cans, while the dashboard had a stick of lip gloss and a pair of sunglasses dangled from the rear view mirror. The front passenger seat had a stack of books, but the folded out map above them prevented Ben from seeing what was underneath. It could have been guidebooks. It could have been something more sinister.

Ben glanced back at the house to check no one was watching and tried the door. It was locked. *Naturally. No hunter would be that careless with the tools of her trade.* Even one who took such a reckless approach to blending in. But that was the hallmark of a hunter—recklessness.

The back seat had a backpack and bottles of drinking water. Prepared for a hike? There was a pair of binoculars and a bird watching book beside them. For a moment, Ben felt doubt.

The revenant scar flashed back into his mind. Ben's mouth tightened. *Very few people walked away from a bite like that.* He continued to the back window.

A blanket was carelessly tossed into the back, along with spare tires and a metallic box that might easily contain a breakdown kit. Might.

Ben's mouth twisted as he spotted what the box rested on. A wooden stake had no place in changing a tire and was too short to prop open a car hood and too thick to act as a tent peg. Nope, there was only one explanation for it—and for the crucifix not entirely hidden by the blanket. George was a hunter.

Ben shaded the window glass with his hand, trying to see what was within. If he knew what George had in her arsenal, he'd know what she was hunting—

"Take a photo. It'll last longer."

Ben's head whipped up.

George sauntered casually down the porch steps. A map was tucked into her pocket and her arms were folded. "No, the car is not stolen, if that is what you're thinking—"

Ben folded his own arms. "You're a hunter."

George's eyebrows raised. "So? That's not against the law either."

"You came to this farm under false pretenses." Ben stared her down. "You aren't a hiker. You lied, took full advantage of the Grangers' hospitality, in order to what? To *spy* on them—"

George leaned against the SUV, rolling her eyes. "You do know how a supernatural investigation works, or do I have to spell it out? Yeah, I'm a hunter. But before I hunt, I need to get my facts. It might surprise you to know this, but most supernaturals don't roll up, card in hand, introducing themselves—"

"There's nothing to investigate here."

George gave Ben a long look and then pointedly shifted her gaze to the trailer in the distance. "The police presence disagrees with you."

"It's like I said inside. No one on this farm's involved in the murder."

"What makes you so certain?"

Ben took out his wallet. He held out a crisp business card. "ARX. Take my word as a professional. You're barking up the wrong tree."

George took the card, a smirk playing on her lips. "*So* sorry. I had no idea I was dealing with a professional."

Ben folded his wallet away. He could ignore her needling as long as it got her off the farm. "Take it from me. The Grangers are not part of this case."

George turned his card over before putting it in her pocket. "So what are you doing here?"

"That's unrelated." Ben fought the urge to snatch the card back. Revealing his identity was a calculated risk. He just hoped that ARX's scorn for freelancers would prevent the woman from getting too far in looking him up—if she even went that far.

"Don't want me poaching your mark? Fine. I can take a hint." George climbed into the driver's seat, closing the door after her.

Ben stepped back, allowing her to back past him.

As she drew level, George wound her window down. "So. What's your professional opinion of the Old Winnaker place then?"

What? Ben frowned. "I don't have one."

George smiled saccharinely at him. "No? And I thought ARX was supposed to be top of the game. Maybe I should be giving you *my* card." She laughed, rolling up the window.

Ben watched her back out onto the highway, before turning back to the house. Instead of feeling relief that the hunter was gone, he felt uneasy. In their brief encounter, the woman had been difficult to gauge. Who knew what she would do—

As Ben reached the top of the stairs, he realized he had a more immediate problem. Ma stood in the doorway. Her hand was locked around the door handle, her knuckles white. She'd been standing there some time. *Long enough to hear my encounter with George?*

Ben looked up at the angry set of Ma's mouth. *She heard.*

"So." Nate swung himself up into the driver's seat of the truck. "The good news is that Ma is not kicking you out."

Ben crossed his arms. He'd been sitting in the truck for so long the seat stuck to his skin. "Don't sound so cheerful, Nate! I've been waiting for you and Ma to finish talking for ages—" He faltered. "Not kicking me out?"

Nate shook his head, still grinning. "Nope. She isn't happy that you used to work for ARX, but I emphasized that ARX helps people who are victims of supernatural attacks and that you're retired." Nate paused. "I also told her that you'd wanted to tell her, but I'd told you not to." He pulled the door closed behind him. "She's still not happy—"

Ben snorted. "I noticed."

"But I told her I'd invited you here to help you put your past behind you and pointed out that it was really lucky we had you here just now."

Nate let his hands rest on the steering wheel. "If we were really involved in this murder, no way we'd invite a supernatural investigator to come visit."

Ben bit his lip. *Did they have that entire conversation dancing around the facts?* He was no longer surprised at how long he'd waited. "Did you tell her the truth about how we met? And what happened in New Camden?"

Nate winced. "What? You think I'm crazy?"

"You're crazy not to!" Ben turned so that he faced him. "Nate, you can't hide that from your family!"

"I have to."

"This is how we got into this mess in the first place—you not talking to your mom!"

"Speaking of talking—is there something we need to discuss?" Nate twisted in his seat to look at Ben.

"Us?"

Nate's gaze rested on Ben. "Ma said that she overheard you running off the hiker that was here before."

"She isn't a hiker, Nate." Ben narrowed his eyes. "She's a hunter."

"A hunter?"

Ben nodded. "Just like the guy who got murdered in your field."

"Are you sure?"

"Of course I'm sure!" Ben ticked off the evidence. "Did you see how she was dressed? Those weren't hiking clothes."

"It's summer," Nate pointed out. "And she was looking at day hikes. Not everyone's got the cash to invest in hiking gear just for a couple of hours in the woods."

"The scar on her neck. That was a revenant bite."

"Last I heard being bitten by a revenant doesn't turn you into a hunter. The opposite actually." Nate leaned back in the driver's seat.

Ben gave him a sour look. "Most motorists keep a spare tire in the back of their car. She had a stake and a crucifix. Explain that, Nate."

"If she's been attacked by a revenant, she's probably keen to protect herself. Just like a lot of women carry mace. Doesn't everyone from New Camden carry salt on them for the same reason?"

"Salt, Nate. Not a stake. Besides, she's not from New Camden."

"Then she maybe wouldn't know that salt is the new garlic." Nate thumped Ben on the arm. "I admit you didn't get the best introduction to Little River, but trust me—things here are completely normal. You can relax, forget about the supernatural."

It was hard to tell if Nate believed that or just desperately wanted to believe it. Ben raised his eyebrows. "Didn't you notice how pointed her questions were?"

"Your imagination—"

Ben shook his head. "When I accused her of spying on your family—"

"You did what?" Nate stared at him. "Shit, Ben."

"What was I supposed to do? She was blatantly playing up to you, fishing for information—"

"Now we get to it."

"Get to what?"

"Are you worried that George is a hunter? Or that she was coming on to me?"

Ben stared at Nate. "She admitted she was a hunter—"

"Hunting's not against the law."

"But her questions—the way she was blatantly hitting on you even though you'd just met—"

"Flirting? Look, a woman hitting on a hot guy isn't suspicious, Ben. It just means she likes what she sees."

"But—"

"It's probably going to happen again," Nate said hesitantly. "I mean, working at Century, I get a lot of attention from guys and girls."

How had the conversation changed direction so rapidly? Ben felt like he had a bad case of whiplash. "That's not what this is about."

"You're sure?" Nate ran his hand through his hair. "It's just... People make some pretty weird assumptions about bisexuals."

Ben felt his cheeks heat. "Oh."

"I'm going to notice hot girls," Nate continued quietly. "Just like I'm going to notice hot guys. That doesn't necessarily mean I'm going to do anything about it." He reached for Ben's hand. "It's up to what kind of a relationship you want."

Ben swallowed.

Nate's eyes were earnest, fixed on Ben. "You want a committed relationship, that's cool. Just say the word."

"I don't think I'm ready for this conversation."

Hurt flickered in Nate's eyes.

"Not like that!" Ben bit his lip. "Not that the idea of a committed relationship with you doesn't appeal. It does. But—" Ben took a deep breath, looking down at his knees. He had to get this straight in his head, and he couldn't do that with Nate looking at him. "I still don't know what I want. What I'm ready for."

Nate gently patted Ben's shoulder. "You want to explore your options? Century's good for that—"

Ben blanched internally. "Nothing about that appeals."

"I can quit Century. Look for another job—"

"Can you?" Ben tapped the wristband Nate wore. Unable to be removed without specialist equipment, it combined credit card reader and emergency alarm with Century's trademark sense of style. All Century's hosts wore them, and they represented a considerable investment for the club—one they would not say goodbye to easily. "What about your contract?"

"They'll let me go. I'm not exactly in the running for employee of the month right now. Not after—well, you know." Nate attempted to shrug.

Ben didn't buy it. "You like your job. You're good at it, and you genuinely enjoy helping the people you meet. Has that changed?"

Nate wormed back in the driver's seat. "It's not the same. I don't think it could be now."

Ben studied him closely. "If you really want to break your contract and leave Century, I'll help you," he said slowly. "But it's got to be your decision, not mine—what you want, not what you think I want. Does that make sense?"

"Yeah."

"You're not happy."

Nate ducked his head ruefully. "The plans you make in your head never come out right in real life, do they? I wanted to impress you with my devotion. Sweep you off your feet."

Despite himself, Ben's mouth twitched. "You swept me as far as Little River."

"Yeah, but—"

"That's enough." Ben put his hand over Nate's. "I much prefer my feet on the ground." He found it very necessary to tuck his hair out of his face. "Just—keep being you. Knowing I have your support while I figure things out is— That means more than any grand gesture. Honestly."

Nate's fingers stroked through his hair. "That I can do." He leaned in. Ben moved to meet him eagerly, trying to express his gratitude in the kiss.

It was a while before Nate pulled back. "So," he said with more of his usual cheerfulness. "First stop, Little River."

☆☆☆

Nate parked outside the General Store. "You're sure you don't want to come in with me?"

Ben shook his head as he slid out the door. "No offense, but I saw the size of the list Ethan gave you. Is he trying to buy out the entire seed stock?"

"It's not going to take that long. Seeds are all on the same shelf." But Nate still grinned. "What are you going to do?"

Ben shrugged, hoping his tone was casual. "Thought I'd take a quick look at the library."

"The library?"

"If I'm staying, I need something to do while you're hanging out with your brother."

Nate's eyes softened. "Yeah? Cool."

The guilt was instant. Ben's answering smile froze in place. If Nate knew he planned on looking up the Winnaker place the hunter had mentioned...

The guilt lasted all the way across the road. Ben stepped through the door hesitantly. *Am I walking into a library or a police station?*

The answer was both. The main doors opened into a reception area that did double duty as a community space. A PC so old Ben wondered for a moment if he'd walked into a museum was placed at a desk, with a notice taped to the monitor indicating there was a thirty-minute limit on the use of the internet. Beside it was a poster promoting road safety and another the importance of reading. On the right side of the reception area, the police station was beyond a door with an electronic lock, a wooden bench set out in front. A poster indicated the numbers to call in case of an emergency. A vacuum cleaner could be heard within.

On the left was an open reception desk. A woman with wispy gray hair spoke energetically into the phone. The shelves beyond her indicated she was the librarian. "All confidential of course—but I can tell you the sheriff's told me to be prepared to close early to accommodate a police team from Chinquapin—well, she would have to. Murder after all... Yes, the Granger farm—" She spotted Ben, nestling the phone against her bosom. "Police?" she asked hopefully.

Ben shook his head, approaching slowly. "Actually, I'm looking for a local history and got told to try the library."

"I'll call you back." The librarian put down the phone. She stood up from the desk, beckoning Ben to step through the sensor gate. "Something I should know?"

"Excuse me?" Ben paused.

She lifted a thick book down from its shelf, setting it on the reading table with a thud. "You're the second person today to want our history."

"Who was the first?"

The librarian pursed her mouth. "A young woman, obviously from the city. Now you..." She considered Ben. "I don't recall seeing you before."

Ben smiled thinly, taking the book. "I'm staying with a friend. Nate Granger."

"Oh!" The librarian blanched. "Well," she said with false brightness. "I'll leave you to your book."

Ben sat down at the table. *Just what has she heard about the murder?* At least Ben's presence within the library seemed to be a deterrent against her picking up the phone again. Ben opened the history to the back index, aware the librarian was watching him closely.

Winnaker— Here. There were a handful of entries, but Ben had no problems finding the one George referred to.

Myth or Moonshine? He raised an eyebrow at the title. *This doesn't bode well.*

The two paragraphs that followed did not deserve the hype. *Although it had a devastating effect on the local economy, the chestnut blight gave rise to one of Little River's more colorful characters. Josiah Winnaker gained local notoriety for his outlandish behavior as the blight reached Castanea County. A third-generation resident of Little River, Josiah inherited the family farm from his father, Joshua Winnaker. However, after an unfortunate series of events, Josiah claimed his farm was cursed by a shapeshifting tree. According to Josiah, the tree was chestnut one day, oak the next. Any attempts to cut the tree down were in vain as the tree simply grew back the next day. The local pastor was called on to exorcise the tree but refused, claiming that the whole thing was pure moonshine.*

Local opinion at the time was that Josiah had been drowning his sorrows with home brew. Winnaker was known to be strongly opposed to prohibition and had appeared before the court on charges of being found drunk and disorderly. Whatever the cause, when the National Parks and Recreation Board expanded the area allotted to the Castanea ranges, Winnaker was one of the first to sell his property. He moved to Charlotte, still insisting that he was driven from his house by 'that damn tree.'

Seriously? Ben flicked through the rest of the book but couldn't find another reference to Winnaker. *That's what she was looking up?*

Not only did trees not shapeshift, but Ben had not once, in all his years of experience, encountered one capable of pulling off a curse. *Does the hunter not know basic monsters? Or is she so desperate she's grasping at straws?*

Maybe Nate's right, and the hunter's just messing with me. Ben turned to the index, looking first for 'myths' then 'ghost stories.' Nothing. Little River was just as quiet as Nate had promised—

"Ben." Nate barged through the library gates. "Let's go."

Ben stood up immediately. "It's not—" A look at Nate's expression, and Ben swallowed. "Okay."

Nate gave the librarian a distracted nod. He didn't speak, even when they were both in the car. Instead he drove in silence, his jaw set.

Ben watched Nate's hands on the steering wheel. His knuckles were white. "What happened?"

Nate's mouth tightened. "Nothing."

"Something obviously happened."

Nate's mouth dropped unhappily. "Maybe I'm just being paranoid."

"Tell me." Ben patted Nate's arm lightly.

Nate hunched forward over the steering wheel. "The entire time I was in the store, it felt—weird. When I walked in, there was this hush. Rose and the woman she was serving fell silent. I said hi, but there was something off about their replies, and I'd swear they were relieved when I went to get the seeds. I'd just about finished with Ethan's list when the door flies open, and Dan bursts in. 'What did I tell you?' he says. 'The police team from Chinquapin includes a supernatural investigator! I always said there was something not right about that family!' Rose hissed at him to shut up, and Dan spotted me. His face went white as a sheet."

"What happened?"

"Didn't stay to find out. Only thing I could think of was getting you and leaving." Nate groaned. "What a mess."

Ben patted his arm. "I'm sorry."

"It's not your fault. I'm just—really angry. I mean, Ma's worked her ass off for this community for years—decades. She always goes in early on a Sunday to arrange the flowers before church and stays late to help clean up after. Me and Ethan, we've grown up here—this is our home!

And these people, our neighbors, they've known us our entire lives—they've decided we're guilty, just like that."

"They're scared. That's all. In cases of the supernatural, people react uncharacteristically."

"I know... Still. It's different when it happens to you."

Ben bit his lip. This was something Nate was going to have to get used to...but how to tell him that? He blinked, realizing that instead of fields, they were driving through forest. "We're not going home?"

"And upset Ma a second time?" Nate's smile was strained. "We'll do the shopping in Rockford. With any luck, the news hasn't reached there yet."

CHAPTER EIGHT

Rockford was a sizeable town—by Little River standards. It had a charming shopping street with stone buildings that were proudly turn of the century, home to galleries and artisan goods, with an eye on the through traffic. Normally, Ben wouldn't have given it a second thought, unless it was to wonder how much further they were from an actual town, but now he found himself sizing up the shops and houses they passed with keen interest.

Nate drove him around it twice. The first time so Ben could appreciate the fact that there was more than one main street, the second time so that Ben could assure himself they weren't being followed. "See? Just like I said. If the sheriff wants us, she knows she just has to wait for us to go home."

Ben decided not to argue. "There's just the two banks?"

"Three—there's another inside the mall. Why?"

"I want to go to all of them."

"How come?" Nate turned into the parking lot for the nearest bank. "Planning on making me feel better about the murder investigation by robbing a bank?"

"Funny." Ben made a rueful face. "You know that there's a limit of how much you can withdraw before the bank flags it as potentially suspicious?"

"Somehow I never pegged you for one of them anti-government 'the feds are out to rob us' types, but sure." Nate stopped the truck and undid his belt.

Ben bit his lip. He could ask later. "I'm thinking I want to use my card to take several small amounts from different ATMs, rather than one big withdrawal that could potentially get reported back to Saltaire."

About to open the truck door, Nate glanced back at Ben sharply. "I thought he washed his hands of us."

"Only because he expected us to end up dead." Ben caught his expression in the side mirror, surprised by how grim it was. He took a deep breath. "As long as he thinks we're dead, we've got no problem."

"But we're not dead."

"And that's the problem." Ben stretched out a hand, trying to grasp the words he wanted. Just the memory of Saltaire made it hard to think past the weight of his vampire sire's power in his mind. "There wouldn't be evidence of my death anyway, as a vampire, and Saltaire's not interested in you. He's arrogant enough to assume that there being no signs of us means his machinations worked, that I could not overcome the vampire's urges and killed you and then destroyed myself from guilt once my hunger was satisfied and my senses returned."

Nate reached for Ben's arm again. "Remind me again why you put up with the guy for so long?"

"I didn't exactly have a choice." But Nate's question lifted some of the memory of Saltaire's oppressive influence. "Anyway, while Saltaire's not interested in the fine print, he runs a company of hundreds of people trained to investigate supernatural related oddities. If my name appears on a watch list because of a large amount of spending and someone at ARX spots and reports it..." He shrugged. "There's every chance that the police investigation will send someone to ARX to check up on my possible demonic contacts. They're going to know I'm alive. All I can do is stay as inconspicuous as possible."

Ben made Nate wait out of view of the security cameras as he made his withdrawals. "That's one thing we've got going for us," he said as he finished the last transaction. "Vampires aren't supposed to show up on film. No way will anyone at ARX believe this is me."

Nate didn't smile. "Ma asked me again how we met."

"She asked me the same question."

"I know. She said she wanted to be sure you were a friend." Nate bit his lip. "She said you'd been asking a lot of questions?"

Ben blinked. "Not supernatural questions. Ordinary ones. About baby photos and plants. I was trying to work out what period of his life Ethan became interested in plants. It might help us narrow down what happened."

Nate put his hands in the back pockets of his jeans. "That sounds a lot like investigating."

Ben tried to gauge Nate's expression. "With everything that's happened, I thought I should look into the situation as much as I could."

"By investigating Ethan."

"You trying to hide him has flagged him as a threat," Ben told Nate. "We need facts—not fears."

"You haven't told your family you're alive."

"That's different! Completely different—and you know why!" Ben took a deep breath. "You can't compare escaping Saltaire to hiding from a murder investigation."

"The police will do their job. They must see Ethan has nothing to do with this." Nate bit his lip. "Please, Ben? Leave it to the police."

Ben hesitated. It went against every instinct he had. "I'm good at this stuff, Nate. I can help." But as Nate's mouth drooped unhappily, Ben realized the request mattered a lot to Nate. "I don't think this is a good idea, but fine."

Nate's relief was palpable in the arm he slid around Ben. "Thanks. I know it's hard when you don't know us, but—thanks, Ben." He took a deep breath. "So. Time to spend all your money."

☆☆☆

Ben would not have recognized the building Nate took him to as a mall. It was all one story, a collection of shops that shared a common roof, and nothing else. There was no food court, no Starbucks, and a complete circuit of the shops took less than five minutes. However, it had stores that stocked clothing in varieties other than denim and flannel, so Ben wasn't complaining. He bought two complete sets of clothes and a backpack to store them in.

Nate took charge of Ben's shopping bags. "Where now?"

Ben spotted a cell phone shop. "There."

There were new models out since the last time he'd updated his phone. Ben settled down to browse the displays with intent.

Nate leaned against the sales counter and spent a good ten minutes establishing that the sales clerk had been a senior in high school when he and Ethan had started as middle-schoolers. Then he proceeded to ask about the status of every single mutual acquaintance they shared. Ben would have rolled his eyes, except that it gave him ample time to make his decision.

Nate straightened up as Ben set down his choice on the bench. "Found one you like?"

Ben nodded. "I'd like two of this model," he told the clerk.

"Two?" Nate started.

"One is for you."

"You can't—" Nate looked up at the clerk. "Excuse us," he said and dragged Ben over to the new iPhone display. "You can't just buy me a phone!"

"Why not?"

"These things are expensive, Ben! I'll never be able to pay you back."

"I don't want you to pay me back. I want you to have a phone."

Nate shook his head. "This is too much."

"Not to me." Ben checked that they were screened for the clerk's gaze by the display before placing his hand on Nate's arm. "After everything you went through to protect me—including wrecking your phone in the first place—this is the least I can do."

Nate looked helplessly at him. "You're sure?"

"What's the problem?"

Nate looked down at his mud-splattered boots and frayed edges of his jeans. "I don't want you to be like my sugar-daddy."

"Sugar—" Ben choked.

Nate continued. "Century, it's all about the money. You and me, it's about us. I don't want that to change."

Ben felt a curious mix of happy and sad all at once. "Me giving you a present won't change that, Nate. I promise. Besides, you having a phone is as much for my benefit as it is for yours."

"How do you mean?"

"Peace of mind. Knowing that you can call for help if you need it, or I can call you..."

"You don't need to call me." Nate slapped Ben on his arm. "I'm right here." But he seemed happy to let Ben make his purchase.

Buying the phones was one thing, setting them up another. Nate could transfer over his previous number and plan, but Ben had to start entirely from scratch. *Much better this way.* It took the best part of an hour, but it was worth it to walk out of the store with a number Saltaire knew nothing about.

"Now what?" Nate nodded towards a bookstore. "You want to get your geek on? We have an electronics store, too."

Ben looked towards the display. He did want to replace the laptop left behind at Saltaire's, but a purchase like that had to be researched... A red-and-white pole caught his attention. "Hold up. I want to get my hair cut."

"Why? Your hair looks great."

"That's a matter of opinion," Ben stepped towards the shop. "And in my opinion, this haircut is hideous." Now that the prospect of not scaring himself every time he passed a mirror was in front of him, Ben was eager.

"It looks good. I'm not just saying that." Nate reached out to tuck Ben's hair out of his face. "Gives you this soft kind of vibe."

"You're really not selling it."

Nate studied him carefully. "You hate it that much?"

Ben caught his hand, tugged him towards the mirror in the window of the hairdresser's. "When I look at my reflection now, I don't see me—who I was before I died. I see the person I was under Saltaire's influence." Ben pushed his fringe out of his eyes. "I hate long hair on me. Always have. I never would have let it grow by choice."

"But when you became a vampire you stopped caring?" Nate looked over Ben's shoulder, studying his reflection intently.

Being the recipient of such focused attention was humbling. Ben dropped his eyes from Nate's. "I forgot to think about my appearance. I had to concentrate on avoiding mirrors, and I stopped thinking about what they were for."

"How'd you dress and shave and stuff?"

"Hair was easy. That was purely on memory. I trusted Godfrey and Hunter to let me know if I'd made a mistake." *Like his current look.* Ben grimaced. "When they decided I needed a shave, it was usually Hunter's stylist who did it."

"Wait." Nate's grin was half-incredulous. "Hunter employs a stylist?"

"You don't think he looks that good without help?" Ben nudged him. "Beth picks out his clothes and keeps him up to date with the latest trends. She doubles as his personal shopper."

Nate shook his head. "Only Hunter."

"It makes sense when you think about it." There was no reason Ben should be this annoyed. Hunter was no longer his brother in blood. "He comes from a time when vampires were staked and torched on discovery. He cares a lot about blending in. Anyway, doesn't Century hire stylists?"

"They call them 'look-curators'." Nate shook his head. "Sorry. This is cracking me up. You think of vampires being all dark and mysterious, you don't think of them having stylists."

"It's not that funny." But seeing Nate smile was a relief. Ben squeezed his hand. "You've got shopping to do for Ma, right? You go ahead and start on that. I'll see if they have an appointment free."

"Trust me. They'll be free—another benefit of small town life." Nate smirked. "You think you'll be able to find the supermarket all right?"

"Nate. I've been in shopping malls larger than this town. I'll be fine." Ben stepped into the salon.

A cloud of perfume rolled out to meet him, making his eyes water. Ben coughed, attracting the attention of the blonde girl working on the woman seated in the barber's chair.

"Here for a cut? Take a seat." She nodded towards the chairs. "Claire's on break, but she'll be back soon."

Ben nodded thanks, sitting down. He smirked as he noticed that among the glossy fashion magazines spread out over the table were a collection of farming and hunting magazines. *I'm not in New Camden now.* Reaching for a magazine, Ben froze.

A familiar pair of combat boots jostled impatiently under the barber's chair, and the black scarf draped carelessly over the magazine stand was instantly recognizable. Ben looked to the mirror. Reflected back at him as she sat in the chair was the woman from earlier. As the hairdresser teased out her thick curls, Ben glimpsed again the scar he'd noticed on her neck earlier. He froze. *What is the hunter doing here?*

Getting her hair cut, apparently. George eyed her reflection without much hope. "You need to really tease out the curls before you cut. Otherwise it ends up uneven."

"I've seen this on YouTube," the stylist assured her with more enthusiasm than believability. "Leave it to me." She returned to her work. "Where were we...?"

"You were just telling me I picked the right time of year to come visit."

The stylist nodded, her hoop earrings jingling. "Right. Not too hot, not too crowded. Give it another month, and with the summer holidays, you'll be lucky to have space for a tent."

The hunter snorted. "Tell the truth, I'd like some company. That murder's got me anxious." She drummed her fingers against the arm of the chair. "I was jumping at every little sound last night. If I hadn't just put a week's payment down on my caravan spot, I'd have turned around and gone right back."

The stylist hummed sympathetically. "I know what you mean. I was the exact same. You don't expect death, not out here."

"I still have half a mind to leave."

Ben eyed the back of the hunter's chair balefully. If she had any thought of leaving, she'd be gone—not getting her hair cut.

The thought didn't seem to occur to the stylist. "You'll be fine. Little River—where the guy was found—is a good half hour's drive from here.

"What about that murder?" One of the flyers asking for information about Olivia Winkler's death was displayed inside the salon. "That says Rockford."

"That's ten years too late." The stylist sighed. "Girl I went to high school with. Fell in with the wrong guy and paid the price."

"Yeah? I heard it was unsolved."

"No one has any idea who the guy was. Olivia was secretive and moody, the kind to make a big deal out of nothing. No one had a clue she'd actually managed to land a guy."

"Her friends didn't know anything?"

"She didn't have any." The stylist shrugged. "She was always off reading. Preferred books to people. No one could have guessed she'd get herself murdered, but it goes to show people can surprise you."

"How do you know it was a guy then?"

"She was dressed up when they found her. Lipstick, makeup…"

The hunter laughed. "That's proof of nothing. She was a teenage girl! When I was that age—"

"You didn't know Olivia. She never bothered before, not even for her confirmation." The stylist nodded. "An odd girl."

Ben glanced towards the door. With the stylist distracted, he could be out the door before either woman noticed. He began to work his way across the seats to the chair nearest the door.

"Plus, there was the magic," the stylist continued.

Ben paused.

"Magic?" The hunter tilted her head.

"Hold still." The stylist readjusted her position. "They found her in a field. She looked normal, like she was asleep, but the grass around her was blackened. It smelt like a fire, but there was nothing but a circle all around her." The stylist's fingers moved deftly as she warmed to her topic. "You could still smell it, even at the funeral. A horrible, thick smell of burning. Minister refused to have her in the church."

Ben looked at the magazine he held without seeing it, conscious that he needed to hide his shock. *A second demonic death.*

The hunter whistled. "That poor girl. Wasn't the guy they found yesterday in a field, too?"

The stylist shook her head. "That's totally different, and I know that for a fact." She jerked her comb in the direction of the second barber's chair. "Liz Parker was in here this morning for her usual coloring. She lives in Little River, and she told me all about it. They had the police in, asking questions. Liz called up the sheriff to find out what she was doing to keep them safe, and the sheriff said that however the man died, there was no sign of struggle in the field, that he didn't die there. Liz said she thought the sheriff emphasized that particularly."

The hunter's foot began to jiggle again. "Interesting. Why do you think that might be?"

"Gossip travels fast round here. Matter of fact, the Grangers—that's the family whose farm this man died, sorry, was found on—have had problems in the past with people spreading rumors. It's old news now, but there was a scandal when the mother got pregnant." The stylist shook her head. "They were an older couple, and he'd been ill. People assumed they couldn't have kids. So when she got pregnant out of the blue, there was talk."

The hunter raised an eyebrow. "An affair?"

The stylist snorted. "Anyone who knew her would have known the answer to that in a second! She was my Sunday school teacher. Just goes to show you how petty people can be... Turns out, they'd been having IVF treatments, and she was too ashamed to tell anyone."

Ben was aware that his mouth was open. He shut it, looking down at the magazine he held. The words swam before his eyes. In one five-minute conversation, George had uncovered more about the Grangers than Ben had in two days of staying with them. *This isn't a haircut. This is an investigation.*

"Wonderful what medicine can do these days," George said.

The stylist nodded. "There were still people who talked, said that there was no way a man as religious as Mr. Granger would go against the Lord's will, but a man will do a lot to make his wife happy, and Mrs. Granger really wanted to be a mother."

"IVF's against religion now?"

"People here tend to be old-fashioned." The stylist glanced complacently at the laptop on the reception desk, wirelessly porting music to the speaker in the corner. "Some of the older generation will tell you that her sons are a judgment on Mrs. Granger for coveting what she didn't have."

"Seriously? Man. No wonder she didn't want to tell anyone she was getting treatment!"

The stylist nodded energetically. "Nobody's business but her own. And I'll tell you one thing, there's none of this 'not God's will' talk when they get the vet in to artificially inseminate their cattle."

"You know the sons then?"

"Not well. I graduated before they started high school. I've cut their hair though, and I tell you, they could not be more different. Nate's good fun, but trying to get a word out of his brother's an exercise in frustration!"

"Nothing unusual about that. You often hear of a loud twin and a quiet twin."

"Ethan takes it to extremes. There's something...odd about him."

Ben held his breath. No way he could leave the salon now. He pretended to be enthralled by the magazine, hoping that it would mask his face should George glance back.

"You're sure you just want a trim?" The stylist paused, running her fingers through George's hair.

"For now," the hunter said firmly. "No offense, but I'm not trusting my hair to YouTube."

"I think a pixie cut would really suit you." The stylist continued to detangle George's hair. "Maybe another time."

George wasn't buying it. "You were telling me how religious folks were?"

"That's the other reason we're sure that whoever killed Olivia wasn't from around here. Folks around here don't hold with magic. They take pride in their faith." The stylist nodded solemnly. "No, you can sleep safe tonight. Besides, the guy in Little River brought it on himself. They say he was a supernatural hunter."

Ben couldn't help it. He glanced at the mirror, drawn to George's reaction.

Her eyes met his, but there was no spark of awareness. Her expression was bleak. To Ben it seemed that she was looking inward, entirely unaware of him. He dropped his gaze back to the magazine, heard her shift in the barber's seat. "A hunter, huh? What is there to investigate around here?"

"That's the thing. We can't imagine. As Liz Parker was saying, there's something there that doesn't add up."

"There's got to be something. Small town like this with a history. What about legends, folklore, ghost stories—nothing like that?"

"We've got stories, of course," the stylist agreed. "But none of that's real."

"You can't stop there." The buckles on the hunter's boots jingled impatiently. "Let's hear them."

Ben mumbled an apology and ducked out the door. *I'm not imagining this.* The hunter was in Little River on business—and she knew about Nate and Ethan. *Nate's got to listen now.*

Nate was waiting for Ben in the truck. He raised an eyebrow as Ben climbed into the passenger seat, pulling the door shut behind him. "What happened to your haircut?"

"I'll tell you as we drive." Ben pulled on his belt. His eyes automatically flicked to the rear-view mirror. "Remember George, the hiker? She was in the salon, pumping for local gossip. She was asking questions about the Winkler murder, the guy found yesterday and local folklore." Ben glanced at Nate. "You and Ethan were mentioned."

"Just as well we're ready to leave."

Ben tilted his head. "That's it? You're not going to tell me I'm paranoid?"

Nate's smile was purely reflexive. "Funny thing happened at the supermarket. And by funny, I mean really fucking weird." He took a deep breath. "People at the supermarket usually stop, say hello, ask me how my mother is. Today...you'd not believe the amount of people falling silent as I turned down the aisle. And when I talked to people, the conversation felt kind of strained. Then when I got to the register, I caught Mrs. Parker from the farm down the road saying, 'I do think it odd that it would be their farm. After all—' I said, 'After all what?' She grabbed her bags and practically ran out of the store."

Ben reached for his hand. "I'm sorry."

Nate's mouth pressed thinly together as he pulled the truck out onto the main road. "You were right. Sorry, Ben. I didn't want to believe you."

"As long as you believe me now." Ben looked back over his shoulder to check they hadn't been followed.

Nate's mouth twisted ruefully. "I'm just glad Ma and Ethan stayed home."

Ben nodded in silent agreement.

☆☆☆

As the mountains came into sight up ahead, grim and inevitable, a black and white car shot past on the other side of the road.

"Was that the sheriff?" Nate glanced at the rear-view mirror.

"I didn't see."

"She saw us. Shit." Nate clenched the steering wheel. The patrol car had done a U-turn and now came after them, horn blaring. "What do I do?"

"You pull over to the side of the road, and you don't panic," Ben told him. "It's too early in the investigation for them to want to arrest you."

Nate gave him a dire look but pulled over. The sheriff's car came to a stop beside them a moment later, Ray winding down the passenger window.

"What's up?" Nate asked. "Did anything happen?"

"We got a call from the timber yard." The sheriff leaned over Ray to answer. "They found what they think could be a magical circle showing signs of being recently activated."

"You've found the crime scene?" Ben sat up.

"What they've found is a patch of grass with burn marks on it," the sheriff grumbled. "Word's got out that we're looking for a supernatural killer, and you know what it's like. Everyone will be calling me up to take a look at their cat that jumped for no reason, or the glowing lights that could be aliens but are more likely the headlights of passing traffic. It'll be the Winkler case all over again."

"But why stop us?" Nate asked. "We went to the mall. We weren't anywhere near the timber yard."

The sheriff snorted. "Ray here had the bright idea" —Ray grinned sheepishly— "that since we had a supernatural expert in our midst, we may as well consult. Would you be able to identify a magical circle on sight, Hawick?"

"Absolutely," Ben said. "But what about the forensic team from Chinquapin? They must have someone who could tell you."

"What, and have them think we country cops don't know a magical circle from a campfire?" The sheriff shook her head. "Besides, they're too important to spend on grunt work like this. We determine it's worth their while, then they might deign to investigate."

"No feelings of insecurity here at all." Ray flashed them a quick grin.

The sheriff gave him another withering look. "I'm going to do another U-turn and head to the lumber yards. You'll follow us?"

Nate nodded. "Right behind you." As Ray wound up his window and the sheriff pulled the car out onto the road, he nudged Ben. "Look at you. Third day out of work, and you're developing a freelance career already."

Ben shook his head. "We need to see this circle first."

The owner of the lumber yard was, much to Ben's surprise, a woman with triceps that rivaled Nate's. "I always take the dogs and do a walk around first thing in the morning," she explained. "Because we're so close to the train tracks, occasionally people who've jumped aboard the train see this as a good place for an overnight stop. I've caught people camping here, absolutely no shame. Double padlocking the gate doesn't deter them, so I got the dogs." She scratched the nearest under his chin. The boxer shut his eyes in pleasure, stubby tail wagging. "Anyway, this morning, I was doing the rounds as normal, and the dogs did not want to walk past this one patch. I yelled. I tugged at their leashes. Eventually, I just picked them up. Prince was shivering. That dog isn't afraid of anything, but he was afraid of this." The owner shook her head. "I had to take a look. That's when I spotted the circle. I can't make heads or tails of it myself, but as the police call went out for anything unusual, I thought I'd give you a crack at it."

The sheriff tugged her hat in thanks. "Where are these possible magical traces?"

The owner led them to a huge pile of wood chips. "It was half hidden beneath the chips. I wouldn't have found it at all if not for the dogs, digging at it. Here."

It was definitely a magical circle. The ground of the yard was mostly dirt tramped down flat, but where the odd tuft of grass grew, it was green. This circle had been scratched in the dirt, and all the grass within or immediately surrounding it was parched and yellow. There was a thick smell, suggestive of smoke, and the lines had sunk into the dirt, leaving it blackened and cracked, as if exposed to great heat.

"Well?" The sheriff asked. "Is it the real deal?"

Ben nodded. "Call Forensics," he said. "This is what killed Harriet."

"How do you know that?" Ray asked.

Ben pointed to the inverted pyramid within the circle. "Right way up, the pyramid amplifies. Upside down, it drains. There are no signs of candles being used to power it, and I don't see any blood, so it looks like it was borrowed power, and the traces of fire suggest that power was demonic."

"Just what we need," the sheriff grumbled. "Ray, you got all that?"

The deputy nodded. "Want me to relay back to Forensics, get a team out here?"

"Well, I'm not wondering about their health. Use your brain, boy." The sheriff turned back to the owner. "You got a security system? Camera, anything like that?"

"Sure do. No alarms went off last night. I'd have known."

"Show me what you've got—no," —as Ben made to follow— "not the two of you. Thanks for the help, Hawick, but we'll take it from here."

☆☆☆

"That's weird."

Ben looked away from the field. The tent that had covered the scene was gone, and there seemed to be fewer police officers in evidence. "Weird?"

"Ma's car's in the drive. She usually has her fellowship meeting about now." Nate parked the truck beside a neat little blue sedan sitting in front of the garage. "Never misses." He grabbed the grocery bags out of the back seat.

Ben gathered up his shopping bags and followed.

Ethan sat on the porch. Ben thought he was just sitting there, but as they neared, Ethan picked up the needles on his lap.

Ben watched as Ethan looped a strand of wool around the needles and they clicked together. There was already a long, shapeless mass resting on his knees, but despite that and the steady click of the needles, Ben could not make himself accept the evidence of his eyes. *Ethan knitting?*

Nate didn't react to the optical illusion at all. He frowned at the living room windows, through which a vacuum could be heard at full volume. "What's up with Ma?"

"Pastor came by." Ethan paused to unwind more wool from the ball resting on the sofa. "Expressed congregation's sympathy—from a safe distance."

Nate peered through the window. "I bet that went over well."

Ethan shrugged. "Ma sent me to find her devotionals book. Pastor was leaving when I got back. Ma's been vacuuming ever since."

Ben studied Ethan thoughtfully. He'd been wondering how aware Ethan was of the net gathering around his family. His words were a simple recitation of fact, but there was a note in his voice that gave his sentences more meaning than the obvious.

"Shit. Okay, um." Nate turned back to Ben. "We're going to want to go in the back door."

Ben's mouth quirked, but he obediently followed Nate around the house.

Nate didn't speak again till they were safely in Ben's bedroom. "I'm going to put the groceries away. You don't mind staying here?"

Ben shook his head. "Is your mother okay?"

Nate leaned on the doorframe, lowering his voice even though the vacuum was still going. "She's going to be upset. Like I said, she never misses her church groups. I'm going to put the groceries away and then talk to her."

"Need any help?"

Nate shook his head. "I got this."

Ben set his new phone charging and lay back on the bed. The vacuum was still going. Was Nate waiting for his mother to exhaust herself before he approached her? Or was he unwilling to interrupt a job in progress?

The ceiling was long, thick planks of wood of a size that Ben didn't remember seeing before. *The chestnut Nate mentioned?* Ben shuddered at the idea of being surrounded by even more trees. *Not that I'm in favor of a blight... But there's got to be a medium.*

There was something niggling at his mind. Something that was not related to the ever-present mountains. As Ben turned his thoughts back over the trip to Rockford, he found himself dwelling on the sheriff's words. *'We'll take it from here.'*

It had been an unexpected shock—like walking straight into a glass door. Only in this case, Ben had stumbled into the division between civilian and paranormal life. *I don't miss being part of that world, do I?* Ben weighed meeting the sun with Nate and walking outside against the routine loss and horror of ARX investigations. *There's no competition.*

But all the same...

Ben reached for his phone. There was enough battery now that he could go through the setup menu. In a matter of minutes, he was tapping 'Little River' into the default search engine.

There was nothing about Harriet's death in the national news sources, and the country news gave it a brief paragraph.

He was a hunter. With access to Saltaire's incredible library, Ben hadn't needed to use the Internet for supernatural research. However, the hunting forums and communities, where the hunters swapped news of bounties, possible supernatural sightings, and tips for approaching hard-to-kill monsters, were a good way to gather gossip about a case and ensure investigators weren't going in blind. Ben brought up the biggest of the hunting sites. *I wonder...*

Harriet's death was the first thread on the page. Ben skimmed it with a frown. Written by a moderator, it was bare on facts. *His partner has confirmed that the dead man in the police reports is Harriet, known to most forum users simply by his handle 'Old Enough.'* Partner? Ben remembered the lost look on George's face. It put the woman's actions into a new light...

No, Ben thought, remembering how she'd inserted herself into the farmhouse. *Lying is still lying.* But would he feel so strongly if it wasn't Nate's family being deceived?

He couldn't answer that question. Ben turned back to the forum.

Harriet's death is a loss to the community in every way. Active on and off the forums, Harriet was always willing to take a young hunter under his wing or join a buddy on a difficult fight. He didn't ask for anything in return for his help. An experienced hunter, Harriet was well aware of the risks of his profession. He had made arrangements for his funeral many years ago. Instead of financial contributions or flowers, his partner has indicated that anyone wishing to honor Harriet's memory should donate to the Fund for Hunters in Difficulty.

Ben scrolled down through the thread. Comment after comment of condolences and shock. Harriet certainly had been around for many years if his death got this big of a reaction. But the common note among all the replies was surprise. No one had known what Harriet was working on before he died.

Time to change tactics. Ben searched for Harriet's username, started working backward through his posts. There were a lot of them. Harriet had gone out of his way to counsel younger hunters, steering the most reckless away from dangerous undertakings and advocating caution. The more Ben read, the more disquieted he felt. It was easy to dismiss hunters as crass, preying on the fears of their clients and the vulnerability of the supernatural community. But he could not dismiss Harriet...

"Hey, Ben." Nate pushed the door open. "Ethan and I were going to throw a basketball around. You want to join us?"

Ben blinked. He hadn't even noticed the vacuum stop. "I'm good, thanks." A basketball in Ethan's hands was not a prospect that excited him.

Nate walked over to the bed, looking down at Ben's phone. "What are you doing?"

"I've found the forum Harriet used to frequent. I've been going through his posts." Ben sat up. "It seemed like he was looking for something."

"Isn't that why most people use the internet?"

Ben shook his head. "This forum has posts on it going back a decade." He set his phone down, reaching for his notebook. "He was vague about what he was looking for. Reports of unexplainable deaths at ten-year intervals." Ben tapped the page with his finger. "I'm almost certain that he was gathering information on one specific demon."

Nate sat down on the bed. He took the notebook, glancing at Ben's notes, but didn't read them. "This sounds an awful lot like investigating, Ben."

Ben clutched his phone tightly. "I'm not asking any questions about your family."

"But what about your fresh start? You've got the chance to put all of this behind you, Ben, have a normal life. Isn't that what you want?"

Ben frowned. "I don't know what I want," he said slowly. "But I know I can't ignore this. If Harriet is right—and his death is a good indication that he was—then the demon responsible for Olivia Winkler's death is due another meal soon."

Nate's forehead furrowed. "Are you saying there's going to be another victim? But Harriet's dead!"

"Harriet doesn't fit the pattern. He was most likely killed by the agent in self-defense."

"How do you know that?"

"The pattern in the circle at the timber mill. It lacked the double circle to summon and contain the demon." Ben tapped the page of his notebook with the relevant notes. "My guess is that the agent was aware Harriet was getting closer to figuring him out and took the precaution of drawing and hiding a circle at the timber yard before they met."

"So they knew each other?"

"There must have been some contact. Enough to make an appointment to meet." Ben held out his hand for the notebook. "If we can retrace Harriet's movements, find out who he talked to, then we might just be able to figure out who he went to the timber yard to meet."

Nate didn't move. "But that sounds like you think whoever killed Harriet—and Olivia—is still here?"

A floorboard creaked. Ben and Nate looked up to see Ethan in the doorway. His expression was more wooden than ever.

"Ethan!" Nate scrambled to his feet. "Sorry, didn't mean to leave you waiting! We got to talking— What's up?"

"The police." Ethan jerked his head in the direction of the front door. "They want to talk to us."

CHAPTER NINE

This interview took place at the Little River police station, fire station, and library. Nate and Ethan stood awkwardly in the reception as the sheriff and the team from Chinquapin argued over whether to interview the twins together or separately. Ethan resolved the argument by pushing Nate into the sheriff's office and walking in after him, leaving the officers to follow or not follow at will. The forensics team was using the briefing room, so Ben found himself sharing the police station's single cell with Ray and a criminal psychologist from Chinquapin.

Deliberate? Ben let himself be fingerprinted, reflecting that if the police were trying to rattle him, they had their work cut out. The cell was small, but the iron bars allowed air to pass through, and he could hear voices from the other rooms. The overhead light might be electric, but it was still light. *Compared to a coffin, this is comfortable.*

Ray leaned over to watch Ben apply his fingerprints to the paper. "Nice and steady. You've done this before."

Ben rolled his eyes. "I'm used to crime scenes." In order to interview Ben and take his fingerprint, a folding table had been squeezed into the gap between the two beds either side of the cell. Ben sat on one, reaching for the box of tissues. "Can I ask why you're taking our fingerprints?"

Ray settled back on the bed opposite. "We found Harriet's truck this afternoon, a forty-minute drive from here. It was abandoned on a disused farm road."

The psychologist glared at Ray. "That's classified info."

"What's the harm? Hawick's an old hand at this. Ten to one, he'd figure it out." Ray shrugged, turning back to Ben. He and the psychologist sat on the bed opposite, and it was not a comfortable fit. She perched on the edge with her notebook, while Ray sat as far as physically possible from her. "Anyway, Harriet clearly didn't drive it there himself."

Ben nodded. They were all thinking the same thing. Harriet's killer had used the truck to transport his body to the farm. "Have you examined it?"

"Naturally. Forensics found his prints, and that of an unknown person."

"Officer Legapsi," the psychologist interrupted. "Do I have to call in a superior officer? You're exceeding your boundaries sharing that information with a suspect!"

Ben raised an eyebrow. "You do realize it's a physical impossibility for me or Nate to be present in Harriet's truck while being interrogated in New Camden by Department Seven?"

"Not when there's magic involved." The woman was pale, but there was an angry red flush stealing over her face. She clutched her clipboard tightly. "The victim died when he stepped onto a demonic circle. There was no need for the murderer to be present—"

"All demonic circles require a contract. The demonic agent either had to speak or write at the exact moment Harriet stepped onto the circle." His hands were as clean as he was going to get them. Ben dropped the tissues on the table. "Not to mention, the exchange of power would create a ripple." Ben caught the woman's eye. "Go ahead. Call Department Seven. Ask them if they would miss a demon summoning taking place right under their noses."

She flinched.

Ben leaned back against the cell wall. "I see you've talked to Gunn."

She shot Ben a look of pure dislike. "Officer Gunn didn't have a lot of positive things to say about you."

"Gunn's a *lemur*." Ben placed his hands together on his lap. "He feeds on negative energy and delights in causing misery. The day he has a positive word about anyone is the day he gives up on life."

She raised an eyebrow. "He said that was what you would say. He also said that your knowledge of the supernatural was accurate and that we could rely on your help to protect innocent lives, but not necessarily to tell us the truth." She paused meaningfully. "The whole truth."

Amazing that being a sixteen-hour drive away did not impact Gunn's ability to cause Ben problems any. He fought the impulse to swallow, hiding his discomfort. "Did he? You know, coming from Gunn, that's a ringing endorsement."

"You're not dealing with Gunn." The woman leaned forward. "You're dealing with the Chinquapin Police Force."

"And us," Ray cut in quickly. "Don't forget about us."

The woman rapped her clipboard down on the table. "This is not an ARX investigation. We call the shots."

"What do you want?"

She leaned across the table. "Why are you here?"

"We've covered this. Nate invited me—"

"Are you investigating the family?"

Ben grit his teeth. "I'm not here to investigate them. I was invited—"

"Give us a break. The Grangers have a reputation in these parts for keeping to themselves. No one can remember them having a guest that wasn't a family member since the husband died. Why would they invite you?"

Ben rested his arms on the table. "I don't know. Why don't you ask Nate?"

"Harriet was a supernatural hunter, too. Did the family approach you to deal with him?"

She was probing, trying to get a reaction. Ben resisted the urge to snap back. "I saw Nate's reaction when we found the body. I've seen enough reactions to extreme situations to know genuine shock when I see it—and I saw it on Nate."

"Your ARX training." She narrowed her eyes. "Whatever non-disclosure ARX has on its employees doesn't hold water in a police investigation. Tell us what you're investigating in Little River."

"Nothing. Once again, I'm here as a private citizen."

She shook her head. "ARX might think that refusing to pass over your employee records will keep them safe, but if this goes to a federal level, we can demand they turn over their files."

My files had been requested—and Saltaire had yet to swoop down on them? Ben clamped down on the many possibilities racing through his head. *Later.* Now he had to concentrate on meeting the psychologist's questions calmly. "Or I might have cut ties with ARX completely, and they're right in claiming that my presence here is not ARX-related."

She scoffed. "We're not going to believe that. You met Nate in what Department Seven describes as abnormal circumstances, and after a brief acquaintanceship, you accompany him to his home sixteen-hours' drive away. You must have some added motivation to make such a long trip with a guy who is little more than an acquaintance."

Abnormal? Ben winced. Is Gunn referring to the necromancer trying to kill us—or Hunter's party?

The psychologist seized on his grimace. "Who was the target of your supernatural investigation? Was it Nathan? Or was it the brother—Ethan?"

Ben sighed. This had gone on long enough. "Fine. If you absolutely must know—and I am only making this statement under protest—it's Nate."

Triumph flashed in the female officer's face. She started to say something, but Ben held up his hand.

"I'm not investigating him. I'm fucking him."

The angry color in her face faded abruptly. At the far end of the bed, Ray choked.

Ben stood. "Sometimes he fucks me. It's pretty great. If you want correlating details, I'd be happy to tell you how great." Both officers just stared at him. "No? Then we're done."

The psychologist made an abortive attempt to stop him. "You can't leave—"

"You're not holding me. And with Department Seven's own evidence putting me directly in the clear, you don't want to try holding me." Ben stepped out of the cell door. "All the time you waste on us, the actual demonic agent is getting further and further away—and closer and closer to their next victim."

None of the officers tried to stop him leaving the station. It wasn't until he was outside and storming down the side of the road that Ben was conscious of being disappointed.

What? Did I want a fight? Ben realized his fists were clenched. *I do. Goddamn it! What is wrong with me?*

He took a deep breath, concentrating on slowing his breathing. The urge to hit something subsided and was replaced by new feelings. Anger at the psychologist's questions, frustration at his inability to do anything. But beneath that was an icy cold sensation. *Fear.* Ben felt its pinpricks travel up the back of his neck, putting him back in the tomb. *What possible reason do I have to be afraid?* Despite the scan discovering traces of demonic contact, he and Nate were clear. There was no way either of them could be charged with Harriet's death—providing the police did their jobs correctly. *Is that what I'm afraid of? That they'll make the wrong arrest?* Ethan was the obvious suspect and getting more obvious every day. *Nate's not going to like that...*

Nate. Ben swallowed. There was the heart of the problem. *I'm not thinking of the case or even myself. I'm thinking of Nate.* Putting his hands in his pockets, Ben started to walk.

ARX had strict no fraternization rules. Ben had always been scornful of agents who allowed themselves to be swayed by their feelings. Lives rested on an agent's ability to make clear, reasoned decisions! *And here I am, doing the exact same thing.*

Outside the interview room, Ben was less impressed with his conduct. *Might as well have just given them a neon sign saying 'Here! A weakness for you to exploit!'* He groaned. As an ARX employee, living and dead, he'd been in far more extreme situations. He'd kept his internal vampire in check for over a year. *And I lose my cool during a standard police interview. What is wrong with me?*

The answer was obvious. Ben gnawed at his lip. *Nate.*

He'd never had any problems keeping things cool and professional until he met Nate. Nor had he had any conflicting feelings about doing his duty. *That wasn't living!* Ben protested immediately. *Being Saltaire's soulless puppet...I could never go back to that.*

But was he any freer now?

Ben's footsteps slowed to a stop. *I'm still trapped.* His instincts told him to investigate, to learn everything he could, but at Nate's request, he'd done nothing. *When Nate's with me, I agree. But when he's not here...* Ben swallowed back a sick feeling. *Did he influence me?*

I'm jumping to conclusions. Nate feels just as strongly about compulsion as I do. No way he'd try to sway me against my will! But the memory of Nate managing his mother into a better mood came back instantly. *That's different! Nate just wants to help people. Help me.*

Ben thought of Nate sitting by him during his nightmare, but the initial glow of the memory was dimmed by a suspicion. *I rely on him too much. That's why I'm so reluctant to go against his decision—I don't want to lose him.*

Ben did not like his conclusion.

He looked around. Either side of the road was nothing but fields. In his anger, he'd walked without paying any attention to the direction he'd taken. Now he could be anywhere. In that brief amount of time, he'd left all the houses of Little River behind him. A mailbox just up ahead of Ben indicated that there was a house at the end of a gravel driveway, but a thick hedge screened it from view. He was alone with the fields, the sky, and the ever-present mountains.

The car's engine was almost a surprise. Ben belatedly realized that standing in the middle of the road to have his emotional stock take was not his best decision. He stepped into the grass at the side of the road as a red sedan approached.

It stopped right there in the road, the driver winding his window down. "Hey," said Ray. "Sorry about that."

"Are you apologizing for standard police practice? Because the psychologist is right. That is going outside your boundaries."

Ray smiled faintly. "Still. My cousin's dating a girl. She got a lot of flack because of it. Um. Anyway—"

"It's fine."

"No, it's not. I don't know much about demons, but the sheriff agrees with you. Says that whoever the agent is, he's not from around here. The Chinquapin team, they just want to get back home as soon as possible. That's why they're putting the pressure on. Hoping for anything they can use against Ethan."

Ben snorted. "That was obvious." He started walking. Ray seemed like he could take a hint.

The car cruised alongside Ben. "You realize you're not just walking away from town, but away from the Granger's farm, right?"

"Clearing my head," Ben said shortly.

"Hop in. I can give you a ride."

"I'd rather walk."

"Don't be like that. Look, it's our fault you're out here so why not let me make it up to you?"

"Will you stop following me in the car?" Ben hunched his shoulders. "It's like you're trying to pick me up."

Ray laughed. "Hey, baby. Want to go check out a possible crime scene?"

Ben's head snapped up to stare at Ray. "What?"

Ray smirked. "Forensics is done with Harriet's hotel room. Didn't find anything worth noting. I got permission to give you a look at it before we pack up his stuff. Interested?"

"What's the catch?"

Ray looked far more innocent than any police officer should. "Catch?"

"I'm a suspect in an ongoing investigation," Ben reminded him. "I'm also a private citizen. You should be taking pains to keep me out of scenes of interest. Not inviting me to them."

Ray shrugged. "You're an expert. We aren't."

Ben studied him thoughtfully. "And it'd score a point for local law enforcement to have one over on Chinquapin?"

Ray's grin broadened. "You didn't hear it from me."

Ben hesitated. *Nate won't like this.* He felt sharp impatience. *If I let what Nate wants or doesn't want make my decisions for me, I might as well be back under Saltaire's shadow.* "All right." Ben climbed into the passenger seat. "Let's go."

☆☆☆

Harriet's Rockford motel room had a lived-in air that had survived rigorous forensic exams. He'd kept it tidy, but his belongings were spread out around the room where he'd left them. A towel hung over the back of the chair at the desk, and the half-open wardrobe door revealed a suit hung up inside. Harriet's suitcase was where he'd left it on the coffee table.

"Sheriff insisted they put everything back as they found it," Ray noted. "They didn't like it of course, but supernatural cases, we get a lot more leeway."

Ben hummed in acknowledgment. He was trying to put his finger on what was off about the room. "Did housekeeping come in after he left?"

"Harriet requested that his room be left as is. He changed the sheets himself." Ray leaned against the door to watch Ben work. "The staff describe him as pleasant and personable. He tipped well, paid up front, and hit that fine median between keeping to yourself and being overbearing. None of them had any idea he was a hunter."

Ben nodded. "That matches what I found on his online profile."

"Not investigating?"

Ben shot Ray a look. "I was curious." He walked over to the bed. It had been stripped, and after a moment's pause, Ben found himself examining the desk. It was empty except for coffee cup with the dregs still in it and a couple of pens. "Laptop?"

"Chinquapin sent it in to get an expert to analyze the data on it."

"Notebook?"

"Must have been on his person. It's long gone." Ray jiggled impatiently. "My guess is the agent burnt it."

"That would be logical," Ben agreed, going to stand in front of the wardrobe. "Whoever killed Harriet approached it cautiously. Luring him to the timber yard at a time when it was empty, transporting his body in Harriet's own truck..." He stopped.

"And then going and ditching the body in an extremely obvious place." Ray jangled his car keys distractedly, but his attention was on Ben. "There's no way that wasn't deliberate."

Ben nodded thoughtfully. "No."

"You think they ditched the body where they did to cover their tracks?"

Ben bit his lip. Department Seven had no reason to hide Nate's supernatural status. "Nate was entirely unaware he had any supernatural links until very recently. When we arrived in Little River, he had yet to break the news to his mother. It's highly unlikely anyone outside the family would know about him."

"And Ethan?" Ray shrugged at the look Ben gave him. "We know there's something there."

"Then you also know that whatever it is, the family doesn't speak about it."

Ray raised an eyebrow. "You don't know?"

"It's not my business."

"Not your business to investigate an unknown supernatural right under your nose?"

"I'm here as a private citizen, trying to put his past behind him and move on with his life."

Ray snorted. "That would be a lot more effective if you weren't in the motel room of a murdered man."

"At your invitation." Ben bit his lip. "I want to help—and I will help. But not by investigating Ethan."

"But if he's behind this—"

"Then the physical evidence in the truck will convict him. But I don't think you'll find Ethan's fingerprints in the truck."

Ray nodded slowly. "The guy goes out of his way to make the case against him obvious. But the sheriff agrees with you." He shrugged. "I don't know. I'd say the religious upbringing and denial of whatever supernatural links he has would make him more likely, but the sheriff isn't letting Chinquapin make an arrest until there's hard evidence."

"Should you be telling me this?"

Ray scratched his neck. "I figure if you know how the case stands, you're more likely to help. Sheriff's being pushed to make an arrest fast. There's already been one threat made against the Granger family."

Ben caught his breath. "A threat?"

"And that's not the only thing. The reason the sheriff and I arrived at the farm so quickly after Nate called to report finding Harriet was that we were already on our way over to you. We'd just received an anonymous call claiming there was a dead body on the farm." Ray drummed his fingers against the door. "Looking more and more like the family has an enemy."

Ben nodded. "That occurred to me. Nate said he can't think of anyone with a grudge against the family, but Nate might not be aware."

"His brother's certainly not winning any popularity contests."

Ben made a noncommittal noise. If Ray was hoping to draw him on Ethan, he was out of luck. He looked through Harriet's clothing. A cold weather jacket, a shirt and suit jacket hung in the wardrobe, but the rest of his clothing was still neatly packed in the suitcase. From the looks of things, he was planning to spend a more than a few days in Rockford. "How long did Harriet take the room for?"

"He paid for three days upfront, then on the third day paid for two more. Told the receptionist he'd found what he was looking for."

"Interesting."

Ray smirked. "Isn't it? He visited Little River the second day of his stay, seeming to imply that whatever he found, it wasn't there."

"How do you know he didn't return?"

"You've met Dan. He had a long talk with Harriet while he was filling up. Trust me. Harriet came back, Dan would know."

Ben turned to search the suitcase. "You said you talked to Harriet in Little River?"

"More the sheriff than me. He was asking about the Winkler case. The sheriff worked on it, and he had some points he wanted to clear up."

"Did he mention any supernatural incidents?" Even accounting for the clothes hanging in the wardrobe, the suitcase would not be full. Ben patted down the sides automatically.

Ray shook his head. "Asked the best way to the old Winnaker farm, and that was it. Seemed like he planned to go there immediately after talking to us. It wouldn't have taken him more than an hour."

Ben looked up sharply. "You've been to the Winnaker farm?"

"Naturally. Had a hell of a time finding it—the place is overgrown."

"And?"

"And nothing." Ray shook his head. "The farmer sold the property to the Parks board after his wife left him. The house fell to ruin, and the forest reclaimed the farmland. Matter of fact, the Parks board bought up a whole bunch of farms adjoining the park back in the sixties. The only mystery is why anyone'd think there was anything spooky about it."

Ben frowned. He could investigate the Winnaker farm on his own. "What happened to Harriet's weapons?"

"How did you know—right, forgot who I was talking to." Ray ducked his head. "The investigating team took the guns. One hunting rifle and a pistol. Harriet was the registered owner and had a license for both. He cleaned them regularly, and he had ammunition, but both guns were unloaded. There was a hunting knife on the body and a machete in the suitcase. Along with a large number of candles, salt, wooden stakes, crucifixes and garlic."

"I can smell the garlic." Ben leaned into the suitcase. "Also—myrrh?"

"That would be the unidentified substance that Forensics is analyzing."

"It is believed to have anti-demonic properties. Because of the religious connotations. As far as I know, it's never been proved conclusively whether or not it's effective, but a lot of people swear by it."

"So it's your opinion Harriet was aware he was looking for a demon?"

"Definitely." The only part of the room Ben had not searched was the bed. He stepped towards it.

"He didn't mention that to the police."

Ben snorted, opening the bathroom door. "He wouldn't. Admitting to hunting a demon puts a hunter at great risk, from the demon and the larger supernatural community. Demons are the most feared precisely because they are the most powerful. Hunters have a bad habit of either dying horribly or becoming agents themselves. Sometimes both."

Ray accompanied Ben to the bathroom door. "So there's backlash?"

"It's not believed possible to kill a demon. Anyone attempting it has to be mad or deluded—and ripe for the sorts of promises demons make. The church attempted to stamp out demonic agents by restricting knowledge on them to their own authorized exorcists, and Department Seven requires anyone who wants to research demons to hold a Class-five magical license and be willing to go to regular meetings with one of their experts."

"And ARX?"

Ben shook his head. "Very few agents were allowed to handle demonic investigations. I wasn't one of them."

"But you tested positive for demonic contact."

"I know." Ben frowned.

"You really have no idea?"

Ben shook his head. "It could be anything that requires a signature or a verbal agreement. Agents leave traces even when the contract signed is benign."

Ray shook his head. "You're sure about that?"

"Of course." Ben found himself echoing Nate's words. "I think I'd remember meeting a demonic agent!"

"I saw the detailed analysis of your sample. They had a proper priest do the analysis. She said that it was marked contact, not residual—not something you picked up from a casual contract."

Ben's mouth was dry. "You're sure?"

"Very sure. The sheriff wanted my opinion on it, we went over the readings together." Ray sounded vaguely apologetic. "According to the priest's report, you were 'demon-marked'—are you okay?"

"Demon marked." Ben's breath caught in the back of his throat. "Making me an agent or a victim?" He shook his head. "That's not— No way it's—"

A memory stirred. Long buried, it flashed across his mind, incomplete but vivid. A room, splattered with blood, a thing that had once been a woman lying in the center of a circle—

"Or you lived for a long time in close quarters with an agent that regularly conversed with demons—yeah, I think you need to sit down." Ray grasped Ben's arm.

"I'm fine," Ben said mechanically. "I'm a professional."

"Even professionals need a breather." Ray steered him towards the bed. "Get your head down and take some deep breaths."

Ben felt a sudden revulsion. He dug in his heels. At the exact same moment, Ray slowed to a stop.

"The chair. I'll move the towel—" He released Ben hurrying towards the chair.

"No," said Ben. "There's something here. A spell is at work."

Ray froze. "What do you mean?"

"Three times now I've approached the bed, and each time I've turned away to do something else." Ben wiped clammy hands on his jeans.

"There's something there that Harriet didn't want anyone to find." He stepped towards the bed. "Help me lift the mattress."

Ray shuddered as he stepped forward. "If this is magic, I will pass. This feels like the worst kind of hangover."

"Don't think about it. When I say go—lift!"

Beneath the mattress was a magical circle, holding a mid-level rune of obscuration. Within it was a gallon-size ziplock bag containing a battered looking book. As soon as light fell on the rune, the compulsion to get away from the bed faded.

"Holy crap." Ray bent over, steadying himself with his hands on his knees as he took deep breaths. "I've never felt anything like that—"

"You're lucky." Ben picked up the bag. *On Monsters, Being a True Account of the Means of Identifying and Battling Unnatural Creatures by A Servant of the Lord Engaged in His Work.*" He looked up at Ray. "Do you know what this is?"

"Judging from the title?" Ray ran a hand through his hair. "I'm guessing it's a book about identifying and battling mon—uh. The existentially different."

Ben continued to clutch the book tightly. "I've heard of this. It's one of the oldest records of supernatural investigation and contains first-hand accounts of the author's work as an exorcist at a time before the Church's growing ascendancy forced the supernatural in Europe underground. Copies are exceedingly hard to find—there's probably only ten or twelve copies still in existence!"

Ray held out his hand. "I'll have to give this to Forensics. No— It's no good looking at me like that. I don't swing that way."

Ben made no move to pass the book over. "Please? I found it. Can't I at least see what Harriet was looking at?"

Ray hesitated and then groaned. "Fine. We didn't go to the effort of finding it just to have Chinquapin get the info first." He unwound a pair of plastic gloves from his jacket pocket. "But I'm holding the book."

Ben nodded. "Fine with me."

About to take the bag from Ben, Ray paused. "This isn't going to curse me, is it?"

Ben fidgeted impatiently on the spot. "Open the book."

Harriet's bookmark was where he'd left it. Ben peered over Ray's arm to read. "*May the fate of this unhappy man stand as a warning to all honest men to beware the blandishments of demons! Discovered in the very act of preparing the hellish trap in which he intended to make the young maid that was to be his victim the next meal of his demonic master, the man Wendel boasted that his unholy ally had granted him the strength of ten men and surely it was so for it took all of twenty men to subdue him and even then he was dragged before the bailiff unafraid and without a proper sense of shame—*"

"Did the church have a vendetta against punctuation? Because that is one long sentence."

Ben frowned faintly, intent on the page in front of him. "*Bound in chains of blessed iron and taken within the sanctuary of the church... And there Wendel did weep most terribly for at last he saw the peril his soul was in and he pleaded piteously for the help of my most excellent brother Pius—*" He drew a sharp breath.

"What? What did you find?"

Ben swallowed. "*The wretched man spake freely to Brother Pius of all he knew and I, his scribe, took down every word as it came from his mouth.*" He looked to Ray. "Do you realize what this is?"

"An account of a demon?"

"From an agent! That—" Ben gripped Ray's arm. "That never happens!"

"You're starting to scare me."

Ben read on. "*It is the nature of demons to be ruled by their appetites. So it was the case with this foul beast, Gaassimolar by name, upon whose head may be laid many dozens of innocent deaths. Most horribly, the demon demanded his agents procure not only an innocent victim, but that their dreadful fate rest upon the utterance of love for him that deceived them most cruelly.*" Ben let go of Ray's arm. "This is it. The demon Harriet was looking for."

"Do you have any idea of your own strength?"

"Don't mind that now." Ben tapped the book. "You need to call the sheriff. If Harriet's right, then Olivia Winkler wasn't just murdered, she was first seduced by Gaassimolar's agent."

"Shit." Ray hastily reached for his phone.

"Correlate her death against unsolved deaths involving a lonely, socially isolated victim and traces of demonic involvement," Ben said. "Get onto Department Seven's supernatural crime database."

Ray raised the book in a 'pipe down' gesture. "I do know how to do my job— Sheriff? Hawick's found something. No— Trust me, you're going to want to hear this."

As Ray relayed the news of their discovery, Ben became aware of a vibration coming from his pocket. *My phone?* He took it out. The sight of the lock screen made his heart sink. *Nate.* Message after message, two missed calls... Ben hit redial feeling sick.

Nate picked up immediately. "Ben? Where are you?"

"Rockford. Ray brought me to Harriet's hotel room."

"But you're all right? Nothing's happened, you're safe?"

"Yeah, we're fine. What's happened?"

He heard Nate breathe out. When he next spoke, his voice was colored with so much bitterness, Ben almost didn't recognize it. "Apparently the sheriff's taking too long to arrest us. After the police got done interviewing us and we went home, a bunch of our neighbors showed up at the house with the intent of hurrying justice along. They had pitchforks, but they replaced the torches with rifles."

"Jesus, Nate! Are you all right?"

"Fine." The reply was unconvincing. "We were lucky. They didn't wait for the Forensics team to finish packing up the trailer, and the police didn't take kindly to their prime suspects being threatened right under their noses. They've been sent packing and threatened with criminal charges of endangerment and trespassing."

Ben looked at Ray. The police officer met his eye and nodded. From his tense expression, the sheriff was filling him in on the incident. "We're coming back at once."

"To do what?" That didn't sound like Nate at all. "There's nothing you can do, Ben. It's over."

CHAPTER TEN

Ray pulled the rooftop flashing lights out of the backseat of his red car and drove as if he'd never heard of speed limits, but the drive back to the farm felt far, far too long for Ben. The sick feeling in his stomach had nothing to do with the many twists of the mountain road, or the knowledge of what Harriet's book, somewhere in the backseat, contained.

Nate was in danger and I wasn't there.

He was out of the car before it rolled to a complete stop, taking in the damage with a sinking heart. Smoke hung in the air and the grass on the front lawn was scorched. The flower bed in front of the house had been trampled, and the front kitchen and living room windows were smashed.

A police officer came down the porch to meet them. "Excuse me, sir. I need to ask you to identify yourself—"

"Hawick's staying with the family," Ray said. "Shit. What happened here?"

As the police officer began to recount what she'd seen, Ben dashed into the house.

Nate sat at the kitchen table, a first-aid kit in front of him. He was laboriously wrapping a bandage around his hand. He looked up as Ben entered the kitchen and then away.

Ben felt a tension within him lift. Seeing Nate for himself reassured him in a way that their phone conversation hadn't. He laid his hand on Nate's shoulder for a moment, before pulling out the chair next to Nate and quietly but firmly taking the bandage from him.

"You'll have an officer here all night." The sheriff nodded acknowledgment of Ben's arrival but continued to speak. In marked contrast to her earlier visit, she stood in front of the coffee maker while Ma sat at the table. "And we're not leaving till we're sure you feel secure."

Ma looked even older. There was a bandage on her cheek, and she didn't have a speck of color in her face. "I taught Sunday School to some of those men! They're our neighbors, friends... Dan came to our wedding!"

"Dan should know better than to run his mouth without thinking. That's disturbing public peace at the very least, inciting violence at the worst... Him and that pastor." The sheriff banged a coffee cup down in front of Ma.

"Don't speak ill of a man of the cloth." Ma's response was automatic, reflexive.

Nate clenched his fist. "What the hell, Ma! He's a jerk, no matter what his job is!"

"Nathan! I don't want to hear that language from you!"

Ben placed his hand on Nate's arm, waiting until he'd relaxed his fist to tie off the bandage. He shifted his seat closer to Nate, putting his hand on Nate's arm.

Nate met Ben's eyes and grimaced. He had a smear of blood on his cheek and an angry red mark, but Ben recognized the grimace for what it was—an apology. He squeezed Nate's hand lightly.

"Pastor's doing the Lord's work. What he thinks is best." Ma looked at the coffee cup in front of her as if she'd never seen one before. "This is—"

"A shock," the sheriff said. "People acting hastily and jumping to conclusions. Don't take it to heart, Emma. They're at fault, and you've got a dozen police witnesses to the fact that it was entirely unprovoked."

Ma shook her head. "You've been very kind to us, but if it's the Lord's Will—"

"If anything was the Lord's will, it was the Forensic Team being right around the corner. Come on, Ma. Snap out of this." Nate leaned against the table to put his hand on Ma's.

"Nate's got the right idea," the sheriff said. "You've got two good sons taking care of you. You'll be fine."

Ma put a hand to her face, as she turned aside, but it was too late. They'd all seen her face crumple.

"Ma." Nate pulled her into a hug. She buried her face in his T-shirt, but it was not enough to muffle her sobs.

"That's the way," the sheriff encouraged. "Let it out."

Ben quietly gathered the bandages Nate had been using into the first-aid kit and picked it up. He'd seen where it was kept in the bathroom and intended to put it back. Ben wasn't sure what instinct prompted him to push the door to the bedroom Nate and Ethan shared open instead.

"Ethan?"

Nate's twin was sitting on one of the beds. He looked worse for wear, pale except where red marks showed up injuries.

"What are you doing in here?"

"Ma told me 'go to your room'." Ethan's voice was even flatter than usual, something Ben had not imagined possible.

"And no one's looked at your injuries?"

Ethan frowned. "They trampled Ma's dahlias."

Ben's mouth twitched. Now was not the time. "I think your mother's more worried about her son than her dahlias." He sat down on the bed. "Give me your arm."

Ethan held it out obediently.

It was like practicing first aid on a mannequin. A really life-like mannequin, but a mannequin nonetheless. Ethan sat motionless and silent throughout the application of disinfectant, bandages, and soothing gel. Ben frowned as he set the latter item back in the first-aid kit. Most of Nate and Ethan's injuries were consistent with being in a fight, but Ethan's burns were something else. Ben couldn't help but think of the scorched grass outside the house. "Does this hurt?"

Ethan grunted.

"I can ask your mother if she has an ice pack. Or we can make one ourselves—"

"Thank you, Ben, but that's not necessary." Ma stood in the doorway. Her eyes were red-rimmed, but she'd regained her self-composure. "I'll mind Ethan. You've had a long day yourself, you'll want to rest."

It was dark outside the window. Ben realized just how late it was by the ache in his body. "Goodnight, Ethan. Sleep well."

Ethan didn't stir. His expression was just as blank as when Ben had entered the room, and his hand rested on his bandaged arm. He looked at the wall, in the direction of the front of house.

The dahlias? Ben turned to the door and received a shock. Ma watched Ethan with something that looked very much like fear.

She looked up, stepping back into the hall and the expression was gone. Ben followed her down the hall with an uneasy feeling. *Fear of Ethan? Or for him?*

"You have everything you need?" The question was automatic, Ma opening the spare room door and waiting for Ben to enter.

"Yes. Don't worry about me at all."

Ma frowned. She looked around the spare room, her gaze resting on the shopping bags. "Are you packed? I don't mean to be inhospitable, but it's time you thought about leaving."

"Because of what happened tonight? Mrs. Granger, don't think for a second that I—"

"I don't think, I know. Someone's going to get hurt, and I don't want it to be you."

That wasn't a threat. It was defeat. Ben rubbed his arm. "I want to help. I can help. I want to stay, as long as you'll have me—"

Ma shook her head. "You can't help, Ben. No one can. This is a judgment on me, and there's nothing you or I or anyone can do about it."

The hairs on Ben's arm stood up one by one. *Judgment?* "What do you mean?"

Ma turned away as if she hadn't heard. "The bus leaves from Rockford at ten fifteen. The sheriff has said she'll see you get on it safely." She started to shut the door.

Ben caught it before she could. "What judgment? Did you do something? Know something? If it's got any bearing on this case—"

Ma looked at him. It was a dispassionate gaze that went through him. "That's nothing to do with you, and it's better that way." She shut the door, leaving Ben in the dark of the spare room.

Ben stood, looking at the closed door, for a long time after her footsteps had faded away down the hall. *A judgment on me...* "She wouldn't. Couldn't." Nate said she was passionate about her faith, and what Ben had seen of her bore that out. But a mother would go to dire lengths to protect a child... And Ethan was proof that Ma wasn't above pushing the limits of her faith.

Ben leaned back against the door. He felt better with the wood as a barrier between him and the rest of the house. *Is her faith a front? Or is she trying to make amends for her sin—whatever it is?* No amends were possible for someone who'd summoned a demon. Their soul was forfeit, claimed by the demon as soon as the agent became unable to fulfill their promised contract. Ma could not fail to know that.

"Investigators rely on facts, not imagination." Ben dug his fingers into his arm to drown out the voice that immediately reminded him he was no longer an investigator. "Ma's scan came up empty. Whatever she's hiding, it isn't magic."

On the other side of the door, he could hear the quiet tread of footsteps and the front door closing. Silence settled throughout the house, the occasional settling of boards taking the place of the house's daytime inhabitants.

Ben slid down the length of the door to sit on the floor. Tired as he was, he knew getting into bed would do absolutely nothing. He was keyed up, wired, thoughts bouncing around inside his head. *Does Nate know that Ma wants me out? Or that she admitted to something potentially ominous? Would the people of Little River make a second attempt at swaying justice? Was Nate upset that Ben was in Rockford instead of being there to help?*

Ben settled himself in a cross-legged pose, and took a deep breath, letting it out slowly and deliberately. Then again. On the third round, the cyclone of his thoughts had been downgraded to a tropical storm. Ben was calm enough to be aware that something was off.

Exhaling slowly, Ben worked his way back through his mental steps. He felt it again, a certain resistance, pushing him back from certain thoughts, just as he'd sensed the obscuration spell. No magic this time, but an instinctive knowledge to draw back from pain.

Demon-marked. Ben swallowed. He retraced the memory that had jumped into his mind in the hotel room.

A room, full of pungent smoke and the cloying, copper scent that made him feel sick. He was afraid, but he stepped forward as if compelled. There were shouts of alarm behind him, and a heavy hand clasped on his shoulder, drawing him away, but it was too late. Ben had seen it, and that instant's glance was enough.

Ben caught himself on the brink of shying away from it. *No. It's time.* He took a breath, was alarmed at how loud and raspy it sounded in the still, sleeping house. He wriggled himself back more firmly against the door. The smooth wood was not as cold as he expected. Ben thought of Nate, replacing the wooden surface with Nate's solid presence. Taking another deep breath, he forced himself to picture the scene in its entirety.

Mother.

☆☆☆

Ben sat quietly on the flight of stairs between the second and third stories. The house was old and full of shadows. The light in the hall below didn't reach more than halfway up the first flight of stairs, or if it did, the dark wood of the banisters and heavy carpet immediately swallowed it. He was almost positive no one could see him, but he wrapped his arms around his legs and rested his chin on his knees to be sure. He couldn't see more than his father's back and shoulders, still wearing the suit he'd worn for the funeral, and Godfrey, changed back into his usual suit. Hunter was entirely out of sight down the hall. But Ben heard them perfectly.

"A quiet affair." Ben strained to catch Austin's words, low and tired. "She'd have hated it. She always said that funerals were far too morbid. A waste of a good party."

"Under the circumstances..." Godfrey's placatory murmur was so faint as to be almost inaudible.

"What are the circumstances?" Hunter's languid question was the most normal of the three of them. "You said the coroner's ruling came in?"

Austin bowed his head. It was Godfrey who answered. "He admitted to some doubt, but I explained the situation. In view of Bennet's youth, he agreed that it was better to keep the affair off the public record. As far as anyone knows, Audrey committed suicide while the balance of her mind was disturbed."

"Department Seven won't like that." Austin crossed his arms. "They already don't like it."

"They don't have to like it." Hunter came into sight then, looking, as he always did, impossibly dramatic, even at a distance of two flights of stairs and a set of banisters between them.

Ben felt his heart give an unhappy lurch—he didn't want to be spying on Hunter, but no one told him anything. They just got impossibly solemn and shook their heads—as if he was still in kindergarten, and not fourth grade and fully aware that his mother had not killed herself.

"This case is no longer their jurisdiction," Hunter continued. "The only ones who know the truth are the three of us—and Bennet."

Ben stayed very still.

"How much does Bennet know?" Godfrey's inquiry was mild.

"Nothing," his father said.

Hunter turned to glance at Godfrey momentarily. "I read the child psychiatrist's report for Department Seven. She expressed concern. In her opinion, he's not reacting like a normal child—"

"How would a normal child react to this?" Austin raised an arm in a sweeping gesture. "What is a normal reaction anyway?"

"She believes that Bennet is concealing something—or protecting someone."

The silence following Hunter's words seemed to seep into the house itself. Ben felt a cold clamminess creep up his arms. There was still time to creep back into his room. They'd never know he had heard.

But he couldn't make himself move.

Austin's shoulders sagged in defeat. "Ben is...was...very close to his mother. She spoiled him and he adored her. It will be hard for him to accept that she's gone. Even harder to accept how she died. It's likely that he's protecting her."

Godfrey exclaimed. "Even though she—?"

"Perhaps we should continue this conversation in the dining room," Hunter suggested casually. "What is that saying? Something about little pitchers...?" His dark eyes rested on Ben's banisters for a second, and then he turned, leading the way into the dining room.

Ben stayed where he was, not daring to move until he'd heard the door close behind them. He counted all the way to a hundred twice, before he stood, making himself go downstairs.

Hunter was draped over the chaise longue when Ben opened the door. "Evening, Bennet. Do you like your new room?"

Ben nodded. He crossed the room to where Austin stood, looking out the window, and put his hand in his father's. "I like the desk. And the bookcase."

"If there's anything you want, feel free to let Godfrey and I know. A TV, perhaps?"

Austin made a sound of protest. "You're spoiling him!"

"It's all right," Ben said quickly. "I don't want a TV."

"But there is something you want?" Hunter turned his crystalline gaze on Ben.

It was like watching the snakes at the zoo. There was something unsettling, something dangerous, something absolutely fascinating about Hunter. Only Austin's hand tightening around him, stopped Ben from taking a step towards Hunter. "I want a new copy of *Dracula*." Ben belatedly remembered his manners. "Please."

"Ben!" Austin hissed, mortified. "You mustn't—"

"My copy's missing!" Ben protested. "And I always read it before bed!"

"Oh, that's easy." Hunter stood. "I'm sure there's a copy of the library. Shall we take a look together, Bennet?"

It was tempting—very tempting. Looking at a real vampire's library with a real vampire! But Ben shook his head, tightening his grip on his father's hand. "Maybe later."

"I'm very sorry." Austin hastily apologized. "I really don't know what's got into him."

Hunter's smile was amused. The hint of a fang was just visible. "No apologies necessary. I—or Godfrey—can show you the library anytime, Bennet. After all, this is your home now."

☆☆☆

Ben's phone buzzed in his pocket, startling him out of the memory. It buzzed three more times as he found it, and Ben shook his head wryly as he looked at the lock screen. *Was giving Nate a phone a bad idea?*

—*Ben*

—*Ben*

—*Going to keep doing this until you reply*

—*Ben*

—*B*

—*E*

—*N*

Ben smiled, tapping in his passcode. —*That's entirely unnecessary, Nate. What's so important it can't wait?*

—*Think you can get to the barn without anyone seeing you?*

Ben stared at the message for a moment. Then he stood, making his way through shadow to the window. The night was clear, the moon casting a faint glow, making the shadows darker. The barn was one solid black profile against the night, unfathomably deep.

Something in Ben woke. His heart beat in anticipation. Navigating the garden in the dark was a challenge even without the police officer stationed outside on guard duty to contend with.

—*Absolutely,* he typed. *Why?*

—*Tell you when you get here.*

Ben placed his phone in his pocket. Fortunately, his sneakers were close at hand. Nate was confident that Ethan liked Ben, but Ben wasn't convinced. He'd taken to keeping his sneakers inside the spare bedroom when he wasn't wearing them to make sure they didn't get lost a second time. Ben pulled them on in the dark. Eyes already adjusted to the night, Ben opened the spare room window.

The garden felt different in the dark. The sweetly scented flowers had retired with the sun, and the cool night air carried a smell that seemed to come from the earth itself. Unseen trees whispered softly in the breeze. The porch creaked as the officer on guard duty paced.

Easy.

Ben slipped quietly across the grass. The floral hedge masked him from view, and he moved with the wind, letting the sound of rustling leaves disguise any sound he made. The open field before the barn gave him slight difficulty, but Ben used the shadows cast by Nate's truck and the barn itself to melt into the night. He pulled the door behind him, heart beating fast but his breathing perfectly under control. The night was his.

The only light in the barn came from a dusty skylight, through which the moonlight fell in one pool. Nate stood in its center, looking at his phone. He was perfectly outlined as if he stood on stage beneath a spotlight—or only seconds away from an alien abduction.

Little River is getting to me. Shaking his head, Ben ghosted across the barn floor to place his hand on Nate's arm. "I'm here."

Nate jumped, hastily grabbing at his phone. "Jesus Christ, Ben! You scared me!"

"Keep your voice down." Ben hoped that the shadows hid his amusement. "Not unless you want our police escort rushing in to investigate."

Nate breathed out, turning to face Ben. "After all the effort of sneaking out here? Pass." He tucked his phone into the back pocket of his jeans.

Ben looked around the barn. The musty air smelled of hay and animals. The floor was mostly clear, but Ben could see hay bales piled up against the wall, and a ladder leading up to some kind of loft. Pieces of machinery, unidentifiable in the dark, loomed strangely. "What's up?"

Nate reached for Ben. "I wanted to talk to you. But now you're here, I don't know what to say." His fingers traveled restlessly up and down Ben's arm.

Ben raised an eyebrow. "Do you really want to talk?"

"Well, yeah. I mean—given everything that's happened, anything else would be weird."

And yet, Nate was still touching him. "Heard of terror management theory?" As Nate shook his head, Ben continued. "You were threatened tonight, confronted with your own mortality. Faced with the prospect of death, our biological imperative kicks into overdrive, making us want to reproduce as quickly as possible."

"Shouldn't we decide whether we're dating before talking about kids?"

Ben nudged Nate with his elbow. "It's only a theory. But if it's right, basically, we're hard-wired to want to fuck."

"This explains so much about why vampires are so popular." Nate drew Ben towards him.

"It's a subconscious urge. Completely natural." Ben lightly placed a hand on Nate's side. "But vampires take advantage of it."

"Really." Nate's voice lowered confidentially. "Planning on taking advantage of me?"

"You forget." Ben leaned in, deliberately speaking to Nate's sensitive neck. "I'm no longer a vampire." He was so close to Nate that he felt the shiver go through him.

Nate leaned over Ben. His voice dripped with calculated insolence. "You're saying we're just some biological urge then?"

Challenging me. Ben felt the spike in adrenaline at the same time as the arousal. He placed his hand on Nate's chest. Nate's breathing was rapid, his body tense. Violence, the urge to fight, assert dominance and reclaim territory seemed equally as likely as sex. *Supernatural being who has hurt you once,* the logical part of Ben's mind reminded him. *You won't survive a tree being thrown at you—if that's all he does.* The voice coiled at the back of Ben's mind, sinuously inserting itself in a cold shiver running across his shoulders. *You don't know him. You don't know what he's capable of.*

I've had it up to here with the unknown. Ben tightened his fingers in Nate's T-shirt, tugging him down to face level. He could feel Nate's startled exhalation on his cheek. *Time to tackle this head on.* "Want to find out?"

The words came out more aggressively than he'd intended, but Nate's response was immediate. "How?"

Even though it was dark, the moonlight not reaching between them, Ben still looked down. He felt for and found the rough denim of Nate's jeans. Nate was hard and hot beneath the fabric. Ben gripped his erection tightly, stroking it through the cloth. "You'd like to fuck me." Nate grunted, an admission of need that went straight to Ben's cock. "You'd like to push me back against the hay and take me."

Nate surged forward as if Ben's words had pressed a button. Mouth on Ben's, he gripped Ben's hips as he ground against him.

Ben didn't realize they'd moved until he bumped into the hay bale. Stretching out an arm for balance, he found nothing behind him. The next second, he was on his back, neck tickled by the blades of hay, and his hands locked around Nate's ass. Nate thrust against him urgently, and Ben arched his hips to meet him, reveling in the mindlessness of it. *Who's thinking now?*

Nate swore as he fumbled with Ben's fly.

Ben had a moment of triumph—Nate was miles more experienced than he was, so seeing him this needy was a thrill—before realization hit. He caught Nate's hand. "No."

Nate came to an immediate halt. "No?"

Ben took a breath to control himself. "You wanted to prove we are more than a biological impulse, right?" Nate made no attempt to rebut him. Ben felt awareness of his power grow as he continued. "We're not going to do that by giving in to our urges."

Nate groaned. "Fuck, Ben. I— I need—"

Ben gripped Nate's shoulder tightly. "Can you control yourself? Do what I tell you—exactly what I tell you?" Nate drew a sharp breath and Ben pressed on. "Then you'll know it's not all biology."

"I don't remember any of this from Ms. Pollock's class."

"Go. Stand in the moonlight." It was a relief to say the words, know they carried nothing more than Ben's own thoughts.

Nate pried himself away slowly, giving Ben a last caress before he stood. His obvious reluctance gave Ben a thrill. He sat up, trusting the dark would hide his smile. After days at the mercy of events out of his control, calling the shots felt very good indeed.

"What now?" Nate stood at the center of the moonlight. His eyes were dark pools, the light not touching them. He looked back over his shoulder, catching and holding Ben's gaze. "Aren't you going to join me?" He ran his hands over his own body in a deliberate caress—and equally deliberate challenge. Nate was taking power back.

Ben felt a rush of affection. Nate was a consummate professional in his own right, thinking of Ben's pleasure in the midst of his own needs.

"It's not your body," he said, the words rough and unconsidered. "It's you."

How was it that the unguarded surprise on Nate's face was more intimate than seeing him naked? Ben rolled off the hay bale and onto his feet, seeking the cover of the shadows. He wasn't sure that he wanted his own expression to be visible.

"So why I am I standing here all on my own?" Nate had recovered enough bravado to give a convincing challenge.

"Clothes off."

Nate turned, trying to pinpoint Ben's location in the dark. "Where are you?" His T-shirt was already halfway up his chest.

"I don't want a show, Nate. I want you naked."

Nate's smile curved dangerously before it was hidden by the T-shirt being jerked over his head. "Who's needy now?" He casually skimmed a hand across his perfectly toned stomach, before letting the T-shirt drop to the floor.

Ben abruptly realized he'd paused to watch entirely unthinkingly. *Nate's good at this. No surprise there.* "The longer you take on this, the longer you have to wait."

"Yeah, yeah. Isn't that the point?" But it seemed to Ben that Nate fumbled with his fly in his haste. Finally, he stood beneath the skylight, completely bathed in the moonlight. His freed erection swayed lightly as Nate shifted. It looked heavy, demanding attention, but Nate lightly stroked his stomach, denying himself the contact he obviously craved. "Naked as ordered. You gonna do something about it?" As the barn creaked, the old boards, shifting, Nate turned eagerly toward the sound.

Wanting me. Worry flashed through Ben. *Am I being cruel?* He stepped out to join Nate beneath the skylight, announcing his presence with a hand on Nate's back. "What do you want, Nate?"

Nate started, but he recovered quickly, turning around to face Ben. "You to hurry the fuck up."

"You don't know what I have in mind." Ben's hand had traveled as Nate turned and lingered over his hip.

"I don't need to know. I trust you." There was no hesitation in Nate's voice, none at all.

Ben caught his breath. Nate's admission was terrifying—as was his immediate reaction to it. *I shouldn't be so turned on by his vulnerability! I could hurt him—use him—*

But I'm not going to. Ben gripped Nate's ass with both hands, rocking against him so that his trapped erection brushed against Nate's, making his intentions clear. "This is about you. Tell me what you want."

Nate ground back. "Fuck me. Hard, fast, furious."

That's not proving anything, said the single part of Ben's brain not occupied by with the immediate need to be inside Nate. "Can you—" Ben groped for the right word, his mouth dry. "—handle that?"

Nate stepped out of Ben's grip, turning around. He bent over, moonlight catching the shift of his muscles as he braced himself, deliberately pressing back against Ben. "I want you to push me right to the edge." His voice was low but absolutely certain. "I can take whatever you give me and more. Let me show you my control."

It was on now. Ben undid his fly, pushing his briefs down to free his erection. "You can't touch yourself. No matter how close you get, you'll keep your hands on your legs."

"Challenge accepted." Nate sounded eager.

A good part of Ben wanted to thrust in right then, catch Nate by surprise. He firmly checked the impulse. *Nate's too willing to be what other people need. I have to make sure this is what he wants.* He ran his hands over Nate's ass, sliding his cock over Nate's crack in a shallow thrust.

Nate hummed, rocking back. The moonlight gave his skin the black-and-white quality of an artistic photograph. Ben ran his hand down the curve of Nate's spine, admiring the way he held himself almost still, despite the tautness of his muscles indicating his need, even as Ben's hand slid across his cheeks. Nate was beautiful.

"You an ass man?"

"What?" Ben was startled.

Nate grinned at him over his shoulder. "Feeling me up like that." His eyes shone darkly. "You're totally getting off."

Daylight Ben would have snatched his hand away in immediate denial, his cheeks burning. Night-time Ben considered Nate's words, his hands continuing to work Nate's skin. *This is a turn on.* "Learn something new." He pressed his length fully against Nate, letting him feel how ready he was. "Lube?"

"Don't need it." Nate's response was immediate. "Fuck, Ben. I can handle it."

Ben squeezed his hip in warning as he stepped back. "I'm not hurting you." He trod on the denim of Nate's jeans and picked them up. Nate usually had something in his pockets—there. The condom was immediately recognizable, but the thin tube could have been a number of things. Ben held it up to the moonlight to see the label and raised an eyebrow. Just as he'd thought. Lube. "You came very well prepared for a guy who wanted to talk."

"Come on, Ben. Don't leave me hanging."

That note of breathlessness in Nate's words sent an immediate reaction through Ben. He rocked against Nate's leg as he hastily coated his fingers with the lube. "Self-control. It won't hurt you to wait."

"It might. God, Ben." Nate readjusted his position, trying to push back as Ben's fingers sought his entrance. "Come on—" The plea ended with ground teeth.

Ben added two fingers, and then a third. He'd managed to subdue his straining cock, but Nate's raw need rocked through him. Precome leaked from his cock, smearing Nate's leg and eliciting another moan. *Not Nate. That was me.*

Nate rocked back, fucking himself on Ben's fingers. "Ben, please. I want you in me, filling me. I'm ready, I'm so fucking ready."

Ben fumbled to pull the condom on. He lined himself up with Nate's hole. "Brace yourself." He slid smoothly into Nate in one thrust.

First it was just the heat, the incredible sensation of being buried deep in Nate, joined with him. Then Nate gasped, purposefully tightening around him. "Ben…"

Ben grunted, pulling back to thrust forward. Nate was fighting for control, trying to take what he wanted. *So why not give it to him?*

"Oh fuck." Nate readjusted his footing, to better meet Ben's thrusts. "Yeah. Don't hold back— *Ben.*"

He wasn't going to last long. Already his body moved of its own accord, slamming against Nate in an urgent rhythm. Ben bit his lip, fighting to clear his head. What was he resisting exactly?

"God, Ben, yes. I need to feel this, feel you—" Nate rocked so forcefully that he was in real danger of falling—and he didn't care.

Ben gripped him by his hips, taking firm hold of them. He could feel the rush starting, gathering force. "Touch yourself," he ordered. "Make yourself come."

Nate didn't respond with words. There was a prolonged gasp, and then his entire body rippled, enfolding Ben in his release. Ben pushed desperately, heedlessly against him. Nate's climax had pushed him over the edge, and then it was all he felt, flooding his senses with glorious sensation.

His legs abruptly decided they'd had enough of standing. Ben pulled out, managing a single step before finding himself abruptly on the barn floor.

Nate laughed breathlessly, following his example. "Jesus, Ben." He brushed the hair out of Ben's face, resting their foreheads together. "Have I told you how freaking hot it is when you take control like that?"

Ben leaned against Nate. Soon they would have to move. Already the hay that littered the barn floor was making itself felt, but now, for this one moment, everything was content. "You may have mentioned it. But you can tell me again."

CHAPTER ELEVEN

"How to put this?" Ben sat on the hay bale from earlier, watching Nate use the flashlight function of his phone to find his clothes. "I don't want to offend you, Nate, but a barn is not really doing it for me romantically."

Nate looked over his shoulder. Ben couldn't see his expression in the dark, but he suspected Nate grinned. "You weren't complaining earlier."

"That was earlier." Ben shifted, trying to find a place free of scratchy hay stalks. He was reluctant to leave—there was a lot unfinished between them—but the hay was uncomfortable.

Nate held up his T-shirt, shaking it out. "Take a look at the loft."

Ben looked over to the ladder. The middle of it was draped in moonlight, but the top was obscured by shadow. "In the dark?"

"Doesn't seem to bother you any." Nate started to pull the shirt on. "Go on. Do it."

Ben paused to size up the ladder. It was true. The dark didn't intimidate him at all. *This is a vampire hangover I don't mind.*

The ladder was firmly wedged in place. Ben climbed onto the upper ledge with ease. The steep sides of the roof were cloaked in darkness, but Ben made out the edges of stacked cardboard boxes. Here and there an odd piece of furniture protruded. An ornate wooden headboard, a child's car seat and an empty bird cage were distinguishable among the shadows. There was a square of light across the loft, coming from a window set high in the wall. It gave definition to the furniture and revealed a loose pile of hay, swept together and covered with blankets and a pillow to create a make-shift mattress.

Ben heard the ladder creak behind him and turned to see Nate—now clothed—climb onto the loft. "What was that about wanting to talk?"

Nate ran a hand through his hair. "I figured after we were done talking, I'd see if you wanted to sleep out here. And if you did—well, something could have happened."

Ben narrowed his eyes, sizing up Nate's uncharacteristic awkwardness. Sex was fine, but inviting Ben to spend the night with him was hard? He blinked as an explanation occurred. "You haven't had a lot of relationships."

"You got me." Nate settled himself down on the mattress. "Sex, yes. Plenty of that. Relationships, only the two."

He looked lonely on the mattress. Even though Ben knew he was probably doing exactly what Nate wanted him to do, he joined him. Nate immediately settled an arm around him, and Ben leaned against his side. "How come?"

"My first boyfriend—first relationship—just disappeared one day. Didn't call, didn't write—didn't tell anyone he was going. I still have no idea why."

"Is that why you dated a girl next?"

"Nah. Amber was your typical dumb high school romance. In retrospect, we had nothing in common—she never wanted to hang out here at the farm, and most of the time we spent together, she talked about all the things she wanted to do as soon as she was old enough to ditch Little River." Nate shrugged. "She dumped me the day after graduation. I was devastated at the time, but in retrospect, I think she'd planned it months earlier, but wanted to make sure she had a date for prom."

"She sounds like you're better off without her." Ben winced. That sounded woefully inadequate. "I'm sorry."

Nate stretched out on the mattress, his arm still looped around Ben's waist. "It's cool. You're way better than them in so many ways—actually being here, for one."

Ben winced. "I had a conversation with your mother earlier tonight. She suggested I should leave."

"She said the same thing to me." Nate threaded his fingers through Ben's. "Told me the responsible thing to do would be to send you back to New Camden on the next bus."

"If your mother wants me to leave—"

Nate shook his head decisively. "She's not going to kick you out. You're a guest."

Ben hesitated. "She said something about a judgment. You have any idea what she means?"

"She's rattled—what happened tonight really shook her. You shouldn't take her seriously." Nate caught himself. "I mean, if you want to leave, I won't stop you. But…"

Ben squeezed his hand, before settling himself down beside Nate. "It's going to take more than a murder investigation to get rid of me."

"That shouldn't make me feel better, but it does." Nate pulled the blanket over both of them.

Is Nate a horrible person at heart, too? Ben settled his head on Nate's shoulder. "A murder won't drive me away, but this hay bed might."

"You'll get used to it." Nate sounded far too pleased with himself.

Ben rolled his eyes. "Goodnight, Nate."

☆☆☆

Ben gasped.

Where am I? He sat in pitch blackness. The air was heavy. Someone—Nate—breathed evenly beside him.

Something buzzed. For a brief second only, the surrounding boxes and the slanting roof beams of the barn were illuminated by the glow of Nate's phone as a text message appeared.

Ben breathed out. *Moon must have gone behind a cloud or something. That's all.*

Nate stirred beside him, murmuring a sleepy protest. At some point in the night, his arm had snuck around Ben's waist.

Ben placed a hand over his face. His skin was cold and sweaty. "Just a dream."

What woke me up? Nothing concrete came to mind, but a lingering sense of threat remained. It occupied the surrounding dark, pressing down on Ben with a hunger that was palpable.

Ben maneuvered himself out from underneath the blanket. *I'm too hot, that's all. That's why I feel clammy.* He took a deep breath. *This is all imagination.*

Nate slept soundly, not stirring as Ben repositioned himself.

No wonder. He's probably exhausted. Ben smiled as he stroked Nate's hair out of his face. After the day they'd had, Nate needed this. *Am I taking care of Nate? Giving him what he needs? Or*—Ben frowned, assessing his own previously contented state—*is he taking care of me?*

Unaware of the suspicion directed at him, Nate sighed softly.

Does it matter? If Nate enjoys taking care of me, the end result is the same. He closed his eyes as he settled back to sleep.

Fifteen minutes later, Ben realized he wasn't sleeping. The threat from earlier had wound its way into his thoughts. *But this time, I'm wide awake.* Staying still, Ben listened for any indication that something wasn't right.

He heard nothing.

Ben's heart sped up. The farmhouse's boards shifted at times, and he'd often heard the rustling of mice in the walls. That the barn, just as old, would lack both these sounds was weird. *What's going on?* The longer Ben lay there, the more convinced he was that something waited in the dark, its gaze focused on the back of Ben's neck.

What will it take for me to get a decent night's sleep? Ben shut his eyes, willing his thoughts clear. He steadied his breathing, focusing on keeping his mind clear. A few minutes of this and he felt himself slip back into sleep.

The lingering influence followed him into his dream. Or was it a memory?

☆

Ben was surrounded by it as he stood in his parents' bedroom in New Camden. He was nine years old, watching his mother pack. She stood with her back toward him. Her suitcase was spread out open on the bed. Ignoring his sobs, she took her dresses from the wardrobe, folding them briskly.

"This is what you want, isn't it?" She didn't look down at him. She emptied the top drawer of the dresser straight into her suitcase.

"No! Please!" He clung to her arm, trying with all his nine-year-old strength to stop her. "I didn't mean that! I'm sorry–"

She shook him off and shut the suitcase. In a few clasps, it was locked, ready to go. Ben watched her pull on her coat with increasing desperation. "No! You can't! Please –"

"But if you don't love me, Benny, then Mommy has no reason to stay."

He tangled himself in her feet, falling over himself in a last ditch effort to stop her from going. "I do! I didn't mean what I said! I'm sorry— I'm sorry! Don't go–"

She paused then, kneeling to face him. Ben's body heaved and shook as if he were violently ill. But she simply tipped his face up to look at her. There was an intensity in her eyes that always scared him a little. "Do you mean that, Benny? You do love me?"

He had nodded, unable to speak.

"Mommy doesn't believe you, Benny. You hurt her feelings very much. No–" she put her finger out, resting it on his lips before he could protest. "You can't just say you love Mommy. You have to prove it." She looked at him again. For a moment, there was something hard, something hungry, looking out at him behind his mother's eyes. "Will you do that, Benny? Will you prove to Mommy that you do love her?"

He nodded, too shaken to do anything else.

She held out her hand. That's my good boy." Taking firm hold of his hand, she led him to the door.

Ben craned his neck to look at the suitcase resting against the wall. "You're not going away?"

"Not if you pass Mommy's test." She led him out the front door, shutting it behind them.

"Where are we going?"

"Why, to your special place, of course. The place you love more than your very own Mommy."

☆☆☆

The light coming in the barn window was faded and gray, reflecting the early morning sky outside. It gave the loft a washed out feeling. Ben, leaning against the boxes behind the mattress, felt permeated by its early morning dullness. He didn't know how long he'd been sitting there before the night gave way to dull half light. After the second bad dream, he'd decided to wait for the dawn.

Nate's breath hitched. Ben looked down at the sleeping man beside him to see Nate's brow furrowed, his eyelids flickering rapidly. He brushed Nate's hair, careful to avoid the bandage. "It's a dream. That's all."

Nate sighed, slipping back into deep sleep.

Ben's hand came to a halt.

When Nate was still like this, the resemblance to Ethan was uncanny. *Identical twins. I really should be over this.* But every time it surprised Ben again. *Why does it bother me so much? I know this is Nate.*

Even so. Identical twins weren't actually identical, right? There was a freckle, a birthmark, something like that. There had to be.

Ben smirked at the thought of asking Nate if he could check him for freckles—*He'd be all over that*—but his smile quickly faded. Even in the daylight, his feeling of foreboding lingered.

Looking around for any distraction, Ben studied the surrounding boxes. It appeared that the police had given the barn a cursory search, the boxes opened, but their contents left undisturbed. A leather cover was just visible, poking out of one of the boxes. *A photo album?*

Moving carefully to avoid waking Nate, Ben climbed off the bed. He paused to shake the hay out of his hair—hay, Ben was discovering, had an incredible tendency to go exactly where it was least wanted—before lifting the album out of the box. Beneath it was a second album, and beneath that, a collection of coats, too small now for any member of the family.

Ben sat on the floor, leaning back against the boxes, and opened the photo album.

Ma sat in a hospital bed, looking down at a tiny baby swathed in cloth. *Didn't she say these photos were getting restored?* The baby was tiny, red and grumpy, like all newborns, but Ma looked down at her child as if she'd never seen anything she liked more. The next photo was of the grumpy baby alone, and then held by Pa, who looked as if he wasn't quite sure what to do with it.

Good thing Nate isn't asking me to identify who is who here. The small, red, thing could be either brother—or neither. Ben frowned as he turned the page. There were no photos of the twins together. *Could it be these aren't the twins?* Ben continued to flick through the book. *All babies look the same. Maybe there was an older sibling who died young.*

The baby celebrated its first birthday apparently alone. As Ben continued through the pages of the album, the baby was christened, sat on various people's laps, and celebrated its first birthday. It produced dark hair, and its eyes became a warm hazel.

Family resemblance, Ben told himself. *Of course, he's going to look like Nate and Ethan. They're brothers.* He reached the end of the album, but something large was tucked in with the pocket for negatives. Ben lifted it out. *A birth certificate?*

GRANGER, ETHAN ROOSEVELT. Born to GRANGER, EMMA CHARITY nee HALSWELL and GRANGER, MITCHELL in ROCKFORD GENERAL HOSPITAL.

The date and signatures followed. Ben gave them a cursory skim, more interested in the discovery of Ethan's middle name. *I can see why he'd hide that.* Did Nate have an equally embarrassing middle name? *Eisenhower? Please let it be Eisenhower.*

But there was no other certificate in the album, just a few cards congratulating Emma and Mitchell on the birth of their son.

Maybe they made a separate album for each son? It would have been a lot of work, but if Ma had crafted the quilt on the spare room bed, then she evidently had time to spare.

The second album picked up where the first one left off. The baby—Ben insisted on calling him Ethan—learned to walk and was soon accompanying his mother outside into the garden. There was no sign of his brother. Or that Ma was expecting again, though Ben was abandoning that theory. The toddler had something about him that was already reminiscent of the twins.

The album followed him all the way up to his fourth birthday then the photos abruptly finished, mid-album. Ben checked, but there was nothing tucked away at the end.

Ben closed the album and laid it flat on his lap.

His hands were clammy. *There's an explanation. Another album, just of Nate's photos. Maybe a third for all the photos of the twins together.* But he knew that was not the case. *Ma lied.* Not only had she lied, but she'd also hidden the album where it would not be seen.

Ben's heart thudded in his chest.

Ma didn't want the photos seen because they meant something, he was sure of it. But what?

Changeling? Ben licked dry lips. There hadn't been a verified case in decades, but people were less likely to associate a child acting oddly with the fae these days. *Ethan's definitely got the signs of being other...* But according to all recorded accounts, the fae kept the human child. Nate wasn't human—unless his powers were a result of time spent with his fae abductors?

Or is the answer closer to home? Ma said a judgment... The album pressed on Ben's lap like a weight. *Demonic involvement?* Nate said he was thirteen when Olivia was killed. The demon worked at ten-year intervals, so he'd have been three when the deal was made. Could Ma have made a pact with a demon for a second child? *Ethan celebrated his fourth birthday alone—it doesn't add up.* Perhaps Ma knew something or had seen something and not come forward to the police about it? A guilty conscience could come from anywhere, and Ben suspected that Ma had a finely honed sense of guilt.

Am I over thinking this? There could be any number of explanations—one of the twins was switched at birth, or a mix-up at the hospital... But if the explanation is normal, why hide the album? No matter how he looked at it, Ben couldn't get past that one fact.

"What's got you looking so serious?" Nate's voice was thick with sleep. He raised his head only high enough to glance at his phone screen. "At—Jesus. Have you looked at the time?"

Ben didn't smile. He felt a feeling of dread settle in his stomach, hard as a stone. "Have you ever seen your baby photos?"

"Baby photos?" Nate tilted his head. "Nah. They were lost when we were little. Pa had a bonfire going one day, and either me or Ethan had the bright idea of throwing more things onto it. The photo album was one of the casualties."

Ben's heart sped up in his chest. Not a surprise that Ma had lied to him. But to lie to Nate? "What about your birth certificate. Ever tried to get hold of it?"

"Actually, that's a funny story. There was a weird mix-up with my birth certificate. When I applied for a copy to get my driver's license, they said I didn't have one. I guess someone at the hospital forgot to record my birth, and it took months to sort out—the hospital refused to admit there'd been a mistake."

"And Ethan?"

Nate waved a hand dismissively. "His was fine. Got his license a full three months before I did, because of it all—the jerk."

Ben's fingers were clamped around the album. "And you don't think that's odd?"

"Obnoxious, yes. Odd, no. You might not think it, but he will remind me that he is the older brother any chance he can." Nate pulled himself up into a sitting position. "What's up? You look...grim."

Ben's mouth drooped. "I've found something."

"Something," Nate repeated. "Supernatural something?" At Ben's nod, he frowned. "What happened to not investigating, Ben?"

"You decided that," Ben shot back. "Not me."

"But you agreed—"

"Because you asked me." There was way more heat in that than Ben had intended. He let out a breath, forcing himself to continue in a much more reasonable tone. "You—it's really hard to say no to you even when I know I should."

Shock followed by hurt flickered across Nate's face. His expressive mouth wavered unhappily before settling in a pout. "What are you saying exactly?"

Ben felt an immediate desire to take the words back, apologize for hurting Nate—*And that is exactly the problem.* He steadied his hands on the photo album. "You're—really intense. I like that a lot. But when we disagree on something..." Ben swallowed. Nate's eyes were fixed on him in a mute appeal that was really hard to ignore. "I end up giving way because I want to make you happy. So I say yes to things I don't agree with."

"Like?"

"Investigating." It felt like Nate was getting farther away even though neither of them had moved. "Yes, I want an ordinary life, but not at the cost of someone else's suffering. I can help, but you're too scared to let me."

Nate's hands gripped the blanket tightly. "I'm thinking of what's best for you, Ben. You've been part of ARX for years. You've lost whatever normal life you had for so long, you don't remember it."

"Which is why I can help. I've got more practical experience and knowledge than anyone on the police team—and I'm doing nothing with it." Ben took a deep breath. "Hiding in fear isn't doing your family any favors. Until you know the truth, you can't rebut whatever rumors your neighbors have concocted. It's in your best interests—and Ethan's—to discover the truth."

"You've been here three days, and you think you know what's best for us?" Nate's voice was hard. "This is our life, Ben!"

Ben winced. "It doesn't have to be this way, Nate. You can break this cycle of fear."

Nate met his eyes in challenge. "Can you promise that what we find won't have negative consequences for Ethan, that he'll be able to stay on the farm?"

Ben was silent a moment. He knew only too well that fear and suspicion wasn't limited to Nate's neighbors. There were plenty of political interest groups—including Department Seven—who were not above using their supernatural constituents to make a point. "No. I can't. But that doesn't mean—"

Nate held a hand up to silence Ben. "Then you know why I can't do anything."

"This is a mistake, Nate." Ben was shaking as he stood. His fingers were locked around the album, but it still felt like it might slip from his grasp.

"But it's our mistake. Not yours." Nate shook off the blanket, climbing to his feet to meet Ben. "I'm sorry, Ben. But you've got to see—"

"I see nothing." Angry? Yes. "I don't agree, and I'm not going to pretend I do."

Nate stepped towards him. "I don't want you to pretend anything, do anything you don't want to—"

"But you're not above manipulating people to get what you want."

Nate recoiled as if Ben had physically struck him. "I would never— Ben." He took a shaky breath. "I lo—"

Ben felt something surge through the surrounding shadows a looming hunger rising to meet them. He moved, instinctively, tossing the album aside as he launched himself at Nate. "Don't say it!"

Nate was caught entirely by surprise. They hit the floorboards of the attic, colliding with the stacked boxes.

"Ow! What the hell, Ben!" Nate shook Ben off him as he sat up. "What was that about?" He glared as he cradled his arm. "What are you trying to do?"

"Did you feel that?" Ben scrambled to his feet. The threat was still there, lingering on his awareness, but it was fading fast. *What had set it off?*

"I feel my funny bone protesting. Seriously, there are better ways to win an argument!"

"There was something there." Ben circled the loft, trying to put his finger on it. "Something—" Ben placed a foot on the make-shift mattress and paused. "Help me move this."

"What are you on about?" Nate gingerly got to his feet. "Seriously, Ben. You're acting like you're possessed or something."

Ben pressed his lips together. *You've got no idea.* He had an inkling of what they would find.

With Nate's help, he drew the straw back in one movement. Stray pieces of hay littered the floor, but the circle beneath them was clearly recognizable even so. Spray painted onto the boards below the bed, it could only be one thing.

"Fuck me." Nate's breath was shaky. "This— Is this...?"

"A demonic circle." Ben frowned. He'd never seen one before, but he'd known what each inscription would look like before they'd drawn back the straw. "I'm willing to bet it's exactly the same as the one that killed Olivia Winkler."

"Shit." Nate drew a deep breath, running his hands over his face. "What's it doing here?"

Ben looked down at the circle. "That's a very good question." His vision seemed to blur. For a second, the hay-streaked boards of the barn were replaced with dusty boards, a circle traced in blood—

The circle was obscured as Nate dragged the hay back over it.

Ben placed his foot down on the hay. "What are you doing? We can't hide this, Nate!"

"We have to! If the police see this, they're gonna think Ethan—"

Ben's fury was white-hot, surprising himself. "So protecting your brother is more important than preventing the demon claiming another innocent victim?"

Nate didn't budge. "He's my brother."

"This is a murder investigation, Nate!"

"Which Ethan is not a part of! The police see this, they're not going to bother looking for the real agent. They've already decided Ethan's it. They just want a solid reason to put him behind bars!"

"You can't suppress evidence. Anything that will lead us to this demon needs to be out there."

Nate placed his hand on Ben's shoulder, looking directly into his eyes. "I promise you. Ethan doesn't have anything to do with this. Please, Ben? Jail will— It's the worst possible thing that could happen to him!"

I should know better. I do know better. Ben summoned all his anger, but faced with the entreaty in Nate's eyes, found it slipping away before a wave of helplessness. Ben shut his eyes. "I can't make that promise."

"Ben—"

"I'm going back to New Camden." Ben heard Nate's gasp but knew better than to look at him. To waver now would be fatal. "I'll take the next bus back."

"But Ben." Nate placed his hand on Ben's arm. "I need you here. Everything—"

"And I need to be able to think for myself—without you influencing me." Ben took a deep breath, looking squarely at Nate. "You can't make my decisions for me. Not now—not ever. I have to go back."

CHAPTER TWELVE

Light fell on him, a stabbing sword across his arm. Ben rolled, dodging his assailant—and found himself inches away from falling off the edge of his bed. "Not *again*."

The location changed, but the nightmare never ended. Ben shut his eyes. His fists were buried in the black silk sheets of his New Camden apartment's master bed. His elbows, supporting his body, trembled, and his chest heaved. His skin was clammy as if he was still dead.

What is wrong with me? Ben's breathing was harsh. He sounded like he was choking, gasping for air. *What good is being alive if I die every time I wake up?*

The cold went deep. The single ray of light escaping through drawn curtains to fall across the bed couldn't touch it. Ben slumped onto his back, placing his hand on his chest. Cold. He hadn't felt this cold since he'd left Saltaire's house. *More like Saltaire's crypt.* For a moment, Ben felt again the approach of dawn settling over his body with an inexorable chill, the life fading from his body as the vampire faded. Cold fingers dragging him underground to a cold, damp grave—

I'm alive. Ben took a deep breath. He swung his feet over the end of the bed and before he could think twice, strode to the window. He threw back the curtains, standing barefoot in the light.

Before him, New Camden went about its morning routine with the prosaicness of a weekday morning. A steady passage of cars and pedestrians streamed past each other below. The humming of motors and occasional horn or screeching tires had a subdued quality about them the night lacked. Ben leaned in to the window, looking down at the city.

"I'm alive." He wrapped his arms around himself, unable to shake off the chill surrounding him. "I am. Alive."

No matter how many times he said it, the only time he believed it—really felt alive—was with Nate.

And Nate was sixteen hours away in Little River.

Ben drew a shaky breath, feeling fear catch in his throat. He breathed out and in again, using the steady rhythm of his breathing to push back his panic. *Alive.* A vampire breathed shallowly, purely on reflex. These breaths went in. Ben wrapped the fingers of one hand against his wrist, squeezing it tightly until his trapped pulse beat against his skin. *Alive. I'm alive.*

Even if I don't feel it.

I might as well be dead. Ben released his wrist. What use was a heart that beat mechanically? His chest felt hollow and cold as the crypt he'd escaped. Not even Ethan had managed to get a rise out of him—

Ethan. Ben rubbed his forehead. That had been an odd encounter. He was still unsure what to make of it.

Ethan took Ben's request to drive him to catch the bus with the stoic indifference that was his trademark. Nate hadn't liked it, but Ben knew better than to give Nate another chance to talk him out of going. He was already regretting his decision, mourning the lost closeness between them. Ethan's silence had been a balm—until they'd come out of the mountains and seen Rockford approaching in the windshield.

Ethan broke the silence. "Don't come back."

Ben was jerked out of his thoughts abruptly. "That's between me and Nate."

Ethan didn't glance at Ben, keeping his eyes on the road ahead. "Nate doesn't see it. I do."

Ben shifted uneasily. How much had Nate told his brother about their disagreement? "See what?"

"You're rotten inside." Ethan's mouth was flat, his opinion delivered in the same tone with which he'd explained grafting. "Rot spreads."

Ben was too numb to feel more than a faint outrage. "I'm not a plant."

"Better you were. You can prune plants." Ethan's brow furrowed. "Cut back the dead wood. You..." He took his eyes off the road to glare at Ben. "Stay away from Nate, or—"

"Or what? You'll cut me down?" Ben's heart beat dully, belatedly waking to the threat. "Did you threaten Harriet too?"

But Ethan's reaction took Ben entirely by surprise. "Who?"

"Harriet. The hunter." There was no recognition on Ethan's face. "The dead guy?"

"Him?" Ethan snorted. "Nothing rotten about him."

Ben took a deep breath. "Ethan. Did you meet Harriet? Talk to him?" At Ethan's nod, Ben swallowed. "Did he come to the farm?"

"Yes."

"Why didn't Ma or Nate say anything?"

"They didn't know," Ethan continued calmly. "He came to see me." He pulled the truck into the car park of the Rockford supermarket. A few people were already waiting with suitcases. "We're here."

Ben clutched the handle of his backpack and made no move to leave. "Why didn't you tell anyone, Ethan?"

Ethan shrugged. "No one asked."

He didn't wait, driving off as soon as Ben shut the door behind him. Ben watched him go with the same conflicted feelings he still felt looking back at the exchange now. He had no better idea how to read Ethan now than he had when Ethan appeared on Ben's doorstep to demand Nate's immediate return to Little River.

At least he left the spade behind this time. Ben brushed his hair out of his face impatiently, turning away from the window. *If only I knew what to do about Ethan—about the circle.* Ben rolled his eyes. *What I am hoping for—a manual? Something to tell me how to think and what to feel?*

He wasn't fast enough to silence the treacherous whisper at the back of his mind. *Anything would be better than this.*

The whisper haunted him as he walked from room to room of his deserted apartment. He'd barely started unpacking, the apartment containing yet to be examined boxes and the bare minimum of furnishings. Looking at it, no one would be able to tell whether he was packing or unpacking. *Is this my life now? A constant state of limbo, unable to go forward or back—*

Ben paused. "Back?"

He looked at the boards beneath his feet. Save for the lack of dust, they were a match for those of his last dream. *Dream—or memory?* This was where it had happened, after all. His mother's death.

Ben reached a hand out to steady himself on the edge of the blunt dining room table. From numb to full speed, his thoughts were racing too fast for him to keep up with. *I knew the circle before I saw it. Did I—remember it?*

He half hoped he wouldn't be able to find the keys, but they were right at the top of the box marked 'desk' in his father's study. Ben slipped them into his pocket, taking a moment to glance over the papers in the folder with them.

Tenant after tenant had cut their rental agreements short and departed citing undue ghostly interference. Eventually, rental agencies had refused to handle the apartment. There was a request by a local paranormal society to rent the apartment for a week in order to investigate its claims of haunting. Not surprisingly, it was declined—Austin had been skeptical of amateur investigators even before his mother—

Ben realized he was shaking.

Why is it so hard for me to face this? He was no longer a child. He was a paranormal investigator, and a good one at that. *I can't blame Nate for being unwilling to confront his past if I can't confront my own.*

Ben placed the papers on the desk and locked his apartment behind him. The key hung heavy in his pocket as Ben climbed the stairs down to the floor below.

☆☆☆

The door to apartment 702 was stiff, clearly not used in many years. Ben, braced for the worst arcane crime scene, was surprised at how normal the apartment looked. Was it the emptiness? There was no furniture, no sound from the refrigerator. The lightbulb hung from the living room ceiling, naked without any shade covering it.

Of course they wouldn't leave it. Ben swallowed. He hadn't seen much. They'd been anxious to keep him away from the apartment. "Not something any child should ever see." But he'd waited, giving no hint of his intentions, a quiet, obedient child, and they'd had no idea he was even there until he stepped past the police guard and walked right into the living room.

It had only been a moment. The guard had grabbed him, physically bundling him outside, and he'd been given back to the child psychiatrist, who had asked him if he was upset and if he wanted anything.

Ben had frowned. "I want my mother," he said. "But that's not something you can help with, is it? She's not coming back."

The child psychiatrist had faltered. "No," she agreed. "She's not."

He'd gathered from overheard phone conversations after the fact that his father had rented the apartment. Ben didn't know which was more incredible. That Austin had done it or that he'd found anyone to take it.

Of course, they never saw it like I saw it. Ben looked around. There had been blood, everywhere. On the walls, the ceiling. As if an enraged beast had attacked, bringing its full ferocity down on the...

Ben swallowed.

There was no furniture, but there was a large rug. Taking a deep breath, he pulled it back.

The floorboards were smooth. Plain. Ben placed his hands to them but could find no discoloration, no sign of harsh cleaning agents.

Am I...wrong? The mind could play tricks. And a kid as young as he had been, exposed to such trauma... Who more likely to imagine things?

But it felt so real. "I know it's here. It has to be here." Ben sat in the middle of the floor." I'm not imagining it." He brushed his hair out of his face. "Think!"

☆

His mother brought him to the apartment. He waited, trying to get his breathing under control, be that good little gentleman she always wanted him to be. *And then she'll go back to normal, and everything will be all right.* She was in the apartment above a long time. When she came back, she carried the leather bag his father kept in the study.

"Aren't those Daddy's special supplies? For work?" Ben blinked. "You know, Daddy doesn't like us to use his study!"

"Daddy won't mind this once. Besides, Benny. You like playing pretend down here with your invisible ghost-friend, don't you? Mommy wants to play pretend, too."

Ben sat in the middle of the floor as his mother drew a circle around them with charcoal. She muttered under her breath as she drew.

Ben didn't understand the words, but they had a placid, repetitive note to them that was soothing in comparison to his mother's frantic mood. "Am I being good?"

"Very good, Benny. It's just a little longer." His mother stood, wiping her hands on her handkerchief. "Tell me what you did in school yesterday."

Ben started the recitation immediately. "First we did math. Then we did science, but it wasn't good science. It was really boring because I wanted to see what happened if you put the vinegar and the baking soda into a car, but Ms. Green didn't even let me try it. When I'm grown up and have a car, I'm going to–" Ben sat up. He reached out, laying a hand on his mother's cheek. "Mommy, are you crying?"

"Mommy is not crying."

Ben frowned. There were two tracks down her face, and there were black lines around her eyes. Like she'd drawn on herself with crayon. "Your eyes are smudged."

"Mommy's mascara. It does that sometimes." His mother wrapped her arms around him. "My own little boy..."

Ben never got used to her sudden, alarming displays of affection. "Who loves you very much," he reminded her. The game wasn't fun, and the sooner they finished it, the better. "What's next?"

His mother was silent a long moment. Her arms tightened as if she wouldn't let him go.

There was a sound Ben could hear, a ticking sound. He didn't remember noticing it before and let go of his mother to look for its source.

But there was nothing in the apartment.

"Do you hear that?"

"Hear what?" His mother put a hand on his shoulder, gently guiding him back to the circle. "Stand up straight." She took a knife from the box of his father's things, gently pricking the tip of her finger with it.

"What are you doing that for?"

"This is a very special game, remember? You have to blood swear that you love Mommy. When you blood swear something, you can never change your mind."

Ben stood while his mother drew a pattern that turned out to be a triangle around him with her fingertip. "This isn't a game, is it?"

His mother didn't answer. Ben looked down. "I didn't mean to say it. I really didn't. I was angry... No one else's mother makes them hold her hand when they cross the street. And Douglas saw, and he laughed at me, and I didn't want him to say something at school—"

"So you cared about your friends more than your mother?"

Ben shut his eyes and nodded.

"Now, don't cry. You can make it up to Mommy. Are you ready?"

Ben opened his eyes. His mother knelt at the other side of the circle. "What do I have to do?"

"Mommy can't tell you. But you have to say three words that Mommy really wants to hear."

"That's all?" Ben took a step towards her eagerly. "I—"

"No!" His mother started back, her arms outstretched. In a moment, she recovered her composure. "You have to say it from the circle, Benny. That's the game."

It doesn't feel like a game. Ben looked down at the circle around him. Was it his imagination, or had the lines moved?

"Benny?"

There was a strange heaviness in the room. The kind of feeling you got, when you stood too close to the plasma globe in the science classroom. Something that seemed targeted at him. "I—"

"That's it, Benny. Make Mommy very happy." His mother looked at him from the doorway. Her face was pale, and there was something that didn't match between her eyes and the way she smiled.

She's afraid? "And if I say it, you promise you'll stay?"

She nodded eagerly. "But you have to say it, Benny. Otherwise I'll know you don't really love me." Her voice took on a coaxing lilt. "Think of all the times I've held you in my arms, sung you to sleep when you were sick or scared. All the times I've taken you to the park and we played games just the two of us." She paused, a note of unhappiness creeping into her voice. "You do love me, don't you?"

"I do! I love—" Ben felt it at his back, that there was someone behind him. He turned.

It was dark in the apartment. Twilight had come without either of them noticing.

"Benny? Let's finish the game, so that Mommy can make dinner."

"I'm scared. I think there's something there."

"Don't be silly, Benny. You know a mother's love is stronger than any monster." His mother took a step towards him, smiling her prettiest. "You are my precious, precious son, and I love you very much." She wrinkled her nose at him in the funny way that always made him laugh. "Don't you feel better now?"

He smiled back, feeling that he had been very foolish. "I love y—"

It was there again, a fearful presence lurking out at him from behind his mother. Her shadow seemed to have grown, moving to fill the room.

"Say it, Bennet."

"I..." He was afraid, too afraid to speak. And he didn't know why he was afraid, only that he was and—

The door swung open.

Ben screamed.

"What's the matter? Ben, are you—" His father stood in the doorway, frozen in place as he took in the scene before him.

Ben didn't hesitate. He flung himself at his father, burying himself in the familiar scent of Austin's suit jacket with a sob that quickly became several.

"What are you doing?" His father's voice had an entirely unfamiliar sound to it, harsh and full of anger.

Ben's chest heaved with fear.

"Only playing a game." His mother sounded shaken herself, but she tried to hide it with a laugh. "Poor Benny... I didn't think he'd take it so seriously!" He felt her hands in his hair. "Easy... Easy now, Benny. Mommy only wanted to teach you to think about what you said."

He looked up at her, relieved to see that the smile was back on her face. "Promise?"

She nodded, reaching for his hand. "And it's very bad for you to play alone down here in this awful apartment. Your Daddy and I, we don't want anything happening to you." She reached for his hand.

"Don't touch him." Austin pushed her back.

The gesture startled all of them.

His mother teetered, staggering back. Her eyes filled with tears. "Darling—"

And then she turned and ran out of the apartment, up the stairs to their house. They could hear her sobbing as she went.

Austin swayed. He looked around the room, seemingly stunned by what he saw. "I can't believe..." He remembered his son with a jolt. "Ben, you're fine? You're not hurt?"

That jarred Ben out of his own shock. "I'm fine! But Mommy— She's really upset. It's my fault. You can't be mad at her! It's only because I upset her."

His father led him into the kitchen, gently, shutting the door behind him. "Tell me about it, Ben. Tell me from the start."

He sat patiently throughout Ben's confused explanation, not saying anything as Ben told him about tugging his hand free to dart across the road to his friends. He stayed silent as Ben described his mother's reaction to him. "The taxi wasn't even near me, really! There was no need for her to fuss like that. And I..." He faltered. "I got mad and I told her that I hated her and she..." Ben wiped his nose with the back of his hand. "She said if that was the case, then she'd just pack her bags and leave." He looked anxiously up at his father. "I don't want her to leave!"

"She drew the circle?" Ben nodded. His father's face seemed older, marked with lines he'd never seen. "No one told her how to do it, she didn't look at a picture?"

Ben shook his head. "She just made it up. We were playing." Ben paused. "It wasn't a game, though, was it?"

His father stood. Ben was surprised to find himself picked up, just as if he'd been a much younger child. "Don't you worry about that, Ben." His father's rough stubble brushed Ben's cheek. "I've got you."

☆

They climbed the stairs to their apartment hand-in-hand.

His father paused with his hand on the doorknob. "You're not afraid?"

Ben shook his head. "I want to see Mommy."

His father knelt, taking both of Ben's hands firmly in his, so Ben had no option but to look it down into his serious face. "Now listen, Ben. You are not to tell Mommy about our conversation. Do you understand?"

Ben nodded. His father's eyes had an intensity that made him feel very uneasy. "I don't see why I shouldn't tell. It was only a game, even if it wasn't a very good one. You said so."

"Yes," said his father. "But you are not to play Mommy's games again. Remember that."

He hadn't made Ben promise, but the way he'd said it impressed Ben. "No more games."

Austin stood heavily taking firm hold of Ben's hand. "Audrey?"

They could hear impassioned sobbing from the bedroom. The door was ajar, the suitcase gone.

Austin put his hands on Ben's shoulders and urged him towards his bedroom. "Read a book. And don't go anywhere with your mother, not without me too."

It seemed ridiculous, even more of an overreaction than his mother had to Ben crossing the road. But Ben nodded. He was tired, too tired to question the strange behavior of his parents. "I'm hungry."

"I'll take care of that." Austin patted him on the shoulder. "Now just be patient and let me talk to your mother first." He didn't wait to see if Ben went to his bedroom but walked straight into the master room. "Audrey, darling?"

He heard his mother's sobs increase in volume and vehemence.

"No, calm down. I'm sorry. I can see you're overwrought. It's my fault—my job. All the late nights, the uncertainty... I could see you've been under a lot of stress lately, but I never imagined—"

"You're not—?" It took a moment to recognize his mother's voice. It was cracked and broken, Ben had never heard it like that before. "When you pushed me away, I thought..."

"I'm so sorry, Audrey. I— Well, with my job you can imagine the conclusions I jumped too. But when I talked to Ben and he explained..." His father's voice took on a soothing hush.

"Ben?" There was a nervous tremble to her reply. "What did he tell you?"

"That he was a very naughty boy." Ben made a face at what sounded suspiciously like a kiss. "And that his silly mother tried to scare him." Another kiss. "And his mother might have got carried away, and scared herself, too."

There was a long pause, and then Ben heard his mother's soft, rich laugh. "I don't know what came over me. Oh, Austin..."

Adults. Ben grimaced and went to get his copy of *Dracula*.

He was reading his favorite part, the bit where Jonathan had just seen Dracula scaling the walls of his castle, when his father knocked on the door. "We're giving your mother the night off," he told Ben. "And ordering pizza."

Pizza was special occasions only, like Ben's birthday. He put down *Dracula* without complaint. "Are we really?"

"Yes," said his father. "And you don't want to upset her by talking about earlier."

Ben gave his father his best withering glare. He wasn't a baby. He knew better than that! But he hurried into the living room, eager to see with his own eyes that his mother was all right.

She was sitting on the sofa, her make-up redone and wearing a new dress. "Movie night, Benny. What shall it be? The Addams Family one or two?" She laughed with delight as Ben flew his arms around her. "Oh, Ben." Her arms tightened around him.

She seemed strangely unwilling to let go of him, even for Ben to run and get plates for them all from the kitchen when the pizza arrived. When he got back, his father was sitting in the middle of the sofa. Ben climbed up next to them. He was allowed to stay up till the end of the movie, even though it was past his bedtime.

"How do you feel?" His father tucked him in and then sat on the bed.

"Fine," Ben said happily.

His father hesitated. "You don't feel nervous sleeping in here by yourself?"

Ben shook his head without hesitation. ARX wasn't going to employ anyone who got scared of the dark.

His father remained, stroking Ben's hair. "Remember, if your mother wants you to go anywhere, yell as loud as you can."

Ben frowned. "Is she going to divorce us?" he asked. Douglas had come home from school one day, and his mother wasn't there anymore. Now he saw her every other weekend.

His father shook his head. "You let me worry about that." He turned off the light and closed the door behind him.

Adults were bizarre. Ben shut his eyes.

He mustn't have been sleeping properly because he heard the sound of the door handle turning and knew at once what it was. But before he could sit up or say anything, his father's voice came sharply out of the dark. "What are you doing?"

His mother gasped, snatching her hand back from the door. "Austin, quiet! You'll wake him," she whispered. "I only wanted to see that he was sleeping fine."

"It'll take more than a fright to scare our Bennet." His father's voice was warm, reassuring. "But if you wake him up, worrying over him, you'll give him a complex."

"I suppose you're right..."

"It's like I said." His father spoke kindly, but like a teacher would—not intending to take no for an answer. "You've been under a lot of stress, and you're imagining things. Let's have a drink."

Ben listened to the clink of glasses in the kitchen and the low murmur of the conversation with a soft, contented feeling. Everything was fine.

His mother didn't come in to get him out of bed. Ben waited, but his stomach got growly, and eventually he couldn't wait any longer. He padded into the kitchen, still in his pajamas, to discover Austin standing at the counter, making pancakes.

Ben frowned at him. "Shouldn't you be at work? You're not even dressed!" Ben looked at the clock with a feeling of alarm. "You're late! I'm late!"

"Change of plans." His father ruffled his hair. "I'm taking the day off. To give your mother a break. You and me are going to visit the zoo."

"On a school day?" Ben took a seat at the table.

"How many pancakes can you eat, Ben? One, two?"

Ben put his elbows on the table. "Three, please. Where's Mommy?"

"She's sleeping in, for once." His father's good humor didn't waver. "Keep your voice low. You don't want to wake her up."

"Are we going to the zoo without her?"

"That's right. Man-to-man. A father and son expedition."

His father never made Ben hold his hand in public and took a more enlightened view of things like climbing trees and ice creams before dinner. "I'll just tell her—" Ben started to slide out of his chair.

"No!" His father collected himself. "No," he said, lowering his voice. "She's very tired, Ben. She needs her sleep."

Ben didn't take long to get dressed. He pulled on his favorite T-shirt and yesterday's jeans and was ready to go. All the same, it didn't feel right going to the zoo without even saying good morning to his mother. Ben peeked out his bedroom door. He could see his father shaving in the bathroom. That would take him a few minutes more. Ben slipped quietly out of his room.

He wasn't intending to wake her. Just see if she was awake. And if she was, then he could tell her about the zoo. Ben opened the door as quietly as he could. The room was dim, the curtains drawn. The unmade bed was shrouded in shadow.

There was no sign of his mother.

Ben went quickly to the wardrobe. Her dresses were all there, and the suitcase she had packed was under the bed. She didn't leave. But where was she?

Closing the bedroom door behind him, Ben checked the other rooms, even opening the door of his father's study. But there was no sign of her.

Ben returned to his bedroom and sat down on his bed. It was very strange. Should he tell his father?

But his father had said—

Austin knocked on the door. "Ready? Put on a jacket, Ben. It's colder outside than you think."

And he hadn't told his father after all. And when he'd come home…

☆☆☆

"I wouldn't imagine a police investigation or forensics team." Ben stood up. "It happened." He looked around the room with renewed determination.

His eye fell on two pieces of wooden boards side-by-side. There was a definite difference in color between them though they were the same in every other way. "Of course." The boards were laid at the same time. There was only one reason why one wooden board would appear more faded than the other.

His father kept a toolbox in his study. It was well stocked, containing both screwdrivers and crowbars. Ben struggled to lever the first board free. As he turned it over, he found the surface was discolored. Dark brown blotches stained the board but did not obscure the intricate pattern beneath.

This is it.

Ben didn't allow himself to think about what he was doing. He went through the process mechanically. It was easier after that first board. Prize the board up, throw it in the pile with the rest, not looking at them closely. If he didn't look at them, he could stave off the knowledge just that little bit longer.

Except, it didn't work like that. He knew what was coming. He'd been prepared for it since the moment he stepped back into the apartment. *I've known, ever since I saw it in the barn.* Ben prized free the last of the boards and stood up. *Maybe I've always known.*

The boards had been nailed down deliberately out of order. That was an old trick. Demonic circles were hard to get rid of. That evil influence sunk into rock, poisoned wood, and killed earth. But disrupting the circle robbed it of its power. Upside down and back to front, the boards were harmless.

Ben tried to think of it as a puzzle. It was quick work to reassemble the circle. In a matter of minutes, he stood, looking down at it. Something clicked into place in the back of his mind.

The feeling of menace was so strong, Ben could have sworn there was something in the room with him, but he knew that it would be useless to turn around. There was nothing there. Nothing but an echo.

He didn't need to compare it to the circle he and Nate had uncovered to know it was the same. His ARX training allowed him to fill in the gaps that his younger self had missed. *A summoning rite reversed to drain the person within the circle's center of their life.* He swallowed. *The runes are written in demonic script. This is probably his signature.* To make sure no one else benefited from the demon's hard work, seducing a human to his will.

Ben reached out his hand for a chair that was no longer there. He staggered and was unable to regain his balance, ending up on his knees on the floorboards. His head felt clouded, heavy. Only one thought made itself known with any clarity.

This is what killed her. The demon.

CHAPTER THIRTEEN

"Knock knock." A shadow slouched in the door of the apartment. "This a private pity party or can anyone join?"

Ben looked up to see a man of average height and above average scruffiness. Everything about him had seen better days, from his battered bomber jacket to the tips of his scuffed boots. Only his eyes, obscured but not hidden by his scruffy fringe of brown hair, were alert. "Gunn?" Ben tried to stand, but he'd been sitting too long. His legs were stiff, unresponsive. "What are you doing here?"

"My job." Gunn sauntered over to look down at the circle, putting down the case he held. "I don't visit you for kicks, you know."

Ben was not glad to see Gunn on principle. The Department Seven officer knew too much and had too few scruples about using what he knew to his own advantage. But it was a relief to have another living presence—comparatively speaking—in the room. "What's the job?"

"Getting a sample analysis of the extant demonic circle linked to the death of Audrey Hawick, aged thirty-two, wife of Austin Hawick, deceased, and mother of Bennet Hawick, pain in the rear—and lately of Little River and a possible demonic case there." Gunn flicked open the case, lifting out a heavy camera. He removed the cap, stepping back to get a shot of the restored array. "Thanks for saving me the hard work of reassembling this thing. Much appreciated."

Ben watched as Gunn took his photos of the array. "Careful. I might make a habit of helping you. And then where would you be?"

"Save your breath. We both know that's an empty threat." Gunn worked efficiently, taking photos of the circle from all angles. Directly above was last.

Ben looked away as Gunn stepped into the circle. *I'd never be able to do that.* His legs felt weak again just thinking of it.

To keep himself steady, Ben leaned against the wall. He concentrated on the things that were different. Instead of the faint smell of orchids that hung around his mother, he concentrated on Gunn's more pernicious odor. Stale, sour, and sulfurous. The combination was only slightly improved by the strong smell of tobacco overlaying it.

But instead of rooting himself in the present, Ben had a flash of memory. When he'd ducked past the guard and been given back to the child psychologist, there had been a lingering smell of tobacco. "Did you work on this case?"

"Yeah, I did. You don't remember me, Benny? I'm hurt." Gunn returned the camera to the case. He pried a sliver of wood free from the center of the circle and then started working on part of the outer circle. "I remember you. A preternaturally silent little crotch-dropping. A normal kid would have cried or kicked up a fuss. You... There was a feeling in the department that there was something uncanny about you. And look how right we were!"

Ben rolled his eyes. Gunn might be a terrible person, but he was a competent police officer. The two slivers were bagged for magical analysis. Next would be a sliver from somewhere else in the room to act as a control. "And the fact that my mother had just been murdered by demonic intervention didn't strike you as a possible explanation?"

"The case had holes," Gunn said. "Holes wide enough you could lose a small child in them." He considered Ben. "I always thought you knew more than you were telling us. Wanted to interview you myself."

"Why didn't you?"

"For some reason, child services said it was 'inadvisable.' They thought I might scar you. Did you ever hear anything so ridiculous?" Gunn scanned the room, settling on a dusty corner for his last sample.

Ben shifted so that he leaned against the wall on one shoulder, watching Gunn. "You called me a crotch dropping just now."

"And? Kids these days get too much coddling. A little trauma now and then is good for the little maggots." Gunn stabbed viciously at the floorboards with his knife.

As the owner of the apartment building, Ben considered saying something. *Not worth it. Never is.* Much easier just to carpet the entire floor once the investigation was closed. "Where's Kenzie?"

"Kenzie?"

"Your partner."

"I know who Kenzie is, Benny. And she's not my partner. She's my subordinate. I can investigate without her."

Ben raised his eyebrows. A werewolf's nose was invaluable, even in a decades-old cold case like this one. There had to be a very good reason Gunn hadn't brought his right-hand woman along with him. "Does Kenzie have kids?"

"The little maggots aren't even hers!" Gunn complained. "Her sister produces them. Her sister should reap the consequences. But no, the pustulant excretions brought back some highly infectious disease from the germ center they patronize, and Kenzie is under doctor's orders not to expose the rest of the city to her bacteria."

Ben very carefully bit his lip. *If I say anything...*

"Depriving the city of a skilled police officer is a crime! If they were older, we could charge them with obstructing justice, but apparently, the law doesn't apply when you're in preschool."

"Who would have thought?"

Gunn glared. He bagged the last sample and jerked his thumb. "Since I'm down my best sniffer, you mind submitting to a brief scan?"

Ben watched him take the scanner out of his case. "Do I get a choice?"

"Between getting scanned or not getting scanned? No. The difference is whether we do this here or down the station after several hours in a cell."

"You don't have grounds to arrest me." But Ben was also interested in the results. In the sheriff's hands, the scanner was little more than a party trick. Gunn, however, was not just an expert in the supernatural, he was supernatural himself. Augmented by Gunn's own talents, the scanner readings were much more accurate. "Hit me."

"Don't say things like that to me, Benny, please." Gunn raised the scanner.

Ben felt a pulse of energy. The hairs on his arms stood at length as if a burst of static shot through him. The scanner produced light blue sparks and a reading that Gunn noted down in his pad.

"Interesting."

Asking Gunn for details was an exercise in frustration, so Ben waited. He was sure he knew what Gunn's next move would be.

Sure enough, the police officer extended the scanner over the circle. Ben felt the same pulse of energy tingle through him, blue sparks dancing across the surface of the circle. The scanner lit up.

Gunn whistled. "See that response? Our demon's been active lately."

"So it is the same." Ben sagged back against the wall.

"Why are you even asking, Benny? You saw the resonance." Gunn wrote down the numbers in his pad quickly. "Demon your mother summoned is the same that killed Harriet in Little River."

"You're sure?"

"I worked on the case. Yeah, I'm sure." Gunn snorted, putting his notepad away. Ben was not surprised to see it replaced by a lighter, Gunn fishing in his pocket for the inevitable packet of cigarettes. "Guess that solves the question of how you wound up demon-marked."

Ben folded his arms. It was always best to meet Gunn as firmly as possible. Weakness was a red flag when he was around. "If you knew about this already, why didn't you tell Chinquapin's Forensics Team the reason I tested positive for demonic contact?"

"I had to be sure." Gunn tapped the circle with his foot. "Wanted to come back here and confirm first."

"And that took you this long?"

"You want to take a crack at us, Benny? You try brokering peace between werewolves. We haven't gone twenty-four hours without a power struggle between packs all week."

"All the more reason to get this out of the way. You didn't need to come here to confirm. The records at the time—"

"Confiscated by ARX."

Ben stared. "What?"

"Like I said, there were holes in the case. Tons of them. Why your mother would go to the trouble of crafting the circle only to lose her nerve and allow the demon to kill her? It doesn't make sense." Gunn's unnaturally yellow fox eyes settled on Ben. "People who trade with demons aren't people who go meekly to their deaths. They struggle right up until the last moment because they know what is waiting for them beyond."

Ben swallowed. The closeness of the room and Gunn's musty smell were beginning to turn his stomach. "But you just said this cleared me—"

"Cleared you, maybe. But your father—now there was a tough nut to crack." Reluctant appreciation tinged Gunn's voice. "Tested positive for exposure only. But he could have told us more, I'd swear it. But before we could even get started on the investigation, there was pressure from above. ARX took over the case. They found it a clear case of suicide. Clear case of cover-up, if you ask me." Gunn sneered. His yellowed teeth had an uncomfortably sharp edge to them. "But that's ARX for you."

Ben was glad that the wall behind him kept him from taking a step back. "Did you find anyone who demonstrated agent levels of demonic exposure?"

Gunn eyed Ben with dislike. "You know we didn't. But if ARX hadn't moved in..." He lit his cigarette. "You're very defensive. Thought you quit ARX."

"I did."

Gunn leered at him unpleasantly. "Having second thoughts? The world a bigger, scarier place without your vampire boss looming at your back?"

"I sometimes wonder if you enjoy being wrong on purpose." Ben crossed his arms, refusing to be baited. "If there was a summoner to find, you'd have found them. There wasn't. Which means—"

He looked at the floor. He couldn't say it. Not with the memory of her lying there, quite normal, except for the hole in her chest—

"Interesting mental block. You don't want to accept her death or that she tried to kill you?"

"Fuck you, Gunn." That response was reflexive, automatic, but it spurred Ben's mind out of its frozen state.

Gunn shrugged. "That sort of thing leaves an impression. Child psychiatrist insisted we had to protect you from the truth, but I always thought you knew."

After a moment, Ben nodded. "There was something...wrong," he said slowly. "Something really pointed about it. I didn't know at the time, but after she died... I knew that it was supposed to be me in the circle." He looked down at the brown stains. "What would have happened, if it—had been me?"

Gunn leered. "Our demon would have been fed, you would be out of existence, and our lucky agent would have got a ten-year respite before needing to find their next victim."

Ben's head whipped up sharply. "Next?" This was what he was most afraid of.

"This isn't a one-off offer. Far as we can tell, this particular demon works on a recurring deal model." Gunn tapped his cigarette against the wall. "Demon finds someone in dire straits. Makes them an offer of the thing they want most. All they got to do is deliver a victim to him in ten years. Masterful, really. Ten years is a long time, and these people are desperate. They agree. After all, ten years is time enough to figure a way out of it." Gunn paused to drag on the cigarette. "But when the time rolls around, they're comfortable. They don't want to give up what they've got. They make excuses to themselves. 'People die of natural causes all the time! Who cares if someone dies a little sooner... It's their own fault, for not being more careful!'"

Ben took a deep breath. It was just as he'd told Ray, he just—hadn't applied it to his own situation. Easier to think of it as a momentary aberration of judgment rather than planned ahead of time. He covered his confusion by walking across the room to open the window. "You're very well acquainted with demonic practice."

"Are you surprised?" Gunn eyed Ben in insolent challenge. "You know what I am."

"I know your feelings about ARX." Ben sat on the windowsill. Compared to Little River, the air coming in from outside was dirty, tinged with car exhaust and warm concrete. Compared to Gunn and his malodorous stench, it tasted like purest mountain air. "Bet you swatted up, determined to find any hole in their case, any evidence of wrong-doing."

For a moment, rueful appreciation gleamed in Gunn's eyes. "I may have kept the case open...on an unofficial basis."

"And?"

Gunn shook his head. "Nothing. All the principals in the case remained in New Camden. If it wasn't your mother, there'd have been a second summoning ten years later. Instead..." Gunn shrugged.

Ben frowned. *Ten years later—I'd have been nineteen.* They'd been living with Hunter then. *Summoning a demon right under a vampire's nose?* Way, way too risky. *Or maybe that's the point? Hunter's power—* "Is there any way to stop it? Once you've made the pact with the demon."

Gunn removed his cigarette from his mouth with an annoyed expression. "Why are you asking me questions a five-year-old child should know the answer too? You studied this for ARX. The only way you get out of a demon's pact is that you don't."

"But if my mother died—"

"If the summoner fails to provide a victim, the demon collects their soul. And I can tell you that is generally not pretty."

"Pretty?" The word struck Ben as incongruous coming from Gunn.

"Didn't they cover this in your fancy lectures?"

Ben frowned. "Demonic practices is a fourth-year paper," he said.

"ARX?"

"I—don't know. I guess we never got around to it."

"And yet, that small-town sheriff made it sound like you knew your way around a summoning rite." Gunn's grin was distinctly unfriendly.

Ben was unimpressed. *Try harder.* "Compared to her? Sure. But that was basic stuff. Identification only. I always figured the in-depth stuff would come later."

"You telling me that ARX's star over-achiever didn't do a little research of his own?" Gunn smirked at him. "I've seen your university record. Your employee history. You don't wait for later. You like to know now."

"All right," Ben said. "You've got me. I didn't look into demonology because I didn't want to know." He swallowed. His chest felt tight as if it wasn't big enough for the feeling it contained.

"And why is that?" Gunn had felt his pain, knew he had an easy victim. "Fear, Benny? Or were you protecting someone? Or—protecting yourself?"

"It doesn't matter now," Ben said harshly—too harshly to be believable, but Gunn was tuned to emotions like a piranha to blood. He already knew. "You said it yourself. The demon wasn't summoned again."

"Oh, it was, Ben. Just not by any of your lot."

Ben frowned. "You mean—"

"Ten years is a long time to wait for your next meal. Particularly if you are an ambitious minor demon with an eye on the next chance." Gunn told his story with relish, enjoying Ben's discomfort to the fullest. "He plays several games. Has two—maybe three, possibly four—agents on the line at once. The Little River deaths were done by another of his agents."

"Is that a fact?"

Gunn patted the camera. "This is by way of the final confirmation. I've seen the photos they took of the Winkler crime scene. That circle's identical." He scratched his chin. "Little River's a long, long way to go, just to get murdered. I bet the scenery's nice. Lots of vegetation."

"This isn't your case. It's none of your business."

"Once your name entered the case, I got interested. Dusted off our records, looked up theirs. Too bad you were in a different part of the country entirely."

Ben didn't bother pointing out that he'd been fourteen and entirely disinterested in girls. "I'm not a suspect in this case."

"Ben, Benny, Bennet. You know you'll always be public enemy number one as far as I'm concerned." Gunn smirked at him.

"Please." Ben crossed the room. He opened the door, motioning for Gunn to use it. "You've got an actual demonic agent out there to catch—not to mention the entirety of ARX to mess with. I'm the last thing on your list of priorities."

Gunn ground the butt of his cigarette into the bare wood boards and swaggered over to Ben. "I know you and your slippery ways. As long as you're a suspect in the Little River case, I intend to keep a very close eye on you."

"I'm no longer a suspect, Gunn. Between the time of death and the fact that I was clearly miles away—" Ben stopped. He had a premonition.

"Yeah," Gunn nodded. "Forensics means shit when magic's involved. Who cares about an alibi when the guilty party can summon their demon boss to take care of their problems?" He poked Ben in the chest. "We have werewolves working the highway between here and Little River. You stepped off the road to summon a demon, we'll know about it."

"An admirable waste of time," Ben said tightly. "Anyway, you'd know if I had recent demonic residue. This—" Ben paused. "This doesn't make sense."

Gunn watched him, a cruelness lingering around his mouth. "What's bitten you?"

"You said I tested positive for demonic residue back then. The same that I tested for just now. But I was screened before I went to work for ARX. If there had been demonic exposure, they'd have known about it."

"And?" Gunn shrugged. "ARX knew."

"But they'd have told me if that was the case! I got a copy of my records. It—" Ben looked down.

"I always thought there was something really fishy about how quickly your dad changed career streams. From being one of ARX's day-time investigative agents to Hunter's personal housekeeper. Made me wonder if a deal of some sort wasn't made." Gunn picked up his case. "A deal involving a clean slate for you, perhaps?"

Ben followed him out into the stairwell. "I'm not involved in this case, Gunn."

The Department Seven officer made his way down the stairs as casually as if Ben hadn't spoken at all. "Yeah. And I'm nominated for a sainthood." His laugh echoed all the way up the stairs.

☆☆☆

After the cramped apartment and Gunn's assorted offensive smells, the supermarket was paradise. Ben walked down the aisles slowly, basking in their uniform cleanliness and order. The cleaning agents, in particular, looked very attractive.

Powerful enough to remove decades of grime in just one application. Ben considered the Spray and Wipe. *Kills odors in seconds? Now we're talking.*

But while spraying Gunn with fast-acting stain remover was incredibly tempting, Ben was on a mission. *I have to think like Godfrey.*

He continued his circuit of the supermarket. Close to Hunter's townhouse, his father had favored this particular store during his time as Hunter's housekeeper. It had a good variety of products, including the hard to find foreign items or luxury goods the residents of the upmarket area desired. *No denying that Hunter has expensive tastes.* It was a dinner night. They'd be entertaining. Which meant fresh ingredients—Godfrey was particular about his role as host.

But would he shop here? As a vampire, Ben hadn't bothered himself with the minute details of the household. He regretted that now. Would Godfrey favor convenience or prefer to patronize a more economic establishment? He paused in the produce section. No one could fault the quality of the supermarket's fresh stock—and that was what Godfrey would care about most, right?

Ben looked down at a display of apples, picturing the man who had been something between grandfather and mentor. Godfrey's wizened form had contained considerable energy and a brain that was sharp despite its owner's advanced age. He balanced meeting the needs of the three vampires around Saltaire's unpredictable schedule, organizing their social engagements, keeping the household running smoothly and regularly maintaining the magical wards on the property. As a talented witch possessed of power unrelated to Saltaire's own, Godfrey's wards not only protected the vampires' property, but allowed them to occupy it without any other vampires suspecting their presence.

Or at least they had. Ben's mouth twitched. Nate had crashed through Godfrey's wards the same way he'd crashed into Ben's life—completely demolishing all safeguards and leaving a trail of wreckage and confusion in his wake.

What if they've moved? Ben gripped the supermarket display. The thought hadn't occurred to him. *If they have—*

He'd never find Godfrey, not without approaching ARX. And his inquiry would get reported all the way to the head office, and it wouldn't take long for them to investigate, discover that he was alive and then—

Then it would all be over.

"Excuse me." The voice was mild and elderly, with something formal in its tone. Ben didn't catch the reply, looking immediately for the speaker.

A middle-aged woman smiled, pulling her shopping cart back so the elderly man could step in front. He didn't hesitate, selecting a fresh bunch of asparagus with a practiced glance and stepping back with a half-bow for the waiting woman. "Thank you."

That old-fashioned courtesy, particularly towards women, was Godfrey all over. Ben felt an ache as he saw the familiar profile lift, Godfrey seeking his next object and moving towards it without hesitation. It should have been obvious—beyond obvious—but it only now occurred to Ben how much he'd missed him.

Godfrey had a basket, not a shopping cart, and he walked right past the tomatoes towards the red bell peppers.

Ben breathed out. Godfrey tailored each of his meals, not to their guests, but to the preferences of the vampires who fed from them. Saltaire liked a Mediterranean diet, of which tomatoes, sun dried or fresh, were a major part. Hunter, on the other hand, favored the soups and stews of his European home.

Ben's suspicions were confirmed as mushrooms and onions were added to the basket. A rich stew, simmered long. And that meant—

"Here." He held out the flank steak. Cooked for hours over a low heat, it would break down into tender, flavorful chunks.

Godfrey turned towards him. "I think you have me confused..." The sentence trailed off, Godfrey's owl-like eyes widening in shock. "Bennet?"

Ben swallowed. It was painful seeing the familiar face whiten in reaction to himself. "It's me."

"But in daylight—" Godfrey reached beneath his coat.

Ben steeled himself for what was to come. *It's not personal. In our profession, surprises like this aren't usually good.*

Godfrey withdrew his rosary. He held it out, the iron crucifix at the end thrust towards Ben.

It took all Ben's self-control not to recoil. Vampires knew instinctively what would hurt them. Exposure to a cross burnt. It was strange to look at it dispassionately. *It's only an object.* He reached out, cupping the cross in his palm. "It doesn't burn. See? I can touch it without pain. I have a pulse. I breathe. I—"

"This isn't possible." Godfrey's voice was hoarse. "It should not be possible."

"I know," Ben took a deep breath. He was rather glad he hadn't cut his hair yet. The barrier of his long fringe was comforting. "It's not possible, but here I am anyway." He looked up. "I—"

Godfrey's arm shook, the crucifix swinging erratically.

Ben took his arm. "I'm sorry, I didn't mean to surprise you!" He looked around. Godfrey was so organized, so alert and wise, that Ben forgot he was old. "There's got to be somewhere you can sit down—"

Godfrey's fingers closed around his arm. Ben was surprised at the strength in them. "You have a pulse. No," he said. "I don't need to sit down. I need to hear all about this."

☆☆☆

They compromised. The shopping center the supermarket was attached to had a cafe. Ben carried the tray of cappuccinos and sandwiches back to their table. "Are you feeling better?"

"I'm not that delicate," Godfrey complained. "You coming back from the dead—again—startled me. It did not shatter me." He tapped Ben's seat. "Sit down. You have a lot of explaining to do."

Ben explained, exactly as if he were still Godfrey's apprentice and he was recounting every step in his process that had led to an unexpected outcome. "Peter performed a substitution rite. My vampire powers for his humanity. He didn't plan on me living long enough to make use of it. As soon as he'd completed the exchange and could be sure that no possibility of backlash existed to him harming me, I would be dead. Again."

"Brilliant," Godfrey said simply. "Ambitious and entirely unprincipled—but that was Peter all over. I no longer wonder that he was frustrated by his treatment at ARX. I only wonder that he didn't succeed." He picked up his cup of coffee but didn't drink immediately. "How did you escape?" His eyes twinkled. "Or does a certain young man with more good intentions than sense come into the equation?"

Ben felt a second stab of pain. "I owe Nate my life," he said shortly.

"Is Nathan all right?" Godfrey put his cup down, sitting up. "His name was not among the official list of victims—"

"Nate's—" complicated "—fine." Ben took a deep breath. "We...had an argument. I'm— We're not talking right now."

Godfrey's eyebrows raised. "I have a hard time thinking of an argument strong enough to deter him. He was very determined to rescue you—even from yourself."

"I'm not here to talk to you about Nate." Ben looked down at his coffee, willing himself calm. "I've got questions."

"I can imagine." Godfrey leaned forward. "As far as I know, what Peter attempted has never been done before, but that is not to say that there haven't been similar experiments. Years ago—many, many years ago, when I was still a field agent, I heard whispers of such cases."

Ben stared at him. "But that's— I did the research myself! There's nothing—"

"This was, as I said, a very long time ago." Godfrey's tone was apologetic. "In the days of my novitiate which should give you some idea of how long ago I'm talking."

"Didn't you leave the Church before you worked for ARX?"

"Actually, it was because of my experience within the Church that I became of interest to Saltaire," Godfrey said. "It was a different time. Not that my superiors were happy I chose to accompany Saltaire on his mission, but they could not dissuade me from it."

Ben frowned. He'd never asked about Godfrey's youth. An entire, unexpected vista had opened before him. He had questions, many questions—and any other time, he'd have demanded more information about Godfrey's earlier years. Now... "How is it you never mentioned these cases until now?"

"The new vampire is, unfortunately, inclined to be preoccupied with what he has lost." Godfrey's voice was apologetic. "He will take too many risks in order to attempt to regain what he has lost. You... Your half-life never sat well with you." His tawny eyes were sympathetic. "I was not sure whether or not it would become an unwholesome preoccupation."

"So you"—Ben looked down at his coffee rather than face that too understanding gaze—"hid the knowledge from me?"

"Curtailed what resources were available to you," Godfrey adopted a matter-of-fact tone. "You would have been given full access to our library—and my memories—in time."

For a moment Ben wanted to ask what the books he'd withheld were. *First things first.* He had a mission. "Like you curtailed my knowledge of my mother's death?"

Godfrey went very still. After a long pause, he put his cup down. "Hunter and I wondered how much you knew. We didn't think it possible, as Austin said, that you'd observed nothing. But at the same time... Well, you were a very sensitive and intelligent boy who had just lost his beloved mother in tragic circumstances. We did not want to upset you. Hunter and I decided it would be best to wait for you to speak of it first. But in fifteen years of knowing you, this is the first you've spoken of it." It wasn't a question. Godfrey knew, as surely as if Ben had said so. "It's happened again."

Ben nodded. "There was a murder—a hunter. It seemed to be tied to a girl who died ten years ago, sacrificed by a demonic agent. But I don't know why yet. All I know is that it's the same demon that murdered my mother."

"The same," Godfrey repeated quietly. "It was always a possibility. It would only have had to wait..." He looked up at Ben. "You're wondering what we know about the case?"

Ben nodded. "I remember what happened. But I don't know why." He took a deep breath. "I was supposed to be the one who died. But Audrey—Mother—something happened. Dad was angry and she died instead." He took a deep breath. "He killed her—and made it look like a demon."

Godfrey's eyes widened. "Is that what you thought?"

Ben nodded. "I know that's what happened. He—" He stopped. It was hard to continue. The words had been locked inside for too long. "He said that she was in bed when we left the house, that she was sleeping, but that was a lie. I know it was because I looked and she wasn't there." It felt wrong to say the words. Ben shut his eyes. *He's dead. It won't hurt him now.*

"Ben—"

"He took me to the zoo. I didn't understand it then. I'd made Mother cry. I should have been in trouble. Instead, he was spoiling me. It's obvious now. He was establishing an alibi. I caught him looking at his watch a lot. And when I was coming back from the bathroom, I saw him dropping a little plastic container—the kind medicine came in—into a rubbish bin. He used gloves to do it, dropped those in too."

"You never said anything." Godfrey's voice was sympathetic.

Ben, startled into a laugh, looked at his companion. "How could I? He'd just murdered my mother!"

"But you covered for him?"

Ben had to drop his gaze. "I was scared. My mother was dead. I didn't understand why, but I knew it was because of me. And if my father went to jail... I'd be entirely alone."

"And rather than lose him, you said nothing." Godfrey laid his leathery old hand over Ben's. "Ben. I am so sorry."

Ben blinked hurriedly. "It's not your fault. You weren't there."

"There were things about the case that didn't add up," Godfrey said, his voice quiet but perfectly calm. Ben listened to it as if it were a recording, noting dispassionately the melodic cadence to the simple words, the way Godfrey carefully enunciated every syllable. *A throwback to his monastic training?* "It seemed too great a coincidence that the one day your father, an employee known for his impeccable health and attendance, chose to take off would be the day his wife tried and failed to summon a demonic entity—and that you and your father would be safely out of the way when she did. Austin was in a senior position within ARX. Hunter and I looked into the matter ourselves. He found the gloves and the medicine bottle, just as you described—fingerprints or the lack thereof are no match for a vampire's nose—or a witch's magic."

Ben drew a shaky breath, but the words didn't come.

Godfrey continued. "On the surface, it seemed clear enough. Austin slips his wife a sleeping drug, takes her downstairs to the empty apartment, lies her on the array he has forced her to draw with her own blood. He leaves with his son, careful to establish an alibi, knowing that at the appointed time, the demon will arrive to claim its victim."

"But—"

"On the surface, it seemed straightforward." Godfrey steepled his long fingers together. "But there is more to the matter than you know. Your father was never a murderer, Ben."

CHAPTER FOURTEEN

Ben stared at Godfrey. For a moment he thought he'd misheard. "I know what I saw—"

"We saw the same," Godfrey told him. "But there is other evidence that you haven't heard about." Godfrey hesitated. "This may be difficult to hear, Ben."

Ben wanted to laugh. He'd carried around the knowledge that his father had killed her for years. This was nothing! But instead of speaking, he found himself sucking in a rapid breath.

"Perhaps we should return to the house." Godfrey looked around to signal the waitress.

"No!" Ben steeled himself. "I don't— I didn't leave Saltaire on the best circumstances. I don't want him to know—"

Godfrey looked at him. "You cannot remain hidden from him forever. You know that, Ben."

Ben put his palms flat on the table. "I just need time. Time to figure out what I want and who I am. Before— You know I can't do that around Saltaire. His influence..."

"I understand," Godfrey said. "You want to establish yourself as an individual before returning to Saltaire's realm of influence."

"And Hunter's, too," Ben added quickly.

Godfrey pressed his lips together. "Well. It grieves me not to share your news, but I will respect your wishes." He sighed. "It's a shame. We are short-handed right now. We've had an increase in cases since the Necromancer killings. Saltaire has gone to Europe in self-imposed exile, leaving myself and Hunter holding the fort. We would be very glad of your help."

It was tempting—very tempting. There had been camaraderie and purpose, the knowledge that he was helping a worthwhile cause, saving lives. Ben shook his head before he could second-guess himself. "I've got control of myself. Tell me about the case."

Godfrey's eyes saw everything. Ben thought for a moment that he was about to refuse, but with a sigh, Godfrey leaned back in his chair. "In the course of my career, I've seen the work of demons such as this many a time. My order specialized in them. A good part of my long distant youth was spent in attending exorcisms, and traveling with my master to look up treatises on the various known species of demons and their identifying characteristics. That was how I first came to Saltaire's attention—as a newly ordained brother, on the trail of the same demon he sought."

Anyone else might make that pronouncement in a coffee shop and not be believed. Godfrey's words sounded the right ring of gravity, even in the midst of the bustling cafe. Ben nodded. Rather than feeling exasperation at Godfrey's detour into the past, he appreciated it for what it was—a chance for Ben to collect himself.

"I've seen many demonic victims," Godfrey said. "There is a difference between those taken by means of a sealed bargain—such as the one your mother attempted—and those who break their bargain. And then there are those who get in the demon—or its agent's—way. The first is comparatively gentle. Death occurs the instant the ritual exchange is complete. The soul is consumed, the flame of existence extinguished. Indeed, I have seen victims who appeared so peaceful that you would swear they had died peacefully of natural causes."

"So that means—" Ben faltered. No one could imagine that the body he'd glimpsed died naturally.

Godfrey nodded. "Your mother's death did not end the demon's rite. But there were no more deaths."

"You don't know that—"

"Actually, Ben. I think we do." Godfrey leaned forward. "We kept your father under close observation. The housekeeping job... Well, at first, it was simply a ruse. During the day I monitored your father, while at night Hunter made sure he did not have the opportunity to create a second circle, find another victim. He didn't even try to make the attempt. If anything, he seemed...relieved."

Ben looked down. "But it's my fault she died. Because I didn't say—" He was unable to voice the words, even now.

"Hunter and I were wondering how to proceed when your father decided to confide in us. He'd come home unexpectedly early from work, found his wife about to sacrifice their son to a demon—"

"No."

Godfrey continued placidly as if Ben had not interrupted. "She laughed it off, tried to pass it off as a joke, but Austin wasn't fooled. He'd noticed that his wife's behavior had become strained and erratic as their ten-year anniversary approached. He didn't want to believe it possible, but he knew what he'd seen. You see, Austin had encountered this particular demon's work before in the course of his work for ARX. That's how your parents met—Austin handled the investigation into the circumstances of Audrey's parents' death."

Ben stared at Godfrey. "They died in a car crash." He hated how lost his voice sounded. He hadn't even known his grandparents.

Godfrey's smile was sad. "I'm afraid not. Austin found that Audrey was the intended victim for a demonic circle created by her father, but when the circle mistakenly claimed his wife, he realized he would be unable to hide his wrongdoings and killed himself. In retrospect, it seems likely that Audrey was the agent all along, and she killed her father to cover her tracks. We will never know her motivations, but I suspect that starved of love and possessions in her youth, she was willing to go to extraordinary lengths to secure them."

"I don't believe it." Ben gripped the edge of the table. "Just because she's dead and can't defend herself, doesn't give you the right—"

"We looked into the case a second time. Audrey's relationship with her parents was rocky at best, and she was obsessed with wealth. After her death, Austin discovered a host of secret bank accounts she'd made. As if she expected to have to hide. It was the hardest blow, and what, I think, made him determined never to speak of her to you. He could forgive a moment of weakness, but not a considered plan."

Forgiveness? "But he killed her!"

"He did exactly as procedure dictates. Left the summoner for the demon to claim."

Ben stared at him.

"There would have been more victims otherwise," Godfrey explained gently. "Your mother was a resourceful woman. She'd managed to hide her pact all the while living right under the nose of a man who investigated supernatural elements for a living. She was also a very attractive woman, who enjoyed playing hostess. It's possible that she hoped to attract someone to take your place in the ritual. Unfortunately for her, a few weeks earlier, someone had asked your father a question about his work at the dinner table, and he'd explained the signs of a demonic ritual. Audrey was furious with him afterward, and increasingly nervous. He said in retrospect it was obvious."

"But the pills—"

"He didn't want her to die as most agents do," Godfrey said. "Aware and knowing what was about to happen. He hoped that if she was unconscious she would be spared the pain. He was very much in love with her, even then."

Ben looked down at the table again. His ears were ringing like they did at high altitude. "I didn't know. He never told me."

"He hoped to protect you," Godfrey said. "Knowing how close you were to your mother—he didn't want your memories of her poisoned by the knowledge that she—"

"Would have killed me to save her own life." Ben's legs shook as he stood, and his hand banged clumsily against the chair. "I have to go."

Godfrey stood. "Is there anything—"

"No! No." Ben took a deep breath. After so long, his self-command was still there. "I just need some time to take this in."

Godfrey reached over the table, placing his lean hand on Ben's arm. "I'm only a phone call away."

Ben nodded, not trusting himself to speak.

He stood on the pavement blankly, not knowing which way to turn. Where was he going? Where was there to go?

As he hesitated, a taxi slowed hopefully. That gave Ben impetus. He climbed into the back seat. "The New Cemetery."

☆☆☆

The New Cemetery was established two centuries prior, when New Camden's inhabitants had reached the limits of the boundaries so optimistically set out for them by the city's founders. It was a lot more practical, lacking, for the most part, the marble crypts and statues of its predecessor.

Austin's grave was plain. The stone still had a smooth, glossy shine to it that time and New Camden's notoriously polluted air had not yet taken away. All traces of the murder from a year prior had been removed, and the damage to Austin's slab skillfully repaired. The grave looked good as new.

So new, the stone had an unfinished quality about it. No mention of his family—Saltaire had been against it, reminding Ben that such details could become deadly to vampires. "We are recognized now," he'd said. "But that may not always be the case. Your father would understand. He always put your safety first."

Ben sat down at the foot of the slab. *Died protecting me. Lived protecting me from the knowledge that my mother tried to trade my soul for ten years more wealth.*

He should feel something. Not this gnawing emptiness within. Something! He should be sad or grateful or full of rage...

"What is wrong with me?" Ben looked at the stone.

In Memoriam
Austin Hawick
This Wasn't On The Job Description.

The corners of Ben's mouth turned up tiredly. *Such a Dad joke.* People would have to know he was a father, even without that information on the stone.

His vision blurred, eyes filling with tears. "Dad." His throat was constricted with all he wanted to say. "Dad, I—"

The words didn't come. Ben tried again, but it was as if there was an outside force acting on him, preventing him from saying the words.

Instead he felt, as if for the first time, the loss of his father.

It's been a year. I shouldn't feel this strongly now. I should be over this.

But he'd spent a year not allowing himself to grieve. And before that...

Ben could remember passing the time with Austin, working with him on preparing meals for Hunter's dinner guests or researching musty tomes for his cases. Austin had always welcomed Ben's involvement, many times expressing an interest in Ben's homework or university essays. Ben always refused.

I always held back from him. Ben scrubbed his hand across his eyes. *I never told— I wanted to protect him! But I never forgave him either.*

So instead, he'd deliberately withdrawn emotional contact from his only remaining family member. "Dad, I'm s—"

How pathetic am I? Ben ground his fingers into a fist. *I can't even talk to a headstone! How can I ever expect to get on with living people if I can't even face the dead?* Ben dug his fingers into his arm in an effort to stave off the thought, but it was too late.

I'm broken. This is me—too broken to be able to live or feel or love. He shut his eyes. *Nate's the only person who could make me feel—and instead of welcoming it, I freaked out.* Was it Nate's choices that scared Ben, or his reactions to them? Anger and frustration and fear were a part of life, as much a part of it as joy and affection. *In rejecting one, did I lose all of it? Is it Nate I'm afraid of—or life itself?*

Ben looked down at the marble slab before him. There was no headstone separating him and Nate, but the distance between them felt just as insurmountable.

He was still there, hours later, when his phone rang. Ben was so surprised he swore, getting dirty looks from the mourners at a neighboring grave. Ignoring them, Ben pulled out his phone, heading for a quiet bench away from the other visitors. "Hello?" His heart was beating fast, his hands clammy. Very few people had the number to his phone. "Nate?"

"Hate to disappoint you." Ben could picture George's smirk exactly, lingering in self-satisfaction. "But it's only me."

"George." Ben took a moment to get his voice under control. When he next spoke, it was shorn of any indication that he'd been surprised. "How did you get my number? Nate?"

"Tried Nate. You two have a fight or something? He was weirdly against giving me your number."

"That's none of your business." Ben forced his voice to relax. "Then how did you get it?"

"Officer Raymond was kind enough to oblige."

Ben frowned. He'd had to leave a number with the police before leaving Little River. "That's private information. They shouldn't be sharing it."

"I'm helping them in their inquiries," George told him. "And you're helping me with my inquiries."

Ben snorted. "Think again," he told her. "I'm through with Little River. I've got no interest in getting caught up in that again—"

"There's been developments you don't know about."

"There's no developments that could change my mind about going back to Little River."

"Not the discovery of a demonic circle in the Granger's barn?"

Ben shoved the sense of alarm away. "What are you talking about?"

"Police made the discovery yesterday. Only one course of action they could take." The phone quality dropped dramatically. Ben guessed that George had shrugged. "Your boyfriend's been arrested for Harriet's murder."

Once again Ben felt as if he'd been shocked out of his body. He heard the words, but they were distant. Or was it Ben himself who was distant. *Nate, arrested?*

'You don't understand, Ben. Jail would kill Ethan... I promise you, Ethan has nothing to do with this.'

"Hello? Hawick? You there?"

"Sorry, George." Ben clenched his phone tightly. "I've got a call to make."

Little River might not be on the map, but it was on the internet. Ben located the number he wanted after a quick search. He hit call and waited, expression as grim as the rows of graves surrounding him.

"Little River Sheriff's Office, Sheriff McCall speaking."

Ben got to the point at once. "You didn't tell me you'd made an arrest."

There was a long pause. Ben could imagine the sheriff tugging her hat down to hide her eyes. "That's not how consulting works. We don't need your permission to make an arrest."

"You could have told me." Ben gripped the phone. "If it's my evidence you're using—" He stopped. None of the evidence he had found pointed to Nate.

"Rest assured that we took everything you told us into consideration," the sheriff said. "And there's our own experts too. We didn't rush into the decision, but there was new evidence found and— Well, we did what we had to."

"The circle in the barn? The idea that the family knew about it is preposterous!"

"Circle? Now who told you about that?"

Ben ignored the question. "Even if you did find a link to the family, there's no reason to think that Nate—"

"Nate?" There was a chuckle. "I think your informant jumped the gun." Before Ben could answer, the sheriff continued. "No, Nate's back in New Camden. Which is a relief. The family is taking it very calmly. Our team here has put Emma onto a good legal counsel with a supernatural background. Ethan's in good hands." The sheriff had the tone of someone who genuinely wished to believe what she was saying.

Ben laid his hand on the arm of the stone bench. "You arrested Ethan? But—"

"The evidence against him is entirely circumstantial," the sheriff agreed. "But it's a damn sight safer for him in there than it is in Little River right now. People are talking. He's the only person in the area with any sort of difference... And well, you saw what fear does to people. Ethan is best out of that."

"But jail?" Ben could hear the echo of Nate's words. Prison would kill Ethan.

"Buys breathing room. Ethan doesn't have to appear in court for at least a month. That's plenty of time to find new evidence in the case."

Ben looked down at his phone to be sure that it was still on. That he'd heard what he thought he just heard.

"Hello? Hawick, you there?"

"Are you saying that you arrested Ethan—even though you don't think he did it?"

The sheriff sighed. "This supernatural stuff... It's all over my head. I'm just a simple country sheriff. I know people, not magic. But all the same...I can't see any son of Emma's getting himself mixed up in anything demonic." Just for a moment, the sheriff's voice wavered. Ben heard the tiredness behind it. "The folks here were pushing for an arrest fast, threatening to take things into their hands if there wasn't one, and pressure from above to control the situation. I made the call, but it doesn't entirely sit right with me. So if there's something to find, we won't stop you finding it." She hung up before Ben could reply.

☆☆☆

Ben braced himself to climb the steps to Century. Every single time he'd visited Nate at his place of work, it had ended in disaster. First the discovery that Nate had remembered Ben and his vampire family, despite Ben attempting to preserve his safety by erasing his memories. Ben snorted. *Yeah. Like that had gone well.* Now, he was inclined to think of Nate's ability to resist as a gift.

Harder to accept: his own decision to leave Nate. Granted, they hadn't even been dating at the time, but Nate had taken it extremely personally.

Have I even changed? Ben looked around Century's foyer. *I am alive now, living. No longer bound by the patterns of my past. So why do I keep repeating them?*

He waved aside the sales representative, making his way through the foyer and into what was once a theater, but was now either New Camden's greatest shame or most well-known success. To be honest, either appellation would have suited Century's marketing team. They traded on both their scandal and their suitability, combining private club, nightclub, and brothel with luxury and exclusivity.

The remodeled theater echoed the establishment's contradictions in its own architecture. The floor was industrial concrete, harshly minimalist, while there was no attempt made to hide the lighting frames. It could have been a modern gallery, except that the long wooden slab that made up the bar was polished wood, salvaged from the original theater, as were the boxes, enclosed tables with seating repurposed from the theater's original chairs. The stage was unapologetically old, with full, thick curtains and gilt edging.

Century had only just opened, so the stage was empty, the curtains drawn, and the club mostly bare. Its hosts and hostesses were gathered around the bar. As Ben approached, one host glided up to meet him with almost predatory quickness.

"Can I help you find what you're looking— Oh, it's only you."

And to think, I was worried that I might have problems finding Aki. Ben looked at his reluctant companion. "Nice to see you too."

Nate's best friend didn't bother to hide his lack of enthusiasm. He was dressed for work, his black hair freshly spiked and a leather collar worn over his silky shirt. "You're wasting your time. He isn't here."

And that answered all of Ben's questions. Easy.

Too easy.

Ben narrowed his eyes. "What makes you think I'm here for Nate?"

Aki rolled his eyes. "You're so uptight, you wouldn't know fun even if it turned in a complete work history and resume. The only reason you're here is to make sure Nate isn't having fun without you."

"I'm not worried about Nate having fun without me."

"Uh-uh," Aki shook his head. "I am willing to fake sympathy for Nate, but he's my best friend. You dumped him. You get nothing."

Ben blinked. "Did he tell you that?"

"It's obvious," Aki shrugged, turning away from Ben to scan the doorway hopefully. "He phoned in a few days ago. Said his family was having some issues, he needed personal leave. Of course, we all knew what 'personal leave' meant." Aki took his eyes off the door and any potential clients to eye Ben. "You guys went from Romeo and Juliet levels of reckless mutual endangerment to broken up in less time than a celebrity wedding. That has to be some kind of record."

"That's the thing everyone forgets about Romeo and Juliet. They never got to see how they could have handled their relationship because they died—" This was off topic. "Anyway Nate and I had a disagreement. Not a suicide pact." Ben blinked. "How did you go from that to 'broken up'?"

"It's obvious, isn't it?" Aki counted off the reasons on his fingers. "You're in New Camden. Nate is not. Nate hasn't touched his phone in days. Nate's phone was a present from you. Nate's ex is asking after him—" Aki straightened up. "Excuse me, Ben. Duty calls." He sauntered past Ben, intent on the man who had just walked through the door.

"Wait!" Ben grabbed Aki by the hand. "What do you mean, Nate's ex?"

"Ben! Let go! I have my student debt to think of!" Aki did his best to shake Ben off.

Ben tightened his grip. "Tell me about Nate's ex."

"Later! I haven't had a decent client and—great. Tybalt's got him." Aki thrust Ben's hand away in disgust. "Thanks for nothing."

Ben looked over his shoulder. Another host had beaten Aki to the client. Evidently the man was well-known. A few others were walking over to join him.

Aki jabbed Ben with his finger. "You owe me."

Ben did not feel particularly apologetic. "I'll buy you a drink." Aki brightened. "But only one drink."

Aki sighed. "You are the literal worst."

"Careful. Or I'll give you a one-star review."

Aki elbowed him. His slight form was more solid than it appeared at first glance, honed athletically. The elbow hurt. "Don't even joke about that."

The bar was crowded, so Ben let Aki talk him into upgrading to a table booth. The added privacy was worth the cost, and it meant Aki had slightly less to complain about, an advantage at any time. Ben waited until Aki was done moaning about New Camden's increased supernatural regulations, the security measures that Century had just rolled out, and the stinginess of the police reward system, before turning the conversation back to Nate. "You said Nate's ex was asking after him?"

Aki smirked, reaching for his glass. He'd gone for a ridiculous cocktail, replete with paper umbrella and straw. "So you'd better not waste any time on making up with him. The guy is rocking the hobo-chic. Blond hair, green eyes, tattoos, piercings, the works... Not to mention, a great bod... Amazing body when you think of it." Aki's eyes lingered with pity on Ben's bone thin arms.

Ben tried to clamp down on the immediate feeling of insecurity. "Sandy?" Nate's anger at Ethan took on unwelcome connotations. Ben remembered how Nate had stormed out rather than talk to Ben about him.

Aki sipped at his cocktail. "He didn't introduce himself, but it had to be him."

"And you're sure he was looking for Nate?"

"Asked about him, was visibly disappointed that Nate wasn't here, kept asking about him even when I said I didn't know when he'd be coming back. Wanted to know everything about what Nate was up to."

"Did you tell him where Nate was?"

Aki shook his head. "That was about the time Nate stopped responding to phone messages. Besides, the guy is all wrong for Nate."

Ben felt a sense of relief. "You think so, too?"

Aki nodded. "Broke," he agreed. "Nate's already in trouble for associating with necromancers and getting killed on the job. He doesn't need to be in trouble for giving out freebies, too."

That's not the point! Ben opened his mouth to point this out, instead heard his voice say, "And you think Nate would?"

Aki sighed, making an obvious effort to be sympathetic. "You've heard the way Nate talks about the guy, right? He's not just Nate's type, he's Nate's prototype. I'm pretty sure that Nate's not going to be making a single smart decision around the guy... So the sooner you put an end to it the better." His advice was only slightly ruined by the fact that he was scanning the club as he spoke, checking out the latest new arrivals.

I should just be glad I kept Aki's attention this long. Ben frowned. Sandy's physical description was entirely at odds with Ben's...everything. "Me? You know Nate and I broke—"

"Nate managed to fall for you despite common sense, more attractive options, and certain death." Aki gave Ben a look just short of being a glare. "The attraction between you two makes absolutely no sense... Which is why you have to do something about this."

"You're worried about Nate?"

Aki put his drink down, sitting up. Shorn of its usual attitude, his voice was softer. "You know how Nate is. Stupidly generous. Sandy... Sandy was the first person to really hurt him. Leaving the way he did without a word. There is no reason at all that Nate should still hold a torch for the guy. But he does. And that... Well, someone's got to save Nate from himself." He slapped Ben on the arm, sliding out of the booth. "My regular's here. It's been great, Ben. Don't call again."

Ben picked up his own soda. Aki had rolled his eyes, but after all the shocks of the day, Ben didn't think alcohol was a good idea. The carbonation was a shock in itself, and Ben took a few slow sips of the drink. With any luck, the sugar would tide him over until he could crash.

What now? There were many reasons Nate might have taken personal leave. Being incarcerated was only one of them. *The sheriff said Ethan...*

But George had said 'your boyfriend.'

I'm not going to be able to rest until I know. Ben stood. He had a long drive ahead of him.

Castanea County Prison was depressing the way all prisons were depressing. The concrete facility was surrounded by open fields, miles from anything else. Ben stood beside his rental car, looking at it. For the first time, the truth of what Nate said about the place destroying Ethan really made sense.

There's nothing here. No life. Just—concrete.

He forced himself to walk up to the building.

His ID was checked three times and there was a phone consultation with Little River and New Camden both before Ben was allowed through security screening. He found himself unaccountably nervous as he sat on one side of the thick plastic looking at the empty chair on the other side.

The door opened, a guard directing his prisoner to the seat. There was a brief moment of hesitation, and then he slumped into the chair, managing to project an air of 'let's just get this over with' despite his wooden expression.

"Fifteen minutes," the guard said and shut the door.

Ben leaned forward. It had only been a moment, but he'd seen a flicker of hurt in that moment of hesitation. "Nate. How on earth did this seem like a good idea?"

He glared back, expression unwavering. "Not Nate." He held up his arm. "See?"

It took Ben a moment to see what was missing. Nate's Century wristband. The personal safety device protected the club's investments as much as Nate's life and couldn't be removed without specialized equipment. Destroying it would double Nate's debt to the club.

For a moment, Ben wondered if he'd imagined what he'd seen. After all, the sight of Ben visiting him would throw Ethan too.

Looking up, Ben caught the other man's eyes on him, before he hurriedly looked away.

"Nate," he said. "You can't fool me. Any more than I've ever been able to fool you."

"Don't tell anyone." Nate leaned into the plastic urgently. "Ben, you can't. They'll think—"

"That Ethan's got to be involved in a big way if you're going to these lengths to protect him?" Ben fixed Nate with a glare. "You are an idiot, Nate. This— Of all the things you could have done, this was the worst!"

"You didn't leave me much choice, did you?" Nate glared. "Anonymous phone tip about the barn— You couldn't have turned us in under your own name?"

Ben stared at him. "Phone tip?"

"Like you don't already know." Nate sneered—or tried to. He met Ben's eyes and stopped. "You didn't?"

Ben shook his head. "I—realized I couldn't blame you for protecting your brother, given that I held my tongue about my mother's murder for years."

Nate pressed his hands against the glass. "Ben. What?"

"I'll tell you about it sometime when we don't have a fifteen-minute time limit." Ben glanced at the clock. "You really thought that I'd turn you in via an anonymous tip?"

Nate didn't meet his eyes. "Who else could it be? No one knew the circle was there. If it wasn't you, then who?"

"Anyone who visited your barn in the last ten years."

Nate's head jerked up. "What?"

"The demonic agent was active in the Little River and Rockford area ten years ago—we know that because of the Winkler murder." Ben leaned forward. "I'm right in assuming that your family was still relatively retiring ten years ago?"

Nate nodded. "We farmed cattle then—beef, not dairy—so we had the vet in occasionally, stock trucks a couple of times a year, and Mr. Cafferty and his sons brought the bull round... You're taking notes? You can't be serious, Ben. These are our neighbors!"

"Who would have a better knowledge of the places in Little River and Rockford likely to be deserted than someone who lives here?" Ben continued to jot down notes on his notebook. "We know for a fact this agent has local knowledge—and that's not all we know." Ben put his pen down.

Nate watched closely, waiting for Ben to speak.

"This demon feeds on a genuine declaration of love from the victim. The agent deliberately cultivates an emotional connection with their victims before betraying them in the worst possible way—"

"That's fucked up." Nate swallowed. His skin was pale. "Ben, I'm sorry—"

Ben shook his head. He had to get this out now, before the emotion building in his throat choked him entirely. "There's something I haven't told you." He took a deep breath.

"Is it about your mother?"

Ben stared. "How did you know?"

"Ray told me about the case when they checked out the barn." Nate hunched his shoulders, looking down at the floor. "I guess I can't blame you for feeling strongly about demons given your mother was a victim of one."

"My mother was the agent," Ben said flatly. "I was the demon's intended victim—and not just any demon. The same one that killed Harriet."

Nate looked like he'd been slapped. "You're not serious."

"Deathly serious." Ben sucked in another deep breath. "Nate, we have an almost unprecedented chance to stop a demon claiming another victim—if we can find the agent. But as long as you're in here pretending to be Ethan, the police think they've got a closed case."

Nate shook his head, slumping back in his seat. "I can't. And you know why I can't. George said the same thing."

"George?" Wheels were starting to turn in Ben's mind. "You'll take advice from a hunter, but not from me?"

"You weren't here!" Nate glared. "What was I supposed to do? Anyway, it's not like I consulted her or anything. She just said that she wouldn't like to be in Ethan's shoes and—why are you looking at me like that?"

"You're not helping Ethan, me—or yourself." Ben stood up. "But that's fine. You being in here works both ways."

"What do you mean?"

Ben held up the notebook. "You can't stop me investigating from in here."

Nate got to his feet. "What are you going to do?"

"Whatever I want. And you don't get a say in it." Ben smiled sweetly. "Think about that, Nate."

CHAPTER FIFTEEN

George was staying in a campground at the entrance to one of the major hiking trails. Her RV, a battered 1970s Airstream Argosy, was not hard to find—it was the only one in the park. She was outside, going through a set of practice sword drills with a staff and grinned as she caught sight of Ben. Her lipstick was a bright pink, obnoxiously cheerful.

For some reason, that made Ben even angrier. "What did you tell Nate?"

"Nice wheels. That a rental?" George let her staff rest on her shoulder. "When you didn't get off the bus this morning, I was worried. Thought I might have miscalculated. Was going to try you again after this, actually." She waved the staff.

Ben was not distracted. "I want an explanation."

"An explanation?"

"You talked to Nate. Next thing I know, Ethan's in prison—"

George shook her head. "I'm not fooled by that any more than you are."

"Was that your idea?"

"I may have made a few...observations...in Nate's hearing." George shrugged. "I'd been visiting our good sheriff, could see which way the wind was blowing. Figured I owed the guy a head's up."

"And thanks to you, he's in jail."

"Hey, I didn't force Nate to throw himself under the bus." George waggled her staff at Ben. "He was weirdly eager to do that himself. Relationship troubles?"

"None of your business." Ben ground out the words through gritted teeth.

George gave him a pitying smile. "Anyway, I had to get your attention somehow."

Ben crossed his arms. "A phone call is usually sufficient."

George shook her head. "Be honest. Your kind, you look down on us freelancers. You'd sooner collaborate on a case with a revenant than work with one of us. Nah, I needed you to listen to me."

"This is not the way to get my attention. Sure, I'm listening, but do you really think I want to work with you after this? "

"I take no responsibility for the choices of your extraordinarily pretty boyfriend." George watched Ben from beneath her long lashes. "It was all his decision...though he is incredibly open to suggestion. I'd keep a better handle on him—"

"Don't talk about Nate like that." Ben realized his fists were clenched.

George noticed. "You want to fight?" She picked up a second staff leaning against the side of the caravan. "We can clear the air before we get down to business."

Ben shook his head. "There is no business."

"Come on. I would never have condoned your boy getting arrested if I wasn't confident I could get him out again. I want to find the real agent, Ben. Before there's another victim." George threw the staff.

Ben caught it instinctively. "I'm not stopping you from doing that, but I'm not going back. I'm retired from the business."

"The police might buy that, but I don't." George gave Ben the briefest of bows before circling him, staff extended. "They haven't lived this life like we have. You don't leave this life behind, Ben, any more than you choose it in the first place."

"You don't know anything about me." Ben's fingers tightened around the staff as he stepped back, circling George as she did him.

"I know enough." She cocked her head back, her eyes laughing at him. "You hold the staff like you've been waiting for this, and you move like you were doing this just yesterday."

Ben looked down at himself in confusion. *I can't—don't want this!*

George charged forward, bringing her staff down.

Ben brought his staff up with both arms, twisting it sideways to distribute the force of George's strike. She grunted, stepping back out of striking distance to aim another blow at Ben's side. Anticipating that, Ben was able to deflect the blow sideways, drawing George off balance, and following up with a kick. It took more effort than he was used to expending—quite apart from lacking a vampire's strength, Ben was sadly out of shape—but his pulse kicked in just the same.

"This proves nothing!" *It was self-defense.* Humans naturally wanted to protect themselves. *Just because Nate doesn't have any self-preservation—* "I'm stronger than that. Strong enough to leave this world behind."

"You're dreaming!" George caught him on the arm, hard enough to sting. "I'm not going to respect your delicate male ego and hold back out of respect for your quarter-life crisis!"

"You seem to think you know me pretty well." Ben's follow-up strike was too angry to be anything but clumsy, and George avoided it with ease. "But you're not going to convince me with wild assumptions like that."

George laughed. "You want me to stop? Fight properly and I'll consider it."

Ben sucked in an angry breath. "Fine."

His weapon of choice was a pistol. You could size the situation up from a distance. There was time to think, less margin for error provided your aim was good—and Ben's aim was very good. But Saltaire had insisted that Ben train in swordcraft. 'Our enemies are old. Their methods are old,' he'd said with the gravity his power gave any statement he made. 'You must be prepared for any eventuality.' Ben had obediently drilled the patterns—block, thrust, retreat, advance, misdirect, feint, parry. There was something in them, something that reached through his anger, through his fear for Nate.

"Knew you'd be good at this." George was faster than Ben had expected. She delivered each blow with confidence, keeping him on the defensive with the focus of a woman who knew exactly what she wanted. "It's that purpose in your movements. Your body knows you're a fighter, no matter what you tell yourself."

"I quit." Ben allowed George to catch him a slight blow on his arm so that he'd have a better chance of catching her staff himself.

She freed herself with more strength than he'd expected. "You're fooling no one. Not me, not your pretty boyfriend."

"He's not my boyfriend."

"Yeah." George added insult to injury with an unhurried grin. "And the Loch Ness Monster really exists. Lie to yourself all you want, but it won't make it true."

I'm getting really sick of this. Ben swung angrily, realizing too late that George had been goading him into a hasty move. He barely managed to block her side-swipe, forced onto one knee as he blocked her follow up strike.

"All this self-delusion's making you sloppy. You can't deny you're a hunter—and you can't hunt in denial. Face the facts."

She's right. Ben took a step back, letting George drive him away from her trailer. *I've missed this.* He'd disagreed with Saltaire's policies, but not his work. *It's a part of me.*

It was like something clicked in his mind. No longer resisting, Ben let himself go with his instinct. He countered George's next blow, directing it to the side. As she twisted with the momentum, he caught the staff a second, rattling blow. His next strike knocked it from her hands entirely.

The staff rolled to a stop between them. There was no further sound beyond their harsh breathing.

Then George smirked at him. "Told you."

Ben tossed his staff after hers. "I'm still not convinced."

"I am. Suspected you'd be good at this, but I needed to be sure." George nodded. Her breathing was rapidly getting under control. "I'm going to level with you. I know I'm over my head, but this isn't a case I can walk away from. I need a partner. And that's you."

"Why should I trust you? For that matter, what makes you think you can trust me?" The question was asked without malice, Ben genuinely curious. "You're making a lot of assumptions based on what you think you know about me."

"You can't afford not to trust me," George picked up the staffs. She motioned Ben to follow her back to the caravan. "We're both after the same thing. We find the demon's agent, and Nate gets out of prison incredibly grateful to you for your efforts on his behalf. I don't know what your argument was about, but I'm pretty sure that clearing his brother of murder charges is going to go a long way to making up for it."

Ben swallowed back the instant longing. He and Nate couldn't go back to the way things were. He'd said too much. "And you?"

"Me?"

"Demonic cases always have a lot of danger. This agent's killed twice that we know of and is ready to kill again." Ben tilted his head to consider George. "You're not risking your life to help me and Nate patch up our relationship."

Something glimmered in George's eyes. She looked down. "I want the demon. I want it dead."

☆☆☆

The caravan was small, which only made the sheer volume of things inside it that much more incredible. Ben sat on the edge of the double bed nervously trying not to touch anything. He was entirely surrounded by mess. A bra lay tangled in the duvet thrown over the bed, a fuzzy slipper beside it. A dressing gown was folded over the back on one of the two built-in chairs. A jug boiled on one of two cooking elements. Every other piece of available space—the table, the window sills, the sink, the floor—was taken up by an assortment of notebooks, writing implements, clothing, magazines, and hair and make-up products.

"What's your poison?" George hunted through the cupboard above the sink. "I think I saw tea in here once—"

"Coffee's fine." There was a large can of instant on the counter.

"I got actual cream. Figured if I was going to entertain, I might as well do it properly."

Ben didn't have the heart to tell her he preferred milk. "Thank you." He accepted the cup and hesitated.

George watched him knowingly. "It's fine. I know what you're thinking. Go ahead and do your fancy magic checking thing."

Ben raised an eyebrow. *Then again, she already knows what I am.* "Do you have a piece of paper?"

Using magic still gave him a thrill. As a vampire, even basic spells like this divination to detect harm in the cup of coffee would have been impossible. It was based on the caster's life energy—energy a vampire lacked. Not even the fact that Ben drew his circle on loose-leaf with a biro rather than ink on parchment phased him—though the intense attention that George gave the rite came close. "It's only a basic divination."

"It may be basic to you, but it's fascinating to me."

Ben frowned, placing a hair from his own head in the center of his drawn circle. "This is a beginner level spell. You really haven't seen it before?"

"Not all of us could afford a magical education." George didn't take her eyes off Ben's work. "And this stuff you can't exactly find in a library."

Ben bit his lip. Knowing how to check that your food and drink was safe should be a basic requirement in an industry that hunted magic users. "The circle's the same every time. The hair gives it a target—me." He placed the coffee cup on the circle and extended his hand over it. The steam warmed his palm as he continued. "The command is simple. 'Do me no harm.' And the result—"

There was a brief blue flash, so quick that if it hadn't been for the corresponding tug, Ben might have thought he'd imagined it. "All good. See that the hair is gone? That—and the feeling of power drawn from you—is how you know it worked."

George whistled. "Can I keep that paper?"

"A moment." Ben lifted his cup off it. He marked the different sigils with a number. "You have to draw it in the correct order."

George studied the paper a long moment before folding it away. "You learned this at Uni?"

Ben shook his head. "I had a teacher." He wondered what Godfrey would make of George. Would he be shocked at Ben sharing the secrets of their trade?

No. Not Godfrey. Ben bit his lip. *Godfrey would want to protect her from herself.* "Is this what you want me for? My magic?"

"Among other things.' George picked up her own cup of coffee, leaning back against her sink. "Compared to you, I must seem like an absolute rookie, but I've been hunting for years. I know what cases I can and can't handle alone, and this one... Well, I've made it as far as I can on my own. I need knowledge I don't have. You have the contacts and the magical ability I need."

"You need your head checked." Ben shook his head, picking up his cup of coffee. "Attempting to kill a demon is..." He couldn't remember reading a case where it had been attempted, let alone when it had been successful.

George's face hardened. "I got my reasons."

"Harriet?"

"He's part of it," George conceded. "But this goes way beyond that." She pursed her brilliant pink lips, frowning at Ben.

"Tell me," Ben said. "I need to understand what you're willing to endanger Nate for."

There was the faintest glimmer of a smirk on George's face. "Not dating, huh?"

Ben raised an eyebrow. "You don't know an elementary protection charm, but you think you can kill a demon—and you're questioning my judgment?"

George's smirk disappeared instantly. "Got to give you that."

Ben watched her thoughtfully. She fought with the experience of a hunter, even if she hadn't been educated as one. "If there's one thing the police, ARX, and the hunting community all agree on, it's that demonic involvement is bad news. Killing one has never been done so far as I know—"

"It's been done," George said. "And it's going to be done again. Harriet and I had a plan." She set her coffee aside, gripping the edge of the sink with both palms. "I met Harriet on the forum way back in the day. I was an angry teenager with a burning desire for revenge. He channeled that rage into more productive outlets, even taught me a bit of sense. Most hunters eventually get over their desire for revenge, and either retire or hunt for profit. Harriet had more experience than anyone I knew, and he was never about the cash or the glory, but he'd never talked about revenge. I realized we were out for the same thing—the same demon." George's mouth twisted ironically. "We compared notes, pooled our knowledge. Harriet had a contact who got him his copy of 'On Monsters.' We figured out a way to not end the agent, but the demon—but to do that, we need the agent to summon the demon."

"Good luck with that."

George snorted. "I don't need luck. I just need a name." She crossed her arms across her chest. "I forget how the Winkler case cropped up on our radar. Harriet came down here to investigate. First we had to figure out whether or not it was tied to our demon or not. Harriet checked out the obvious local suspect—"

"Ethan?" Ben set his coffee down. "What did he find?"

George shook her head. "After we find our agent. Now, Ethan might have made a great contender for an agent himself—only thirteen at the time of Winkler's death, but by all accounts, he looked older. Could have appealed to a teenaged girl. He's rumored to have abilities no one is quite sure of—again, hallmark of a demon is to grant an agent power and wealth. Doesn't specify that they have to be monetary."

"But you don't think Ethan's involved."

George shook her head. "Harriet eliminated him from the investigation entirely."

"How?"

"I'll give you his notes once I know who the agent is and not a moment before then. Sorry, Ben—" George didn't sound even slightly sorry. "—but a girl needs insurance."

Ben nodded slowly. If it hadn't been for Ethan's confirmation that he'd met Harriet, he'd have left—or would he? Knowing what he did, could he walk away from the prospect of killing the demon, ending the cycle of victims once and for all—no matter how unlikely? "Go on."

"That's it? You're not going to lecture me about the possible danger or the damage to your boyfriend's emotional wellbeing?"

"No one forced Nate to get himself arrested," Ben said. "He's a grown man. He can make his own bad decisions." *As can I.*

George stared at him. "That must have been one hell of an argument you guys had." Her arm brushed her cup of coffee, and she picked it up almost absent-mindedly. "Anyway. After satisfying himself that Ethan wasn't involved, Harriet looked into the case. He concentrated on the Rockford side of things, visiting her family, the scene of the crime. That's where he made his discovery—"

"What discovery?"

"That's what I need you to find out." George wrapped her fingers around her cup. "Harriet was the face of our operation. He made all the inquiries. I'm the bait. If the agent works out I'm looking for him, then our plan's doomed."

"It's not looking all that great now." Ben remembered his coffee, taking a sip before continuing. "You told me yourself you're out of your league. The agent we're up against took out Harriet—so not only does he have experience of his own, but he's going to be on guard—and we don't even know where he is."

"I've got a secret weapon," George said. "But to remain a weapon, it—and me—have to remain secret. I know you've got no reason to think I can do this, but please, help me. All I need is the guy's name."

Ben narrowed his eyes. If George was looking to make a demonic contract of her own, there were more direct ways to go about it—ways that did not involve bringing her actions to the notice of an ARX—former ARX—agent. "How do you expect me to find that?"

George's smile was brilliant. "Retrace Harriet's steps. You can start by visiting the Winkler family. They still live in town. I can give you the address now. Then there's the scene of the crime—I'll send you the pin."

"The police will have done all this," Ben protested. "Multiple times. You really think I'll find something?"

George thumped him on the shoulder. "You're a hunter, aren't you?"

Ben shook his head. "You're giving me far, far too much credit."

"I don't think so." George watched him closely. "See, the hunters I talked about, the ones in New Camden? They don't like ARX, but the sheer amount of grudging respect they give it speaks for itself. You guys are good."

"We're trained to investigate. Not work miracles."

George smirked at him. "Hunters have a lot of interest in the competition—naturally. Especially ARX's night staff. And there's the funny thing. Seems they had a hunter by the name of Hawick who hasn't been seen since the necromancer killings—"

"You already know I worked for ARX—"

"But you left out the part where you worked nights. Even I know what that means." George grinned at Ben's discomfort. "And yet here you are. A vampire able to walk around in broad daylight. No—" She held up a hand to stop Ben's protest. "I'm not going to turn you in or ask how you did it. All I want is your help."

☆☆☆

The Winkler house was one of several identical houses. The paint on the weatherboard was peeling, but the yard was scrupulously tidy. A jeep was parked in the driveway, and laundry fluttered half-heartedly on the line as Ben parked. He saw the curtains twitch even before he rang the bell.

The Winklers didn't rush to answer the door. Ben looked around. Two sets of boots, caked with dirt, stood on the porch. Clearly the truck wasn't just for show. Were they farmers? Or farm adjacent? George hadn't shared whatever she knew about them.

Finally the door opened. "What do you want?"

Ben looked up at a stern-faced man. "Ben Hawick." Ben had a business card ready. "I'm investigating a recent death in Little River." He was counting on the familiar ARX logo to reassure and the toll charge of phoning New Camden to prevent anyone looking up his credentials. "Are you Mr. Winkler?"

The man took the card. He had the weathered hands of someone who worked the land. "We're not responsible for that hunter's death. He came round here to ask questions that once, but that was it. We're not liable— We didn't even know the man!"

"Exactly," Ben said crisply. "No one is suggesting that you did." He nodded to his card. "I want to know what you can tell me about Harriet's visit. That's all."

Mr. Winkler's mouth tightened. "ARX is insurance, isn't it? Supernatural insurance? We're not buying—"

"Insurance is part of our services," Ben agreed. "But in order to offer protection against supernatural threats to our clients, we have to know supernatural threats. Which means that in cases like this—where things go wrong—we investigate." Not technically untrue—but ARX agents usually limited themselves to cases that involved their clients.

"And you're not going to try and sell us anything?"

"Look at the card," Ben told him. "It says 'investigator.' Not 'sales.'" He paused. "You're under no obligation to talk to me," he admitted. "None at all. And you've probably had enough of talking with the police. But if you can spare me a couple of minutes, I'd really appreciate it."

Mr. Winkler looked down, his mouth setting into a grim satisfied line that lacked the something needed to become a smile. "You might as well come in."

A woman, presumably his wife, stood in the kitchen doorway, wiping her hands on her jeans. "Mrs. Winkler?" Ben repeated his introduction.

Mr. Winkler waved him towards a stiff armchair. "What do you want to know?" He sat on the sofa, and after a moment's hesitation, his wife joined him.

"Harriet came here to ask you about the death of your daughter, Olivia, right?" Ben was conscious of the need to sit up very straight. "What made you decide to talk to him?"

"Our local police had got nowhere fast," Mr. Winkler said. "They go through the motions of reopening the case every few years, but that's all it is. They're not going to solve it. The way the man Harriet put it, we had nothing to lose. Not like there was an ongoing investigation or anything."

"What did you talk about?" The room was plain, furnished with uninspired knick-knacks that could have been seen in hundreds of similar houses. The owners of the room didn't seem like they were prone to imagination.

"He wanted an account of Olivia's last days from us," Mrs. Winkler piped up. "In our own words. The sort of detail that gets left out of the court reports."

"He'd looked at the police reports?" Ben raised an eyebrow.

"Sure seemed like it." Mr. Winkler stroked his chin. "As he already knew most of it, there didn't seem any harm in telling him what was left."

"Would you mind going over Olivia's movements again?" Ben asked. "As close to what you told Harriet as possible."

The Winklers had clearly given this conversation several times. They barely paused, giving their account smoothly, as if they'd rehearsed it.

Ben listened thoughtfully. None of it was news to him—or, he thought, to Harriet. The guy had done his research. Still—he'd obviously found something. "Was it odd for Olivia to go off by herself?"

Mrs. Winkler shook her head. "She was usually by herself. She wasn't happy at school. She wasn't happy at home. She was a difficult teenager. Not like her sister..." Mrs. Winkler sighed, looking towards a photo on the mantelpiece. "That's her, there. You can see what I mean."

Ben stood to examine the photo. In the family group photo, Olivia was the only one not smiling. She stood a few steps distant from the group, an anxious girl with a thin, pinched mouth.

"She was going through a difficult patch," her mother continued. "Awkward. She'd discovered boys, but none were interested. She had a way of feeling sorry for herself that put people off. She could be quite exasperating, but none of us thought she was going to be murdered."

"Did she act differently in any way leading up to her death?" Ben asked.

"She did." Now they were on the subject of Olivia, Mr. Winkler was content to let his wife talk. She did with confidence. "As I told Harriet, she seemed a lot happier. I wondered who the boy was, but Olivia didn't tell me. I wasn't that worried. There's only so many people in Rockford. I knew that I'd hear about it in good time."

"How do you know it was a boy?"

"She took to wearing my perfume," Mrs. Winkler explained. "A fresh bottle, half-used in a matter of weeks! I had to have a word with her." She looked stricken. "That was the last time I talked to Olivia. Telling her she couldn't take it without permission. She blew up at me. She didn't come home that night after school. I thought she was angry. But when she never came home, even after it got dark..."

"The police will tell you how she was found," Mr. Winkler said. "We never saw her."

Ben sensed that the interview was over. He stood up. "Thanks for your time."

He drove out of town before pulling over to the side of the road to call George. "Well, I'm done with the Winklers."

George was less than impressed with the fruits of Ben's interview. "I could have told you all of that, and I've never even spoken to these people."

"It does confirm that the agent is someone who seduced Olivia. She took to wearing her mother's perfume before her death. Her family thought this was uncharacteristic." Ben glanced at the rear view mirror out of habit. The surrounding countryside was deserted, but it never paid to get too comfortable. "There's got to be a certain type of person willing to seduce a fifteen-year-old."

"Hate to break it to you, but creepy guys are a dime a dozen." George sniffed. "I can name you twenty right now, blowing up my phone with their pedo-ass shit."

Ben blinked. He hadn't given too much thought to George's plan, but now he had an inkling. "You're acting as bait for this agent?"

"He needs a victim for his ritual." George shrugged. "That's not what he's going to get."

"That is—" *Wrong on cosmic levels.* "—a really, really bad idea."

"Which is why he's never going to see it coming," George said. "You've still got the death site to check out, right? Get on it." She hung up.

Do I attract people with no self-preservation instincts? Or are the anti-integration lobby groups right and the supernatural presence just encouraging more reckless behavior in people? Ben waited for a truck to pass and pulled out onto the road. "At least no one can say it's dull." After Little River, New Camden might actually seem relaxing.

☆☆☆

Olivia died in a field. Ben parked the truck at the side of the road and climbed a fence to get to the spot. He found it at once. The blanket fragments mentioned in the police report were long gone, as was the shape of the circle in the grass, but the scars remained. The ground within the circle, and quite a lot of that surrounding, was cracked and dry. Nothing would grow there, not unless a purification rite of some kind was performed.

Ben looked down at the barren grass.

Olivia had been excited. Maybe nervous, but for the ritual to have worked, she must have been genuinely infatuated with whoever killed her. For a brief, very brief time, she'd been happy.

How can he do that? How— Ben clenched his fists, feeling himself start to shake. He'd been able to view the case dispassionately until he'd seen Olivia's photo. That anxious, worn look, the odd one out in a happy, confident family, it had struck a chord too close to home for Ben.

Ben mentally caught himself. He shook his head, setting his hands back in his pockets. *I'll have to ask George if Harriet was an awkward teenager.*

He looked around the rest of the field. It was far from town, out of sight from any houses, and with the slight dip that the circle was in, anyone sitting would have been shielded from view from the road. A spot perfectly suited to the agent's needs — and once again, impossible to guess how he came across it.

A local? But the police had employed specially trained sniffer dogs to seek out any traces of sulfur or brimstone. They'd found nothing on any Rockford resident.

Someone scouting out the land would have been noticed. Ben glanced around the field, hoping against hope for any inspiration. No one mentioned anyone suspicious...

Ben's rented car stood out as the only man-made thing in his surroundings. The fences, made from posts of natural timber, seemed like they'd escaped the bush, which strained at the ill-maintained boundary. A couple of seedlings were visible above the grass.

No surprise the field's neglected, given its history. Maybe that was why Ben felt so uneasy, so aware of his isolation. With nothing between him and the elements, he was entirely unprotected. Anything could happen —

A voice howled.

Nothing human made that sound! Ben spun towards the forest. He braced himself, mentally running through possible causes — *Banshee haunt isolated places — farms aren't usually on the list! Far too inland for morgenau* — before he became aware of an undercurrent of sound, rushing towards him like thousands of feet marching in unison. The forest didn't even ripple, but Ben caught fleeting glimpses of a shape passing — and passing — through the trees.

"This is it." Harriet must have been here at the same moment Ben had, caught the exact same phenomenon. "A train!"

If someone hopped on and off the train lines, they'd be able to size up the surrounding countryside without anyone being the wiser. Ben thought rapidly. *There was a railway crossing before we entered Little River too — it all adds up.* Was this the break Harriet had found? Ben started towards the car. *Only one way to find out.*

☆☆☆

"Is that laptop secure?"

George jumped as Ben swung open the door of the Airstream, kicking off his shoes in the doorway. She was sitting at the table, music blaring from the speakers of the laptop. Another amateur mistake—a hunter needed to be able to hear their surroundings, even in daylight. Now, it was already evening, the sun setting as Ben drove back to the campground.

"Don't bother saying hi or anything!" She caught sight of Ben's expression. "You found something."

"I think so—but I want to make sure first." Ben slid into the seat opposite George and took out his phone.

George turned the music off. "Who are you calling?"

"Department Seven." As he dialed, Ben was aware that George was watching him with avid attention. "Don't get excited," he told her. "It is extremely unlikely I'm going to get anything but a headache out of this— Yes, Department Seven? I'd like to speak to Officer Gunn."

George whistled. "Going straight to the top."

Ben looked at her. "How do you know Gunn?"

"I lurk on a lot of forums. Hunters in New Camden argue about everything. Disliking Gunn is the one thing they seem to agree on." George paused. "Is he really that—"

"Yes," Ben said, turning quickly away as he was taken off hold. "Gunn?"

"Officer Gunn is sadly unavailable right now." The voice was female and officiously bland, but Ben thought he recognized it. "If this is an official matter, I can relay you to the appropriate staff member—"

"Kenzie?" Ben asked.

There was a pause as the speaker digested his question. "Hawick?"

"Right. What's happened to Gunn?"

He held the phone away from his ear as Kenzie barked in laughter. "Chicken pox."

"Really?" It was incredibly unprofessional to be grinning this much. Not only that but incredibly irresponsible. Ben knew full well chicken pox in adults was a much more serious occurrence, with greater risks... Although it was hard to imagine any of those risks affecting a *lemur* like Gunn.

"Turns out that Gunn's from a time before immunizations," Kenzie continued.

Ben could not stop grinning. "He's on sick leave?"

"We got five days." All of Kenzie' crisp professional attitude couldn't prevent a note of happiness creeping into her voice. "Five glorious days without him. We're looking into giving him measles next."

"Mumps, too." Ben caught George's eye and remembered he had work to do. "I'm calling about the supernatural crimes database. I was hoping you wouldn't mind running a search for me."

Ben could hear the frown in Kenzie' reply. Unlike her superior officer, she followed the rules. "Access to the database is restricted to Department Seven or personnel approved by us. You need to fill out a permissions form—"

"Send me one with the data," Ben said. "I know it's irregular, but time is short— We're up against a demonic agent on a timeline. I'm looking for details of demonic killings related to the case in Little River and my—mother's death."

He could feel the skin on the back of his neck crawl as George stared at him.

"Looking up related crimes, searching for a pattern?" Kenzie sounded thoughtful.

"That's right. I want any unexplained or unsolved supernatural murders that fit the profile of the Olivia Winkler case—victim young, socially isolated, killing occurred in a deserted location—along a train line."

"That's it? A train line?"

Ben ignored George, waiting for Kenzie' response. "Look, the sheriff here consulted me on the case already. I promise any results I find that might have bearing on the case I'll take to her."

"All right," Kenzie decided. "I'll run the search. I should have the results for you tomorrow morning. Where do you want them sent?"

Ben gave her his e-mail address. "Thanks, Kenzie."

"Give my regards to your boyfriend."

"He's not—" It was too late. Kenzie had hung up. Ben sighed, turning to report to George. "Officer Kenzie is going to—"

"Your big break is trains?"

"It makes a lot of sense, okay? Olivia Winkler died in a field really close to the train tracks, the timber yard is right on the tracks. By hopping on and off the trains at will, the agent could scope out the lay of the land without attracting too much attention."

"Huh." George mulled it over. "Hopping on and off—you're ruling out train staff."

Ben nodded. "Although it's possible that they might know something about our guy."

"I'll take a look at traveler forums while we wait," George decided. "And in the meantime, you can tell me what you meant by your mother's death." She fixed Ben with a stern glare.

It was much too late for backing out, Ben realized. "My mother. It's—a long story."

"We got time. Plenty of it. Police move fast when delivering parking fines, but that's it."

"If I'm telling you about my mother, I want to hear your story."

"What makes you think I have a story?"

Ben raised an eyebrow. "You're here."

"What, a girl can't be addicted to a little danger?" George sighed. "Have it your way. I didn't have a great childhood."

"What you told the Grangers about hiking with your father...?"

George shook her head. "Both my parents were addicts, they were in and out of our life. My older sister raised me and my baby brother. She quit school to put food on the table, was more of a parent to us than our real parents combined. She worked herself to the bone to see that we finished high school and finally, when we're both off at college, and she's got a chance to have a life of her own, she falls for a user. Not drugs—this guy used her for everything he could. She cooked his meals, paid his rent, bought his fancy sneakers—but that wasn't enough. In the end, he took her soul, too."

George's mouth was a thin, flat line, her face stark with remembered sorrow. "The official investigation stalled. Miami's a big city, there's hundreds of ways you can have contact with a demon and not know. He bragged about being untouchable— He fucking bragged." George took a moment to get herself under control. "I started looking for any evidence that he knew more. I didn't know it then, but Harriet was already investigating, on his own dime. We teamed up— There's stuff people will say to a girl that they won't to a man and vice-versa. We found what we needed to prove that he was complicit in her death. My sister was found barefoot in the kitchen." George looked down. "She hated bare feet. She wore slippers if she was at home. We looked around. Bastard bought her shoes, left them at home as a surprise to her then went out with his friends. Called her to see if she was enjoying them. The circle was written on them." George's lip curled. "When she thanked him—"

"It's the same demon then." Ben frowned.

George nodded. "As far as I can make out, it is. Harriet's been after it for decades. Anyway, the bastard's doing time for murder. He's going to be in there still when his time runs out. Not even good behavior will save him. He spilled his cowardly guts to Harriet, told us all he knew about Gaassimolar. That got us enough to go on to profile the victims, identify related cases—and eventually, brought us to Rockford." George shook her head. "Most fucked up thing about this is that if we succeed and end this demon, we're going to save that fucking murderer's life."

"But you're not going to walk away and let him die?"

"I won't lie. The thought of him getting his is really tempting... But when it comes down to it, Sis would never have condoned it." George shook her head. "I can't accept that there's going to be more victims. As long as Gaassimolar's out there, he's going to keep working his scam, and people are going to keep accepting it. And that—" She shrugged. "I can't accept that."

Ben nodded slowly, acutely aware of how ready he'd been to walk away from the case. "My mother. Well." He grimaced. "My parents owned an apartment block in New Camden. We lived on the top floor, but there was an apartment on the floor below that wouldn't stay occupied for longer than a week. Naturally, rumors went around the building that it was haunted. Soon as I heard that, I had to explore it. I loved anything related to the supernatural, so I spent hours in that apartment, trying to coax the ghost out to play. Eventually I succeeded." A faint smile creased Ben's face at the memory. "Jean—the ghost—was lonely, I think. One small child was not as threatening as the adults that came through with furniture, completely rearranging the apartment and filling it with noise. He played hide and seek with me. Everything was fine until my ninth birthday. My mother was always very protective, now it seemed like she guarded me constantly. I wasn't allowed to play by myself in the apartment anymore. I rebelled, and to punish me, my mother threatened to leave. She packed her suitcase and was all set to walk out the door—unless I made a special promise to love her forever."

"A promise made in the middle of a demonic circle?" George stared at him. "Shit."

It was easier to talk than Ben had imagined. Instead of choking him, the words came more easily. Part of it was because George listened like someone who knew. Part of it was that this wasn't the first time. *Has my silence been hurting me?* Ben detailed his father's discovery and what followed, a part of his mind marveling at how matter of fact he sounded. *These events... They're sad. I still grieve for my parents, but...they no longer define me.* He finished his story.

"That is fucked up." George reached across the table to thump Ben on the arm. "I'm sorry. But hey, if it helps any, I haven't noticed any danger signs from you."

Ben's smile was rueful. "That means a lot."

"It means more than you think." George nudged him playfully. "I was going to make you sleep in your car. Now..."

Ben froze. "Now?" George knew about Nate. She wasn't flirting with him, was she?

George laughed at his expression. "There's an air mattress in here somewhere. You can crash on the floor."

Ben looked down at the mess. About to protest that the motel in Rockford wasn't that far away, he caught sight of the divination he'd drawn George, pinned to the RV wall. *For a hunter to trust anyone is a big deal. To go to the lengths of inviting them to stay...* "I'd be honored."

"Don't feel too special. You're going to be pumping the damn thing yourself." George stood. "Now, where'd I put that thing..." But her smile was at odds with her words.

Chapter Sixteen

It was bright. Too bright.

Ben froze.

The muffled light was dawn. His body was rigid, impossible to move. He was trapped, alive in a dead body, helpless to prevent anyone from opening the curtains—

Move! I have to—have to—

Ben fought the cold rigor mortis settling over him. It gave way abruptly, and Ben thrashed on the ground—

"Jesus!" The voice shocked him into stillness. "Are you all right?"

Ben looked down at himself. He was shaking, his skin cold and clammy, George's duvet draped over his legs. *Fear,* he realized. *Not death.* "Sorry," he mumbled. "Sorry. It was—" He swallowed. "A bad dream."

"In this profession? We all have nightmares." George sat up. Out of respect for what she termed Ben's 'delicate sensibilities,' she'd slept in a T-shirt and sweatpants. "Least you didn't wake up screaming." She swung her legs over the edge of the bed. "Coffee?" She reached for the jug.

Ben had to shift position so that George could reach the kitchen unit. The air mattress took up most of what floor space the RV had. "Did I wake you?"

"I was half-awake already. Nightmares of my own." George looked down at him. "Kind of surprised I didn't wake you, actually."

"What kind of nightmare?" Ben rested his back against the caravan seats. He shut his eyes, trying not to compare its support to Nate's arms, but the stab of loss was immediate.

Nate—

"The usual." George shrugged, rinsing out two mugs in preparation for the coffee she was about to make. "Whatever horrific stuff I've seen in the day job plus a good dose of 'You're going to die and it's going to be horrible'."

As she turned her back, Ben caught sight again of the scarred patch on her neck. He stood.

"They usually fade over time, but ever since Harriet died, they've been more frequent. I guess—" George froze.

Ben took his hand away quickly. "Sorry," he said. "I should have asked."

George let a breath out, placing a hand over the scar on her neck. "You're very lucky you didn't get a kick in the nuts just then."

"I'd have deserved it," Ben said frankly. Until he'd felt George tense, he hadn't even thought about the implications of touching her. "I thought 'vampire' and reacted automatically. It's— It is vampire, isn't it?"

George nodded. "Revenant. One of my first solo gigs. Harriet didn't want me to take it, but I wanted to prove I could handle it. All I proved was that I made a very attractive meal to vampires. Luckily, Harriet had second thoughts about letting me handle the job on my own. He was there to end the thing before it ended me." She glanced at Ben. "Where's yours?"

He pulled back his hair so that she could see the two puncture marks in his neck.

"No fair. I get a scar, you get almost nothing."

"Dead flesh reacts different to living," Ben reminded her. "It's not on purpose."

"Even so." George bit her lip. "If you die—again, I mean—"

Ben knew where the question was going. "I'll become a vampire again," he said. "I don't see how I couldn't. I've been exposed to so much of it in the last year... I'm pretty sure it's inevitable."

"And that doesn't freak you out?" When Ben shook his head, George tilted hers. "Because you've experienced it?"

"Worse," Ben said with certainty. "I know exactly what it will be like."

George looked at him. Her mouth was half-open, for once without lipstick. She looked as if she was on the verge of asking but aware she might regret the question.

"You're not yourself." Ben looked down. He picked up a biro resting on the table, tapped it against some papers just to assure himself his body was his to control. "You're never alone. It's like having another person right there with you, in your head, looking out from behind your eyes, always waiting for its chance to get out."

"But I thought you were one of the—" George caught herself.

Ben smiled at her, but from the look on her face, he didn't think it was successful. "One of the lucky ones? No such thing. You fought a revenant, right? Getting up close and personal with one is bad enough. Imagine coexisting with one inside your own skin..."

George shuddered. "Harriet said the same thing. That if his time came, he didn't want to be brought back. Not that I would, of course, but—"

Ben understood that. In a world where monsters of myth and legend were reality, cancer had lost none of its power. The immortal life of vampires held no hope to humans and their numbered lifespans. It was a strange joke, made stranger by the lack of punchline. Still, there were those who hoped, fought against all reason, to find some kind of life in the undead, realizing too late that they simply prolonged their inevitable death. Any hunters with such beliefs inevitably lost them in the business of their work. Seeing what unnatural life did to those in its thrall was the best argument against resurrection.

"It's not extended life so much as a prolonged death," Ben said. "Being in control of my thought processes didn't change that, it just meant that every moment I was aware of what I was and what I was not. I died again, every single dawn. You can feel it, the exact moment when your body turns against you and you become—"

"Enough." George shook her head, picking up her cup. "This is only my first cup of coffee. I need to be on my second before I'm ready for this level of doom and gloom." But she was thoughtful as she sipped her drink. "You killed many vamps?"

"Lots." An alarming amount when you considered it really. But for that one year, it had been his only saving grace. Yes, he was a monster, but he could spend that vampiric killing instinct on those more monstrous than himself... "Why? You're not worried about my qualifications?"

George shook her head. "I need someone to make sure I don't walk."

Ben's fingers closed around the pen. He wasn't expecting the request.

"Harriet was going to. I assumed I'd die before him." George frowned, picking at the fuzz on the sleeve of her fluffy dressing gown. "You never met Harriet. He was a great guy. Calm, never bothered by anything. I guess it was convenient to imagine he'd always be here. Always complaining about the coffee, that I spent too much time flirting, not enough time on the job... He was good at it. Too good to be dead this soon."

Ben swallowed. There was an unmistakable note of mourning in George's voice.

After a moment's pause, she continued. "I can't ask my family, and Harriet was my only friend in the biz. When I die, I need someone to put me down before I hurt anyone. I'm tainted. The revenant's bite–"

"I know." Ben took a deep breath. He'd thought this life was behind him, but there was no way he could turn down this request. "I can do it."

The smile George gave him was genuine. "I'll do the same for you," she promised. "Unless you've already got someone lined up."

"Actually, I don't." It was one of the first things he should have done leaving ARX. Ben frowned. There was only one person he could have asked, and...

He couldn't inflict this on Nate. Providing, of course, he could even make Nate see the necessity of it.

Nate loved me even as a monster. Ben bit his lip. *Risked his life to save me as a vampire.* He could not imagine Nate standing by his grave with an ax, waiting.

"So that's settled." George spoke loudly to cover her genuine relief. "You want to look at my messages with me while we wait for Kenzie to get back to you? You can help me decide who to pass on to the authorities as possible predators, and who to flag for further investigation."

Ben cautiously joined George on her side of the table. "Sounds like fun—" He stared at her screen. "That is a lot of messages."

"Brace yourself, Benjamin. You're going to learn things about humankind you never wanted to know."

"It's Bennet, actually." Ben stared at the laptop screen with dismay. "And you're really going to meet these people?"

"Not unless I absolutely have to." George brought up the first series of messages. "Eager to get our hypothetical fifteen-year-old alone, but pushing the fun, not the romance. My gut says pred."

"Can we look him up elsewhere?" Rockford's laptop selection came to mind again. Ben drummed his fingers against the table. A laptop was preferable to no laptop, even if the selection was severely limited...

"I'm going to do something I don't do for just anyone. Get out your phone, Bennet. I'm giving you my Wi-Fi password."

A depressing indictment on the state of mankind followed. Was there no end to the amount of people willing to encourage a supposedly teenage girl to share intimate pics or meet up with them in person? Ben's anger numbed into a deep disgust. George was tireless in clicking 'report as inappropriate.' The worst offenders she set aside to be brought to police attention.

"What happens if you do find the agent?" Ben asked, watching as George shifted another possible, a man with blond dreadlocks and a metal eyebrow stud, to the 'possible agent' file. "Obviously you're not fifteen. He's going to know something's off when you show up."

"Once I find the guy, I got a new line to sell him." George was already clicking her way through the next series of messages. "A poor, bewildered young woman, who has left the religious community in which she was strictly raised, and is finding herself lost and alone in the big, bad world. In desperate need of a protector, and far too ready to confuse gratitude with love."

"It's too dangerous."

"What, and hunting revenants isn't?" George turned to face Ben. "I'm a hunter, remember. And a capable hunter. I can handle—"

Ben's phone rang. He grabbed it, hitting accept call. "Kenzie?"

"Hawick." There was a formal note in her voice. "Before I can send the file, I have to read you a caution."

Ben felt his heart beat. The only way Kenzie would need to read him a caution was if they'd found something. "What did you find?"

"Demons and their associates are a known risk to human life and well-being, recognized as such by the Council for Supernatural Understanding. In accordance with the guidelines laid down by Federal Law, I have to remind you that fraternization with demons in any form is considered a Class A offense and is prosecuted harshly under the laws of this country. I must also remind you that pursuing knowledge of demonic law and practices related to the summoning thereof, and possession of classified material related to their summoning without an appropriate license is an offense punishable by imprisonment. Any evidence of demonic involvement discovered should be communicated to the police without delay. Do you understand the risks and liabilities involved in accepting these files?"

Had she got that memorized? Ben sat up straight, nodding even though Kenzie couldn't see him. "Yes, Ma'am."

"And you are still willing to receive them?"

"Absolutely."

Kenzie did not sound at all surprised. "I'll send them now. I've already forwarded the results of my search to the sheriff's office. You're on to something, Hawick. A string of unsolved deaths within the railway, going back at least seventy years—all at regular ten-year intervals."

"Seventy years?"

"The guy's good at what he does," Kenzie said with a growl. "We had no idea these deaths were linked. Won't know for sure until we've looked into these cases, but on the surface, it looks pretty clear cut. It's all one agent—and we'd have had no idea if you hadn't spotted the railway line."

"Right place, right time," Ben said. "That's all it was."

"Local police are too used to the place. The train could have gone right past them, and it would only have registered as background noise." Kenzie hesitated. "Now you're a free agent, you considered working for the Department? You could do a world of good."

"Never," Ben said immediately. "Working with Gunn— You know that's not a possibility."

Kenzie sighed. "There's a reason we banned him from the recruitment procedures. Still. You ever change your mind, let me know right away."

Ben ended the phone call to find that George was waiting, the laptop already opened to a fresh window and turned towards him. "You caught that?"

"I caught enough to know that we've got a serious lead." George held herself in check with impatience as Ben logged into his mail and downloaded the file. "Let's have it."

The map was grim but perfectly clear. The correlation was too neat to be coincidence. Ben and George studied it in silence for a long moment before, with a sigh, George brought up the first of the victims. "Fourteen years old. Jesus Christ, people suck."

Ben frowned, studying the list of names of the victims. Most were girls, but there were two boys among them. He looked back to the map, mentally charting the position of Nate's barn onto it.

It fit the pattern exactly.

"George, I'll leave looking into the files to you."

"What?" George's gaze jerked away from the computer. "You just found the break we've all been searching for, and you're walking away from it?"

Ben retrieved his car keys and phone from the table. "I've got a visit to make."

☆☆☆

"Visiting twice in two days." Nate leaned back in his chair, crossing his arms over his chest. The plain T-shirt of the prison uniform was ill-prepared for Nate's powerful biceps, riding up to allow a full view of his muscles. Aki's words popped into Ben's mind. *A great bod... Amazing body when you think of it actually.* Just one more thing Ben and Nate did not have in common. "Didn't think you cared about me." There was hurt in the challenge.

Ben put his hand on the plastic. The barrier between them was painful, but in some ways, without the temptation to put his hand on Nate's shoulder and ease his sorrow, it was easier to speak. "You know I care."

"Do I?" There was definite challenge in the look Nate gave him.

Even on the wrong side of the plastic barrier, Nate possessed confidence that Ben couldn't even dream of attaining. Secure not just in himself, but in Ben's perception of him. For the first time, Ben questioned the hunch that had brought him back to the prison. Nate was simply too confident to be taken advantage of.

But as the silence between them stretched out, Ben saw a flicker of something that put him in mind of the anxious kid of the photo album... "Tell me about Sandy."

Nate raised both eyebrows. "Sandy? Why Sandy?"

"Aki mentioned he was in New Camden, trying to find you."

"Are you accusing me of cheating now? You're the one who decided we weren't dating—not to mention the fact that I'm in solitary over here."

"You shouldn't be in solitary." Ben glanced around, but there was no guard he could speak to. "That's a serious breach of procedure—"

"Well, not *solitary* solitary. But it might as well be. There's a special, more secure ward for supernatural prisoners. Right now it's just me and some kind of werewolf? I don't know. The guy seems like he wouldn't hurt a fly."

"Don't annoy a werewolf, Nate."

"I'm not going to! Anyway, I'm here as Ethan, remember? Who could possibly get mad at him?"

I'm not touching that. Ben gave Nate a flat look. "When did you meet Sandy?"

"You sure you want to hear this? I mean, we're not dating—" Nate caught Ben's expression and sat up. "What's going on? You found something?"

"That's what I need to work out."

"Well, you're barking completely up the wrong tree." Nate settled back in the chair. "Sandy's got nothing to do with the demonic murders at all."

"If you want to convince me, you've going to have to elaborate."

"Fine. Though for the record, I'm willing to talk about my romantic history without the excuse of supernatural investigations."

Ben resisted the impulse to roll his eyes. "As long as you talk." He glanced at the clock in the visiting room. They had limited time.

"It must have been our first year of high school. I was just about as miserable as you would expect." Nate shrugged. "New school, lots of new classmates who hadn't grown up with Ethan and weren't used to him. They picked on him, and our Little River classmates, eager to make friends, joined in the fun. Didn't help that we were a head taller than anyone else in our classes—we stuck out in all the wrong ways. Ethan didn't care—he never has—but I cared a lot." Nate brushed his hair out of his eyes. "At the same time, I realized for the first time just how different me and Ethan were. At a time when I needed a friend more than anything else, my best friend was growing rapidly apart from me. It sucked. I didn't think it was ever going to get better."

Ben nodded. "And then you met Sandy?"

Nate nodded. "He was camping beneath our bridge. Trespassing, technically, but I wasn't going to turn him in."

"You met him under a bridge."

"I was going to take you there. Thought you'd appreciate it." Nate smirked at him. "It's popular with travelers, literally covered in graffiti—like our own little piece of New Camden."

"Shut up." But despite everything, Ben had to fight a smile. He looked at his notebook, reminding himself that he was a serious investigator. "Sandy was a...traveler?"

"Yeah." Nate's gaze drifted to the ceiling, a smile playing across his mouth. "He was the coolest guy I'd ever met. No one in Little River had a tattoo. He had seven. He let me see them all." A note of enthusiasm had crept into Nate's voice. "And piercings."

"You became—friends?"

"Yeah. Best thing that ever happened to me." Nate glanced quickly at Ben. "It was soon after Dad got sick. He needed help running the farm. I persuaded him to give Sandy a chance, and he agreed to take him on for a season. We fixed him up a place to sleep in the barn—" He faltered.

"So, he did know about the barn."

Nate sat up, shaking his head vehemently. "It's not like that. Ben, you can't think that!"

"Did you hang out with Sandy in the barn?"

"Yeah, but—there was nothing demonic about that at all! It's monstrous—"

"Demons are monstrous." Ben clutched his notebook. "You became close friends. According to Aki, you had a serious crush on him?"

"More than a crush." Nate scratched the back of his neck. "It's kind of embarrassing now, but I worshiped the guy. No one'd ever paid attention to me before, so it was all totally new." Nate ducked his head. "It completely turned my life around. For the first time ever, I felt like I mattered—and it showed. I stopped shying away from talking to classmates, put my hand up in class. I made friends. People liked me—and it was all thanks to Sandy. Not that I cared about any of that. At the time, Sandy was all I needed."

Ben swallowed. His chest had squeezed painfully tight like something was choking him from the inside out. With effort, he kept his tone detached. "When did you become more than friends?"

"I don't know. Since I'd never met anyone like him, it never occurred to me it wasn't an ordinary friendship until he told me."

Ben took a deep breath. "Did he ask you if you"—his voice shook—"loved him?"

"Yeah."

The guard rapped on the door behind Ben. "Two minutes."

Ben stood up. "Nate, did Sandy ever ask you to prove your love?"

"No. Nothing." Nate frowned. "I mean, we talked about sex. Teenager with a hot boyfriend...I was all about it. Sandy thought it should be special. Meaningful. He wanted it to be romantic. He told me he was going to get things set up. And then he just"—Nate shrugged—"disappeared."

"And you haven't heard from him since?"

Nate shook his head. "My guess at the time was that he'd found out my real age and freaked out. I told him I was fifteen—didn't want him thinking I was some dumb kid. Ethan and I, we looked a lot older than the rest of our class—no one could have guessed we were only thirteen. Which hurt a little, but at the same time, I took it as further proof he cared and wanted to do the right thing."

"Really." Fifteen was still underage. Did Nate not see how wrong this was? As Ben met Nate's expression, he answered his own question. Nate believed totally in what he was saying.

"So you see that Sandy couldn't possibly be the agent," Nate said, as the guard rapped on the door to announce Ben's time was up. "A demonic agent wouldn't have cared about anything beyond getting his next victim. Right, Ben?"

Nate had no right to look at him so trustingly. None at all. "I have to go."

☆☆☆

Ben found the bridge without problem. The road divided the Granger's farm from the neighboring property, and the bridge, a heavy concrete construction, was part of it. Ben left his rental car at the side of the road and climbed over the fence to get a better look.

Either side of the river, the land rose sharply, meaning that the road and bridge were higher than the surrounding fields. A lot of concrete had been provided to stop the gaps, and the bridge that eventuated was a massive industrial eyesore, completely out of place in the rural valley.

Ben eyed it skeptically. *Nate was joking. He had to be.* Yeah, Ben was from New Camden, and possibly feeling more than a little homesick for his city—but he still had eyes. *He can't possibly think I would like this, can he?*

Or was there more to the bridge than met the eye? The fence had been patched with mesh and board, presumably to stop farm animals swimming in or out. One of the boards was easily lifted up, and Ben squeezed through the gap to find himself in a large open space. The concrete supports that held up the bridge had necessitated a sturdy base, so either side of the river—tiny in comparison to the scale of the bridge—was a large, concrete slab upon which the river had deposited a coating of very fine sand. Light shone in through the gaps at the top of the fence, illuminating the space.

Shoe marks in the dirt indicated the space had been visited recently. From the number of footmarks, Ben guessed the police had made a better search of the farm itself than of the barn. And no wonder—the amount of paint on the underside of the bridge revealed it was a popular haven for drifters. Ben gave the circle of ashes amongst the dirt a cursory inspection, deciding that they were the result of nothing more alarming than a campfire, and turned his attention to the graffiti.

Most were tags, the kind that adorned any part of New Camden that didn't have security cameras pointed at them. A few seemed to be advice of some kind, or commentary on the general state of the nation, the travelers having strong opinions of the society they'd opted out of. A couple were genuine artists, a striking mandala-like design taking up a good chunk of prime eye-level concrete, and a recognizable caricature of the sheriff—she didn't seem to be popular. But there was nothing that gave Ben any further clue.

He found himself standing by the ashes of the campfire again. The police hadn't camped here. Had the fire been made before or after their search? *I just don't know.*

Ben sighed, shoving his hands into his pockets as he looked around the under bridge. *What I need is to know what happened ten years ago. And for that...* He squeezed back through the boards, returning to his rental car. *Nate's not the only member of his family with an opinion about Sandy.*

☆☆☆

Ma's normally tightly bound hair was in disarray, strands escaping in every direction. She made a half-hearted effort to fix it but forgot it once Ben stated his errand. "Sandy? Of course I remember... It was a while ago now, but we don't have many guests and him leaving like that left Mitch and I in a bit of a fix over the farm."

"Can I come in?"

Ma stepped out of the doorway without hesitation. "It's a bit of a mess," she said. "Now that it's just me at home, I can't find it in me to keep up the house."

The sink, full of unwashed dishes, indicated that was the truth. "How about I wash and you dry," Ben suggested, "and you can tell me about Sandy as we go."

Ma protested, but in the end, the need for conversation overrode her hospitality. "Sandy wasn't the sort of person I would normally approve of," she admitted. "And he had a lot of influence over Nate. Mitch didn't think there was anything in it—the sort of harmless hero-worship a boy has—but I felt that Nate spent too much time alone with him. Still, he could quote the Bible easy as you like, and he sang in church as sweet as a choirboy even if he looked an absolute disgrace. He worked hard too, and there was nothing I could fault in him, but all the same... It was a relief when he left."

"And you don't know why he left?"

Ma shook her head. "We never had a formal contract worked out, just a loose sort of agreement. But I do think that if he'd got bored of it, he could have told us."

As Ma put away the newly washed dishes, Ben opened the fridge. "When was the last time you went shopping?"

Ma shook her head. "I can't. The way people look at me..."

"You can't go on like this. Write me a list." Ben patted her arm. "You gave me a place to stay when I needed it," he said. "This is the least I can do."

"You won't be popular around here if you're seen helping me," Ma warned. "The pastor himself stood up and said I was an ungodly woman, raising my sons to be demon-bound hedonists."

"The pastor needs a primer on the differences between demonic entities and natural magic," Ben said. "I guess it's just as well I'm not a believer."

Ma needed time to write her list. The empty house, so different to what it usually was, weighed on Ben. He headed outside. At least the mountains were only usual levels of oppressive. As he walked through the garden, a splash of color caught his eye. Ben paused in front of a flower bed.

The last time I saw this...wasn't it trampled into the dirt? He looked around, but there was no sign of damage to the garden at all—or even neglect. Ben knelt by the nearest flower, tugging it towards him. *Is this a dahlia?* Whatever it was, it was in perfect health.

Ben looked around. Not just the flower bed, but the entire garden looked in perfect order.

He hadn't asked Ma or Nate where Ethan was. Nate might be able to pass as his brother, but there was no way Ethan could ever pull off his younger twin. *So where is he?* The amount of dishes in the sink indicated clearly that Ma was alone in the house.

There was no sign of Ethan in the orchard. Ben climbed the stile, following the hiking trail through the woods.

It's too quiet. When he'd walked the trail with Nate, there had been birdsong, the rustling of leaves. Now it felt like the entire forest held its breath. Ben's footsteps sounded unnaturally loud and every twig he stepped on snapped with a resounding echo. *Something is there.*

Ben stopped walking.

It had been there since he'd first arrived in Little River. The pressure he'd felt standing in the garden looking up at the trees. Ben wiped his palms on his jeans. *This isn't imagination. This is—a presence. A powerful presence.* And he was right in the middle of its territory.

Ben breathed out, steeling himself. In the absence of distracting sounds, it was easier to identify the direction of the presence. Like playing hot and cold with an unknown supernatural entity. Taking a second to nerve himself, Ben stepped off the path and into the woods.

This is the stupidest thing I've done in ages. He would get lost within seconds—and who was to say the being he was tracking would even stay in the same place? Every step Ben took away from the path was an invitation to disaster.

And still, he kept walking.

If nothing else, there's a compass on my phone—

Ben stumbled, finding himself on his knees in the leaf bed. As he crawled to his feet, he discovered his foot was caught on something. A piece of wire stretched out in the dirt. Ben tugged at it, discovered that it was attached to a decaying post. "A fence?"

Pushing back the brush, Ben discovered further posts, almost entirely covered by moss or dead leaves, the wire rusted. He looked around, but no other signs existed to indicate private property. He continued on his way, careful to check where he walked.

There were other fences. There was even a barn, the roof collapsed in, and the branches of an apple tree extending out of it. The rusted remains of a truck were parked nearby.

Ben rested one foot on the bumper and considered the truck. He'd never seen anything like it on a road. The high wheel guards and the pinched shape of the engine put it somewhere roughly in the forties, maybe fifties. The amount of rust and the bush growing within it agreed with Ben's assessment. *This was a farm.* If the truck was any indicator, it had been a farm roughly seventy years ago. And now, it wasn't just abandoned. The forest had swallowed it up to an alarming degree.

Is this seventy years of forest? It should have taken years, surely for the trees to creep slowly across the fields, but the trees Ben passed were well established.

He took a moment to study them. Oak? He was pretty sure they were oak. The wavy shape of the leaf was just as he remembered from Mason's Park. *Oak is a sturdy protector against misfortune.* Ben reminded himself of Godfrey's teachings. He looked at the ground, hoping to find an acorn he could pocket for luck.

Instead, he found a spiky, green shell. Ben picked it up, turning it over in his hands before deciding to crack it open. Inside were three smooth brown nuts. Ben prized one loose for a closer look.

Chestnut? All the chestnut trees were gone, weren't they, killed by the blight Nate had mentioned?

Ben looked around, but the only trees he could see were oak. He put the nut in his pocket and continued his exploration.

The silence grew more pronounced. Now that he was among it, Ben wondered if the hostile edge had been his own instinctive response to something bigger, something outside his knowledge. He made his way through the trees, feeling he was approaching the source. An overgrown tangle of apple trees revealed the remains of an orchard, and a splash of color up ahead indicated a garden. The flowers had escaped the stone fence that had once marked the perimeter to grow freely amongst the forest. Ben quickened his pace as he caught sight of a building in the trees. *The Winnaker farmstead. It must be.*

The house was just as it had been left all those decades ago. The windows were caked with dirt and moss grew freely over the porch and steps. Tree leaves littered the porch and the roof, still in one piece but now home to a precariously perched rowan. Ben studied the plant a moment, remembering he'd once had a rowan to thank for saving his life, and then looked around the clearing. It wasn't the house as he'd expected, but something else...

Ben turned, trying to find it.

At the center of the clearing was the largest oak tree he'd ever seen. It dwarfed the surrounding trees, growing straight and proud, clearly the ancestor of the surrounding oaks. It was a veritable King—Queen? How did you identify a tree?

Ben stepped closer. As he did, he felt the pressure solidify into something he could only classify as an awareness. His skin felt supercharged, like he was approaching a turbine—

"You." Ethan's voice was hard, edged not with anger but something that went deeper. Ben turned to see him standing in the doorway of the abandoned house. "I warned you. Stay away."

Ben felt a surge of electricity all down his spine. "You can't tell me what to do, Ethan."

"Maybe I can't—out there." Ethan approached without hurry. That was the most unsettling thing. It felt like a thunderstorm building around them, the air crackling with rapidly gathering power, but Ethan was the same as he ever was. "But there's no church here. No police, no school, no bank. Just us."

The last syllable drifted, taken up by the rustle of leaves through the trees, stirring for the first time. Ben looked up, saw the branches ripple without any breeze to stir them.

Ethan's hand settled on Ben's shoulder, startling Ben back to his immediate danger. "But you're in our place now. Our rules."

Ben couldn't shake himself free of Ethan's grip. "Are you threatening me?"

"Telling you." Ethan pushed Ben backward until he collided with a tree trunk. "Out here, we don't take kindly to rot."

"Do you understand the difference between a tree and a—" Ben froze.

The rough bark of the oak shifted beneath him, wrapping around his skin. As Ben watched, he could see the bark crawl over his legs and arms, trapping them entirely within the tree. Ben struggled, but it was entirely too late.

"What are you doing?"

Ethan watched impassively as the tree trapped Ben. "Got to make sure disease doesn't spread."

CHAPTER SEVENTEEN

The canopy of leaves above Ben's head parted, lifted by the midafternoon breeze. Birdsong sounded. In the distance, Ben caught the flutter of wings. The lazy breeze carried the honeyed scent of the flowers to him, as time passed in a leisurely unhurried way. It was an absolutely idyllic moment—except for the part where Ben was trapped and pretty sure that Ethan intended to kill him.

How does this keep happening? Getting murdered once was bad luck. The second, unsuccessful attempt at his death could be written off as coincidence. *But this?* Ben narrowed his eyes, watching as Ethan laid another armful of boughs to the rapidly growing pile in front of him. *This is entirely too much.*

At least Ethan wasn't gloating. He didn't even seem to be enjoying his task, stacking the wood with every evidence of regret. Though, as Ben noticed Ethan's hand lingering over a withered branch, he wasn't entirely sure that Ethan's sympathy wasn't solely with the cut branches. "What are you doing?"

Ethan drew his hand back. "Bonfire." He placed the next branch on the pile.

"Wait a minute. You're about to build a fire in the middle of a forest? I'm a city kid, and even I know what a bad idea that is!" Ben tried again to free himself from his bark restraints. "You never had Smokey the Bear in Little River?"

Ethan's mouth twitched, even as he snapped a branch to better shape his bonfire. "I can mind a fire."

"Great. I feel so much safer now." Ben caught himself too late—antagonizing Ethan was not going to help his situation any. *I have to make him see reason.* "It seems like such a waste. Can't you—" *What was a Nate word?* "—compost them?"

Ethan raised a branch so that Ben could see that yellow spread from a brown patch in the center of a leaf. "Diseased." He dropped it back in the pile. "Composting spreads it. Burning kills it."

This is not good. Ben watched the bonfire grow with increased apprehension. Did burning also kill rot? Whether it was Ben's demonic involvement as an almost-sacrifice or his vampiric past that Ethan sensed didn't matter. Fire would kill him. "You are aware that I'm not a plant? I'm not diseased or rotten—just different!"

"Different's not good." Ethan paused, his brow furrowed. "Don't know much, but I know that."

"Not necessarily! There are all types of people—"

"Not like me." Ethan continued his task, every bit as matter-of-fact as if they were discussing different varieties of apple. "You weren't there at the house when they came. If they could have cut me down, they would. They've been trying—you don't know how they've been trying—but they found a way at last." Ethan's mouth twisted unhappily.

"Threatening your family? Ethan, that's intimidation. It's a crime. The police will help—"

"Who took Nate away? Told Ma it might be better if the rest of the family kept a low profile?" Ethan angrily brandished a sorry looking twig at Ben. "Wasn't Dan and his lot."

"The sheriff is just doing her job, Ethan. She doesn't know. And how can she, when your entire family is determined to lie to her—lie to everyone?" If Ben could have freed his hands, he would have made fists. As it was, he felt the sandpaper-like surface of the tree scrape across his skin as he tried vainly to move them.

"Nate's gone," Ethan continued as if Ben hadn't spoken. "And I have to stay here." He glowered at the pile of branches.

Calm, Ben told himself. *This may be your only chance.* "You miss Nate, right? You want to help your brother?" He tried to look as engaging as he could. "You can. If you tell the sheriff that Nate took the scan and sample on your behalf, take the test yourself, it'll prove you—and therefore Nate—had nothing to do with Harriet's murder. They'll have to let him go."

Ethan's frown increased. "Ma said the only way to help Nate was to stay out here until she called me back. Said it was safest, that with them thinking I was locked up, they wouldn't trouble us."

"But Nate's getting plenty of trouble. You don't want that, do you?"

"Nate's safest where he is." Ethan returned to his task of stacking the branches. "You have to isolate the disease to stop the spread."

"Isolate?" Prison was definitely a form of isolation, but Nate wasn't diseased—was he? "Are you saying—" Ben strained against the tree trunk as an explanation occurred. "Ethan, are you protecting Nate from Sandy? You know what he is?"

"Rotten," Ethan said, a grimace turning down the corners of his mouth. "All the way to his core."

Ben stared. All the time, Ethan had the knowledge that Ben had worked so hard to attain. "You—" Like a jigsaw puzzle, pieces fell into place. "All those years ago—did you drive Sandy away?"

A smirk settled across Ethan's face as he nodded. "Sure did." He didn't try to disguise his satisfaction with himself. "Knew he was bad from the start, but didn't think much of it—most people are a little bit wrong inside."

"Wrong inside?"

"Fear, want, envy." Ethan shrugged. "I don't know. Too much of it warps you. Like a plant without light to grow, or not enough nitrogen in the soil."

"Um."

"Sandy was the worst. But I avoided him. But when he got his rot in Nate, I had to stop it fast." Ethan flexed his powerful hands. "I'd have liked to rip him out by his roots."

Ben tried not to think about just how strong Ethan was. "But you didn't."

"Next best thing," Ethan dusted off his hands on his jeans, letting go of the branches. "Threw him in the river."

"Seriously?" Getting his ass handed to him by a thirteen-year-old? No wonder Sandy had a grudge against Ethan.

Ethan nodded, a definite smile playing around his mouth. "Told him he could come back when he was clean and not a day before. He didn't like that. Not at all."

"I can imagine."

Ethan nodded. "He made a thing." He raised his hand palm up as if grasping for something not there. "A creature of smoke and ash and pain."

"He summoned a lesser demon?" Sandy had been the demon's agent for at least seventy years, time enough to gain that knowledge and power—but it was still a shock. *George needs to know what she's up against!*

"Didn't last long whatever it was." Ethan's shrug spoke volumes. "Ended up as fertilizer. Used it on the sweet potato crop."

Ben stared. If he hadn't been half trapped inside a tree, he'd not have believed what he heard. As it was, even with the rough grasp of the bark a constant reminder that Ethan broke all the rules, Ben still struggled to believe his ears. "Are you saying you defeated an attack by a lesser demon—as an untaught natural practitioner aged *thirteen*?"

Ethan turned away, his expression hardening. "Those are your words. Not mine."

"No, no, no, no! Ethan—that's a good thing! A really good thing." An unbelievably good thing. Ben took a deep breath to try to calm himself.

"Ma doesn't like it. She says it's meddling in what shouldn't be meddled with."

Ben grimaced. This was going to be hard to get right. "Your mother's a good woman. But she's not magically trained. I'm not sure she knows just what you're capable of." *I'm not sure anyone knows.* "Identifying the wrongness within Sandy, driving him away, fighting his monster... There's not many people alive who could do that."

Ethan's nod had a grudging quality. "Sandy didn't like it. Not one bit." His smile crept back, thoroughly unrepentant. "Didn't think I'd ever see him again." He frowned, turning back towards the overgrown orchard.

Ben watched him walk away with an acute feeling of shock. Nothing in his training had prepared him for this. Power on that scale was the province of senior vampires or demons, beings not usually encountered without plenty of warning. This—

Ethan's lying. He's got to be. There was no way what he described was possible! But Ethan didn't care enough what people thought of him to adjust his behavior. Would he care enough to lie?

Ben thought of Ma's tangible anxiety. *Possibly,* he decided. *For all of his coldness towards people, he's got a soft spot for Ma—and Nate.* He went along with both their lies for a happier existence.

But at what cost? Ethan was no longer in view, but Ben could hear the chop of his ax as he worked his way through the orchard. He sucked at his lip, trying to imagine the implications. Growing up surrounded by lies— *Now that sounds familiar.*

Ben shook his head in a futile attempt to get his hair out of his eyes. It was no good. The idea had taken root. *I punished Dad for lying by holding myself apart from him—and look at me now. I don't trust enough to let myself love or be loved.* If it wasn't for the tree's grip, he would have sagged forward, letting himself feel the full weight of this discovery. *I can't blame Nate— It's me.*

A distant crack recalled Ben's thoughts to Ethan. *You can apologize to Nate—by getting yourself and him out of trouble.* He turned his face in the direction of the unseen orchard. *Ethan's grown up with lies...* Ma and Nate obviously cared a lot about him, but did that only increase the pressure on Ethan? *Lies told with love are still lies...*

Ben tried to imagine it. His aptitude for study had always been met with praise, and although Austin expressed concern that Ben didn't spend more time with his peers, he was proud of every single one of Ben's achievements. *Ethan on the other hand... He's had to hide, even from those who most love him, all his life.* Nate complained about Ethan's diffidence towards his magic, but Ben saw it in a new light. *If all your life you have to hide, you'd have an antagonistic relationship with whatever is forcing you against your true nature.* Add in a pervasive religious atmosphere with no real understanding of magic, and it was too easy to see how Ethan could associate his magic with negative reactions.

That's really got to suck. Nate claimed Ethan didn't care, but Ben wasn't so sure. *Always holding yourself in check, disguising your true nature, living in fear of what may or may not be coming—*

Something stirred in reaction to Ben's thought. Something—outside of Ben.

Ben stilled his mind instantly. His ARX training in identifying and resisting influence came instantly to the fore. *Something's there.* Ben clamped down on his reaction and let his mind drift back over his train of thought. There were no leaps, none of the gaps of logic or memory that indicated influence. *Something listening?* Alert now for any signs of his mental eavesdropper, Ben let his thoughts drift. *I was thinking about hiding...about the unhealthy effect of living in fear—there!*

The presence realized it had been found, drawing back.

Don't go! Ben made his thoughts as welcoming as possible. *Please, I want to talk!* He shoved back the knowledge that he was rapidly running out of time, that Ethan might return to start his bonfire at any moment. *I just want to know what you're doing.*

There was no response, the presence continuing to withdraw.

Attempting to connect with something within your mind was against all the recommended advice, but Ben tried to take mental hold of the presence. *Please—*

He got a sudden, blinding vision. Sun, filtered through dozens of green cells. It faded, the awareness sinking back behind a rough barrier of tough bark.

Ben's mouth felt dry. *A—tree?*

Not just any tree. Ben craned his neck, trying to look up at the tree that bound him. *This...this isn't supposed to be possible!* All living things had the capacity for magic, but trees lacked the awareness to use it—didn't they?

The tread of Ethan's footsteps snapped Ben's attention back to the immediate situation. He watched as Ethan placed his burden of branches down and began adding them to the bonfire. Before getting to work on his task, Ethan reached out a hand to one of the surrounding oak trees in a gesture that would not have looked strange between friends.

Ben tilted his head. "Ethan. You—really like to help plants, don't you."

Ethan snorted, clearly not considering that worthy of response.

Ben pressed on. "Instead of cutting back injured or diseased branches, have you thought about using your power to heal the tree instead?"

Ethan glared at Ben. "Using it is wrong."

"Why? Because Ma and the pastor say so?" At Ethan's nod, Ben continued. "You wouldn't punish a plant for growing according to its nature, would you?" Ethan paused, holding the branch. "You shouldn't punish yourself either. You should embrace your nature—"

"Planting trees in the wrong environment causes stress." Ethan frowned, looking not at Ben but at the surrounding trees. "Makes them more susceptible to diseases."

"That's what I mean! You've been living in the shadow of this fear all your life." The canopy rustled overhead, and Ben pressed on quickly, sure he felt some spark of interest in the surrounding air. "This fear—it's like a blight. It's making you unhappy, Nate unhappy, Ma unhappy—" Ben faltered. The eavesdropper was back, not troubling to hide its presence now. Ben tried not to think about it, concentrating on Ethan. "It's making all of you sick. But it doesn't have to be that way."

Ethan stood in silence, his head bowed in thought. Above them, the leaves whispered, sounding like a rush of voices.

Ben held his breath.

"People are afraid." Ethan started. "They wouldn't be afraid if it was natural."

"They don't know what your magic is," Ben said. "They think all magic is like Sandy's—harmful. You can show them they're wrong."

"They threatened us," Ethan continued. "Tried to cut us down. Over and over, they tried."

Cut us down? Ben threw a glance around the clearing. The surrounding oak trees looked just like any other tree he'd seen, but he was starting to suspect they were anything but. "Fear. It's blighting them too, making them scared and afraid." He bit his tongue, wondering how to proceed.

Ethan turned to him, waiting and there was something of Nate in his expectation of help.

"It's not going to be easy." Ben swallowed. "At all." Ethan continued to watch him. "People prefer to live with fear than to face it. But the only way to escape this blight you're living under is to face it."

"You know how to do that?"

Ben nodded. "There's a friend of mine, George. She has evidence that will clear you—prove to the sheriff that you had nothing to do with Harriet's death." Ben hesitated. "It won't convince everyone. But I think it'll mean a lot to Ma."

Ethan nodded, drawing himself up in a way that indicated business. "Let's go." He set down the branch he still held, wiping his hands on the back of his jeans as he strode forward purposefully—right past Ben's tree.

"Ethan?" Ben twisted, trying to catch a sight of him. "You have to take me with you— Ethan!"

His footsteps had faded away.

Ben wriggled, trying vainly to free himself from the trunk. *Has he seriously just left me here? He's going to be arrested and no one will think to look for me—*

The bark let go its hold on him. Ben stumbled forward, tottering dangerously in the direction of the unlit bonfire before managing to right himself. Regaining his balance, he turned to see Ethan remove his hand from the trunk.

A smile played around Ethan's lips. "Only joking." He turned. This time he did walk away into the woods.

Ben took a deep breath, before following him. *What on earth have I done?*

☆☆☆

"Sandy. That's it? No last name, date of birth, identifying information...?"

Ben juggled the phone on his shoulder as he pulled his belt on. He sat in his rental car in the driveway outside Nate's home, waiting while Ethan explained to his mother what they intended to do. "He's been described as having blond dreadlocks, green eyes, and being politely spoken to a degree at odds with his appearance. He's also been known to summon demonic entities when threatened."

"Now there's an interesting party trick." George sounded distracted. Probably taking notes.

"I've done what you asked me to do, George." Ben watched Ethan and Ma appear on the porch, Ma apparently remonstrating with her son. Ethan didn't hesitate, walking directly towards the car. "Time to uphold your part of the deal."

"Yeah, yeah. Give me a second." There was a rustling sound as various papers were sorted through. "Okay. We're going to need Ethan himself. Good luck finding him."

The car dipped as Ethan climbed into the back of Ben's rental car.

Ben permitted himself a smirk. "Not the problem you imagine."

"If you say so." George didn't sound impressed. "We'll need a priest, too. You already prepared one of those?"

"One moment." Ben muffled the phone against his shirt as Ma climbed into the passenger seat. "What's the name of the local pastor—Whitlock? Any idea where we could find him?"

"The pastor? I don't know if this is a good idea." Ma gazed anxiously at Ben. "Ethan says your friend knows a way we can prove that he's not involved with the case?"

Ben nodded. "I'm not entirely sure what she has in mind," he admitted. "But she said she has proof that will clear Ethan and get Nate out of jail."

Ma's fingers closed around the seatbelt, but she made no move to put it on. "It isn't just the proof that concerns me. Ethan—" She cast an anxious look back at her son. "They might find something that's not related," she said. "I don't want to see my son taken away."

Ben bit his lip. This was the root of the problem—what Ma and Nate had tried so hard to protect Ethan from. If Ethan's true potential for power was known, there was no knowing what might happen. "Whatever we find out today, it won't change who Ethan is. Your son, Nate's brother—his powers won't take that from you. Your fear might."

Ma's eyes widened. She turned to stare at Ethan.

Her son shrugged. He took up half the back seat, all by himself. "My call. I say we do it." His tone was unruffled as he combed his hair out of his eyes. "You don't fight blight by pretending it's not there."

Really? Ben shot Ethan a quizzical look in the rear-view mirror. He didn't make all his decisions based on gardening practices, did he?

"You know your mind best," Ma agreed, sliding her belt home. "But I'll be happier when I've got both of my boys home." She began to finger comb her long hair into order, using the car's mirror. "Council meeting today, at the church hall. Just off the main street. I can't go into the church like this—look at my hair!"

Ben raised his phone. "Pastor's at the church hall. Meet there?"

"All right," George agreed. "I'll pick up the sheriff on the way." She didn't wait for an affirmative, simply hanging up the phone.

Now the sheriff, too? Ben eased the car into the room, feeling the full responsibility of his charge. Get Ethan locked up and Nate would never forgive him. *That's one thing Ma and I are in full agreement on. Both of us will be a lot happier when this is over.*

It took a matter of minutes to arrive in Little River. Ben spotted George's car parked outside the police station, fire department and library, and knew she wouldn't be far behind. He pulled up outside the church. "Here."

Ma undid her belt with a snap. Her face was set in a stern mask, and she climbed out of the car, not speedily, but without hesitation. She reminded Ben of something. But what?

A hunter. Ben fumbled with the car keys. *She's bracing herself for battle.* He felt sorry for Pastor Whitlock.

The church was quintessential country, painted white with a cheerful red roof and stained-glass windows that glowed green, like fresh grass. Ma led them down the well-maintained path and cheerful looking bushes to the hall, a long, squat building, sharing the church's color scheme, but none of its proportions. Ma didn't knock, she just opened the door and walked in. Ethan followed, leaving Ben no choice but to do the same.

They interrupted a meeting. The pastor, wearing his clerical collar with a short-sleeved shirt and slacks sat at a table with two men and three women, going over what appeared to be a roster. He stood as they entered. "Emma. I thought I made myself clear. You're no longer welcome here."

"No longer welcome," Ma said. "And here I've been a member of this church since I was baptized in it." She looked at the group at the table, her mouth tightening. "Nice to see that you haven't wasted any time figuring out how to replace me."

"As if we'd let anyone who sheltered a murderer worship in our church—" The woman appeared to notice Ethan for the first time, flinching back against her chair.

"Emma," the pastor said. "I must ask you and Nathan to leave."

Ma crossed her arms. "Ethan and I aren't going anywhere."

"Then you leave me no choice." The pastor reached into his pocket.

"If you're calling the police, the sheriff just pulled up outside," Ben said helpfully. "And if you're going for a crucifix, that's not going to work either."

The pastor sent Ben a puzzled frown, but before he could muster an argument, the sheriff stepped through the door, removing her hat as she did. "Afternoon, Pastor, Council. Hopefully we won't keep you long."

"Sheriff! There's been some sort of mistake! This is Ethan—"

"So I've heard." The sheriff's tone was dry. "Apparently, our twins need a refresher on the laws surrounding impersonation."

"You mean fraud," Ray said helpfully, following the sheriff into the hall with a case that Ben recognized.

A scanner? Now the presence of the pastor made sense.

The sheriff stepped aside for her deputy. "I mean identity theft."

"Which is a form of fraud." Ray smirked. "You sure it's the twins that need the refresher, Sheriff?"

She shot him a withering look as George slipped into the hall after them.

The pastor took that moment to interrupt. "Sheriff, I must protest this intrusion! As the spiritual leader of this community, I cannot tolerate the existence of this"—he motioned towards Ethan—"thing in our midst!"

"Of course," the sheriff murmured. "So I'm sure you won't object to lending us your expertise for a moment."

"Expertise?"

Ray patted the case he held. "We have here a scanner used to detect magical energies."

"Scanner?" Ma studied the case. "The one you used on us at the farm?"

"The very same." Ray didn't ask before placing the case on the table. The council members shrank back as he snapped the case open.

"But they've already been checked," the pastor said. "Your results—"

"That's it." The sheriff reached out for the scanner. "I'm an officer of the law, not of the supernatural. In my hands, this only gives a bare indication of magical presence. For example." She held the scan up to Ben. "Hawick. Any objection to giving the good folk a demonstration?"

"None at all." Ben straightened up.

The scan flashed blue.

"Demonic energy!"

Ben rolled his eyes. "Exposure to any sort of magic will have that reaction."

The sheriff nodded. "Hawick's an ARX agent, as you may have heard. He's licensed to deal with supernatural cases."

No longer licensed—and she knows it. Ben shot the sheriff a second look. *What was she playing at?*

Whatever the true state of Ben's practitioner status was, the sheriff's statement seemed to relieve her audience. "And you, Emma. We'll show the folks what a clean slate looks like."

Forget steel. The look Ma gave the pastor as she stepped forward to be scanned could have cut diamonds. She didn't speak. The lack of reaction from the scanner did that for her.

"All clear." The sheriff turned towards Ethan.

Ben steeled himself. *This was the moment of truth.* In the sheriff's hands, the scanner would not distinguish between natural or demonic energies. Ethan had used his magic to trap Ben within the plant. Once he tested positive for magical use, he'd never be classified as normal again. *It has to be done.* But Ben struggled to breathe. Depending on the strength of the reading, Ethan could be taken into custody immediately—

"There is a difference between being holy in the sight of the law," the pastor said. "And holy in the sight of the Lord."

The sheriff lowered the scanner, turning towards the pastor. "I see you anticipate my request."

"Request?" The pastor blanched.

Ben held his breath.

Ray motioned to George. "George here was the late Mr. Harriet's hunting partner. She has in her possession a diary that indicates that Harriet visited Little River, met Ethan, and using a scanner of a similar model to the one I'm using, concluded that he had no traces of demonic involvement and took his investigation elsewhere."

Ma had gone very pale. Ben took a step towards her, but Ethan was faster, putting an arm around her.

"But you scanned them yourself!" the pastor protested.

"And that's where the problem comes in. For the scanner to give accurate results, it needs to be in the hands of a spiritual professional. You." The sheriff accentuated her point by wagging the scanner cheerfully.

The pastor gulped. "I couldn't possibly..."

"We'd be greatly obliged if you did." The sheriff reached to tug at the brim of her hat, forgetting she'd already removed it. "Tell them, George."

"Harriet wasn't an ordinary hunter," George said. "He trained for the priesthood before finding his true calling as a hunter. He was ordained in order to better perform exorcisms and have access to the church's records of the supernatural." She raised a battered journal with a leather cover. Harriet's diary. "In his hands, a scanner was a lot more precise. He could calibrate it to exact streams of magical energy. So you see, we need a priest in order to replicate his results."

"You'd be helping a police investigation, Whitlock," the sheriff said. "Not only your civic duty, but your moral one, too, I think." She paused, thoughtfully. "Unless you'd prefer I ask Father Lewis to assist..."

"There's no need to bring the Baptists into this." Was it civic duty or the fear of another priest stealing his thunder that prompted the pastor to take the scanner? "I know my duty." He looked down at the scanner. "Is it on?"

"Let me turn the knob to demonic frequencies... Now just slide the power button—there." Ray guided the pastor. "We'll use Hawick as a test."

Ben gave Ray a flat look. He wasn't sure how he felt about being relegated to 'control' subject—or was that demonic poster child? He steeled himself as the scanner was pointed at him again. *Nate would do the same for me.*

"The light changed! Did you see that? It flashed red!" The pastor took a step back. "That has to be demonic influence!"

"Got it in one," George said. "Too bad, Ben's influence is already on record." Everyone else seemed to have taken on the tense atmosphere of the room, but George was unapologetically cheerful.

"Thank you, pastor. And now, Emma."

Ma stepped forward. She crossed her arms, lifting her chin in mute challenge.

The pastor hesitated. "I'm not sure this is necessary. We're not investigating—"

"It's procedure. If you don't mind..." The sheriff trailed off to watch the pastor raise the scanner reluctantly. The lack of reaction surprised no one.

"And now Ethan." The sheriff motioned him forward.

Ben felt a moment's pity for the pastor. Ethan's bland expression was just as intimidating as Ma's angry challenge. He only hesitated a moment, however, pointing the scanner squarely at Ethan and pressing.

And pressing again.

"Nothing's happening." The pastor frowned at the scanner.

"It looks like you've confirmed Harriet's finding. Ethan's got no demonic involvement at all."

"But that can't be the case! It's jammed—malfunctioning somehow." The pastor pointed the scanner at Ben. It immediately flared red.

"No malfunction," George said. "Now, if we're finished here, Sheriff, I've got a person of interest report to lodge."

"Not so fast," the sheriff raised her hat to the pastor and the silent, watching council members. "We have a young man who needs to be reunited with his family first. Ray—"

Ray saluted. "I'll follow with the scanner, Sheriff."

"See, Ma?" It was Ethan who broke the silence. "No need to worry." He followed the sheriff out the door.

Ethan leaving jarred the rest of them into action. George tucked Harriet's diary back into the inside pocket of her jacket and hurried after the sheriff. Ben stepped back to let Ma follow ahead of him. She laid her hand on his arm in unspoken thanks.

"Emma." The pastor emerged as Ma and Ben joined Ethan in the rental car. "Wait." Apology evidently wasn't easy for him. He tugged at his collar as Ma wound down her window. "It appears we may have been mistaken."

"Mistaken?" Ma gave him a hard look.

"I think I speak for the congregation as a whole when I say we would like you to return, put this regrettable incident behind us."

"Which regrettable incident is this?" Ma said. "The one where you accused me of consorting with the devil and threw me out of your church, or the one where you incited a mob to attack my children?"

The pastor shot a wary glance at the sheriff. "Tempers might have been running high, the situation got out of hand... But you must understand—"

"I understand," Ma said. "That I've given years of my life to this church, and in my hour of need, it wasn't this church that answered my prayers."

"We're only human, Emma." The pastor struck an ingratiating note. "Forgiveness is a great virtue—"

"Perhaps you should make it the subject of your next sermon. Which I—and my sons—will not be attending." She wound the window up, drowning out the pastor's protests. "Let's go," Ma said. "We're done here."

Ben bit his lip to keep from whistling. Ma was mad.

"You never let us miss church." Ethan's tone was laconic.

"Things are going to be different now," Ma said grimly. She twisted in her seat, reaching for Ethan's hand. "I'm so sorry, Ethan. Of all people, your mother should have known you best, and instead I let my fear get the better of me. It won't happen again—but will you ever be able to forgive me?"

Ethan attempted to endure the attention with his usual indifference. "Ma. You're fussing." But the rear-view mirror revealed that he blinked rapidly.

What do you know—there's a human in there after all. Ben returned his eyes to the road. As he glanced in the mirror, he caught the sheriff looking after them. *Is she—smiling?* The sheriff tugged her hat down over her eyes, but Ben was convinced he'd seen a brief flicker of her mouth.

Did she do that on purpose? Ben thought back to their standoff with the pastor. He'd assumed that the sheriff had been distracted before she could scan Ethan herself, but if she'd purposefully emitted it...

She knows. Or at least, she suspects that Ethan's magical—and she's okay with it. Ben released his death grip on the steering wheel. He could tell Nate his brother's secret was still safe.

CHAPTER EIGHTEEN

Ben eyed the plate before him with a feeling of apprehension. *There's generosity—and then there's this.* If the amount of food on the table was any indicator, Ma intended to celebrate the return of her sons by feeding them all the meals they'd missed while Nate was imprisoned in one go.

"You trying to make sure I don't leave home again by filling me so full I can't leave the table?" Nate shared Ben's thoughts. "Look at this! The mashed potatoes alone are the size of my head." But he picked up his fork anyway.

"A lot of mothers wouldn't even bother cooking for a son who put her through all the worry I've had." Ma placed a jug of gravy on the table, pausing to smooth Nate's hair. "You're lucky you're getting anything at all."

"So that's it." Despite his complaints, Nate was making serious inroads on his dinner. "You're planning on giving us a stomach ache by way of revenge."

"Sit down, Ma." Ethan was working his way steadily through his serving of cheesy baked broccoli. "Your food's getting cold."

Ma patted Ethan's cheek affectionately as she took her seat. "It's very good to have a full house again." Her smile rested with evident pleasure on her children.

Ben watched. In his many years of working for ARX, he'd assisted many families after the death of a loved one. They'd saved lives, put vengeful spirits to death, but they'd never done anything like this—reuniting a family.

He liked it.

"Eat up, Ben, there's plenty to go around." Ma didn't manage more than a few mouthfuls before she was back out of her seat. "There's sausages to come."

"This is enough, thank you."

"Nonsense." Ma slid a freshly cooked sausage out of the frying pan and onto Ben's plate. "You're one of the family now, you don't need to hold back."

Family? Ben's mouth quirked. Ma certainly hadn't made any distinction between the massive servings she'd given Ethan and Nate and Ben's heaped plate. He looked to see if Nate shared his amusement, instead caught Nate hastily looking away.

Ben looked down at his plate. There'd been no chance to talk to Nate privately. Things were still unresolved between them. *We can't go back to how we were before.* But what did that leave them?

Ben blinked as Ethan reached over, taking up his plate. In one quick movement, he removed the bulk of Ben's meal, leaving him with the sausage and an entirely manageable portion of mashed potatoes.

Ben stared at him, but Ethan steadfastly resisted meeting his eye. "Like Nate said. More for us."

Ben picked up his knife and fork. "Nice to know I'm good for something." He felt Nate looking at him, turned to meet Nate's eyes.

This time, Nate smiled.

Ben had finished his much more reasonably sized meal and was trying to convince Ma that he didn't need seconds when a vehicle pulled up outside. Nate stood up to look out the window. "It's a truck with a trailer—one of those old RVs."

"Silver?" Ben stood. "That'll be George. I'll see what she wants."

George wound down the truck window. "I'm not staying. Just dropped by to let you know I'm headed to New Camden."

"Am I supposed to wish you luck?"

George grinned at him. Today's lipstick was a rich burgundy. "Jealous that you're missing out on the excitement? You know, if you're good and promise not to steal my thunder, I might let you be my sidekick."

"Your sidekick?"

"Too dangerous for you? That's right, I forgot you're retired." George smirked at him. "I suppose I could find some paperwork for you to file as my secretary."

"Pass."

George shrugged, drumming her fingers along the side of the truck. "Had to ask. You change your mind, you have my number."

"And you've got mine." They weren't friends. George had endangered Nate and risked Ethan, and Ben wasn't entirely sure that she wasn't going to drag him into more danger just by association. But all the same, he found himself grasping to find the right words for her. "Be careful, George."

George laughed. "If I was careful, I wouldn't be in this profession." She wound up the window.

Ben stepped back to watch her back out onto the road. The lazy afternoon breezes were just starting to cool, stirring the evening air pleasantly and tugging at Ben's shirtsleeves. He lingered on the lawn, watching the changing color of the fading sunset play across the clouds. The mountain peaks caught the light, but the slopes were already a mass of shadow. Slip away now and he wouldn't be noticed. Nate, Ethan, and Ma were so complete in their happiness, they wouldn't even notice—

"Hey." The porch creaked as Nate leaned on the end of it. "It's safe to come back inside. Ma's stopped cooking. She's making up the spare bed."

Ben walked slowly across the garden. "I was planning on heading back to New Camden. Your family—they've only just got you back. I don't want to intrude." *It's the truth. So why, when Nate looks at me, does it feel like an excuse?*

"You're not intruding. Ma, Ethan, they both want you to stay. Okay, that's an exaggeration." Nate scratched the back of his neck. "Ma wants you to stay. Ethan probably wouldn't notice one way or another."

Ben's mouth flickered. He was pretty sure Ethan would notice. *Does that mean I've made it with Nate's family?* "What about you?"

"You don't know?"

Ben wrapped his arms around himself. "I said some harsh things. I know you're not trying to manipulate me—"

Nate sat on the edge of the porch. "Maybe not on purpose. But my day job is entirely based on making people not just like me, but need me. I—" He hesitated, brushing his hair out of his eyes. "Sandy left without a word. Amber dumped me without any warning. You— Maybe I am coming on too strong. I'm terrified you're going to leave just like they did."

"Nate—"

Nate shook his head. "When I told you about them in the barn, I'm not going to lie, a big part of me was hoping that you'd say you weren't going to leave. This time—" He looked down at his knees. "I don't want a promise you're not ready to make or you to feel sorry for me. I just want you to know that I did a lot of thinking while locked up, and I didn't like some of the conclusions I came to. It's not fair to you to bring my past into our relationship. So, yeah. I want you to stay, but I also don't want to pressure you."

Ben pulled himself up on the porch to sit next to Nate. He gripped the edge of the wood to keep from reaching for Nate's hand. To be so close, and not touching seemed—wrong. "I— My mother was an agent of this same demon. I was very nearly her victim."

He heard Nate exclaim but didn't trust himself to look at him. "I have a lot of negative associations with love because of—the incident." He winced at the sound of his own voice. Formal and frozen, as if he was talking about someone else. *I could tell George! Why is it so hard to tell Nate?* Ben swallowed. "Logically I know you're looking out for me, but sometimes, I let my fear get the better of me. I'm sorry."

"You don't need to— Shit." Nate had no reservations about taking and squeezing Ben's hand. "That—"

Ben's smile was rueful, as he turned to Nate. "I'm starting to realize that I have more issues than simply the vampire ones."

"How do I subscribe?"

"Nate!" Ben elbowed him. "That's *terrible*."

"I'm sorry. Couldn't help it. But." Nate grinned at him. "We already knew we're complicated. We don't have to figure things out right now."

Ben made a noncommittal sound. Nate's fingers stroked his wrist. The gesture was probably unconscious, but it was calming, making him feel relaxed—more relaxed than Ben had any right to feel in the current situation. "If I stay—we're probably going to have sex."

"Definitely."

Ben squeezed Nate's hand in warning. "Every time we do, I...get more comfortable with you, closer to you. I'm...really starting to depend on you."

"Is that such a bad thing?" Nate sounded curious rather than defensive.

"What if we decide to break up? It's going to be devastating. Or if we need each other too much—"

"Ben." Nate brushed Ben's hair out of his eyes, and Ben automatically looked up to meet Nate's eyes. "We don't know what the future's going to throw at us. The only thing we know is right now."

"Are you saying I'm over thinking?"

"I'm saying that planning for circumstances that haven't happened yet, and might never happen, is an exercise in stress. Figure out what you want right now, what is best for you, and go from there."

Ben swung his heels against the porch, looking out at the rental car across the garden. It was a long drive back to New Camden, and he was tired—too tired to make the long trip. If it hadn't been for his uncertainty about Nate, Ben wouldn't have hesitated to take up Ma's invitation.

And Nate...

Ben placed his hand on Nate's arm and moved it down in a gentle caress, observing that Nate's fingers tightened on the wood of the porch much like Ben's had earlier. "Holding yourself in check?"

"I don't want to make your decision for you."

"I know you don't." Ben placed his hand over Nate's. "Trusting you with my life was easy. I don't know why it's so hard to trust you with my heart."

"No one said this was easy. Or made sense."

Ben's mouth quirked. "I guess not. Then— I'd like to stay tonight."

"Only tonight?"

Ben made himself firm. "If I don't figure out what I want—who I am—I'm going to be forever wondering if I'm giving in to you."

"I hear there's this thing called compromise. Apparently relationships are based on it."

Ben struggled to keep his mouth flat. Smiling now would ruin everything. "You're right. But in order for us to have a proper relationship, I need to figure out what's important to me—what I won't compromise. Do you understand?"

"I know this is going to sound needy and desperate, but is there anything I can do?" Nate looked down. "I understand you needing space, but part of me still feels like I'm never going to see you again."

"Maybe this will be good for both of us. You'll see that we don't have to be always together in order to be together."

"I can text you right? And call?"

Ben nodded. "We can still meet."

"You mean like on dates?"

Ben's mouth quirked. "We haven't actually been on a date yet, have we?"

"No wonder we're messed up. We've been doing this entire relationship back to front." Nate stood up, squeezing Ben's hand. "Come on. If we've only got the one night, let's not waste it."

☆☆☆

Considering how little sleep Ben got, there was no way he should have felt as peaceful or rested as he did the following morning. He wasn't entirely sure he wasn't half-asleep still. The day had a muted, unhurried feeling to it. Ben might have thought he was still dreaming—if his nightmare hadn't woken him.

No one spoke much over breakfast, but it was the companionable silence of friends, rather than fraught with tension. Ben took advantage to indulge his thoughts. Was his current cozy feeling the result of waking up with Nate wrapped around him—or the result of the activity that led to Nate staying the night with him, in clear defiance of Ma's rules? It was a hard problem to solve, and Ben gave it his full attention.

Ma put down her coffee cup. "Nate, Ben. If you've finished with your breakfast, I'd like a word with you."

Ben put down the piece of toast he was struggling with instantly. Ma's statement killed what little appetite he had. He glanced at Nate. *So much for Ma's rules being lifted?*

"What's up?" Nate also put down his coffee.

Ma took a moment before replying. "Nate. You've never been to the old Winnaker property, have you?"

"What, the old farm?" Nate shook his head. "I know where it is—Pa showed us the boundary—but he said we shouldn't ever play there. That the house wasn't safe, that we should leave it alone."

Ma considered him. "I think it's time you went," she said at last. "Ethan'll take you. Ben, you stay here with me."

Ethan stood at once, putting his plate on the counter, but Nate shot Ben a puzzled look. "I don't know. If it's Ben's last day—"

"Ma's right." Ben put his hands on his knees where they couldn't be seen beneath the table. "You should go."

Nate still hesitated. "Are you going to be here when I get back?"

Ben nodded. "I won't leave without saying goodbye."

Nate was visibly relieved. "Thanks." He followed his brother out the door. "You have me nervous now, being all mysterious. If this is a new strain of apple..."

Ben listened to Nate's complaints gradually fade out of hearing. His fists were clenched under the table. Everything in him wanted to go with Nate, protect him from—what exactly? *I don't know. I don't know what it is or if Nate needs protecting from it—and even if I did, that's not my call to make.* Choosing to stand on his own had one distinct disadvantage. *I can't protect Nate. I have to let him live his own life.*

Ma's sigh startled Ben. "It's been a long time coming." Ma stood, automatically gathering up the breakfast dishes. "But it's time."

Ben stood. "Can I wash?"

Ma looked as if she would refuse but decided against it. "Thank you." She placed her hand on Ben's arm as he carried his own dishes to the sink. "You've done a lot for my sons—both of them," she said. "I hope Nate has told you that you're welcome here—no matter what the two of you decide to do."

"That means a lot." Ben hesitated. He didn't know how much of what was behind Ben's decision to return to New Camden Nate had shared with his mother.

But Ma spoke before he could. "There's something you should know about us, Ben. I haven't told anyone what I'm about to tell you. Mitch and I, we couldn't ever have children. I was heartbroken when I found out—we tried various options, but nothing worked. I was getting desperate, and then a hiker stopped by." She picked up the dishcloth, drying the dishes as she talked. "He was a retired forest ranger, finally hiking the trails that he'd been working on all those years. We ended up inviting him to stay for lunch and he told us the strangest tale. He'd heard it from another ranger. When the area became a national park, the state looked into buying up the land around it, to preserve the forest. Most folks refused to sell for the price they were offering. But Winnaker jumped at it. Sold his entire farm and was glad of it. The ranger thought this was odd, and so he got to talking to Old Winnaker. Winnaker was reluctant to talk at first, but a couple of beers later, he told the ranger the farm was cursed and the park was welcome to it."

Ben realized that he'd stopped washing to stare at her. "Cursed?"

"That's what he said. Seems there was a chestnut tree on his farm, not too far from his house. This was before the blight, when the woods around here were so full of chestnut trees that people went out with a rake to gather nuts. Nate's told you about the blight?"

Ben handed Ma the next dish. "He's mentioned it a couple of times."

"It's hard to comprehend the difference it made here. More than the nuts, the chestnuts were Little River's main source of lumber—an entire industry gone, just like that. Half the town left with the chestnuts. I wasn't born then, but I heard it from my parents." Ma placed the dried plate on the bench but didn't immediately reach for the next. "Anyway, this happened as the blight reached us. Old Winnaker got up one morning, and in place of the chestnut tree, there was an oak. He gathered the pastor to be a witness, swore up and down that the chestnut tree had turned itself into an oak. Folks thought he was daft, that the stress of the blight had got to him. Tensions were high as you can imagine, with news of the blight approaching and nothing nobody could do to stop it. Signs had already been seen on some of our trees." Ma placed a hand on the counter. "No one had time to listen to Winnaker's crazy stories much less believe them. So he decided to get rid of the tree himself. It was a big oak, so wide that three men couldn't get their arms around it. Wider than Winnaker could cut down in one day. He tried and tried, but when he returned next morning to finish the job, the tree was healed. It became an obsession with him. He swore the tree was alive and against him. Well, he didn't have a good temper to start with, so no one was really surprised when his wife ran away, and his children all left home. But Winnaker blamed the tree. He tried poison, he tried fire, but no matter what he tried, the tree remained. Once the forest park took over the farm, he left Little River and never returned."

Ma put the dishcloth on the counter. "I think I need another cup of coffee. Will you join me, Ben?"

"Of course." There was no way Ben was missing the end of Ma's story.

Ma took her time, blowing on her coffee before taking the first sip. "It's a relief to talk about this at last. Ethan... I've always been afraid to ask Ethan how much he knows."

Ben looked up from his own coffee with a feeling of shock. When Ma had said she hadn't told anyone, he'd assumed that didn't include her family. "What happened?"

"We went to the Winnaker farm." Ma leaned back in her chair. "After hearing the ranger's story, Mitch and I were curious to see the tree for ourselves. Mitch knew exactly how to reach the farm, so we went there. You've been there yourself, so you know what we found."

Ben nodded. "There's—something there. A definite presence."

"I felt it, as strongly as if it was a person standing right beside me. Mitch and the ranger, they didn't feel a thing. They were arguing over whether or not they'd got the right place—the farm was too overgrown to only have been abandoned forty years. But I knew. I could feel it. I put my hand on the trunk. I couldn't understand it, but I knew it was lonely somehow. It was wanting something. Maybe it felt my want for a baby—we'd just had a call from the hospital that morning. The latest test had come back negative, and it seemed hopeless. Anyway, I think the tree understood. Something fell on the ground near me, a chestnut shell. I put it in the pocket of my skirt, not saying anything about it to the ranger, but that night, I told Mitch I thought it was a sign. He thought I was out of my mind, but he humored me. We ate the nuts together. Nine months later, our son was born."

Ben realized he was holding his breath. He swallowed, his throat uncomfortably tight. "Your son?"

"He was the quietest child you ever saw." Ma's smile was fond, her eyes settled on the wall beyond Ben. "Hardly cried at all, and the sweetest way of looking at you. He was everything I'd ever wanted. As he grew up, the district nurses and the other mothers said there was something different about him, but to me he was perfect. It didn't matter that he didn't talk, that he was the last of his antenatal group to learn to walk. He was my precious, precious son. He loved helping me in the garden, would follow after me everywhere. Mitch would take him into the orchard with him, and they could spend hours there. I never knew a child so happy." Ma's expression clouded. "And then Mitch had the heart attack. We were entirely taken by surprise. You'll think me a horrible mother, but in the panic of calling the ambulance, and taking care of Mitch till they arrived, I didn't have a thought to spare for our boy. He was so good and so quiet always, that it wasn't until the ambulance had left, and I was packing a bag to send to the hospital for Mitch that I remembered he was still out in the orchard."

She was being very careful to avoid saying 'Ethan.' Ben gripped his cup of coffee tightly. He wasn't sure where this was going.

"When I found him—" Ma took a moment to steel herself. "He was covered in blood. His thumb was missing—cut clean off." She shook her head, her mouth tightening. "Mitch had been grafting, and he'd copied his father. I was distraught as you could imagine. I don't know how much time I spent searching for the missing thumb, praying we'd be in time for the hospital to reattach it but—he wouldn't show me where it was. Only when we were back at the house and I was starting to call the ambulance did I realize that my son wasn't acting as though he was hurt. He was calm, uncomplaining as I cleaned him up and bandaged his wound. I thought of the tree and for the first time... I wondered."

Ma looked at Ben. Her face was tired. "You'll think me heartless for not rushing him to the hospital. I was afraid. He was my world, and I was afraid that if people knew just how different he was, I would lose him. I couldn't bear the thought of it. So I did nothing." She sighed, looking down at the woody grain of the table. "Mitch was furious when he found out. By then it was too late to do anything, but he told me off for jumping to conclusions, demanded to see the wound for himself. You can imagine our shock when we removed the bandage to find that his thumb was growing back."

Ben stared at her. Neither of the twins was missing a thumb. He didn't even remember seeing a scar.

"A few more days and it was good as new. Nothing to show that anything had happened. Mitch and I had many discussions about whether or not to consult the pastor, but in the end, it came back to fear. We didn't want to lose him."

Ben placed his palms flat on the table. He needed to steady himself. "What happened next?"

"Mitch had to take things easy. The doctor forbade him from doing any strenuous work. It was a month before he went back to the orchard—and he immediately came back to the house so white and trembling that I started to call the ambulance thinking he'd had another attack. He stopped me, told me I had to go, look in the orchard. I did." Ma laced her fingers together over around the coffee cup. "There was a baby in the orchard."

"A baby?"

Ma's brow furrowed at the memory of the discovery. "He was a tiny, skinny little thing, about a year old, but completely naked and fast asleep in the orchard grass. I couldn't believe that Mitch had just left him there, and I bent to pick him up. That's when I realized he was growing from the tree by this thumb."

Ben stared at her.

Ma met his eyes directly. "You're probably wondering how I could just leave the baby like that. Well, he seemed perfectly healthy where he was, except for a slight, greenish tinge, and I was that shocked, I didn't know what else to do. Mitch and I talked it over back at the house. Once I got over the fright, I wanted to bring the baby inside. Mitch wouldn't hear of it. 'This is no ordinary baby, Emma,' he said. 'We don't know how it works. We might hurt the poor thing.' He convinced me to wait, promising that if it seemed like the baby was in a bad way, we'd help it. He let me put a blanket over the baby, and one or the other of us checked on him every day. He grew fast—a lot faster than a baby should. Within days he was the size of a toddler.

"At the same time, our son had developed a fondness for playing outside on his own. He'd disappear for hours into the orchard. Some of his clothes disappeared, and he got in the habit of taking food from the pantry. Mitch insisted we let him be and waited to see how things played out. And then one day, I called our boy in for dinner, and he had a second little boy, exactly like him but for his thinness. 'He's my friend,' our boy explained. 'Can I keep him in the shed?'"

Ma shrugged, or at least, she tried to. "You can guess what happened. We took the second little boy in, and the two became inseparable. Within days it was impossible to tell one from the other. We had a hard time explaining the second child to our neighbors. We said there'd been a mix-up at the hospital, but I'm afraid a lot of our neighbors suspected Mitch of having an affair. It must have been hard for him, but he said it was better that than letting the truth be known about our sons—and by that time, they were both our sons."

"Who—"

Ma shook her head decisively. "We don't know," she said. "The plant child ate so well and learned so quickly that within days I couldn't tell who was who and they both answered to 'Ethan.' When they started school, we picked one to be Ethan and one to be Nathan, but I could not tell you now which was the son I bore and which the son we found."

She was lying. Ben watched her avoid his eyes. He knew she was lying—but he couldn't fault the motives behind the lie. Any mother would want to give her children the same equal footing. "What are you going to do?"

"What I've always done." Ma picked up her cup of coffee. "Love them both."

☆☆☆

Retracing his steps through the forest would have been easier if there had been steps to trace, or if the forest had not been quite as full of trees. Everywhere Ben looked the trees looked much the same as the trees he walked past minutes earlier.

Even the forest felt different. Some of the pressure had lifted, the presence strong but no longer so concentrated. Ben quickened his pace as he saw the fence up ahead. *Almost there.*

The difference Ben felt was not his imagination. As he approached the house, Ben paused, looking around him. *Weren't there oak trees here before?* Instead of the oaks, there were long, thin trees that stood as straight as soldiers being inspected. Looking up into their branches, Ben could see spiky green pods. *Chestnuts?* He looked for the large oak.

In the center of the clearing which the large oak had previously dominated, was an immense tree, its trunk so huge that four men would have struggled to get their arms around it. Standing in front of it in silent contemplation were Ethan and Nate. Ben hesitated. Although neither twin spoke, he had the feeling he was interrupting.

Nate glanced at him as Ben walked up beside him. His eyes were suspiciously bright. "Ben. You're not going believe this." Nate looked up at the tree, and Ben followed his gaze. "It's a chestnut tree. These are all chestnuts. But there's not supposed to be any chestnuts left! The blight—"

The tree towered. It was taller than the oak had been, standing proud and strong—but Ben didn't sense any of its earlier overpowering intensity. Was it the feeling of being constantly constrained, held in check that had produced the pressure that hung over the valley?

Nate grasped for Ben's hand. "This— I don't know how to explain this. It feels like I've been here before—that this place is inside me. But I know I've never been here. Am I losing my mind?"

"There is a lot of magical energy in this forest." Ben squeezed Nate's hand, leaning against him. "Every living thing has the potential for magic. It's usually associated with people, but some animals have demonstrated ability to use it. Black cats, for example. There's no reason why a tree couldn't possess magic. Or that, knowing that it was threatened, do what it could to protect and preserve itself and its fellow trees, gathering the energy of its dying kin, and disguising itself and its offspring as oak to avoid the chestnut blight and remaining here ever since."

Nate's hand rested on Ben's shoulder. His presence seemed to be a support. "And you think this is why Ethan and I are—different? We're not trees."

Ben thought hard. Was there any way to explain what wasn't his story to explain?

Ethan took his brother by the wrist and placed Nate's hand on the chestnut's trunk. "They're ours. And we're theirs."

Ben watched silently. He didn't know what Nate felt, but he saw the confusion in his face clear. Something inside Ben eased. *He's going to be okay.* There was a chestnut-sized lump in this throat, and Ben swallowed it with difficulty. He wanted independence for himself. He couldn't grudge Nate his.

"But why now?" Nate asked. "If they've always been here—why stop hiding now?"

"It's time," Ethan said, placing his own hand on the tree. "No more hiding. For any of us."

CHAPTER NINETEEN

After so much peace, quiet, and scenic beauty, New Camden hit like a shot of adrenaline. Ben stepped out of the over air-conditioned coffee shop and back into the atmosphere of exhaust, hot tarmac, and rush that was the city in summer, with relief. He knew these streets and where he belonged in them.

Making his way down the pavement toward his apartment building, a file of laptop brochures in his hand, Ben gloried in the knowledge that none of the eyes glancing his way lingered for more than a second. After a momentary impression, he would be forgotten before he'd even reached the opposite side of the road. There was no Dan to notice and comment, no neighborhood gossip to care about—and no Nate.

Ben slowed his pace.

Waking alone in the apartment had been hard. He didn't remember the nightmare, but it had followed him all day, even as he went about what would be his new routine—eating a solitary breakfast of toast, checking his list of things to get for the apartment, and starting the search for a replacement laptop. It was all necessary, all his own choice, but all the same... Something was missing.

"Hey, asshole! You going to answer your goddamn phone or what?" The garbage man paused, bin raised to the collection truck, to glare at Ben.

Crap. Ben snapped back to himself. He was standing in the middle of the pavement, his phone blaring in his pocket. He hastily juggled his coffee and file to grab it. An unfamiliar number. "Hello?"

"Central Hospital. Is this Bennet Hawick?" The speaker was female, brisk and unfamiliar.

"Speaking." Ben doubled back towards a quieter corner. "What's this about?"

"You're listed as emergency contact for a patient of ours. Georgina Martin."

"I don't— George?" Ben tightened his grip on the phone. "What's happened to George?"

"She's in critical condition. Given her underlying condition, we need to make arrangements for our other patients' safety."

Ben stood very still. By underlying condition, she meant George's revenant bite. *Damn it, George. When I promised to put you down, I didn't imagine it would happen so soon!*

"Are you able to come to the hospital immediately?" There was a pause. "Mr. Hawick? Are you still there?"

Ben forced himself to breathe with difficulty. "I'm here. I'll be on my way at once."

☆☆☆

The nurses were calmly professional as they went about adjusting their patient's drip, checking her oxygen and making sure that the call button was within easy reach, but Ben couldn't help but notice that they worked with one eye on the window and the setting sun beyond. He listened to the procedure the head nurse outlined for him in the event of a medical emergency and accepted the stake she provided him in the case of an undead one.

"You're comfortable with the radio?" she asked. "There will be a doctor on the other end of it all night. Your friend's case has already been circulated to everyone on night duty, so if you need assistance, we'll be ready."

Ben looked down at the handset. It was a similar model to those used by ARX operatives—perhaps the hospital had employed ARX for their security needs. "It's fine."

"Once we leave, you will be alone in the ward. The doors are reinforced steel and cannot be opened from the inside. Do you remember the location of the call button?"

Ben nodded. "I've got it."

"In the event of an emergency, our priority will be securing the safety of our other patients. By agreeing to remain, you take full responsibility for your own safety."

"I signed the liability form." Ben was surprised by his own abruptness. "I know what I'm doing."

The nurse hesitated. The rest of her team had already left the room. Ben could hear them making their way down the corridor, footsteps quick and no chatter. She seemed about to say something, but a look out the window decided her against it. "Good luck, Mr. Hawick."

Ben heard the vault-like clang of the steel doors locking into place. In the wake of the nurses' absence, the room felt much bigger than it had been. He stood at the end of the bed and looked down at George.

She was almost entirely hidden by the bandages and hospital gown. The burns were superficial and the surgeon expressed confidence that they would heal without the need for surgery—if she survived the night.

Ben gripped the stake tightly. He'd listened to the doctor on autopilot, picking up the odd word here and there. Head injury. Coma. Internal bleeding. Unpredictable. If George survived the night, she had a fighting chance of a full recovery—but it was the night that was the problem.

The bite scar was still visible, even under the scattering of fresh bandages. Because of the risk revenants posed to staff and other patients, hospitals confined patients infected by vampires to secure wards, leaving them to take their chances during the night. There was a camera at Ben's back, intended to monitor George from the hospital's security center, but there would be no help coming to either of them. The hospital had given George all the help they could, but now the fight was hers alone. If anything went wrong…

Ben's mouth twisted. "How much more wrong do we need, right, George?" He placed his hand over hers.

Her skin was cool. She'd been found, collapsed within a dumpster outside a busy downtown restaurant. Staff had called an ambulance immediately. Their quick action and George's own tenacity had saved her life—she'd managed to successfully hide herself from whatever had attacked her.

The doctors had shaved large parts of her hair to get access to her head wounds, but a singed smell clung to what remained. Burnt hair, mingled with a lingering scent of copper and sulfur.

Ben's nose twitched. The sulfur was so strong, he wondered why he hadn't noticed it before. It put him in mind strongly of—

"Amateurs." Gunn leaned in the room doorway with his arms folded. "You can't warn them. Chasing a demon's certain death whichever way you play it."

Ben schooled his expression into one of indifference. "She's not dead yet."

"Operative word being 'yet'." Gunn wasn't smoking. Despite himself, Ben was impressed. Either Gunn had more respect for human life than Ben had ever imagined, or the head nurse had managed to impress on him the hospital rules. "Visiting hours are over, Benny." Gunn looked pointedly at the stake in Ben's hands. "You here to do the night watch?"

Ben nodded. "I promised I would."

Gunn snorted. "Could have saved myself a trip. Then again, I'm not entirely sure you have the guts to go through with it. I hear she's a friend?"

Ben looked down at George. In the hospital gown and without her make-up, she looked much, much younger than she was. "It's because she's my friend that I will." He flexed his fingers around the stake. "Knowing what is ahead of her if I don't— There's no way I'm letting that happen."

"Even if it means putting a stake through her heart? They struggle, you know. They don't go quietly."

"I *have* done this before," Ben reminded Gunn.

He grinned at Ben, making no apology for his remarks. "Just like riding a bike?"

"Do you know anything about what happened?"

Gunn shrugged, straightening up. "Apart from the obvious? We got a team working on tracing her online movements. Theory is that she successfully managed to attract our agent into a meeting, but the date soured pretty quickly. We found the initial site of the attack in a few alleys over from where she was found—the entire scene scorched. Any circle there might have been is gone. We did find a pile of ashes and a few scraps of paper."

"Harriet's notebook," Ben guessed. "They hunted together."

"Sheriff in Little River suggested George had some kind of plan in mind for the demon. Any idea what that was?"

Ben shook his head. "I'm guessing it was in Harriet's notebook. But whatever it is, it doesn't matter. Demons can't die."

"Oh, Ben. How can someone so twisted still be so delightfully naïve?" Gunn wagged his finger at him. "Everything dies. Demons included."

"But there's no records—"

"Maybe you're not looking at the right records, Benny-boy. And on that note, while I would love to hang out with my favorite waste of space, paperwork calls." Gunn cast a last look at George. "I'll leave you two lovebirds to your wake."

"Love—" Ben looked up in foreboding.

Nate stood in the hall beyond Gunn. He looked apprehensive.

Ben felt sick. "How long have you been here?"

"Gunn got me past security, and the nurses let us in when they left. You—" Nate swallowed. "You're here to kill her?"

"Put her down, Nate. If she dies and rises—" Ben looked at George, lying still on her bed. "—she'll already be dead."

"Because of the vampire bite?" Nate clenched his fists. "But you were a vampire yourself!"

"And that is why I'm here. I know better than anyone else what is in front of George if she rises. Friends don't let friends become vampires, Nate."

"Shouldn't you wait and give her time to adjust? She might be one of the good ones—"

"There are no good vampires. Only slightly better behaved ones." Ben was aware he was clenching his free hand hard enough that his nails were digging into his skin. He deliberately relaxed his posture, repositioning himself in his sentry position over George. "Anyway, George and I had this conversation in Little River. She's a hunter, she's faced revenants and vampires in the field, seen first-hand the harm they do. She wanted to be sure she wouldn't walk."

"I still can't believe it."

"What are you doing here?"

Nate took a hesitant step towards George's bed and looked down. Ben saw his neck tightened as he swallowed, clearly powerfully affected by George's injuries. "The sheriff called on my way back to New Camden. She mentioned being surprised that George listed you as next of kin, and I thought I should be here to help you. Didn't realize what helping you entailed."

After a moment, Ben pulled up one of the seats to George's bedside. With the stake resting on his lap, he would still be able to address any transformation promptly. "Sit down, Nate. We have to be prepared for the worst, that's all. George is tough, and the doctors gave me a positive diagnosis before they left."

"Typical. I come in order to help you, and you end up taking care of me." Nate sank back into the seat Ben had used for most of that afternoon.

Ben felt easier with the bed between them—and then immediately guilty. Driving a stake through George's heart was fine, but he drew the line at using her as a barrier. "I've got experience you don't," he reminded Nate. "I would—and do—feel just as out of place in Century."

Nate studied George's sleeping face. "You were mentally prepared for this because you knew it was coming?"

Ben shook his head. "I knew broadly what George planned, but she wouldn't share the details. She's extremely lucky to be alive at all."

Nate lifted his gaze to Ben. "How can you be friends with someone, knowing you might have to kill them?"

Ben's hand gripped the stake. "You just do. It's a fact of life of being a vampire—a possibility when any kind of supernatural influence is involved."

"Hunter?" Nate watched him closely. "What if he started to behave dangerously?"

"Wouldn't hesitate," Ben said promptly. "I know him too well to think he would want to live with the knowledge that he succumbed to the vampire completely. He'd do the same to me."

"But you called each other brothers!"

"It's an awful responsibility. But as his brother, knowing better than anyone else what he must feel, I couldn't stand by and let him hurt anyone."

Nate gripped the armrests of his chair with both hands. "You stopped Hunter from killing me in the graveyard when you didn't know what I was."

"Yes." Ben was grateful for the support of the seat back. It allowed him to meet Nate's comment with the appearance of calm. "And that's why you're so bad for me, Nate. I don't think I could kill you—even if it was necessary."

"You've really got to work on your flirting." Nate's voice cracked. He wasn't entirely able to pass off his cool tone. He sucked in a second, abrupt breath. "If anything happens to you now—if you died, I mean—would—" He stopped.

Ben winced. "If I died now, there's no way that I wouldn't become a vampire. I have been exposed to their influence too long not to."

"And if that happens, do you want us to—"

"Destroy me." Ben looked down at the stake he held. "I never want to return to that shadow life."

"But you were a good vampire! You didn't hurt anyone—"

"Under Saltaire's influence," Ben reminded him. "Without it, there's no guarantee I would be able to exert enough self-control over myself to contain the monster."

Nate sat in silence. He didn't look at Ben or George, running one hand along his arm as he stared at the floor.

Impulsively, Ben leaned across George's bed to put a hand on his arm. "It's not something I'd ever ask you to do, Nate."

Nate looked up. His smile was shaky. "Don't think I could. Even knowing that's what you want." He sighed and sat straighter, seemingly attempting to regain his composure. "Does that make me weak?"

"It makes you human." Ben patted Nate's arm. "I want to protect that in you."

"Still looking out for me." Nate's hazel eyes regarded him steadily. "You realize that by your own logic, you being unable to kill me makes you human, too."

Ben stared at him. *Is Nate right? Am I doing something right after all?*

A loud beep jarred him out of his thoughts. Ben glanced from George—whose condition did not seem immediately altered—to the monitors surrounding them.

"What was that?" Nate got to his feet at once. "Is she—?"

"I don't know." Ben motioned to the monitors. "I know what these monitors do, but there are many variables that could cause an irregularity in her heartbeat."

"Do we call a nurse?"

"No nurse is setting foot in here before sunrise."

"But—"

"We have to wait it out, Nate. And trust that George isn't giving up without a fight."

Nate reluctantly returned to his seat.

Minutes went by without any further sound from the monitors. Whatever they'd detected, it had passed.

"Why don't you bring your chair round over here?" Nate suggested. "It's going to be a long night. May as well get as comfortable as we can."

Ben sat on the very edge of his seat. "I think it's better we didn't. A little discomfort can be a good thing. Keeps you alert."

Nate gave him a look of pure skepticism. "You know who else thrives on discomfort? Gunn told me pretty much the exact same thing once."

Ben bit back the impulse to protest having anything in common with Gunn. He disliked the man and his methods immensely, but if Nate was hoping for a kneejerk reaction, he was out of luck. "Maybe he was trying to tell you something."

"What do you mean?"

Ben turned over the stake in his hands. "You rate comfortable too highly. That's a problem." He could see the protest forming in Nate's expression and continued quickly. "You want to please everyone, make everyone happy, so you do things impulsively based on what other people want—"

"There's nothing wrong with wanting to take care of people!"

"There is when it comes at your own expense!" Ben deliberately forced his voice into a lower, calmer state. George's recovery wouldn't be aided by the sound of them arguing. "You're so willing to take care of others you don't consider the cost to yourself. How can I depend on you—trust you—when I can't be sure you'll be there when I need you?"

Hurt blazed in Nate's eyes, but he managed to keep himself in check. "You know I wouldn't do what I did for Ethan for just anybody. He's my brother!"

"But you continually put other people first. It's like you've got no idea of your own worth!" Ben was grateful to his long hair for falling in his eyes. He had to say this, but it was a lot harder, looking directly at Nate's face. "You're not even mad at Sandy, and he tried to kill you—"

"You don't know that!" Nate shot back immediately. "You have no proof!"

"Nate, the circle's location in the barn beneath his bed, his intended seduction of you—"

Nate shook his head. "You said it yourself, anyone who came to our house in the last ten years could have done it."

"This is exactly what I mean." Ben sat back, crossing his arms over his chest. "You're ignoring the danger to yourself in order to protect someone else!"

"Because no one else is even giving him a chance! You haven't even talked to Sandy, heard what he has to say."

"George was looking for Sandy."

"She was looking for the *agent*," Nate corrected. "We don't know for sure who she found."

Ben shook his head, settling back in the chair. "It's no good, Nate. This is exactly why we can't be together. I need to figure out who I am and *you* need to develop a spine."

☆☆☆

It was the longest night of Ben's life. Coming from a former vampire, that said a lot. Sitting angry vigil with Nate not talking to him, not even looking at him... The tension between them was so strong, Ben couldn't believe George didn't sense it, that it didn't trigger another alarm.

The metallic thunk of the security doors unlocking heralded the arrival of the team of nurses. Nate got to his feet, shouldering past the head nurse as soon as she opened the door.

Ben watched him go. He wasn't hurt or relieved. He was tired—more tired than he'd ever believed possible. He shook himself, trying to listen to what the nurse was telling him. "I'm sorry. Come again?"

She looked up from George's bedside. "You look white as a sheet. In fact, I'm not so sure we shouldn't send you for a quick observation yourself."

"I'm fine. George?"

She looked down at her patient. "Better for the night's rest," she said. "As you know, it's the first hours that are the most crucial. You can go home and sleep with your mind at ease. She's doing as well as anyone could have hoped." The nurse put a hand on Ben's shoulder, steering him towards the door. "Now, you need to go home and take care of yourself."

Ben took a taxi back to his apartment. He made it as far as his bed, but not as far as undressing. When the phone rang, he was still facedown on the duvet, exactly where he had fallen onto the bed.

Ben felt around for his phone fighting against the groggy mist of being awake too soon. His room was dim, long shadows stretching the length of the room. His fingers closed around the smooth shape of the phone, and he swiped 'Answer.' "Hello?"

"Hawick?" The sheriff was as brisk as ever. "We got a positive ID on the unidentified prints in Harriet's van. Thought you'd like to know."

Ben sat up, swinging his legs over the side of the bed. "Can you tell me who?"

"One Samuel Abraham Miller, known as Sandy to his friends. Assuming he has any. His date of birth is listed as 1921."

"Which lines up with the agent having been active for over seventy years."

"Remarkably youthful for a man his age. I don't think there's any doubt that we've got our culprit," the sheriff agreed.

Talked to Nate? Ben dug his fingers into his arm before he could make the remark.

"There's something else you should know. As you may have guessed from our identification of his prints, Sandy has something of a criminal file. A long history of misdemeanors—loitering, of lewd conduct, petty theft, trespassing—nothing big. But he was found guilty of a charge of sexual misconduct with a minor and received a sentence of fifteen years, that was reduced to nine on good behavior. He was only just released a few weeks back."

"A few weeks?"

"Yes." The sheriff cleared her throat. "Which got me thinking. You don't meet much innocence in jail."

"No," Ben agreed. "You don't. He doesn't have much time to secure a victim."

"If you're right about the game he's playing—and there's no reason you wouldn't be—then Sandy must be getting desperate. What's more, with the attack on the hunter yesterday, he'll be on his guard, too wary to target someone new. Does his victim has to be an innocent? Or will anyone do in a pinch?"

"Anyone who can suffer will do." Ben's body felt like lead. "He's going to go after Nate."

"I was really, really hoping you weren't going to say that." The sheriff collected herself, resuming her usual matter-of-factness. "Is he with you?"

"No. But I'll find him."

"I'll alert Department Seven to the situation. Godspeed, Hawick." She hung up before Ben's startled brain could muster an appropriate response.

He stared down at his phone for several seconds. His mind had kicked into overdrive, sorting through the implications. Sandy's visit to Little River, his pursuit of Nate at Century, all indicated that Sandy, rather than giving up his goal, had become increasingly desperate.

And Nate is wide open. The thought spurred Ben to move. He dropped his phone into his pocket, going to his father's office. Austin had left his hunting supplies behind in the move. Ben had no trouble finding a knife or salt, stowing them within the pockets of his jacket. He hesitated before adding candles and matches—what good were they against demons? *If I don't know what I'm up against, I don't know what I'll need.* Ben added the candles and the crucifix that happened to be in the box. He hoped this was enough.

He dialed Nate as he stepped out the door and into the lift. The call diverted to an answering message. "C'mon, Nate." Ben dialed again. He held his breath as it began to ring. Nothing. "I'll do this as many times as necessary until you pick up," he threatened, dialing a third time as he stepped outside—and into night.

The phone connected to Nate's answering message for the third time. Ben hung up.

I slept the entire day? Ben looked down at his phone, registering the time. No wonder Nate wasn't answering his phone. He'd be at Century, probably working. Ben stepped forward, raising a hand to signal a cab. *Please, Nate. Don't do anything stupid until I get there.*

☆☆☆

Century was packed. People stood wall to wall, every single one intent on blocking Ben's way. He shouldered past them, ignoring their dirty looks as he made a circuit of the dance floor. Nate's height and physique should have made him obvious—but none of the men who caught Ben's eye in the strobe light on the floor or leaning against the bar were Nate.

After the third disappointment, Ben realized he wasn't being logical. He marched up to the bar. "I want a catalog."

He was handed a tablet. The host beside him gave Ben a considering look as he scrolled through the escort options and drifted further down the bar. Ben didn't care. He'd found Nate's profile and with a tap, brought up his availability.

Nate was listed as on duty, but his schedule was grayed out. Ben tapped a time slot, discovered that he was unable to make a booking. *What's going on?* Ben scrolled down, discovered that he could book Nate for the following night. *If he has a client, that's a good thing. He'll be busy.* Too busy for Sandy? Ben hesitated. *I need to be sure.*

He returned to the menu, selecting the host he wanted. This time he was in luck. The host was available. Ben made his booking and waited.

Aki draped himself across the bar. "We have to stop meeting like this. And I seriously mean that. You know we get full powers of veto over our clients, right?"

"I just need some info, Aki. That's all it is."

Aki sighed. "Fine. But I want an hour at premium rate for this."

"An hour?"

Aki motioned to the crowd around him. "My net social worth is decreasing with every minute that we are seen together. It's going to take at least an hour for the crowd to disperse and my credibility to recover."

Ben narrowed his eyes. While he wasted time quibbling with Aki, anything could be happening to Nate. "Fine." He pushed the tablet down the bar to Aki. "Where's Nate?"

Aki's face took on a pitying expression. "Jealousy doesn't look good on anyone. You should have taken Nate up on his offer of exclusivity when you had the chance."

Of course Nate had told Aki about that. Ben forced himself to remain calm. "Take a look at his schedule. Is that normal?"

"Nate is popular with his regular clients. And he's been absent for a few weeks." Aki brought up Nate's schedule with a few quick taps. "He's a professional. You have to understand that—huh."

Ben felt his stomach lurch. "I'm right. That's not normal."

Aki shook his head. "Getting the whole night booked is a big deal. He'd have told me if he had." Aki tapped in his employee login code, brought up a more detailed report. "Yeah. Nate's taken himself off the schedule."

"And that's—unusual?"

"We have the option at any time— Our job, we have to take care of ourselves. But this...Nate was saying at the start of the evening how much he needed this."

Ben forced himself to think past the spike of pain, pay attention to Aki's words. "Did he say anything else?"

"He didn't. I'm guessing his ex did."

Liquid ice flooded Ben's veins. "Sandy was here?"

Aki shrugged. "Saw them together at the start of the night. They looked pretty cozy." He held out the tablet to Ben with a shake of his head. "Sorry, not sorry. This is exactly what I told you would happen. You took too long making up your mind, and Nate's ex swooped in and picked Nate up on the rebound."

Ben fought to keep his thoughts together. Aki didn't know the full story. "Is Nate with Sandy now?"

"Well, I didn't see them leave together. Actually, I know they didn't 'cause I saw security start to head towards them, and Nate's new paramour made tracks. At the time, I assumed that he hadn't paid the cover charge. I gave Nate shit over that, and he told me he'd said he'd meet him after his shift."

"After his shift?"

Aki nodded. "We were going to hit the floor, but then I got a client."

"Is Nate still in the club?"

"You're being really possessive for someone he's not dating."

"It's important."

Aki rolled his eyes turning back to the tablet. "No, he's—not here. Not even in our room." Aki tapped in a few more commands, his frown increasing. "That's not— He's not showing up on the maps at all." He was about to say something else, but a look at Ben's expression stopped him. "Something's happened?"

Ben nodded. "Call Department Seven. Ask to speak to Gunn or Kenzie and tell them exactly what you've just told me."

"And you couldn't have told me that earlier?"

"I said it was important."

Aki shot Ben a disgusted look. "When we've found Nate, you and me are going to have to have a long chat about properly communicating— Yes, hello? I'd like to speak—"

Ben left Aki talking to Department Seven. He called Nate twice more as he left the club. Nothing. Ben struck out onto the city streets.

Nate left the club— Why? What had Sandy told him? It was too easy to imagine. Sandy was a master of his game and would know exactly what Nate needed to hear. The only question was where they'd go. *Somewhere private, unobserved.* Ben turned off the populated main street and down a shady side street. *Somewhere dark where the circle would not be visible.*

The problem was that New Camden had too many dark, secluded corners. Ben turned down one shadowy alleyway and then another. *I'll never find them.* New Camden was huge, and Ben was on foot—

A shadow darted across the ground in front of him. Ben reached for his knife. "Stay back!" *I don't have time for revenants—*

But the shadow faded with the sound of a car traveling away. Ben looked down at the pavement in front of him. *Get it together!* He was panicking, jumping at headlights! *You're better than this. You have to be better than this. Nate—* Ben forced himself to push down the tight fear in his throat. *Nate needs you to get your head together.*

The cold grip of the knife provided some reassurance. It was a remnant of his time as a hunter. *I'm still a hunter. George was right. I need to think like one.*

Pinching the bridge of his nose, Ben reviewed what he knew. By now, Gunn was aware of the situation. The Department Seven officer disliked Ben but would not endanger Nate. Department Seven would be searching the city for Nate and Sandy. Their reach was wider than Ben's alone, and they had at least one werewolf on the team. For perhaps the first time in his professional career, Ben felt himself thinking fondly of a werewolf's tracking and hunting potential. *I would not like to be Sandy when Kenzie finds him.*

Which left Nate.

Aki was surprised that Nate left. At the time, Ben's panic had been foremost, he hadn't given that fact the attention it deserved. Now, he stood with his back to the stone wall of the alley, so that he could give it proper consideration without leaving himself entirely open. *Aki knows Nate's moods. Nate was intending to stay at the club at the start of the night—and told Sandy he'd meet him after his shift.* Something happened after Sandy left. *Who?* Century had reacted to the threat of vampires by taking Nate off the floor—but Nate had taken himself off the roster. *The sheriff?* Ben shook his head. Nate would dismiss the sheriff's arguments about Sandy just like he'd dismissed Ben's. He could feel the panic creeping in. *Who would Nate talk to? There's only—*

Ethan.

If Ma was surprised at Ben calling so abruptly, she didn't comment on it, passing the phone over immediately. "Ethan? Ben wants to talk to you."

The pause before Ben heard the phone picked up was the longest wait of his life. "Why are you calling?"

Ben didn't have time to spare for Ethan's phone manners. "It's important. Did Nate call tonight?"

"Yes."

"Did he ask you if you'd chased Sandy away?"

"Yeah."

Ben clutched his phone so tightly his fingers ached. "What did you tell him?"

"Everything."

"Thanks." Ben hung up. The relief was so dizzying, he actually swayed. Nate knew! His strongest argument in Sandy's defense was gone! "That's why he didn't leave with Sandy! He suspected—and now he knows!"

But Nate's current location was still a mystery—as was his state of mind. *Can I be sure that Sandy still won't be able to manipulate him?* The tone of Nate's voice as he talked about everything Sandy had done for him flashed into Ben's head. The answer was no.

Ben replaced his phone in his pocket, thinking hard. *Nate's got to be hurting. Lost.* Sandy had been a big part of his life and having that ripped away would leave him all kinds of confused. *Aki's his best friend! Why didn't he turn to him?*

Ben bit his lip. Aki had numerous good friend qualities—but sympathy was not among them. *Which leaves what? This isn't Little River. Where would Nate go if he was in trouble and wanted to think?*

A place flashed into his mind, followed by an instant shudder. *No. Not there.* Ben forced himself to move even though every fiber of his body fought it. Mason's Park.

CHAPTER TWENTY

Ben had never wanted to return to Mason's Park.

It wasn't the dark, although it was darker here than the streets and alleys. The sporadic street lamps that dotted the pathways did not penetrate the thick forest beyond the jogging path. It wasn't even the alarming crack as a twig snapped, or the shuffle of movement—animal or other—within the woods. The ever-shifting branches overhead were just background noise.

Ben didn't need a torch to light his way or vampire senses to guide him. He had walked this path many, many times since that first panicked race to reach Nate before he died, retracing his steps over and over, searching for the thing he'd not done that might have changed everything. As Ben stepped into the clearing before the oak, he half expected to see Nate sprawled on the ground, his skin turned white by the moonlight into a mockery of bone, and his throat slit. The air seemed to be thick with copper. Ben choked on it, tasting blood. *Nate—*

It wasn't just that he'd failed to protect him. Ben forced himself forward until he stood where he'd stood, looking down at Nate's corpse. It was that Ben had left him—and Nate had known he'd left him.

I didn't know. Ben saw Nate again, still and growing cold, his blood sickly sweet and congealing, calling to the vampire within Ben to feast. He was dead. Should have been dead. But all that time he'd been aware of every action Ben took—or didn't take.

"If I'd known, I'd never have left you." Ben's words, so much louder than the surrounding night, startled him. *Stupid! You're no longer a vampire! You have to be careful. You can't give your location away to any predator within listening distance like this—*

Ben felt an angry stinging in his eyes. *Who cares if a revenant does find me?* Nate wasn't here. He'd failed to find him. Failed to find him a second time, from an even more pointed danger. Nate's unsuspected inhuman nature had protected him against a human death, but from Sandy—

"You came." Nate's voice sounded hollow.

Ben's gaze jerked up, from the dirt to the branches of the oak. In the hollow formed by diverging branches, Nate sat next to a scrubby looking bush. *A flying rowan.* It had protected the two of them once from Peter's threats. Something in Ben eased at the sight of Nate, and he blinked hastily. *I'm not too late.*

"How did you know I'd be here?" Nate shook his head. "How did you know I needed you?"

The first time he and Nate had sheltered by the oak, Ben's vampire strength had enabled himself to scale the oak without difficulty. Now, Ben was left at the bottom, looking up at Nate. "Are you drunk? You don't sound like yourself."

"No, I—can't think straight. Give me a moment."

Ben, looking up, had a moment's warning. He stepped back.

Nate dropped heavily out of the tree, landing on his feet, but stumbling forward onto one knee.

Ben caught him by his shoulder. "Are you okay?"

Nate didn't try to stand. "I can't think. My thoughts keep hitting a wall."

"What's happened?" Had Sandy attacked Nate? Ben stepped back, scanning Nate for injury. "Are you hurt?"

"Not physically." Nate wrapped his arms around himself. "But I feel like the rug's been pulled out from under my entire identity." He looked up at Ben. "I was nobody before Sandy loved me, nobody. And you were right. He was using me the entire time. He never felt anything for me at all."

Ben winced. Nate should never sound so lost. "Aki said he came to see you at Century."

"At first it was great. I never really expected him to look me up. Thought he was just making conversation back in Little River. Seeing him again, seeing his interest in me... I was just so happy. It was more proof that he couldn't be connected to what happened in Little River. I figured the agent would be trying to get as far away from anything to do with us as possible because he'd know we'd be on our guard. So yeah, I had my guard down. I was relaxed and just enjoying seeing him—" Nate winced. "I was about two seconds away from telling him about all the crazy shit that he'd missed in Little River when he kissed me—just like I'd always wanted him to kiss me. And while I was still trying to get my head around it, he told me he'd been waiting ten years for that kiss. That he'd freaked out when he realized just how young I was. But he'd left to protect me. And that he'd never forgotten me once over the years, and at first, he'd meant to come back, but then he'd worried that maybe I'd misconstrued his leaving or found someone else."

Ben listened. Every word Nate spoke felt like a nail in his coffin. He clenched his fists, unable to act or speak the fear he felt.

"It was everything I'd ever wanted to hear." There was a note of wonder in Nate's voice that hurt more than any harsh words they'd ever exchanged. "Being with Sandy again— I was taller, but apart from that, it was like nothing had changed. Like he'd never left. He told me exactly what I needed to hear. And if I hadn't met you, I'd probably have fallen for it."

Ben's frozen heart sputtered back into life in an explosive burst. "Nate—"

Nate put his hand over Ben's on his shoulder. "He came on too strong—way too strong. Pushed to get me to meet him alone. Said he needed to know if there was still a chance for us." Nate looked anxiously at Ben. "I said yes just to get him to go. I needed time to think."

"And that's why you came here."

Nate slowly got to his feet. "This oak has protected me more than once. It helped me figure out a way to find you. But now—I don't know what to do." Nate placed a hand against the oak's trunk. "I'm scared. I don't know if I can face him again, but if I don't..." Nate turned to Ben. "He's going to kill someone else, isn't he?"

Ben rested his hands in the pockets of his jeans, where Nate wouldn't see that they were clenched. "Yes. He is."

"God." Nate placed a hand over his face. "That should be all the reason I need to act, and I still can't. Here I am, thinking I had anything at all to offer you and everything about me is a lie. I'm not human, I'm not brave, I'm not—*anything*."

"You're the best thing that's ever happened to me— Listen to me, Nate!" Ben gripped his arm. "You're kind, confident, attractive, smart in ways that can't be measured by university degrees, sexy—"

"But none of that is real! My confidence is built around an empty shell. Sandy made me believe I was worth loving—"

"You are worth loving. Look at me." Ben reached up, pulling Nate's hand away, so their eyes met. "You were kind before you met Sandy. I saw it in the photo albums, Nate. Those photos of an anxious thirteen-year-old, who didn't dare reach out to the classmates he wanted to befriend. Even when you were too shy to talk to people, you still watched them, you listened, you learned them. I bet you spent more time thinking of your classmates than they ever did you. That's where your understanding of people comes from, Nate—you." Ben thumped Nate on the shoulder. "Your knowledge of how to make people happy, that comes from being unhappy yourself and knowing just what the right gesture can do for someone. It was your choice to act on that knowledge to help people—and their happiness that gave you your confidence in yourself."

"Sandy—"

"Maybe Sandy sped up the process," Ben said firmly. "But it was always there inside you." He squeezed Nate's shoulder. "Think about it. You meet a lot of people at Century with broken hearts. How many of them are confident because of it?"

Nate blinked. There was a new light in his eyes, and he gave Ben a thoughtful look. "They're upset and angry, wanting revenge. Or their confidence is shattered, and they need help rediscovering themselves."

"The opposite of confidence. That didn't come from Sandy, Nate. That came from you."

Nate shut his eyes. His hand rested heavily on Ben's shoulder as he took a deep breath and let it out deliberately. "Thanks. I—needed to hear that." When he opened his eyes, there was purpose in them. "I know what I have to do now."

"And that is...?"

"Confront Sandy."

"We can call Department Seven. Leave it to them." Ben pulled out his phone. "Gunn is already scouring the city for you—"

Nate put his hand over Ben's, preventing him from dialing. "I have to do this. Department Seven will just scare him off, and he'll start again with another victim. That's what happened to George, right? Sandy tried to use her as his next victim."

"George thought she had a way to end the demon itself," Ben said. "We won't know what happened until she wakes up."

"But if Sandy thinks he has a chance with me, I can keep him on the line until his time runs out." Nate looked at Ben. "He can't have too much time left, right?"

Ben stared at Nate. "Are you—sure?" Nate had felt sorry for Peter, a guy actively trying to kill them both. "He'll beg you to save his life. Try anything that might persuade you—"

"Come with me?" Nate's hand was still on Ben's. "I know it's a bad idea. But at the same time— I can't let him hurt anyone else." Nate looked down. His hair fell across his eyes, screening them from Ben. "I'm afraid you're right. That he's going to persuade me that my life is nothing without him, that it's a fair trade, my life for his. You— I need you there. To be stronger than I am."

His skin was cold, but his hands were steady. Nate seemed decided.

No way I'm letting him do this alone. Ben dropped his phone in his pocket. "Lead the way."

☆☆☆

Sandy waited in a warehouse a fifteen-minute walk south of Century. Ben frowned at the building. *If only it was further away.* The rough plan that he and Nate had hashed out and communicated to Gunn felt incredibly inadequate as he stood beside Nate. "You're sure this is it?"

"The door's open. It's got to be." Nate's tone was strained, and he wiped his hands on his jeans before he stepped forward.

Ben followed suit, grabbing Nate's hand as he did. He squeezed it, guessing that Nate would benefit from the tactile reassurance. "We've got this."

He hoped Nate believed him. Ben was not entirely sure he believed himself.

The warehouse was pitch dark, except for the squares of light, outlined with precision on the warehouse floor, thanks to the street light positioned immediately outside. It looked too perfectly delineated to be real as if they'd wandered into an old detective comic strip. Ben looked around, half expecting to smell cigar smoke or see a fedora-wearing gunman slide out from behind one of the packing crates.

Instead, Sandy sat on one of the crates, waiting for them to approach. He was younger than Ben had expected, his fine blond dreads gathered back in a loose ponytail. He had fine, delicate eyebrows, studded with metal, and his green eyes sparkled, even in the darkly lit warehouse. He was lean and confident, a smile of almost playful amusement tugging at his mouth as they approached. His eyes flicked up and down over Ben, and his smile twisted scornfully. But as quickly as Ben had registered it, the smile was gone, Sandy grinning as he fastened his gaze on Nate.

"I'm so glad you came, Nate." Even his voice was nice, light, softly spoken but calculated to charm. "And brought your—boyfriend?"

Nate shot Ben a startled glance. There was no way that Sandy would be happy about this news—and yet he sounded interested. "We're not—It's sort of—"

"We're dating." Ben left no hesitation in his reply. Sandy was dangerous in a way that only a demonic agent was dangerous. The less uncertainty Nate possessed in facing him, the better. Ben let his hand rest on Nate's arm. *I am not giving this man any weapon against Nate.*

But Sandy's grin caught them both by surprise. His words were disarmingly frank. "I wondered! Your angry friend at the club wasted no time in telling me I didn't have a chance—"

Ben blinked. *Thanks, Aki?*

"But I still had to try. You were my last hope, Nate... But enough of me. You're here to tell me I'm out of luck?"

The look Nate sent Ben was entirely confused. Ben didn't blame him. In all the scenarios they'd discussed on the walk to the warehouse, Sandy's blithe acceptance of his horrible fate wasn't one of them.

Ben frowned, shaking his head. *It was a trap.* "What do you mean by 'out of luck'?" The important thing was to keep him talking.

Sandy's smile was secretive. "I knew my luck would run out eventually. It always does," he confessed. "And I always knew it would be you." He looked directly at Nate. "No more fitting penance for my sins than to die by the action of the one I love."

"You know why we're here?" Nate gripped Ben's arm. "And you're not angry?"

Sandy shook his head, his dreadlocks swaying. "I could never be angry at you. Honestly, I've been praying for someone stronger than myself to put an end to this nightmare."

"Praying?" Ben didn't take his eyes off Sandy. "You made a demonic pact."

Sandy's eyes flicked back to Ben for the briefest moment. Ben was pretty sure he saw contempt before Sandy turned back to Nate. His tone was confiding. "You don't know this—nobody alive knows this—but I was brought up religious. Now, I guess you'd call it a cult. Back then, it was the only way of life I knew. Our town's name was Worthy, and that's what we were—the select few, worthy of being saved—so long as we listened to everything our prophet said. He had a direct line to God, so he said, and wasted no time in passing on His decrees. Rules like don't make eye contact with a woman not your wife, don't speak to anyone outside the community, only read books chosen for us by an Elder and work, work, work because the only thing that would save us was our obedience.

Sandy settled himself more comfortably on the crate. "My father was found to be unworthy and cast out, and my uncle became the head of our family. He took his new responsibilities seriously, very seriously. He could see that I was troubled in mind, and me being a teenager, I expect he thought he knew the cause. He recommended what had helped him—confessing all to the prophet and working through my allotted punishment." Sandy's mouth twisted. "I guess they were expecting me to confess to seeing a bare ankle or having impure thoughts such as wanting to talk to a girl. Liking boys? That was more than they knew how to handle."

Beside Ben, Nate shifted. "What did they do to you? Cast you out?"

Fuck. Sandy's too good at this. Nate sounded worried. Ben tightened his grip on Nate's hand in warning.

"And expose me to a world where I might act out my perverse desires? Not on your life, Nate." Sandy's shoulders drooped. "I was beaten and then imprisoned. When neither of those worked, I was exorcised. Nothing happened, so the prophet concluded that I must be complicit in my perversion and punished accordingly. It was left for God to judge me, so the prophet and his elders took me into the forest where I would be left, without food or water, for God to consider my case and decide whether I should live or die. And to help God make the right decision, they beat me. This time they didn't hold back. They left me dying in those hills, with not another soul to help me—or so they thought."

The warehouse was stock silent. Ben was aware that Nate was listening intently, just as he was. *Snap out of it!* He directed his anger into a study of his surroundings. Brimstone undercut the stale smell of the warehouse, as did another smell—fresh paint? Ben looked around the shadows, wishing he'd brought a flashlight. Sandy could have drawn his circle anywhere...

"So there I was, waiting to die, thinking of all the things I'd never have— The love of another person. Freedom to live as myself. Turning twenty. Drinking alcohol. Seeing someplace that wasn't mountains. This fox came up to me, started talking. I was that far gone that I didn't even think how weird it was. A pattern came into my head. If I drew it, I'd be free, and everything I wanted would be mine."

Sandy frowned. "I'm not entirely sure what happened after that. I've spent eighty years trying to forget. I know my broken body was like new again and that when I walked back into Worthy I was greeted as a miracle—a sign. There was a celebration. No one wondered what I might be a sign of." Sandy's face was tinged with sorrow, and his eyes turned downward. "I shared my vision of the circle, and they wasted no time in drawing it. Big enough the entire community could stand in it. The prophet tried to warn them—for once in his life, he was right about something! But they didn't listen. Me coming back in defiance of his ruling was a sign. They were already calling me the new prophet, and fool that I was, I believed that I was meant to lead them to a new life of freedom. I stood before them proudly as they assembled on the circle. For the first time ever I was accepted and adored. The fox was at my heel, telling me what to say in words that only I could hear. 'Do you trust me?' I asked my people. 'Do you love me?'"

"Jesus, Sandy! They—?"

Ben winced at Nate's words. No amount of warnings could stop Nate from feeling for people—even when it endangered himself. *Sandy knows we know how the demon works. He must know he can't trick us.* But instead of searching for a new victim, Sandy was giving Nate his life history. *It's obviously a trap. The only question is how it is sprung.*

"They all died." Sandy shut his eyes. "All but the prophet. He damned me, cursed me, swore at me—called me demon spawn, accused me of consorting with the devil. And that's when I understood what had happened to me." Sandy slid off the crate. "Been running from it ever since, escaping it any way I can. Nothing deadens the knowledge of it, not for long. Nothing... But knowing there's someone who genuinely cared about me might ease my passing."

"Don't take another step." Ben pulled his phone out of his pocket. He hit the flashlight function, raising it up to illuminate the warehouse's concrete floor.

There was nothing there. Nothing but bare concrete.

Am I wrong? Ben lifted the phone back and forth, searching for anything amiss. *Sandy can't be telling the truth— I know he isn't! Demonic agents don't give up. They have too much to lose...* "He's faking," he warned Nate. "Smell the brimstone."

He could feel it now, a dark presence in the shadows, a growing interest centered directly between his shoulder blades.

"My time is near," Sandy told Nate. "Gaassimolar draws closer. That's what you smell—him, coming for me. Look, I'll prove that I've got nothing to hide." He knelt to get something that clinked out of a satchel leaning against his crate. With the spray paint in hand, Sandy walked to one of the squares of light. "So you can see exactly what I'm doing." Using the spray paint, he traced out the ritual circle without any hesitation at all.

Ben felt the hairs rise on his arms as he watched. He couldn't help but wonder how many times Sandy had done this, for how many victims.

"There." Sandy set the canister down and stepped into the finished circle. "Does this make you feel happier, Benjamin?"

"My name isn't Benjamin." Ben followed Nate over to where Sandy stood.

"Into the light." Sandy beckoned them closer. "So you can see exactly what you're getting into." For a moment, his determined cheerfulness seemed strained. He was in command of himself before Ben even registered the thought. "Now. I know I have no right to ask this, and I don't want to cause trouble between you and your boyfriend, but I have to know before I go. Was I ever anything to you?" As Nate hesitated, Sandy pressed on, his voice cracking with his emotional plea. "Please be honest— Give a doomed man on brief second of light. Make this entire wretched life have meant something—"

"Sandy—" No matter what doubts Ben had about Sandy's sincerity, there was no mistaking that Nate was honestly conflicted. Ben could feel him waver, see his creased brow clear as a decision was reached. "I—"

"Don't you dare, Nate." Ben stepped deliberately on Nate's foot. He hit dial on his phone.

Gunn answered immediately. "Are we allowed to join your party yet?"

"The lamp outside," Ben ordered. "Kill it."

He felt Nate's start of surprise, saw Sandy grit his teeth, but before either of them could react, a shot rang out, followed by shattered glass and complete darkness.

No, not complete darkness. As the afterglow of the street light faded away, a muted glow was seen. Ben heard Nate shift, obviously looking down at the circle beneath his feet with shock. "Glow-in-the-dark paint?"

"Clever," Ben said. "But not clever enough. Get out of—"

Sandy leaped towards Ben. "Don't move." His pleasantly mild speech gave way to a rough bark. He dug his fingers into Ben's hair, jerking his head back. Ben felt the sharp edge of a knife across his throat. "Let there be light."

With a faint crackle, that of a fire being stoked, the warehouse was perfectly illuminated.

"Ben!" Nate took a step towards them. "Let him go!"

"Move and he dies." Sandy tightened his grip, drawing back and pulling Ben with him.

The edge of the knife had a compelling effect on Ben's thoughts. It was hard to think beyond it. "This isn't going to work, Sandy. You can't extort Nate's love—even if he still qualified as innocent."

"Shows what you know." Sandy tightened his grip on Ben's hair, keeping him off balance. "Yeah, he's not innocent now, but he was when we first found him. My master is curious to taste ten years of innocence betrayed. He's granting me an exception to the normal rules."

"An exception?" Nate sounded hopelessly lost.

Sandy shifted to look at him. "You should feel flattered. He's never done this before. We put a lot of work into you, Nate, and he's making you an offer he's never given anyone else."

Nate stood frozen in place in the glow-in-the-dark circle. "Ben—" He attempted to collect himself. "Even if I say the words, they won't mean anything. They're not true."

Sandy's grip tightened. "Don't let a guy down easy, Nate. No, maybe you don't love me, but I'm betting it's a different story for this one." The knife edge caught Ben's skin. He felt a flash of pain, followed by an immediate wet heat. "What's it going to be? Let two people die? Or do you want to save your boyfriend's life?"

Nate made an instinctive movement towards them, checking himself on the brink of stepping out of the circle. "What do I have to do? Just say—?"

"The words," Sandy avoided them deftly. "With all the conviction you can muster. If they mean anything, the circle activates." His tone became persuasive. "Only you can make this choice."

Why does Sandy dodge the words? Ben looked down and saw the spray painted circle beneath his feet. *Not going to get caught in his own trap.* For a moment he saw again the wooden boards with his mother's blood on them. "Don't believe him. I have a history with this demon, too."

Sandy tugged his hair warningly. "Don't try to be clever."

"It's the truth. You feel it, don't you?" Another presence could be felt, an awareness stirring in the shadows and throbbing through the lines of the circle beneath their feet. "It's waited ten years for Nate, but it's had longer for me—thirteen years."

"What is three years to a demon? Nate—"

"I was younger, the betrayal of my feelings more complete." With every word, Ben felt the hungry presence draw nearer. It had waited like this for him in the barn, would always wait. "I've never been able to say those words, to allow myself to feel for another. That— You won't find pain like mine again," he promised the unseen demon.

"It's another trick!" Sandy's voice was harsh. "Don't listen to him!"

Hot air billowed around Ben's ankles. The circle had begun to smoke and brimstone was in the air. "I was right. You do remember me."

"It has to be a trick," Sandy insisted. "No one willingly chooses this." He spoke to the shadows, turning back to Ben with a snarl. "Listen. I call the shots here."

The power surrounding them seemed to convert instantly to light and smoke. Flames licked the warehouse floor, trapping Nate in his circle as they burned in place. Ben felt heat at his legs and looked down to see the fire, burning black as the shadows but hot as any flame, surrounding him, too.

"Men have grown bold, Master," Sandy wheedled. "Bold enough to think they can make a mockery of you. Time to show New Camden what it is to pick a fight with a demon."

There was no audible response, but Ben, straining his senses for anything, thought he felt agreement in the air. Power surged. A sound followed. A drum—no, drums—building steadily closer. It was only when one screeched, that Ben recognized the sound as wings. Looking up, he saw that the window was outlined by a red glow beyond it. *More flames?* Shapes flew down, seemingly a swarm of giant bats. The shouts from outside were joined by the sound of rapid gunfire.

Ben's blood surged in exultation. *In the distraction of battle, I could take my choice of prey! Humans too distracted by the fight to notice their death behind them—*

What the hell was that thought? Ben put a hand to his head, attempting to clear it.

"No sudden movements," Sandy warned him. "Don't expect any help from your friends outside." The flames parted as Sandy stepped out of them, the knife remaining behind, hovering at Ben's throat. "I've got power you've never even imagined."

"Is that why you're doing this?" Nate's fists clenched again, this time with anger rather than alarm.

"When it's kill or be killed, you find yourself doing things you never believed you could." Sandy's voice returned to its incongruously pleasant tone. "I'm not ready to die yet—even for you. So hurry, say the words, Nate. Don't try to be clever. That girl, your friend, thought she could pull a fast one on me. She regrets that now."

"Don't talk about George like that!"

"Anyone stupid enough to challenge a demon head on doesn't deserve pity!" Sandy shook his head. "She had no chance—what use is a vampire in daylight?"

George's secret weapon—could it be the vampire within her? Ben and Nate locked eyes, startled. Ben saw the alarm in Nate's eyes, knew they were thinking the same thing.

It's not daylight now.

Ben breathed in the spilled copper of his wound. The vampire was close to the surface, hungering for blood. *Did the wound call it? The presence of a threat?* Whatever the source, the vampire was ready to fight.

"Ben!" Nate's tone broadcast his alarm loud and clear. "You can't do this! I don't want to lose you! I—need you."

Ben smiled at Nate. The relief he felt—*Nate remembered not to say it!*—was greater even than the knife at his throat. "Me, too. Listen. You'll have to trust me like I'm trusting you. You'll make the right choice— I know you will."

The circle throbbed beneath his feet as if it had a heartbeat.

"Don't listen!" Sandy cried out. "Don't accept him! Something's not right— He's too calm!"

"I am what you've made me," Ben said. "It's time we met." He looked up, meeting Nate's eyes. "I love you."

☆☆☆

He was on fire from the inside out. Ben cried out, staggering onto one knee as molten pain wrapped around his chest. He felt it like fingers, squeezing at his heart, while simultaneously raking through his thoughts. His vision blurred, his consciousness burning away. He heard the metallic clatter as the knife fell to the floor, but he didn't remember it or why it mattered.

Acrid smoke, so bitter it made tears rise in his eyes, billowed thickly in front of him, steaming away to reveal a flash of gold. It was thread, wound into a robe of the rich purple once reserved only for kings. The demon's lip curled in a smile as he stared down at him within the counter circle, impossibly handsome, impossibly cruel. He appeared as a man in his prime, draped in the marks of power of a former age.

Ben had only a few seconds to observe. His vision was spotting, seemingly burning away from inside his skull. He could feel the burning spreading faster, knew instinctively that when it burnt out, he would be gone with the flames, nothing remaining of him except the pain.

"An interesting vintage." The demon spoke in the calm tones of a connoisseur. "If somehow lacking...I wonder if the earlier aborted harvest prevented this fruit from reaching its true potential?"

"How long?" Sandy wet his lips. "Thirteen? He said he'd had thirteen years to develop."

They were talking about him as if he was already dead. Ben braced himself against the stone floor. It was getting harder to think.

"You presume much." The demon's eyes reflected the black flames of the fires that burned surrounding them. "This death was not of your making. If I grant you a respite, it will be out of my generosity."

Sandy's apology was choked out. Ben let the sounds wash over him. They were increasingly distant now. The pain had slowed, the demon stringing out his meal.

Ben looked up. Nate was on his knees, his eyes fixed on Ben. He shook as if he was the one being unraveled.

"The end is close now," the demon observed, conversationally. "He is aware, but only just. If you have any last goodbyes, speak them now or forever regret."

There was still enough left of Ben to be outraged. Using his death to aim at Nate? He snarled in fury, feeling the last vestiges of his self give way.

☆☆☆

The vampire launched himself at the demon. He only had the time it took for the demon to feed. *I have to make this count!*

The demon saw the danger too late. He turned to meet the vampire's assault, but trapped within the circle, it couldn't flee. "Unhand me, vermin! I am a prince!" He yelped, as the vampire's fangs scored his flesh, sending a crimson spark of blood jumping in the flame light.

Blood! The immediate thirst was too great to resist. The vampire forgot his revenge, aiming instead to sink his teeth into the demon's flesh. He missed the demon's neck, but caught his shoulder, punching through the flesh with his fangs.

"Release me!" The demon swung clumsily with the sword at his side, still in its gaudily decorated scabbard. He connected with Ben's head, and the vampire released him, leaving an angry tear that dribbled thick blood behind. The vampire swallowed, tasting the rich crimson in his throat before he was able to take his eyes away from it and look at the demon.

Blood ran freely down his arm. The demon cursed, as he struggled to grip the scabbard with his injured hand and free his sword. Once, no doubt, he'd been a feared warrior and the sword had slid free of its scabbard with the ease of constant attention, but centuries of inactivity had dulled blade and wielder both.

"Use your power! Call up a monster to deal with him!" The demon's agent called to him. He had slunk back against the boxes that littered the warehouse. The vampire spared him only a passing sneer. He need not fear this one coming to his master's aid!

"My forces are engaged," the demon snapped. "They do not return to me." He stepped out of the way as the vampire lunged again, circling each other in the confined space. Unable to leave so long as he still fed and unable to finish his meal as long as the vampire lived, he was trapped, and he knew it.

The vampire hissed, exulting in the situation. The demon was a rare prize, an apex predator, and he had it within his grasp. He feinted one way and, as the demon turned, made his move. The demon struggled, but the vampire possessed all the advantage. This time his teeth tore the demon's throat.

The demon screamed, the harsh cry quickly becoming an unpleasant gurgle. The vampire sunk his teeth into the back of his neck, holding the demon up as he took what he could. The demon's body jerked in his arms. Not a fight, but the spasms of a body already dying. The blood rushed into his mouth warm and rich, if loaded with a bitter after taste.

Death—or demon? It was a heady drink, and when the vampire felt the final trembling of the body cease, he let it fall without regret.

The demon started to steam. His beautiful clothes began to shrivel and wither to nothing, like plastic too close to a flame. The rest of it followed, the body curling up, fetus-like, as it contorted, a foul gray smoke billowing thickly from it, and the foul stench of sulfur threading the air.

Where his blood hit the floor was a sticky black mass, like tar. It smoked too, and the vampire was curious enough to step closer, see that it ate away at the stone. *Interesting.* He studied himself, but the demon blood within him did not have the same corrosive effect. He bared his fangs in triumph. He felt full and powerful, his hunger entirely sated.

The demon's agent whimpered. The smoke was billowing from him too, as the demon's power dissipated. With a sound approaching a sob, he left the cover of the box he hid behind and lurched towards the door. Like the demon, his body seemed to be constricting, tightening around him.

The vampire leaped after him. He was not interested in feeding, but it was instinctive to chase what fled. Instead he was intercepted. The vampire found his arm caught in a grip he couldn't shake free and turned to find himself held by the third man.

"You asked me not to let you hurt anyone." The man's voice tugged at something inside him. The vampire did not attempt to flee, listening instead to the voice. "Pretty sure that applies to Sandy, even if he is an asshole. Department Seven's right outside. He's not getting far. You on the other hand..."

The vampire purred his satisfaction. He remembered Nate. He ran his hand up Nate's arm, enjoying the mere feel of him, the fact that he didn't draw back. *Not afraid. He knows me.* The vampire's smile curved. He saw the glitter of his fangs reflected in Nate's eye. *Knows we belong.*

Nate ripped a sleeve from his T-shirt. "Let me." He dabbed at the vampire's face, clearing away the traces of blood. "Man, it is a good thing you wear so much black. We might actually be able to get away with this— What are you doing?"

The vampire had caught Nate's finger in his mouth and sucked at it, lavishing it with care. His eyes fixed on Nate's, and he saw a flush spread across his skin with distinct satisfaction.

"Um. Is this really the best time for this?"

With the blood of the freshly killed demon flooding his veins with power and life, there was no better time! The vampire pulled Nate close. The press of Nate's warm body, his startled exclamation, the evidence of his life all combined to wake in the vampire a second life, a surge of need, just as powerful as that for blood had been. He ground against Nate, letting him feel his need.

"Fuck, Ben." Nate rocked against him. "You— This is the vampire in you, right? I should not find it hot." He checked his urge and stood still. "We can't. This isn't—a good idea."

The vampire growled, gripping Nate tightly through his jeans. The man could hold himself in check, but he could not prevent himself growing hard. He stroked Nate's hard length through the fabric, drawing a gasp from him.

"I'm not saying it's not an attractive option, but—the fight, Department Seven... We should help them."

The vampire paused to assess the sounds of battle. The overwhelming throb of hundreds of wings had died away, leaving the shouts and screeches of the remaining combatants, peppered by gunshots. The battle no longer woke an interest in him. What he wanted was right in front of him. The vampire tugged the zip of Nate's jeans down, struggling with the button.

"Shit, Ben. You're really serious about this." Nate's hand closed over the vampire's. "Okay, um. Over here."

The vampire resisted the tug until he realized where Nate intended to lead him. There was an attraction to the light, where his claim would be obvious to any who saw them, but the shadows had their own appeal, allowing more leeway. He hummed approval, interested by the way Nate's fingers tightened around his wrist.

As soon as they were within the shadows, Nate turned, reaching eagerly for the vampire. *Few humans gave themselves to death so willingly.* The vampire rewarded him by meeting his embrace. He ran his fingers over the human's body, exulting in it even as he hungered for more of it.

"When did you get so good at this?" Nate gasped as the vampire sucked at his neck. "Fuck."

Although Nate had hidden them in the shadows, he was not able to quiet his need. Perhaps just as well. The stale traces of brimstone clung to Nate, a reminder of the demon's attempts to possess him. The vampire growled, thrusting against Nate. He would claim him so thoroughly that nothing remained of the demon at all.

Nate gasped. "Fuck me." It was an exclamation, not a request, Nate sinking to his knees before the vampire. Nate's fingers hurried to undo the fly of the vampire's jeans, shoving the briefs aside to free his erection. Unable to see in the shadows, he took firm hold of the vampire's base, using it to guide the tip into his waiting mouth.

The vampire hummed approval. Nate's eagerness was satisfying, and he could smell the man's own arousal. It cut through the fog of need in his mind, replaced the urgent need to fight, to fuck, to feed with an awareness that he could afford to take his time. He stroked Nate's cheek gently.

In return, Nate's tongue laved his tip with all the tenderness of a lover. The noise of the ongoing battle seemed no more distinct than the thrum of New Camden's traffic, and the vampire allowed himself to think of nothing but Nate's mouth. He stroked his hair.

He'd chosen his partner well. Nate was skilled as well as unafraid. In a few moments, he'd brought the vampire to the edge of completion, but as the vampire shuddered, feeling his need build, Nate eased off, his mouth traveling instead to the vampire's sac. The vampire thrust impatiently, his cock sliding against Nate's cheek. "You should finish what you started."

"In time." Nate turned his face, letting the vampire's cock slide over his lips. He held the vampire by his base, following the line of his frenulum with his tongue. He ignored the vampire's attempts to hurry him, deliberately spinning out his pleasure.

Memories began to surface. The vampire slowed his thrusts to a steady roll, distracted by the thought of lying tangled with this man in the sunlight. They were lovers, then, if not more. He was trusted with something important, something related to the demon he'd destroyed.

There had been danger. The vampire's fingers tightened in Nate's hair. "Up." He ran his hands over Nate's body, searching for any injury. His nose twitched, and the vampire permitted himself a smile. *What vampire would miss the scent of blood?*

But as he kissed Nate, careful to keep his fangs from piercing the man's delicate skin, the vampire was aware of a difference. Some of his urgency had faded, replaced with an awareness beyond hunger.

A vampire finds life only in those actions that most resemble living. Feeding, fighting, and loving. The vampire parted his lips, inviting Nate to explore. Was prolonging this encounter giving the vampire more of the living to ground himself? He knew he would do whatever necessary to protect the man pressed against him, knew that danger remained for them both.

And then Nate's fingers grasped him firmly, and all thoughts but that of his building need vanished. Kept on the brink for so long, the vampire did not need much to push him over. He leaned heavily against Nate as his vision cleared, and he returned to himself. The demon's scent was drowned now by their shared sweat and the vampire's finish. Taking a moment to savor his satiation, he thought he'd like to return the favor, reaching for the bulge in Nate's jeans.

"No time." Nate caught his hand, but the vampire thought he found it difficult to do.

"No?" He tightened his grip, felt the tremor that went through the man with a sharp increase in appetite.

"Oh fuck. No. Um. Not *here*." Nate struggled to keep himself from grinding against him. "Trust me. If you can wait till we get home, I'll make it worth it."

'Home.' That was almost as interesting a thought as 'worth it.' The vampire gave one last lingering caress then released him. "I'm holding you to that."

Chapter Twenty-One

An insistent whine pierced the night, and the lights outside took on an insistent, pulsing rhythm. Some form of reinforcements had evidently arrived. The vampire reluctantly followed Nate from the shadows.

Before they'd made it halfway across the floor, a voice raised in greeting. "There's my favorite demon bait! Still with the living, I take it?"

The vampire bared his fangs in a snarl. There was a sour note in this man that was only too reminiscent of the demon they'd fought, and his saunter was calculated to offend. Everything about him, from his gaze, too sharp and calculating, to his self-importance was insolent. Beneath this front, something coiled serpent-like, sensed but not seen. *I would tear you to pieces,* the vampire promised, positioning himself between Nate and this new threat.

"Don't start anything," Nate warned him in a voice pitched for the vampire's hearing alone. "Gunn would love an excuse to take you back for further questioning. Let me talk. You can vent the extra anger when we're away from here."

The vampire retracted his fangs with difficulty. Watching the *lemur* approach went against every instinct he had—not to mention the woman trotting at his heels! The ripe smell of spoiled meat, strong enough to be detected even despite the stench left by the demon, was peculiar to werewolves, and the vampire resented acutely the presence of another predator. He bared his teeth—and felt a firm hand grip his ass. Startled, the vampire turned to find Nate standing close by. His familiar scent, intermingled with the scent of his arousal and their earlier activity, reminded him that he had a vested interest in not antagonizing either of their companions.

"Should you even be on duty?" Nate asked the officer. "I heard you were sick."

"What, and miss all the fun? I see the two of you have been busy." Gunn looked down at the demon's corpse. "You decided to throw a mummy unwrapping party without us?"

The demon was gray and shriveled as if he had been dead thousands of years, not minutes. He looked child-sized, parchment-thin skin hanging off its bones. Nothing remained of his finery. His blood hissed, subsiding into a sticky mass on the floor.

"I think it's a demon," Nate supplied helpfully. "I'm pretty sure it's dead."

Gunn shot him a flat look, before turning to his subordinate. "Kenzie, you want to confirm—"

His second-in-command was no longer behind him. She leaned an arm against one of the crates and was noisily sick.

"For crying out loud! We employ you to hunt monsters—not subsidize your illnesses!" Gunn turned on his subordinate.

Kenzie muttered something in a low growl. The vampire wasn't sure, but he thought he caught the words 'try saying that with my nose' and winced. From a werewolf's perspective, the warehouse would be unbearable.

"I think Kenzie has the right idea." Nate moved towards the door. "Can we get some fresh air?"

"Not so fast." Gunn narrowed his eyes. "Tell me what happened here."

"Short version, Sandy's demon tried to eat Ben. Ben really didn't agree with him. He burnt up instead— Please, Gunn? I don't know how much longer I can keep this down."

Advertising weakness in front of Gunn was never a good idea. "And the long version?"

Seeing the *lemur* bare his teeth in triumph, the vampire readied himself to defend Nate.

Nate elbowed him gently. "If I throw up on your jacket, you're paying the dry-cleaning yourself, Gunn. I'm broke."

The lemur transferred his attention to Ben. "You on the other hand... You're looking really good for someone a demon took a stab at. Very good in fact..." Gunn tilted his head. "What's wrong? You're looking... human for once."

The vampire attempted a shrug. "I'm relieved. The demon's dead. We're both..." It was really hard to care about word choice when every instinct was concentrated on the need to strike first, get his teeth into the *lemur* before it could react. "Fine."

"There's something off about this." Gunn circled him. "And you're not leaving until I know what that is."

That was a definite threat! The vampire turned with him, readying himself to meet the man's attack.

Instead he bumped into a warm body at his side. Nate placed a hand on his back, out of sight of the lemur's sharp eyes. A reminder. "You guys can exert your egos all you want, but I'm heading outside for some air." He offered his arm to the werewolf, who gratefully leaned on him.

Too gratefully. The vampire didn't spare Gunn a second thought, following Nate and the wolf outside. He resented the way the wolf's hand lingered over Nate's arm, and every second it took Nate to find a quiet place for her to sit. Around them, sporadic fires were being stamped out courtesy of men in bright orange uniforms. Here and there, the remains of large, bat-winged creatures lay scattered on the ground. The vampire spared only a passing thought for them, far more concerned with inserting himself protectively at Nate's elbow.

Gunn dogged their steps. "Now, perhaps—"

"Sir!" An officer, only a little bit charred, threw a salute as he stepped up to Gunn. "We apprehended a man trying to leave the scene! He doesn't match the physical description of the suspect, but he was behaving erratically."

"Do I have to do everything? Fine." Gunn turned reluctantly. "Let's see him."

The man was thrust forward. He was elderly, his skin hanging in loose folds from his frail body, his limp, gray dreadlocks giving him a disreputable appearance. His eyes were filled with fear, not confidence, but the vampire recognized him instantly.

"Sandy," Nate said at once. "That's him."

"This is Sandy?" Gunn folded his arms. "Nate, my respect for your romantic choices is officially zero."

"Please." Sandy's voice was hoarse, the words rasped out painfully. "I'm just an old man. I never wanted this—"

Kenzie levered herself to her feet. She readied the cuffs she held with the ease of habitual use. "Samuel Abraham Miller, you are hereby charged with the assault and attempted murder of Georgina Martin, the murder of Olivia Winkler, Alex Harriet, and others, of summoning a demon, engaging in demonic fraternization with the intent to cause harm, endangerment of a minor and more."

"You have the right to a lawyer," Gunn agreed. "But good luck finding one willing to touch your case. Even those vultures have standards."

Sandy was placed into a patrol car, Gunn and Kenzie climbing in with him. Having secured the agent, their first priority would be placing him beyond the reach of further demonic intervention.

As soon as the doors shut behind them and the car drove away, the scene lightened.

It could have been relief at securing the object of the operation and preventing further loss of life—but the vampire suspected that the true cause of relief was Gunn's departure from the scene. Around them, officers were turning back to their work with renewed vigor. It was only a matter of time now before all the fires were extinguished, and the bat-creatures cleaned up.

Nate leaned over to whisper in the vampire's ear. "Let's go now, before anyone remembers to take our statement."

The vampire bared his teeth in agreement.

The light filtered softly through his thoughts until he could no longer ignore it. Ben stretched out a hand, lazily shielding himself from the light. For a moment, he thought he dreamed still. There was no way that peace this strong could be his in reality.

The movement caused a chain reaction. Ben became aware of other aches, the small kind that were more pleasant than painful because they came with the memory of satisfaction. That protest in his arm brought an image of himself, his arms locked around Nate, urging him further. The lingering stiffness in his legs indicated Nate had obliged—or was that a memory from Ben turning the tables? Ben shifted, content to bask in the vague bliss of the memories.

"Hey."

Ben turned his head.

Nate sat with his back against the headboard. In contrast to the content Ben felt, Nate looked tired. His skin looked washed out, making the red patch on his neck—a hickey—even more prominent.

Ben felt his face flush. "Hey." He struggled to sit. "You—woke early?"

"Didn't sleep. I didn't know what'd happen when the sun rose." Nate's voice had a hoarse edge. "What else could I do? That obviously wasn't you—*normal* you—but you had a heartbeat."

Heartbeat? Ben stared at Nate as the implications of his words sank in. He sat up, losing the sheet tossed lightly over him as he pressed his fingers to the vein in his throat.

His heartbeat answered him, a steady thump beneath his fingers. Ben breathed out, shutting his eyes in relief. *I'm alive—*

Memories began to surface. Snarling at the passers-by on the street who'd made a pointed remark about Nate's Century bracelet. Licking Nate's cheek so the taxi driver was in no doubt about who belonged to whom. Pressing Nate up against the door of the apartment the second it shut behind them... Heat flooded Ben's cheeks. The memories were too vivid to doubt their truth, but the thinking that colored them was foreign. *The vampire.*

"When the circle activated and the demon appeared, it—drained me of my life. I started to die. But instead of dying, I became a vampire—the living dead." Ben felt as if his vision aligned, previously half-suspected facts lining up with the focus of truth.

"You didn't know this would happen?"

Ben looked at Nate. "I had a hunch. George and Harriet had a plan. When Sandy mentioned vampires it hit me— The vampire was their secret weapon. It could kill the demon from within the circle. After that—" he stopped. "I hoped that if there was a chance I'd retained my...mind...you'd know it."

"And if not?"

Ben couldn't answer.

Nate sighed, dragging a hand across his face. "Until you spoke, I didn't know if I was imagining the awareness in your actions or not. I was scared, but at the same time—if I was about to lose you, I didn't want to give up even a second with you. Even...if it wasn't you." He put up a hand, forestalling the words Ben was about to say. "No. If I don't say this now, I never will."

Ben's fingers dug deeply into the sheets. A feeling of dread settled over him.

"It...hit me then. I finally get what you meant in the barn. I'm not strong enough to be the person you need. I'm not strong enough, but I want to be."

Ben forced himself to stay still. He'd just got control of himself back. He wasn't going to lose it, giving way to his feelings of panic. "What do you mean? Is this—" He struggled to say the word.

"Not goodbye for good," Nate promised. "Just for now. It's going to take time for me to figure out what I need to do. And you need to find yourself."

"Right." It was his plan. Why did it hurt so much coming from Nate? Ben nodded, refusing to give way to the pounding in his chest.

Nate stood. Ben heard him step across the floor but refused to look up. He didn't trust himself not to give way.

Nate's hand rested on his shoulder. "It's not forever." And then his warmth was gone, and Ben heard the bedroom door close behind him.

☆☆☆

"So." George no longer smelled of singed hair and demon. She was allowed to sit up, greeting Ben and his offering of chocolates cheerfully. "Sorry for leaving you a half-finished job, but the Department Seven officer who interviewed me this morning told me that you'd settled things all right."

Ben permitted himself a smirk. Despite everything else, they'd done the impossible—killed a demon and ended an eighty-year-old killing spree. "It's cool. It's what we do."

George grinned, leaning back against the pillows. "Harriet would be pleased. You know, it's weird." She tugged at her badly mangled hair. "In our best-case scenario, I'd still be dead, Harriet would be the one carrying on. I don't really know what I'm doing here."

Ben sat in the same seat he'd occupied that long, uncomfortable night watch. "Are you going to be all right?"

"I'm a survivor." George shrugged. "I've got some work to do. Would feel a lot better knowing I had a partner to work on it with..."

"Not happening."

"Had to try. Which reminds me— I got something for you. Open that cabinet there."

Ben knelt to open the small bedside drawers. Inside was a jacket Ben had last seen hanging in Harriet's motel room. He glanced at George.

"Harriet left me his stuff. Department Seven returned a few of them. Look underneath."

Ben's hand touched a book. He pulled out Harriet's copy of *Of Monsters*.

"I want you to have this," George said.

"Are you sure? This is—"

"Harriet's legacy," George said. "You never met the guy, but you finished his life work for him. The demon took his brother. I know this is what he'd have wanted."

Ben looked down at the book. For the second time that day, he was having a hard time speaking. "Then, I accept."

"Good. And just remember— You owe me, now." George smirked at him.

Ben stared at her. *Have I been had?*

☆☆☆

He was no nearer to answering that question as he reached his apartment. Possession of the book without a license was an offense. As an ARX agent, Ben had been cleared to deal with dangerous literature...but demons were a league of their own. *Does George intend to blackmail me? I could be charged with possession...* The smart thing to do would be to turn the book over to the authorities at once—or to apply for the requisite license through Department Seven.

I'm going to be there anyway... Legal proceedings ate time and paper, even when lodged against deadly hell creatures. Ben had survived one round of interviews, but he knew there would be others. He sank into the sofa, opening the book.

When was the last time I just...read?

It had been a year at least. Ben's mouth quirked. Reading a proscribed medieval text was not everyone's idea of fun. *I have to start somewhere.*

He started at the beginning. The author, a novice monk, flushed with pride at being selected to join the expedition headed by Brother Pius, a veteran exorcist with years of experience in the business of seeking and eradicating the supernatural, was vocal in his self-congratulations, including in generous detail all the particulars and furnishings of the party he was to be a member of. His companions were less enthusiastic, knowing very well that few of Pius's companions returned from his secretive expeditions. Half their small party was lost almost immediately in fierce battle with creatures the novice described as 'trolls'—a mistake in the translation? Or was their more truth in folklore than Ben was aware of?

Ben quickly became engrossed with the novice's account of the trials that followed. Not even the cumbersome medieval spellings or the frequent pious asides could detract from the interest of the account. Every village they arrived at seemed to have its own peculiar supernatural misfortune. Monks died of battle wounds, succumbed to the temptations of the fiends they fought, or eloped with comely village girls. The novice dealt with these at first with the optimism of youth, then the resolution of faith, and finally with philosophic resignation and a certain wry humor that reminded Ben very much of something just out of mind.

Recognition was just within reach when he reached the final chapter. The novice, now a brother, was the last of those to remain with Brother Pius. The two had made their way to a village, all the people of which had deserted it ten years previously, but which Pius was certain contained the means by which they might finally lay hands on the demon Samigina that had so far evaded their just pursuit. The novice had doubts.

For some weeks previous, I had observed that we were pursued by a man, seemingly of noble class, if not of manner—proud and cruel, with an air of abiding sorrow, and who seemed most assiduously keen to make our acquaintance. That my most observant brother, usually so quick to draw my attention to persons of interest, should appear utterly indifferent to such a singular man—and singular he was, though my quill struggles to express in what manner—and even scold me for bringing him into the conversation at all, only made me more curious, and keeping a watch on the shadowy lord, I realized I was not mistaken. He appeared each night a few hours after sunset, and though I asked, I could find no one to tell me his name or his lodgings.

Ben tapped the page thoughtfully. *Vampire?* In all of their travels, the novice had yet to report encountering one. At this point in history, vampires were relatively unknown in Europe. It was not strange the novice shouldn't make the immediate connection—*Or am I jumping to conclusions based on my own experiences?* Ben turned the next page and felt an eerie sense of dislocation.

Pius bade me prepare for a lengthy ordeal, ordering me to fast and meditate and purge myself of all worldly thoughts before the vigil he planned in the abandoned church. Your humble Brother Scribe was, I confess, less concerned with the vigil than eager to see if my supposition was correct and our noble shadow would follow us as far as this deserted town.

In searching for any sign of the nobleman, I saw Pius crafting a circle with many strange runes, that made me ill to look upon, and pausing often as he did, looking about him with such a clandestine air, that truly I became quite uneasy. Why I should have shrunk from hailing my fellow, and inquiring of him the meaning of his actions, I cannot say, but I returned to my room to pray, uneasy in spirit and oppressed by what I had seen.

And by and by, the sun set, and Pius came to fetch me to the church. He was in a fine mood, assuring me that he had every faith in our success, and yet he seemed to be always looking at something in the shadows as he spoke. I grew even more concerned and had just resolved to say something when behold! We reached the abandoned church and to my amazement and Pius's anger, the doors stood wide open, and all the candles were extinguished. Pius was a great deal vexed, for he said we had need of a great deal of light for the long night before us, but I told him that I carried an extra supply in my saddlebags and went to fetch it. And to my intense astonishment, who waited for me in the stables but the nobleman himself?

He apologized and said that he trust that I should forgive him in time and before I could enquire what sin I must absolve him of, he had struck me a glancing blow and I fell to the floor, stunned. I woke, not more than quarter of an hour later, stripped of my robes and quite alone in the stable. Thinking to warn Pius I made my way back to the church. To my dazed eyes I saw Pius enacting the vigil with a hooded, robed figure and I realized the nobleman had taken my place in the vigil! But it was no holy rite that Pius enacted.

My blood ran cold as I watched the shadows grow, the air growing thick with the presence of those that prey on men. And just as the awful scene reached its climax, and Pius raised his hands in the final chant, I saw a figure gilded in the finery of sin and proud as Lucifer himself appear within that awful circle—Samigina itself! At once, the hooded figure jumped up, letting its hood fall back to display a face no less terrible than that of the demon. It leaped at it, as a terrier leaps on a rat, and this awful beast did rend savagely the demonic creature. Pius himself shrieked dreadfully. "Betrayed! I am betrayed and undone!" He ran for the door of the church. Here I jumped up and, scarcely knowing what I did, tackled my false brother to the ground. He did not resist, but lay moaning and crying, and I looked to see how the demon fared. It was dead or dying, and the creature that killed it approached. Its face was smeared with blood and the animal light shone in its eyes, but it restrained itself with difficulty, turning its face so I might not see its fangs.

"I had hoped to spare you this sight," he said. "You are not hurt?"

"No," I said. "But I cannot say the same for my brother."

"Your brother has sought to betray you," the noble sneered. "Well, this is Christian charity if nothing else! Let us look at him."

But when I succeeded in turning Pius over, we found him dead.

The noble would fain have hurried me away to the next town, but I would not leave Pius—bless his soul, wherever it may be!—and stayed to bury him and burn the thing that remained of the demon.

It is my belief that in his many years of dedication to his pursuit of delivering the innocent people of these wild lands from the burden of the supernatural, Pius was tempted to make a pact of power of his own, reasoning what was one soul lost when so many others hung in the balance? When I ventured to share this opinion with my companion, he smiled and made no reply. The noble told me much that explained the mysteries of the last few weeks and much else besides—that Pius must have made a deal with this demon many years since and has delivered it a burden of souls, that the noble has been tracking it for many years, that had he not taken my place in the circle, this humble scribe would be nothing more than a few humble lines on a stone in an abandoned churchyard, and that my noble lord is not human but a member of that species that even demons fear, that which, if it is spoken of at all, is termed vampyr...

Ben stared down at the page he'd just read. A monk crossing paths with a vampire... He swallowed. *Godfrey...?*

The blaring of his phone made him jump. Ben snatched it up, his heart pounding. "Hello?"

"This is not a pleasure call, Bennet."

Gunn was using his full name? Ben raised his eyebrows. If he was about to arrest him, Gunn wouldn't be playing nice—well, nice by Gunn standards anyway. "Have you ever made a pleasure call?"

"Graphic detail is your boyfriend's department. Anyway." Gunn cleared his throat. "I have my social worker hat on today."

Ben pursed his lips. He knew Department Seven was severely understaffed, but he still had a hard time imagining Gunn in this role. "Every single other person in the department was unavailable?"

"Shut up. I'm doing my yearly good deed." It was hard to read Gunn's tone. "You own the building you live in, right? And you rent apartments to the supernatural?"

"You know we—I—do." It was his father's policy, and even after his death, Ben had seen no reason to change things. "An agency handles the tenancy agreements—"

"But it's your call, right? I got an urgent case for your consideration, Mr. Landlord."

"I don't have any free apartments—" Ben stopped. The apartment where his mother died was empty. "702?"

"That's the one."

"It's haunted."

"These guys are desperate," Gunn said. "And I'm desperate to get rid of them. It's this or finding a suitably sized cardboard box."

Ben narrowed his eyes. Any tenants that Gunn recommended were bound to have a catch. "What's the story?"

"Victims of the heightened restrictions after the necromancer killings. Our charming pair are deemed a security risk by their former lodgings and are in desperate need of a place to crash. They have no references, no bond, one has a personal history that is best described as vague, the other a mountain of student debt. I mean, I personally have no qualms throwing them to the wolves, but got to do my due diligence."

"Bare minimum effort, you mean." But Ben was already feeling sorry for whoever had been consigned to Gunn's care. "No promises, but I'm willing to look at them."

"Great. We're waiting outside the apartment." Gunn hung up.

Ben looked at his blank phone. For the second time that day, he was sure he'd been had.

He hid the book under a sofa cushion—*so obvious no one would think of looking for it there, right?*—and grabbed his keys from the table. As he descended the stairs to the seventh floor, Ben caught the echoes of some very familiar voices. *Now I know I've been had.*

"This is a really bad idea," Nate insisted. "Ben's got enough on his plate without unwanted tenants."

Aki drummed a heel impatiently against the welcome mat. "Unwanted tenants? Give yourself more credit than that, Nate! We might even be able to trade on your relationship for reduced rent."

Nate shook his head. "Ben's not like that."

"Thanks, Nate." Ben climbed down the last of the stairs as they turned to meet him. He ignored Aki's start of surprise and Nate's alarm, focusing instead on Gunn, dropping cigarette ash on the stairwell. "You couldn't have told me who the tenants were?"

Gunn bared wolfish teeth at him. "You should at least hear them out. I'm not exaggerating when I tell you that they're running out of options."

Nate tried to hide his duffel bag and suitcase by standing in front of them, but Aki had an entire set of suitcases with him. "Please? We'll be good tenants. No wild parties or any of that— We get enough excitement on the job."

"Century's kicked you out?"

"Of the employee dorms." Aki shrugged, carelessly flicking his employee wristband. "But not our contracts. Nate is now considered a security risk, and well—" Aki scowled. "I couldn't let him loose on New Camden alone. You know the trouble he gets into."

"Aki exaggerates," Nate cut in quickly. "I'm sure we'll find something. We haven't been around the hostels yet."

Gunn's lip curled. "You'll find them an even stricter proposition than the rental agencies. Since the necromancer made his base in a hotel, the entire hospitality industry's come down hard on supernaturals. Especially unknown supernaturals."

And part of the conditions of Nate's Class 3 listing was having an address and being available for spot inspections. Ben did not like the way this added up.

"It's our problem," Nate insisted. "Not Ben's. Look, he's not interested in tenants. Let's just consider our options somewhere else."

"Wouldn't have thought you'd be in such a hurry to leave," Gunn drawled. "What's the matter? Trouble in paradise?" His eyes glittered with obvious relish.

That explains Gunn's interest in the matter of Nate and Aki's housing. Feeding on misery, he'd sensed that Nate's unhappiness had something to do with Ben and was intent on making the most of the ensuing drama. Ben motioned towards the stairs. "Nate. Can I have a word?"

"You don't have to do this," Nate said as they climbed the stairs to Ben's apartment. "I'm sure Gunn's exaggerating."

Ben shook his head. "Finding housing in New Camden is hard enough, even without throwing being supernatural into the mix." He found the key in the bundle in his father's study, held it out to Nate. "Here."

Nate didn't take it. "You need to figure out who you are. You can't do that when I'm around. Remember?"

Ben wrapped his fingers around the key. "I remember. I also remember you saying you didn't want to influence me."

Nate ducked his head. "We need to stay apart. So you can figure out who you are, and so I can get my shit together, be stronger—be someone you can rely on."

"I do rely on you." Ben reached out, intending to place a hand on Nate's arm. "Nate—"

Nate put a hand up, forestalling him. "I knew you didn't want to go back to being a vampire. But I still let it happen, telling myself it was okay, that you'd get control back, that you'd remember."

"And I did." Ben wrapped his arms around himself. "The demonic rite didn't kill me. I survived."

"But neither of us knew that would happen. And if it hadn't—" Nate looked up, meeting Ben's eyes. "There was no way I could ever kill you. Not after hearing you say you loved me."

The tight fear in Ben uncurled, letting go of him. "I said I would never ask you to do that, Nate. I mean it. I'm trusting you with my life, not my death."

Nate stared at him, open-mouthed.

Ben smiled, reaching out his hand to brush Nate's hair out of his eyes. This time Nate didn't draw back. "You stopped me hurting Gunn, Kenzie—even Sandy. The more time I spent with you, the more of...me...I remembered. You kept me from losing myself to the vampire." Ben dropped his hand. "I've still got a long way to go until I'm ready for a relationship with you. But until then..." He held out the key. "There's no reason we should be strangers."

Nate watched his face carefully. "You're sure?"

Ben nodded. "We're stronger together than we are apart."

Nate took the key. His fingers lingered over Ben's. "We're not dating."

"No."

"Would you say we're not not-dating?"

Ben's mouth twitched. "How many negatives is that?"

"Aki's going to ask."

Ben brushed Nate's arm as they turned back to the stairs. "Fine, then. We're not not-dating."

About the Author

Gillian St. Kevern writes anything from YA to contemporary comedies, but her first love is always the paranormal. Her stories feature quirky characters, twisty plots and often travel in unexpected directions.

Gillian has just returned to New Zealand after eleven years teaching English in rural Japan. From being entirely surrounded by rice paddies, she is now entirely surrounded by sheep. She is attempting to stave off reverse culture shock by finally learning to drive, playing with her adorable niece, and, of course, writing! To keep up to date with her new releases, including The Dead Living, the third book in the Thorns and Fangs series, subscribe to her mailing list:

Email: gillian.stkevern@gmail.com
Website: www.gillianstkevern.com/
Twitter: www.twitter.com/GillianStKevern
Facebook: www.facebook.com/gillian.stkevern
Mailing list: www.gillianstkevern.com/newsletter-sign-up.html
Goodreads: www.goodreads.com/author/show/8337607
Pinterest: www.pinterest.com/gillianstkevern/

Also by Gillian St. Kevern

For the Love of Christmas!
The Ugliest Sweater
Ibiza on Ice

Thorns and Fangs
Thorns and Fangs

NINESTAR PRESS, LLC

www.ninestarpress.com